"**THE NORTHERNERS** is the first anthology of stories about the far reaches of the Canadian northland. The ten tales in these pages are authentic, atmospheric, [and] packed with action.

"We think you'll agree this is frontier adventure fiction at its most absorbing."

Bill Pronzini and
Martin H. Greenberg
From the Introduction

THE NORTHERNERS

Edited by
Bill Pronzini and
Martin H. Greenberg

FAWCETT GOLD MEDAL • NEW YORK

Acknowledgments

"Captives of the Arctic Wastelands," by Victor Rousseau. Copyright (c) 1936 by Glen-Kel Publishing Co., Inc. First published in *North-West Stories*. Reprinted by permission of Forrest J. Ackerman.

"Black John Gives a Tip," by James B. Hendryx. Copyright (c) 1942 by Short Stories, Inc.; copyright (c) 1944 by James B. Hendryx. Reprinted by permission of Hendryx Unltd. and the estate of James B. Hendryx.

"Webs for One," by Ryerson Johnson. Copyright (c) 1942 by Esquire, Inc. First published in *Coronet*. Reprinted by permission of the author.

"Mistress of the Midnight Sun," by Dan Cushman. Copyright (c) 1950 by Glen-Kel Publishing Co., Inc. First published in *Northwest Romances*. Reprinted by permission of Scott Meredith Literary Agency, Inc., 845 Third Avenue, New York, N.Y. 10022.

Contents

Introduction

"Northerns"—stories set in the rough-and-tumble frontier days of Alaska, the Yukon, the Canadian Barrens, Hudson's Bay, and other Far North locales—were quite popular during the first half of this century. The widespread publicity given to the Yukon Gold Rush of 1898, and to the Alaskan Gold Rush shortly afterward, focused attention on that part of the world; and it sent such writers as Jack London, Rex Beach, and, later, Robert W. Service, scurrying northward in search of story material as well as precious metals. Such works as *Call of the Wild*, *The Spoilers*, and *The Trail of '98* in turn spawned thousands of adventure stories, hundreds of novels, and numerous films featuring northland prospectors, fur trappers, wilderness pilots and explorers, dog-sledders, traders, gamblers, outlaws, and of course the brave men of the Northwest Mounted Police.

So popular were Northerns in the years prior to World War II that entire pulp magazines such as *North-West Stories* (later *Northwest Romances*), *Real Northwest Stories*, and *Complete Northwest Novel* were devoted entirely or almost entirely to "vigorous, tingling epics of the great Snow frontier." *North-West Stories* acquired such a loyal following that it had a much longer life than most pulps, lasting nearly thirty years (1925–1952). Northerns could also be found in most issues of such adventure pulps as *Short Stories*, *Argosy*, *Adventure*, *Blue Book*, and *Action Stories*; in several of the Western titles, notably Street & Smith's *Western Story*; and in such slick-paper periodicals as *Collier's* and *The Saturday Evening Post*.

Many prominent authors of traditional Westerns wrote Northerns, among them Luke Short, Charles Alden Seltzer, and William MacLeod Raine. A number of other writers built substantial careers specializing in this type of story. James Oliver Curwood was one; James B. Hendryx, William Byron Mowery, George Marsh,

Robert Ormond Case, Samuel Alexander White, and Frank Richardson Pierce are others of note.

The Northerners is the first anthology of stories about the far reaches of the Canadian northland. The ten tales in these pages are authentic, atmospheric, packed with action, and carry the bylines of most of the prominent writers mentioned above, as well as such others as Ryerson Johnson, Victor Rousseau, and Dan Cushman.

We think you'll agree this is frontier adventure fiction at its most absorbing.

—Bill Pronzini and
Martin H. Greenberg

The Northern fiction of Jack London (1876–1916)—in particular the novels The Call of the Wild *and* White Fang, *and the story collection* The Son of the Wolf: Tales of the Far North—*are still as universally popular today as they were when first published more than three-quarters of a century ago. One of the reasons is London's firsthand knowledge of his subject matter; another is his unique and graphic portrayal of man's constant struggle against the elemental savagery of his environment. He was also masterly at creating memorable characters and unusual relationships, as in "The Wit of Porportuk," the ironic tale of an old man's hunger for the beautiful daughter of an Indian chieftain.*

The Wit of Porportuk

****

Jack London

EL-SOO had been a mission girl. Her mother had died when she was very small, and Sister Alberta had plucked El-Soo as a brand from the burning, one summer day, and carried her away to Holy Cross Mission and dedicated her to God. El-Soo was a full-blooded Indian, yet she exceeded all the half-breed and quarter-breed girls. Never had the good sisters dealt with a girl so adaptable and at the same time so spirited.

El-Soo was quick, and deft, and intelligent; but above all she was fire, the living flame of life, a blaze of personality that was compounded of will, sweetness, and daring. Her father was a chief, and his blood ran in her veins. Obedience, on the part of El-Soo, was a matter of terms and arrangement. She had a passion for equity, and perhaps it was because of this that she excelled in mathematics.

But she excelled in other things. She learned to read and write English as no girl had ever learned in the mission. She led the girls in singing, and into song she carried her sense of equity. She was an artist, and the fire of her flowed toward creation. Had she from birth enjoyed a more favorable environment, she would have made literature or music.

Instead she was El-Soo, daughter of Klakee-Nah, a chief, and she lived in the Holy Cross Mission where there were no artists, but only pure-souled sisters who were interested in cleanliness and righteousness and the welfare of the spirit in the land of immortality that lay beyond the skies.

The years passed. She was eight years old when she entered the mission; she was sixteen, and the sisters were corresponding with their superiors in the order concerning the sending of El-Soo to the United States to complete her education, when a man of her own tribe arrived at Holy Cross and had a talk with her. El-Soo was somewhat appalled by him. He was dirty. He was a Caliban-like creature, primitively ugly, with a mop of hair that had never been combed. He looked at her disapprovingly and refused to sit down.

"Thy brother is dead," he said shortly.

El-Soo was not particularly shocked. She remembered little of her brother. "Thy father is an old man, and alone," the messenger went on. "His house is large and empty, and he would hear thy voice and look upon thee."

Him she remembered—Klakee-Nah, the headman of the village, the friend of the missionaries and the traders, a large man thewed like a giant, with kindly eyes and masterful ways, and striding with a consciousness of crude royalty in his carriage.

"Tell him that I will come" was El-Soo's answer.

Much to the despair of the sisters, the brand plucked from the burning went back to the burning. All pleading with El-Soo was in vain. There was much argument, expostulation, and weeping. Sister Alberta even revealed to her the project of sending her to the United States. El-Soo stared wide-eyed into the golden vista thus opened up to her and shook her head. In her eyes persisted another vista. It was the mighty curve of the Yukon at Tanana Station, with the St. George Mission on one side, and the trading post on the other, and midway between the Indian village and a certain large log house where lived an old man tended upon by slaves.

All dwellers on the Yukon bank for twice a thousand miles knew the large log house, the old man, and the tending slaves; and well did the sisters know the house, its unending revelry, its feasting, and its fun. So there was weeping at Holy Cross when El-Soo departed.

There was a great cleaning up in the large house when El-Soo arrived. Klakee-Nah, himself masterful, protested at this masterful conduct of his young daughter; but in the end, dreaming barbarically of magnificence, he went forth and borrowed a thousand dollars from old Porportuk, than whom there was no richer Indian on the Yukon. Also Klakee-Nah ran up a heavy bill at the trading post. El-Soo recreated the large house. She invested it with new splendor, while Klakee-Nah maintained its ancient traditions of hospitality and revelry.

All this was unusual for a Yukon Indian, but Klakee-Nah was an unusual Indian. Not alone did he like to render inordinate hospitality, but, what of being a chief and of acquiring much money, he was able to do it. In the primitive trading days he had been a power over his people, and he had dealt profitably with the white trading companies. Later on, with Porportuk, he had made a gold strike on the Koyukuk River. Klakee-Nah was by training and nature an aristocrat. Porportuk was bourgeois, and Porportuk bought him out of the gold mine. Porportuk was content to plod and accumulate. Klakee-Nah went back to his large house and proceeded to spend. Porportuk was known as the richest Indian in Alaska. Klakee-Nah was known as the whitest. Porportuk was a moneylender and a usurer. Klakee-Nah was an anachronism—a medieval ruin, a fighter and a feaster, happy with wine and song.

El-Soo adapted herself to the large house and its ways as readily as she had adapted herself to Holy Cross Mission and its ways. She did not try to reform her father and direct his footsteps toward God. It is true, she reproved him when he drank overmuch and profoundly, but that was for the sake of his health and the direction of his footsteps on solid earth.

The latchstring to the large house was always out. What with the coming and the going, it was never still. The rafters of the great living room shook with the roar of wassail and of song. At their table sat men from all the world and chiefs from distant tribes—Englishmen and colonials, lean Yankee traders and rotund officials of the great companies, cowboys from the Western ranges, sailors from the sea, hunters and dog mushers of a score of nationalities.

El-Soo drew breath in a cosmopolitan atmosphere. She could speak English as well as she could her native tongue, and she sang English songs and ballads. The passing Indian ceremonials she knew, and the perishing traditions. The tribal dress of the daughter of a chief she knew how to wear upon occasion. But for the most part she dressed as white women dress. Not for nothing was her needlework at the mission and her innate artistry. She carried her clothes like a white woman, and she made clothes that could be so carried.

In her way she was as unusual as her father, and the position she occupied was as unique as his. She was the one Indian woman who was the social equal with the several white women at Tanana Station. She was the one Indian woman to whom white men honorably made proposals of marriage. And she was the one Indian woman whom no white man ever insulted.

For El-Soo was beautiful—not as white women are beautiful, not as Indian women are beautiful. It was the flame of her, that did not depend upon feature, that was her beauty. So far as mere line and feature went, she was the classic Indian type. The black hair and the fine bronze were hers, and the black eyes, brilliant and bold, keen as sword light, proud; and hers the delicate eagle nose with the thin, quivering nostrils, the high cheekbones that were not broad apart, and the thin lips that were not too thin. But over all and through all poured the flame of her—the unanalyzable something that was fire and that was the soul of her, that lay mellow-warm or blazed in her eyes, that sprayed the cheeks of her, that distended the nostrils, that curled the lip, or, when the lip was in repose, that was still there in the lip, the lip palpitant with its presence.

And El-Soo had wit—rarely sharp to hurt, yet quick to search out forgivable weakness. The laugher of her mind played like lambent flame over all about her, and from all about her arose answering laughter. Yet she was never the center of things. This she would not permit. The large house, and all of which it was significant, was her father's; and through it, to the last, moved his heroic figure—host, master of the revels, and giver of the law. It is true, as the strength oozed from him, that she caught up responsibilities from his failing hands. But in appearance he still ruled, dozing ofttimes at the board, a bacchanalian ruin, yet in all seeming the ruler of the feast.

And through the large house moved the figure of Porportuk, ominous, with shaking head, coldly disapproving, paying for it all. Not that he really paid, for he compounded interest in weird ways, and year by year absorbed the properties of Klakee-Nah. Porportuk once took it upon himself to chide El-Soo upon the wasteful way of life in the large house—it was when he had about absorbed the last of Klakee-Nah's wealth—but he never ventured so to chide again. El-Soo, like her father, was an aristocrat, as disdainful of money as he, and with an equal sense of honor as finely strung.

Porportuk continued grudgingly to advance money, and ever the money flowed in golden foam away. Upon one thing El-Soo was resolved—her father should die as he had lived. There should be for him no passing from high to low, no diminution of the revels, no lessening of the lavish hospitality. When there was famine, as of old, the Indians came groaning to the large house and went away content. When there was famine and no money, money was borrowed from Porportuk, and the Indians still went away content. El-Soo might well have repeated, after the aristocrats of another time and place, that after her came the deluge. In her case the deluge was old Porportuk. With every advance of money he looked upon her with a more possessive eye, and felt burgeoning within him ancient fires.

But El-Soo had no eyes for him. Nor had she eyes for the white men who wanted to marry her at the mission with ring and priest and book. For at Tanana Station was a young man, Akoon, of her own blood and tribe and village. He was strong and beautiful to her eyes, a great hunter, and, in that he had wandered far and much, very poor; he had been to all the unknown wastes and places; he had journeyed to Sitka and to the United States; he had crossed the continent to Hudson Bay and back again, and as seal hunter on a ship he had sailed to Siberia and for Japan.

When he returned from the gold strike in Klondike, he came, as was his wont, to the large house to make report to old Klakee-Nah of all the world that he had seen; and there he first saw El-Soo, three years back from the mission. Thereat Akoon wandered no more. He refused a wage of twenty dollars a day as pilot on the big steamboats. He hunted some and fished some, but never far from Tanana Station, and he was at the large house often and long. And El-Soo measured him against many men and found him good. He sang songs to her, and was ardent and glowed until all Tanana Station knew he loved her. And Porportuk but grinned and advanced more money for the upkeep of the large house.

Then came the death table of Klakee-Nah. He sat at feast, with death in his throat, that he could not drown with wine. And laughter and joke and song went around, and Akoon told a story that made the rafters echo. There were no tears or sighs at that table. It was no more than fit that Klakee-Nah should die as he had lived, and none knew this better than El-Soo, with her artist sympathy. The old roistering crowd was there, and, as of old, three frostbitten sailors were there, fresh from the long traverse from the Arctic, survivors of a ship's company of seventy-four. At Klakee-Nah's back were four old men, all that were left him of the slaves of his youth. With rheumy eyes they saw to his needs, with palsied hands filling his glass or striking him on the back between the shoulders when death stirred and he coughed and gasped.

It was a wild night, and as the hours passed and the fun laughed and roared along, death stirred more restlessly in Klakee-Nah's throat.

Then it was that he sent for Porportuk. And Porportuk came in from the outside frost to look with disapproving eyes upon the meat and wine on the table for which he had paid. But as he looked down the length of flushed faces to the far end and saw the face of El-Soo, the light in his eyes flared up, and for a moment the disapproval vanished.

Place was made for him at Klakee-Nah's side, and a glass placed before him. Klakee-Nah, with his own hands, filled the glass with fervent spirits. "Drink!" he cried. "Is it not good?"

And Porportuk's eyes watered as he nodded his head and smacked his lips.

"When, in your own house, have you had such drink?" Klakee-Nah demanded.

"I will not deny that the drink is good to this old throat of mine," Porportuk made answer, and hesitated for the speech to complete the thought.

"But it costs overmuch," Klakee-Nah roared, completing it for him.

Porportuk winced at the laughter that went down the table. His eyes burned malevolently. "We were boys together, of the same age," he said. "In your throat is death. I am still alive and strong."

An ominous murmur arose from the company. Klakee-Nah coughed and strangled, and the old slaves smote him between the shoulders. He emerged gasping and waved his hand to still the threatening rumble.

"You have grudged the very fire in your house because the wood cost overmuch!" he cried. "You have grudged life. To live cost overmuch, and you have refused to pay the price. Your life has been like a cabin where the fire is out and there are no blankets on the floor." He signaled to a slave to fill his glass, which he held aloft. "But I have lived. And I have been warm with life as you have never been warm. It is true, you shall live long. But the longest nights are the cold nights when a man shivers and lies awake. My nights have been short, but I have slept warm."

He drained the glass. The shaking hand of a slave failed to catch it as it crashed to the floor. Klakee-Nah sank back, panting, watching the upturned glasses at the lips of the drinkers, his own lips slightly smiling to the applause. At a sign, two slaves attempted to help him sit upright again. But they were weak, his frame was mighty, and the four old men tottered and shook as they helped him forward.

"But manner of life is neither here nor there," he went on. "We have other business, Porportuk, you and I, tonight. Debts are mischances, and I am in mischance with you. What of my debt, and how great is it?"

Porportuk searched in his pouch and brought forth a memorandum. He sipped at his glass and began. "There is the note of August 1889 for three hundred dollars. The interest has never been paid. And the note of the next year for five hundred dollars. This note was included in the note of two months later for a thousand dollars. Then there is the note——"

"Never mind the many notes!" Klakee-Nah cried out impatiently. "They make my head go around and all the things inside my head. The whole! The round whole! How much is it?"

Porportuk referred to his memorandum. "Fifteen thousand nine hundred and sixty-seven dollars and seventy-five cents," he read with careful precision.

"Make it sixteen thousand, make it sixteen thousand," Klakee-Nah said grandly. "Odd numbers were ever a worry. And now—and it is for this that I have sent for you—make me out a new note for sixteen thousand, which I shall sign. I have no thought of the interest. Make it as large as you will, and make it payable in the next world, when I shall meet you by the fire of the Great Father of all Indians. Then the note will be paid. This I promise you. It is the word of Klakee-Nah."

Porportuk looked perplexed, and loudly the laughter arose and shook the room. Klakee-Nah raised his hands. "Nay," he cried. "It is not a joke. I but speak in fairness. It was for this I sent for you, Porportuk. Make out the note."

"I have no dealings with the next world," Porportuk made answer slowly.

"Have you no thought to meet me before the Great Father!" Klakee-Nah demanded. Then he added, "I shall surely be there."

"I have no dealings with the next world," Porportuk repeated sourly.

The dying man regarded him with frank amazement.

"I know naught of the next world," Porportuk explained. "I do business in this world."

Klakee-Nah's face cleared. "This comes of sleeping cold of night," he laughed. He pondered for a space, then said, "It is in this world that you must be paid. There remains to me this house. Take it, and burn the debt in the candle there."

"It is an old house and not worth the money," Porportuk made answer, looking straight at the old man.

"There are my mines on the Twisted Salmon."

"They have never paid to work," was the reply.

"There is my share in the steamer *Koyukuk*. I am half owner."

"She is at the bottom of the Yukon."

Klakee-Nah started. "True, I forgot. It was last spring when the ice went out." He mused for a time while the glasses remained untasted and all the company waited upon his utterance.

"Then it would seem I owe you a sum of money which I cannot pay . . . in this world?"

Porportuk nodded and glanced down the table.

"Then it would seem that you, Porportuk, are a poor business-man," Klakee-Nah said slyly.

And boldly Porportuk made answer, "No; there is security yet untouched."

"What!" cried Klakee-Nah. "Have I still property? Name it, and it is yours, and the debt is no more."

"There it is." Porportuk pointed at El-Soo.

Klakee-Nah could not understand. He peered down the table, brushed his eyes, and peered again.

"Your daughter El-Soo—her will I take and the debt be no more. I will burn the debt there in the candle."

Klakee-Nah's great chest began to heave. "Ho! Ho!—a joke— Ho! Ho! Ho!" he laughed homerically. "And with your cold bed and daughters old enough to be the mother of El-Soo! Ho! Ho! Ho!" He began to cough and strangle, and the old slaves smote him on the back. "Ho! Ho!" he began again, and went off into another paroxysm.

Porportuk waited patiently, sipping from his glass and studying the double row of faces down the board. "It is no joke," he said finally. "My speech is well-meant."

Klakee-Nah sobered and looked at him, then reached for his glass, but could not touch it. A slave passed it to him, and glass and liquor he flung into the face of Porportuk.

"Turn him out!" Klakee-Nah thundered to the waiting table that strained like a pack of hounds in leash. "And roll him in the snow!"

As the mad riot swept past him and out of doors, he signaled to the slaves, and the four tottering old men supported him on his feet as he met the returning revelers, upright, glass in hand, pledging them a toast to the short night when a man sleeps warm.

It did not take long to settle the estate of Klakee-Nah. Tommy, the little Englishman, clerk at the trading post, was called in by El-Soo to help. There was nothing but debts, notes overdue, mortgaged properties, and properties mortgaged but worthless. Notes and mortgages were held by Porportuk. Tommy called him a robber many times as he pondered the compounding of the interest.

"Is it a debt, Tommy?" El-Soo asked.

"It is a robbery," Tommy answered.

"Nevertheless, it is a debt," she persisted.

The winter wore away, and the early spring, and still the claims of Porportuk remained unpaid. He saw El-Soo often and explained to her at length, as he had explained to her father, the way the debt could be canceled. Also he brought with him old medicine men, who elaborated to her the everlasting damnation of her father if the debt were not paid. One day, after such an elaboration, El-Soo made final announcement to Porportuk.

"I shall tell you two things," she said. "First, I shall not be your wife. Will you remember that? Second, you shall be paid the last cent of the sixteen thousand dollars—"

"Fifteen thousand nine hundred and sixty-seven dollars and seventy-five cents," Porportuk corrected.

"My father said sixteen thousand," was her reply. "You shall be paid."

"How?"

"I know not how, but I shall find out how. Now go, and bother me no more. If you do"—she hesitated to find fitting penalty—"if you do, I shall have you rolled in the snow again as soon as the first snow flies."

This was still in the early spring, and a little later El-Soo surprised the country. Word went up and down the Yukon from Chilkoot to the Delta, and was carried from camp to camp to the farthermost camps that in June, when the first salmon ran, El-Soo, daughter of Klakee-Nah, would sell herself at public auction to satisfy the claims of Porportuk. Vain were the attempts to dissuade her. The missionary at St. George wrestled with her, but she replied:

"Only the debts to God are settled in the next world. The debts of men are of this world, and in this world are they settled."

Akoon wrestled with her, but she replied: "I do love thee, Akoon; but honor is greater than love, and who am I that I should blacken my father?" Sister Alberta journeyed all the way up from Holy Cross on the first steamer, and to no better end.

"My father wanders in the thick and endless forests," said El-Soo. "And there will he wander, with the lost souls crying, till the debt be·paid. Then, and not until then, may he go on to the house of the Great Father.''

"And you believe this?" Sister Alberta asked.

"I do not know," El-Soo made answer. "It was my father's belief."

Sister Alberta shrugged her shoulders incredulously.

"Who knows but that the things we believe come true?" El-Soo went on. "Why not? The next world to you may be heaven and harps . . . because you have believed heaven and harps; to my father the next world may be a large house where he will sit always at table feasting with God."

"And you?" Sister Alberta asked. "What is your next world?"

El-Soo hesitated but for a moment. "I should like a little of both," she said. "I should like to see your face as well as the face of my father."

The day of the auction came. Tanana Station was populous. As was their custom, the tribes had gathered to await the salmon run and in the meantime spent the time in dancing and frolicking, trading and gossiping. Then there was the ordinary sprinkling of white adventurers, traders, and prospectors, and in addition a large number of white men who had come because of curiosity or interest in the affair.

It had been a backward spring, and the salmon were late in running. This delay but keyed up the interest. Then, on the day of the auction, the situation was made tense by Akoon. He arose and made public and solemn announcement that whosoever bought El-Soo would forthwith and immediately die. He flourished the Winchester in his hand to indicate the manner of the taking off. El-Soo was angered thereat; but he refused to speak with her and went to the trading post to lay in extra ammunition.

The first salmon was caught at ten o'clock in the evening, and at midnight the auction began. It took place on top of the high bank alongside the Yukon. The sun was due north just below the horizon, and the sky was lurid red. A great crowd gathered about the table and the two chairs that stood near the edge of the bank. To the fore were many white men and several chiefs. And most prominently to the fore, rifle in hand, stood Akoon. Tommy, at El-Soo's request, served as auctioneer, but she made the opening speech and described the goods about to be sold. She was in native costume, in the dress of a chief's daughter, splendid and barbaric, and she stood on a chair, that she might be seen to advantage.

"Who will buy a wife?" she asked. "Look at me. I am twenty years old and a maid. I will be a good wife to the man who buys me. If he is a white man, I shall dress in the fashion of white women; if he is an Indian, I shall dress as"—she hesitated a moment—"a squaw. I can make my own clothes, and sew, and wash, and mend. I was taught for eight years to do these things at Holy Cross Mission. I can read and write English, and I know how to play the organ. Also, I can do arithmetic and some algebra—a little. I shall be sold to the highest bidder, and to him I will make out a bill of sale of myself. I forgot to say that I can sing very well, and that I have never been sick in my life. I weigh one hundred and thirty-two pounds; my father is dead and I have no relatives. Who wants me?"

She looked over the crowd with flaming audacity and stepped down. At Tommy's request she stood upon the chair again, while he mounted the second chair and started the bidding.

Surrounding El-Soo stood the four old slaves of her father. They were age-twisted and palsied, faithful to their meat, a generation out of the past that watched unmoved the antics of younger life. In the front of the crowd were several Eldorado and Bonanza kings from the upper Yukon, and beside them, on crutches, swollen with scurvy, were two broken prospectors. From the midst of the crowd, thrust out by its own vividness, appeared the face of a wild-eyed squaw from the remote regions of the upper Tanana; a strayed Sitkan from the coast stood side by side with a Stick from Lake Le Barge, and, beyond, a half-dozen French-Canadian voyageurs, grouped by themselves. From afar came the faint cries of myriads of wild fowl on the nesting grounds. Swallows were skimming up overhead from the placid surface of the Yukon, and robins were singing. The oblique rays of the hidden sun shot through the smoke, high-dissipated from forest fires a thousand miles away, and turned the heavens to somber red, while the earth shone red in the reflected glow. This red glow shone in the faces of all and made everything seem unearthly and unreal.

The bidding began slowly. The Sitkan, who was a stranger in the land and who had arrived only half an hour before, offered one hundred dollars in a confident voice and was surprised when Akoon turned threateningly upon him with the rifle. The bidding dragged. An Indian from the Tozikakat, a pilot, bid one hundred and fifty, and after some time a gambler, who had been ordered out of the upper county, raised the bid to two hundred. El-Soo was saddened; her pride was hurt; but the only effect was that she flamed more audaciously upon the crowd.

There was a disturbance among the onlookers as Porportuk forced his way to the front. "Five hundred dollars!" he bid in a loud voice, then looked about him proudly to note the effect.

He was minded to use his great wealth as a bludgeon with which to stun all competition at the start. But one of the voyageurs, looking on El-Soo with sparkling eyes, raised the bid a hundred.

"Seven hundred!" Porportuk returned promptly.

And with equal promptness came the "Eight hundred" of the voyageur.

Then Porportuk swung his club again. "Twelve hundred!" he shouted.

With a look of poignant disappointment the voyageur succumbed. There was no further bidding. Tommy worked hard but could not elicit a bid.

El-Soo spoke to Porportuk. "It were good, Porportuk, for you to weigh well your bid. Have you forgotten the thing I told you—that I would never marry you!"

"It is a public auction," he retorted. "I shall buy you with a bill of sale. I have offered twelve hundred dollars. You come cheap."

"Too damned cheap!" Tommy cried. "What if I am auctioneer? That does not prevent me from bidding. I'll make it thirteen hundred."

"Fourteen hundred," from Porportuk.

"I'll buy you in to be my—my sister," Tommy whispered to El-Soo, then called aloud, "Fifteen hundred!"

At two thousand one of the Eldorado kings took a hand, and Tommy dropped out.

A third time Porportuk swung the club of his wealth, making a clean raise of five hundred dollars. But the Eldorado king's pride was touched. No man could club him. And he swung back another five hundred.

El-Soo stood at three thousand. Porportuk made it thirty-five hundred and gasped when the Eldorado king raised it a thousand dollars. Porportuk raised it five hundred and again gasped when the king raised a thousand more.

Porportuk became angry. His pride was touched; his strength was challenged, and with him strength took the form of wealth. He would not be ashamed for weakness before the world. El-Soo became incidental. The savings and scrimpings from the cold nights of all his years were ripe to be squandered. El-Soo stood at six thousand. He made it seven thousand. And then, in thousand-dollar bids, as fast as they could be uttered, her price went up. At fourteen thousand the two men stopped for breath.

Then the unexpected happened. A still heavier club was swung.

In the pause that ensued the gambler, who had scented a speculation and formed a syndicate with several of his fellows, bid sixteen thousand dollars.

"Seventeen thousand," Porportuk said weakly.

"Eighteen thousand," said the king.

Porportuk gathered his strength. "Twenty thousand."

The syndicate dropped out. The Eldorado king raised a thousand, and Porportuk raised back; and as they bid, Akoon turned from one to the other, half menacingly, half curiously, as though to see what manner of man it was that he would have to kill. When the king prepared to make his next bid, Akoon having pressed closer, the king first loosed the revolver at his hip, then said:

"Twenty-three thousand."

"Twenty-four thousand," said Porportuk. He grinned viciously, for the certitude of his bidding had at last shaken the king. The latter moved over close to El-Soo. He studied her carefully for a long while.

"And five hundred," he said at last.

"Twenty-five thousand," came Porportuk's raise.

The king looked for a long space and shook his head. He looked again and said reluctantly, "And five hundred."

"Twenty-six thousand," Porportuk snapped.

The king shook his head and refused to meet Tommy's pleading eye. In the meantime Akoon had edged close to Porportuk. El-Soo's quick eye noted this, and while Tommy wrestled with the Eldorado king for another bid, she bent and spoke in a low voice in the ear of a slave. And while Tommy's "Going . . . going . . . going" dominated the air, the slave went up to Akoon and spoke in a low voice in his ear. Akoon made no sign that he had heard, though El-Soo watched him anxiously.

"Gone!" Tommy's voice rang out. "To Porportuk, for twenty-six thousand dollars."

Porportuk glanced uneasily at Akoon. All eyes were centered upon Akoon, but he did nothing.

"Let the scales be brought," said El-Soo.

"I shall make payment at my house," said Porportuk.

"Let the scales be brought," El-Soo repeated. "Payment shall be made here where all can see."

So the gold scales were brought from the trading post, while Porportuk went away and came back with a man at his heels, on whose shoulders was a weight of gold dust in moose-hide sacks. Also, at Porportuk's back walked another man with a rifle, who had eyes only for Akoon.

"Here are the notes and mortgages," said Porportuk, "for fifteen thousand nine hundred and sixty-seven dollars and seventy-five cents."

El-Soo received them into her hands and said to Tommy, "Let them be reckoned as sixteen thousand."

"There remains ten thousand dollars to be paid in gold," Tommy said.

Porportuk nodded and untied the mouths of the sacks. El-Soo, standing at the edge of the bank, tore the papers to shreds and sent them fluttering out over the Yukon. The weighing began, but halted.

"Of course, at seventeen dollars," Porportuk had said to Tommy as he adjusted the scales.

"At sixteen dollars," El-Soo said sharply.

"It is the custom of all the land to reckon gold at seventeen dollars for each ounce," Porportuk replied. "And this is a business transaction."

El-Soo laughed. "It is a new custom," she said. "It began this spring. Last year, and the years before, it was sixteen dollars an ounce. When my father's debt was made, it was sixteen dollars. When he spent at the store, the money he got from you for one ounce, he was given sixteen dollars' worth of flour, not seventeen. Wherefore shall you pay for me at sixteen and not at seventeen." Porportuk grunted and allowed the weighing to proceed.

"Weigh it in three piles, Tommy," she said. "A thousand dollars here, three thousand here, and here six thousand."

It was slow work, and while the weighing went on, Akoon was closely watched by all.

"He but waits till the money is paid," one said; and the word went around and was accepted, and they waited for what Akoon should do when the money was paid. And Porportuk's man with the rifle waited and watched Akoon.

The weighing was finished, and the gold dust lay on the table in three dark yellow heaps. "There is a debt of my father to the company for three thousand dollars," said El-Soo. "Take it, Tommy, for the company. And here are four old men, Tommy. You know them. And here is one thousand dollars. Take it, and see that the old men are never hungry and never without tobacco."

Tommy scooped the gold into separate sacks. Six thousand dollars remained on the table. El-Soo thrust the scoop into the heap and with a sudden turn whirled the contents out and down to the Yukon in a golden shower. Porportuk seized her wrist as she thrust the scoop a second time into the heap.

"It is mine," she said calmly. Porportuk released his grip, but he gritted his teeth and scowled darkly as she continued to scoop the gold into the river till none was left.

The crowd had eyes for naught but Akoon, and the rifle of Porportuk's man lay across the hollow of his arm, the muzzle directed at Akoon a yard away, the man's thumb on the hammer. But Akoon did nothing.

"Make out the bill of sale," Porportuk said grimly.

And Tommy made out the bill of sale, wherein all rights and title in the woman El-Soo were vested in the man Porportuk. El-Soo signed the document, and Porportuk folded it and put it away in his pouch. Suddenly his eyes flashed, and in sudden speech he addressed El-Soo.

"But it was not your father's debt," he said. "What I paid was the price for you. Your sale is business of today and not of last year and the years before. The ounces paid for you will buy at the post today seventeen dollars of flour, and not sixteen. I have lost a dollar on each ounce. I have lost six hundred and twenty-five dollars."

El-Soo thought for a moment and saw the error she had made. She smiled, and then she laughed.

"You are right," she laughed. "I made a mistake. But it is too late. You have paid, and the gold is gone. You did not think quick. It is your loss. Your wit is slow these days, Porportuk. You are getting old."

He did not answer. He glanced uneasily at Akoon and was reassured. His lips tightened, and a hint of cruelty came into his face. "Come," he said, "we will go to my house."

"Do you remember the two things I told you in the spring?" El-Soo asked, making no movement to accompany him.

"My head would be full with the things women say, did I heed them," he answered.

"I told you that you would be paid," El-Soo went on carefully. "And I told you that I would never be your wife."

"But that was before the bill of sale." Porportuk crackled the paper between his fingers inside the pouch. "I have bought you before all the world. You belong to me. You will not deny that you belong to me."

"I belong to you," El-Soo said steadily.

"I own you."

"You own me."

Porportuk's voice rose slightly and triumphantly. "As a dog, I own you."

"As a dog, you own me," El-Soo continued calmly. "But, Porportuk, you forget the thing I told you. Had any other man bought me, I should have been that man's wife. I should have been a good wife to that man. Such was my will. But my will with you was that I should never be your wife. Wherefore, I am your dog."

Porportuk knew that he played with fire, and he resolved to play firmly. "Then I speak to you not as El-Soo but as a dog," he said; "and I tell you to come with me." He half reached to grip her arm, but with a gesture she held him back.

"Not so fast, Porportuk. You buy a dog. The dog runs away. It is your loss. I am your dog. What if I run away?"

"As the owner of the dog, I shall beat you—"

"When you catch me?"

"When I catch you."

"Then catch me."

He reached swiftly for her, but she eluded him. She laughed as she circled around the table. "Catch her!" Porportuk commanded the Indian with the rifle, who stood near to her. But as the Indian stretched forth his arm to her, the Eldorado king felled him with a fist blow under the ear. The rifle clattered to the ground. Then was Akoon's chance. His eyes glittered, but he did nothing.

Porportuk was an old man, but his cold nights retained for him his activity. He did not circle the table. He came across suddenly, over the top of the table. El-Soo was taken off her guard. She sprang back with a sharp cry of alarm, and Porportuk would have caught her had it not been for Tommy. Tommy's leg went out. Porportuk tripped and pitched forward on the ground. El-Soo got her start.

"Then catch me," she laughed over her shoulder as she fled away.

She ran lightly and easily, but Porportuk ran swiftly and savagely. He outran her. In his youth he had been swiftest of all the young men. But El-Soo dodged in a willowy, elusive way. Being in native dress, her feet were not cluttered with skirts, and her pliant body curved a flight that defined the gripping fingers of Porportuk.

With laughter and tumult the great crowd scattered out to see the chase. It led through the Indian encampment; and ever dodging, circling, and reversing, El-Soo and Porportuk appeared and disappeared among the tents. El-Soo seemed to balance herself against the air with her arms, now one side, now on the other, and sometimes her body, too, leaned out upon the air far from the perpendicular as she achieved her sharpest curves. And Porportuk, always a leap behind, or a leap this side or that, like a lean hound strained after her.

They crossed the open ground beyond the encampment and disappeared in the forest. Tanana Station waited their reappearance, and long and vainly it waited.

In the meantime Akoon ate and slept, and lingered much at the steamboat landing, deaf to the rising resentment of Tanana Station in that he did nothing. Twenty-four hours later Porportuk returned. He was tired and savage. He spoke to no one but Akoon, and with him tried to pick a quarrel. But Akoon shrugged his shoulders and walked away. Porportuk did not waste time. He outfitted half a dozen of the young men, selecting the best trackers and travelers, and at their head plunged into the forest.

Next day the steamer *Seattle*, bound upriver, pulled into the shore and wooded up. When the lines were cast off and she churned out from the bank, Akoon was on board in the pilothouse. Not many hours afterward, when it was his turn at the wheel, he saw a small birchbark canoe put off from the shore. There was only one person in it. He studied it carefully, put the wheel over, and slowed down.

The captain entered the pilothouse.

"What's the matter?" he demanded. "The water's good."

Akoon grunted. He saw a larger canoe leaving the bank, and in it were a number of persons. As the *Seattle* lost headway, he put the wheel over some more.

The captain fumed. "It's only a squaw," he protested.

Akoon did not grunt. He was all eyes for the squaw and the pursuing canoe. In the latter six paddles were flashing, while the squaw paddled slowly.

"You'll be aground," the captain protested, seizing the wheel.

But Akoon countered his strength on the wheel and looked him in the eyes. The captain slowly released the spokes.

"Queer beggar," he sniffed to himself.

Akoon held the *Seattle* on the edge of the shoal water and waited till he saw the squaw's fingers clutch the forward rail. Then he signaled for full speed ahead and ground the wheel over. The large canoe was very near, but the gap between it and the steamer was widening.

The squaw laughed and leaned over the rail. "Then catch me, Porportuk!" she cried.

Akoon left the steamer at Fort Yukon. He outfitted a small poling boat and went up the Porcupine River. And with him went El-Soo. It was a weary journey, and the way led across the backbone of the world; but Akoon had traveled it before. When they came to the headwaters of the Porcupine, they left the boat and went on foot across the Rocky Mountains.

Akoon greatly liked to walk behind El-Soo and watch the movement of her. There was a music in it that he loved. And especially he loved the well-rounded calves in their sheaths of soft-tanned leather, the slim ankles, and the small moccasined feet that were tireless through the longest days.

"You are light as air," he said, looking up at her. "It is no labor for you to walk. You almost float, so lightly do your feet rise and fall. You are like a deer, El-Soo; you are like a deer, and your eyes are like deer's eyes, sometimes when you look at me, or when you hear a quick sound and wonder if it be danger that stirs. Your eyes are like a deer's eyes now as you look at me."

And El-Soo, luminous and melting, bent and kissed Akoon.

"When we reach the Mackenzie we will not delay," Akoon said later. "We will go south before the winter catches us. We will go to the sun lands where there is no snow. But we will return. I have seen much of the world, and there is no land like Alaska, no sun like our sun, and the snow is good after the long summer."

"And you will learn to read," said El-Soo.

And Akoon said, "I will surely learn to read."

But there was delay when they reached the Mackenzie. They fell in with a band of Mackenzie Indians and, hunting, Akoon was shot by accident. The rifle was in the hands of a youth. The bullet broke Akoon's right arm and, ranging farther, broke two of his ribs. Akoon knew rough surgery, while El-Soo had learned some refinements at Holy Cross. The bones were finally set, and Akoon lay by the fire for them to knit. Also he lay by the fire so that the smoke would keep the mosquitoes away.

Then it was that Porportuk, with his six young men, arrived. Akoon groaned in his helplessness and made appeal to the Mackenzies. But Porportuk made demand, and the Mackenzies were perplexed. Porportuk was for seizing upon El-Soo, but this they would not permit. Judgment must be given, and, as it was an affair of man and woman, the council of the old men was called—this that warm judgment might not be given by the young men, who were warm of heart.

The old men sat in a circle about the smudge fire. Their faces were lean and wrinkled, and they gasped and panted for air. The smoke was not good for them. Occasionally they struck with withered hands at the mosquitoes, that braved the smoke. After such exertion they coughed hollowly and painfully. Some spat blood, and one of them sat a bit apart with head bowed forward, and bled slowly and continuously at the mouth; the coughing sickness had gripped them. They were as dead men; their time was short. It was a judgment of the dead.

"And I paid for her a heavy price," Porportuk concluded his complaint. "Such a price you have never seen. Sell all that is yours—sell your spears and arrows and rifles, sell your skins and furs, sell your tents and boats and dogs, sell everything, and you will not have maybe a thousand dollars. Yet did I pay for the woman, El-Soo, twenty-six times the price of all your spears and arrows and rifles, your skins and furs, your tents and boats and dogs. It was a heavy price."

The old men nodded gravely, though their wizened eye slits widened with wonder that any woman should be worth such a price. The one that bled at the mouth wiped his lips. "Is it true talk?" he asked each of Porportuk's six young men. And each answered that it was true.

"Is it true talk?" he asked El-Soo, and she answered, "It is true."

"But Porportuk has not told that he is an old man," Akoon said, "and that he has daughters older than El-Soo."

"It is true, Porportuk is an old man," said El-Soo.

"It is for Porportuk to measure the strength of his age," said he who bled at the mouth. "We be old men. Behold! Age is never so old as youth would measure it."

And the circle of old men champed their gums, and nodded approvingly, and coughed.

"I told him that I would never be his wife," said El-Soo.

"Yet you took from him twenty-six times all that we possess?" asked a one-eyed old man.

El-Soo was silent.

"Is it true?" And his one eye burned and bored into her like a fiery gimlet.

"It is true," she said.

"But I will run away again," she broke out passionately a moment later. "Always will I run away."

"That is for Porportuk to consider," said another of the old men. "It is for us to consider the judgment."

"What price did you pay for her?" was demanded of Akoon.

"No price did I pay for her," he answered. "She was above price. I did not measure her in gold dust, nor in dogs and tents and furs."

The old men debated among themselves and mumbled in undertones. "These old men are ice," Akoon said in English. "I will not listen to their judgment, Porportuk. If you take El-Soo, I will surely kill you."

The old men ceased and regarded him suspiciously. "We do not know the speech you make," one said.

"He but said that he would kill me," Porportuk volunteered. "So it were well to take from him his rifle and to have some of your young men sit by him, that he may not do me hurt. He is a young man, and what are broken bones to youth!"

Akoon, lying helpless, had rifle and knife taken from him, and to either side of his shoulders sat young men of the Mackenzies. The one-eyed old man arose and stood upright. "We marvel at the price paid for one mere woman," he began; "but the wisdom of the price is no concern of ours. We are here to give judgment, and judgment we give. We have no doubt. It is known to all that Porportuk paid a heavy price for the woman El-Soo. Wherefore does the woman El-Soo belong to Porportuk and none other." He sat down heavily and coughed. The old men nodded and coughed.

"I will kill you," Akoon cried in English.

Porportuk smiled and stood up. "You have given true judgment," he said to the council, "and my young men will give to you much tobacco. Now let the woman be brought to me."

Akoon gritted his teeth. The young men took El-Soo by the arms. She did not resist and was led, her face a sullen flame, to Porportuk.

"Sit here at my feet till I have made my talk," he commanded. He paused a moment. "It is true," he said, "I am an old man. Yet can I understand the ways of youth. The fire has not all gone out of me. Yet am I no longer young, nor am I minded to run these old legs of mine through all the years that remain to me. El-Soo can run fast and well. She is a deer. This I know, for I have seen and run after her. It is not good that a wife should run so fast. I paid for her a heavy price, yet does she run away from me. Akoon paid no price at all, yet does she run to him.

"When I came among you people of the Mackenzie, I was of one mind. As I listened in the council and thought of the swift legs of El-Soo, I was of many minds. Now am I of one mind again, but it is a different mind from the one I brought to the council. Let me tell you my mind. When a dog runs once away from a master, it will run away again. No matter how many times it is brought back, each time it will run away again. When we have such dogs, we sell them. El-Soo is like a dog that runs away. I will sell her. Is there any man of the council that will buy?"

The old men coughed and remained silent.

"Akoon would buy," Porportuk went on, "but he has no money. Wherefore I will give El-Soo to him, as he said, without price. Even now will I give her to him."

Reaching down, he took El-Soo by the hand and led her across the space to where Akoon lay on his back.

"She has a bad habit, Akoon," he said, seating her at Akoon's feet. "As she has run away from me in the past, in the days to come she may run away from you. But there is no need to fear that she will ever run away, Akoon. I shall see to that. Never will she run away from you—this the word of Porportuk. She has great wit. I know, for often has it bitten into me. Yet am I minded myself to give my wit play for once. And by my wit will I secure her to you, Akoon."

Stooping, Porportuk crossed El-Soo's feet, so that the instep of one lay over that of the other; and then, before his purpose could be divined, he discharged his rifle through the two ankles. As Akoon struggled to rise against the weight of the young men, there was heard the crunch of the broken bone rebroken.

"It is just," said the old men, one to another.

El-Soo made no sound. She sat and looked at her shattered ankles, on which she would never walk again.

"My legs are strong, El-Soo," Akoon said. "But never will they bear me away from you."

El-Soo looked at him, and for the first time in all the time he had known her, Akoon saw tears in her eyes.

"Your eyes are like deer's eyes, El-Soo," he said.

"Is it just?" Porportuk asked, and grinned from the edge of the smoke as he prepared to depart.

"It is just," the old men said. And they sat on in the silence.

Like Jack London, Rex Beach (1877–1949) wrote of the Yukon and Alaska frontiers from personal experience. As a result, such novels as The Spoilers, The Barrier, The Iron Trail, The Winds of Chance, and Valley of Thunder are filled with vivid descriptions, memorable characters and locales, and an unvarnished sense of the hardships and satisfactions of life in the Far North at the turn of the century. The same is true of Beach's short fiction, as "The Stampede"—a story of men caught up in the headlong pursuit of gold—effectively demonstrates. Beach's other fine northland tales appear in such collections as Pardners (1905), Laughing Bill Hyde and Other Stories (1923), and North of Fifty-Three (1924).

The Stampede

★★★★★★★★★★★★★★★

Rex Beach

From their vantage on the dump, the red gravel of which ran like a raw scar down the mountainside, the men looked out across the gulch, above the western range of hills to the yellow setting sun. Far below them the creek was dotted with other tiny pay dumps of the same red gravel over which men crawled, antlike, or upon which they labored at windlass. Thin wisps of smoke rose from the cabin roofs, bespeaking the supper hour.

They had done a hard day's work, these two, and wearily descended to their shack, which hugged the hillside beneath.

Ten hours with pick and shovel in a drift where the charcoal-gas flickers a candle flame will reduce one's artistic keenness, and together they slouched along the path, heedless alike of view or color.

As Crowley built the fire, Buck scoured himself in the wet snow beside the door, emerging from his ablutions as cook. The former stretched upon the bunk with growing luxury. "Gee whiz! I'm tuckered out. Twelve hours in that air is too much for anybody."

"Sure," growled the other. "Bet I sleep good tonight, all right, all right. What's the use, anyhow?" he continued, disgustedly.

"I'm sore on the whole works. If the Yukon was open, I'd chuck it all."

"What! Go back to the States? Give up?"

"Well, yes, if you want to call it that, though I think I've shown I ain't a quitter. Lord! I've rustled steady for two years, and what have I got? Nothing—except my interest in this pauperized hill claim."

"If two years of hard luck gives you cold feet, you ain't worthy of the dignity of 'prospector.' This here is the only honorable calling there is. There's no competition and cuttin' throats in our business, nor we don't rob the widders and orphans. A prospector is defined as a semi-human being with a low forehead but a high sense of honor, a stummick that shies at salads, but a heart that's full of grit. They don't never lay down, and the very beauty of the business is that you never know when you're due. Some day a guy comes along: 'I hit her over yonder, bo,' says he, whereupon you insert yourself into a pack-strap, pound the trail, and the next you know you're a millionaire or two."

"Bah! No more stampedes for me. I've killed myself too often— there's nothing in 'em. I'm sick of it, I tell you, and I'm going out to God's country. No more wild scrambles and hardships for Buck."

A step sounded on the chips without, and a slender, sallow man entered.

"Hello, Maynard!" they chorused, and welcomed him to a seat.

"What are you doing out here?"

"D'you bring any chewing with you?"

Evidently he labored under excitement, for his face was flushed and his eyes danced nervously. He panted from his climb, ignoring their questions.

"There's been a big strike—over on the Tanana—four bits to the pan."

Forgetting fatigue, Crowley scrambled out of his bunk while the cook left his steaming skillet.

"When?"

"How d'you know?"

"It's this way. I met a fellow as I came out from town—he'd just come over—one of the discoverers. He showed me the gold. It's coarse; one nugget weighed three hundred dollars and there's only six men in the party. They went up the Tanana last fall, prospecting, and only just struck it. Three of 'em are down with scurvy, so this one came over the mountains for fresh grub. It'll be the biggest stampede this camp ever saw." Maynard became incoherent.

"How long ago did you meet him?" Crowley inquired, excitedly.

"About an hour. I came on the run because he'll get into camp by eleven, and midnight will see five hundred men on the trail. Look at this—he gave me a map." The speaker gloatingly produced a scrap of writing paper and continued, "Boys, you've got five hours' start of them."

"We can't go; we haven't got any dogs," said Buck. "Those people from town would catch us in twenty miles."

"You don't want dogs," Maynard answered. "It's too soft. You'll have to make a quick run with packs or the spring breakup will catch you. I wish I could go. It's big, I tell you. Lord! How I wish I could go!"

They were huddled together, their eyes feverish, their fingers tracing the pencil markings. A smell of burning food filled the room, but there is no obsession more absolute than the gold lust.

"Get the packs together while me and Buck eats a bite. We'll take the fox robe and the Navajo. Glad I've got a new pair of mukluks, 'cause we need light footgear; but what will you wear, boy? Them hip-boots is too heavy—you'd never make it."

"Here," said Maynard, "try these." He slipped off his light gossamer sporting boots, and Buck succeeded in stamping his feet into them.

"Little tight, but they'll go."

They snatched bites of food, meanwhile collecting their paraphernalia, Maynard helping as he could.

Each selected a change of socks and mittens. Then the grub was divided evenly—tea, flour, bacon, baking powder, salt, sugar. There was nothing else, for spring on the Yukon finds only the heel of the grubstake. Each rolled his portion in his blanket and lashed it with light rope. Then an end of the bundle was thrust into the waist of a pair of overalls and the garment closely cinched to it. The legs were brought forward and fastened, forming two loops through which they slipped their arms, balancing the packs or shifting a knot here and there. A light ax, a coffeepot, frying pan, and pail were tied on the outside, and they stood ready for the run. They stored carefully wrapped bundles of matches in pockets, packs, and in the lining of their caps. The preparations had not taken twenty minutes.

"Too bad we 'ain't got some cooked grub, like chocolate or dog biscuits," said Crowley, "but seeing as we've got five hours' start over everybody, we won't have to kill ourselves."

Maynard spoke hesitatingly. "Say, I told Sully about it as I came along."

"What!" Crowley interrupted him sharply.

"Yes! I told him to get ready, and I promised to give him the location an hour after you left. You see, he did me a good turn once and I had to get back at him somehow. He and Knute are getting fixed now. Why, what's up?"

He caught a queer, quick glance between his partners and noted a hardness settle into the lined face of the elder.

"Nothing much," Buck took up. "I guess you didn't know about the trouble, eh? Crowley knocked him down day before yesterday and Sully swears he'll kill him on sight. It came up over that fraction on Buster Creek."

"Well, well," said Maynard, "that's bad, isn't it? I promised, though, so I'll have to tell him."

"Sure! That's all right," Crowley agreed, quietly, though his lip curled, showing the strong, close-shut, ivory teeth. His nostrils dilated, also, giving his face a passing wolfish hint. "There's neither white man nor Swede that can gain an hour on us, and if he should happen to—he wouldn't pass."

Be it known that many great placer fortunes have been won by those who stepped in the warm tracks of the discoverers, while rarely does the goddess smile on the tardy; in consequence, no frenzy approaches that of the gold stampede.

Passing Sully's place, they found him and his partner ready and waiting, their packs on the sawbuck. Crowley glared at his enemy in silence while the other sneered wickedly back, and Big Knute laughed in his yellow beard.

Buck's heart sank. Could he outlast these two? He was a boy; they were reckless giants with thews and legs of iron. Knute was a gaunt-framed Viking; Sully a violent, florid man with the quarters of an ox. Through the quixotism of Maynard this trip bade fair to combine the killing grind of a long, fierce stampede with the bitter struggle of man and man, and too well he knew the temper of his redheaded partner to doubt that before the last stake was driven, either he or Sully would be down. From the glare in their eyes at passing it came over him that either he or Knute would recross the mountains partnerless. The trail was too narrow for these other men. He shrank from the toil and agony he felt was coming to him through this; then, with it, there came the burning gold hunger; the lust that drives starving, broken wrecks onward unremittingly, over misty hills, across the beds of lava and the forbidden tundra; on, into the new diggings.

It neared eight o'clock, and, although darkness was far distant, the chill that follows the sun fell sharply.

As they swung out on to the river, their fatigue had dropped away and they moved with the steady, loose gait of the hardened "musher." Buck looked at his watch. They had been gone an hour.

"The race is on!" said he.

Though unhurried, their progress was likewise unhindered, and the miles slipped backward as the darkness thickened, hour by hour. Straight up the fifty-mile stream to its source, over the great backbone and into the unmapped country their course led. If they hurried, they would have first choice of the good claims close about the discovery; if they lagged, Sully and his ox-eyed partner would overtake them, and beyond that it was unpleasant to conjecture.

"We'll hit water pretty soon!" Crowley's voice broke hours of silence, for they were sparing of language. They neither whistled nor sang nor spoke, for Man is a potential body from which his store of energy wastes through tiny unheeded ways.

True to prophecy, in the darkness of midnight they walked out upon a thin skin of newly frozen ice.

"Look out for the overflow! She froze since dark," Crowley cautioned. "We're liable to go through."

On all sides it cracked alarmingly, while they felt it sag beneath their feet. It is bad in the dark to ride the ice of an overflow, for one may crash through ankle-deep to the solid body beneath or plunge to his armpits.

They skated over the yielding surface toward safety till, without warning, Crowley smashed in halfway to his hips. He fell forward bodily, and the ice let him through till he rolled in the water. Buck skimmed over more lightly, and, when they had reached the solid footing, helped him wring out his garments. Straightway the cloth whitened under the frost and crackled when they resumed their march, but there was no time for fires, and by vigorous action he could keep the cold from striking in.

They had threaded up into the region where spring was further advanced, and within half an hour encountered another overflow. Climbing the steep bank, they wallowed through thickets waist-deep in snow. Beneath the crust, which cut knifelike, it was wet and soggy, so they emerged saturated. Then debouching on to the glare ice, the boy had a nasty fall, for he slipped, and his loose-hung pack flung him suddenly. Nothing is more wicked than a pack on smooth ice. The surface had frozen glass-smooth, and constant difficulty beset their progress. Their slick-soled footgear refused to grip it, so that often they fell, always awkwardly, occasionally crushing through into the icy water beneath.

Without warning Buck found that he was very tired. He also

found that his pack had grown soggy and quadrupled in weight, tugging sullenly at his aching shoulders.

As daylight showed, they slipped harness and, hurriedly gathering twigs, boiled a pot of tea. They took time to prepare nothing else, yet even though the kettle sang speedily as they drank, from around the bend below came voices. Crowley straightened with a curse and, snatching his pack, fled up the stream followed by his companion. They ran till Buck's knees failed him. Thereupon the former removed a portion of the youngster's burden, adding it to his own, and they hurried on for hours, till they fell exhausted upon a dry moss hummock. Here they exchanged footgear, as Buck now found his feet were paining him acutely, owing to the tightness of his rubber boots. They proved too small for Crowley as well, and in a few hours his feet were likewise ruined.

Noon found them limping among the bald hills of the river's source. Here timber was sparse and the snows, too, had thinned; so to avoid the convolutions of the stream, they cut across points, floundering among "niggerheads"—quaint, wobbly hummocks of grass—being thrown repeatedly by their packs which had developed a malicious deviltry. This footing was infinitely worse than the reeking ice, but it saved time, so they took it.

Now, under their stiff mackinaws they perspired freely as the sun mounted, until their heavy garments chafed them beneath arms and legs. Moreover, mosquitoes, which in this latitude breed within arm's length of snowdrifts, continually whined in a vicious cloud before their features.

Human nerves will weather great strains, but wearing, maddening, unending trivialities will break them down, and so, although their journey in miles had been inconsiderable, the dragging packs, the driving panic, the lack of food and firm footing, had trebled it.

Scaling the moss-capped saddle, they labored painfully, a hundred yards at a time. Back of them the valley unrolled, its stream winding away like a gleaming ribbon, stretching, through dark banks of fir, down to the Yukon. After incredible effort they reached the crest and gazed dully out to the southward over a limitless jangle of peaks, on, on, to a blue-veiled valley leagues and leagues across. Many square miles lay under them in the black of unbroken forests. It was their first glimpse of the Tanana. Far beyond, from a groveling group of foothills, a solitary, giant peak soared grandly, standing aloof, serene, terrible in its proportions. Even in their fatigue they exclaimed aloud:

"It's Mount McKinley!"

"Yep! Tallest wart on the face of the continent. There's the creek we go down—see!'' Crowley indicated a watercourse which meandered away through cañons and broad reaches. ''We foller it to yonder cross valley; then east to there.''

To Buck's mind, his gesture included a tinted realm as far-reaching as a state.

Stretched upon the bare schist, commanding the back stretch, they munched slices of raw bacon.

Directly, out toward the mountain's foot, two figures crawled.

''There they come!'' and Crowley led, stumbling, sliding, into the strange valley.

As this was the south and early side of the range, they found the hills more barren of snow. Water seeped into the gulches till the creek ice was worn and rotted.

''This'll be fierce,'' the Irishman remarked. ''If she breaks on us, we'll be hung up in the hills and starve before the creeks lower enough to get home.''

Small streams freeze solidly to the bottom and the spring waters wear downward from the surface. Thus they found the creek awash, and, following farther, it became necessary to wade in many places. They came to a box cañon where the winter snow had packed, forming a dam, and as there was no way of avoiding it without retreating a mile and climbing the ragged bluff, they floundered through, their packs aloft, the slushy water armpit-deep.

''We'd ought 'a' took the ridges,'' Buck chattered. Language slips forth phonetically with fatigue.

''No! Feller's apt to get lost. Drop into the wrong creek—come out fifty mile away.''

''I bet the others do, anyhow,'' Buck held, stubbornly. ''It's lots easier going.''

''Wish Sully would, but he's too wise. No such luck for me.'' A long pause. ''I reckon I'll have to kill him before he gets back!'' Again they relapsed into miles of silence.

Crowley's fancy fed on vengeance, hatred livening his work-worn faculties. He nursed carefully the memory of their quarrel, for it helped him travel and took his mind from the agony of movement and this aching sleep-hunger.

The feet of both men felt like fearful, shapeless masses; their packs leaned backward sullenly, chafing raw shoulder sores; and always the ravenous mosquitoes stung and stung, and whined and whined.

At an exclamation the leader turned. Miles back, silhouetted far above on the comb of the ridge, they descried two tiny figures.

''That's what we'd ought 'a' done. They'll beat us in.''

"No, they won't. They'll have to camp tonight or get lost, while we can keep goin'. We can't go wrong down here; can't do no more than drownd."

Buck groaned at the thought of the night hours. He couldn't stand it, that was all! Enough is enough of anything and he had gone the limit. Just one more mile and he would quit; yet he did not.

All through that endless phantom night they floundered, incased in freezing garments, numb and heavy with sleep, but morning found them at the banks of the main stream.

"You look like hell," said Buck, laughing weakly. His mirth relaxed his nerves suddenly, till he giggled and hiccoughed hysterically. Nor could he stop for many minutes, the while Crowley stared at him apathetically from a lined and shrunken countenance, his features standing out skeleton-like. The younger man evidenced the strain even more severely, for his flesh was tender, and he had traveled the last hours on pure nerve. His jaws were locked and corded, however, while his drooping eyes shone unquenchably.

Eventually they rounded a bluff on to a cabin nestling at the mouth of a dark valley. Near it men were working with a windlass, so, stumbling to them, they spoke huskily.

"Sorry we 'ain't got room inside," the stranger replied, "but three of the boys is down with scurvy, and we're all cramped up. Plenty more folks coming, I s'pose, eh?"

The two had sunk on to the wet ground and did not answer. Buck fell with his pack still on, utterly lost, and the miner was forced to drag the bundle from his shoulders. As he rolled him up, he was sleeping heavily.

Crowley awakened while the sun was still golden; his joints aching excruciatingly. They had slept four hours. He boiled tea on the miners' stove and fried a pan of salt pork, but was too tired to prepare anything else, so they drank the warm bacon grease clear with their tea.

As Buck strove to arise, his limbs gave way weakly, so that he fell, and it took him many moments to recover their use.

"Where's the best chance, pardner?" they inquired of the men on the dump.

"Well, there ain't none very close by. We've got things pretty well covered."

"How's that? There's only six of you; you can't hold but six claims, besides discovery."

"Oh yes, we can! We've got powers of attorney; got 'em last fall in St. Michael; got 'em recorded, too."

Crowley's sunken eyes blazed.

"Them's no good. We don't recko'nize 'em in this district. One claim is enough for any man if it's good, and too much if it's bad."

"What district you alludin' at?" questioned the other, ironically. "You're in the Skookum District now. It takes six men to organize. Well! We organized. We made laws. We elected a recorder. I'm it. If you don't like our rules, yonder is the divide. We've got the U. S. government back of us. See!"

Crowley's language became purely local, but the other continued unruffled.

"We knew you-all was coming, so we sort of loaded up. If there's any ground hereabouts that we ain't got blanketed, it's purely an oversight. There's plenty left farther out, though," and he swept them a mocking gesture. "Help yourselves and pass up for more. I'll record 'em."

"What's the fee?"

"Ten dollars apiece."

Crowley swore more savagely.

"You done a fine job of hoggin', didn't you? It's two and a half everywhere else."

But the recorder of the Skookum District laughed carelessly and resumed his windlass. "Sorry you ain't pleased. Maybe you'll learn to like it."

As they turned away he continued: "I don't mind giving you a hunch, though. Tackle that big creek about five miles down yonder. She prospected good last fall, but you'll have to go clean to her head, 'cause we've got everything below."

Eight hours later, by the guiding glare of the Northern Lights, the two stumbled back into camp, utterly broken.

They had followed the stream for miles and miles to find it staked by the powers of attorney of the six. Coming to the gulch's head, to be sure, they found vacant ground, but refused to claim such unpromising territory. Then the endless homeward march through the darkness! Out of thickets and through drifts they burst, while fatigue settled on them like some horrid vampire from the darkness. Every step being no longer involuntary became a separate labor, requiring mental concentration. They were half dead in slumber as they walked, but their stubborn courage and smoldering rage at the men who had caused this drove them on. They suffered silently, because it takes effort to groan, and they hoarded every atom of endurance.

Many, many times Buck repeated a poem, timing his steps to its rhythm, rendering it over and over till it wore a rut through his brain, his eyes fixed dully upon the glaring fires above the hilltops. For years a faintness came over him with the memory of these lines:

> Then dark they lie, and stark they lie, rookery, dune, and floe,
> And the Northern Lights came down o' nights to dance with the
>   houseless snow.

Reaching the cabin, they found an army of men sleeping heavily upon the wet moss. Among them was the great form of Knute, but nowhere did they spy Sully.

With much effort they tore off the constricting boots and, using them for pillows, sank into a painful lethargy.

Awakened early by the others, they took their stiffly frozen footgear beneath the blankets to thaw against their warm bodies, but their feet were swelled to double size and every joint had ossified rheumatically. Eventually they hobbled about, preparing the first square meal since the start—two days and three nights.

Still they saw no Sully, though Crowley's eyes darted careful inquiry among the horde of stampeders which moved about the cabin. Later, he seemed bent on some hidden design, so they crawled out of sight of the camp, then, commencing at the upper stake of Discovery, he stepped off the claims from post to post.

It is customary to blaze the boundaries of locations on tree trunks, but from topographical irregularities it is difficult to properly gauge these distances, hence, many rich fractions have been run over by the heedless, to fall to him who chained the ground.

Upon pacing the third one, he showed excitement.

"You walk this one again—mebbe I made a mistake."

Buck returned, crashing through the brush.

"I make it seventeen hundred."

The claim above figured likewise, and they trembled with elation as they blazed their lines.

Returning to camp, they found the recorder in the cabin with the scurvy patients. Unfolding the location notices, his face went black as he read, while he snarled, angrily:

" 'Fraction between Three and Four' and 'Fraction between Four and Five,' eh? You're crazy."

"I reckon not," said Crowley, lifting his lips at the corners characteristically.

"There ain't any fraction there," the other averred, loudly. "We own them claims. I told you we had everything covered."

"You record them fractions!"

"I won't do it! I'll see you in—"

Crowley reached forth suddenly and strangled him as he sat. He buried his thumbs in his throat, forcing him roughly back against a bunk. Farther and farther he crushed him till the man lay pinioned and writhing on his back. Then he knelt on him, shaking and worrying like a great terrier.

At the first commotion the cripples scrambled out of bed, shouting lustily through their livid gums, their bloated features mottled and sickly with fright. One lifted himself toward the Winchester, and it fell from his hands full cocked when Buck hurled him into a corner, where he lay screaming in agony.

Drawn by the uproar, the stampeders outside rushed toward the shack to be met in the door by the young man.

"Keep back!"

"What's up!"

"Fight!"

"Let me in!"

A man bolted forward, but was met with such a driving blow in the face that he went thrashing to the slush. Another was hurled back, and then they heard Crowley's voice, rough and throaty, as he abused the recorder. Strained to the snapping point, his restraint had shattered to bits and now passion ran through him, wild and unbridled.

From his words they grasped the situation, and their sympathies changed. They crowded the door and gazed curiously through the window to see him jam the recorder shapelessly into a chair, place pen and ink in his hand, and force him to execute two receipts. It is not a popular practice, this blanketing, as the temper of the watchers showed.

"Serves 'em right, the hogs," someone said, and he voiced the universal sentiment.

That night, as they ravened over their meager meal, Knute came to them, hesitatingly. He was greatly worried and apprehension wrinkled his wooden face.

"Saay! W'at you t'ink 'bout Sully?"

"I don't know. Why?"

"By yingo, ay t'ink he's lose!"

"Lost! How's that?"

In his dialect, broken by anxiety, he told how Sully and he had quarreled on the big divide. Maddened by failure to gain on Crowley, the former had insisted on following the mountain crests in the hope of quicker travel. The Swede had yielded reluctantly till, frightened by the network of radiating gulches which spread out beneath their feet in a bewildering sameness, he had refused to go farther. They had quarreled. In a fit of fury Sully had hurled his pack away, and Knute's last vision of him had been as he went raving and cursing onward like a madman, traveling fast in his fury. Knute had retreated, dropped into the valley, and eventually reached his goal.

There is no time for reliefs on a stampede. The gentler emotions are left in camp with the women. He who would risk life, torture, and privation for a stranger will trample pitilessly on friend and enemy blinded by the gold glitter or drunken with the chase of the rainbow.

For five days and nights the army lived on its feet, streaming up gullies where lay the hint of wealth or swarming over the somber bluffs; and hourly the madness grew, feeding on itself, till they fought like beasts. Fabulous values were begotten. Giant sales were bruited about. Flying rumors of gold at the cross roots inflamed them to further frenzy.

A town site was laid out and a terrible scramble for lots ensued.

One man was buried in the plot he claimed, his disputant being adjudged the owner by virtue of his quicker draw. It was manslaughter, they knew, but no one spared the time to guard him, so he went free. Nor did he run away. One cannot, while the craze is on.

Five days of this, and then the stream broke. With it broke the delirium of the five hundred. The valleys roared and bawled from bluff to bluff, while the flats became seas of seething ice and rubbish. Thus, cut off from home, they found their grub was gone, for everyone had clung till his food grew low. As the obsession left them, their brotherhood returned—food was apportioned in community, and they spoke vaguely of the fate of Sully.

For still another half fortnight they lay about the cabin while the streams raged, and then Crowley spoke to his partner. Rolling their blankets, they started, and, although many were tempted to go, none had the courage, preferring to starve on quarter rations till the waters lowered.

Ascending for miles where the torrent narrowed, they felled a tree across for a bridge and, ascending the ridges, took the direction of camp. In a new and broken country, not formed of continuous ranges, this is difficult. So to avoid frequent fordings, they followed the high ground, going devious, confusing miles. The snows were largely gone, though the nights were cruel, and thus they traveled.

At last, when they had worked through to the Yukon spurs, one morning on a talus high above, Buck spied the flapping forms of a flock of ravens. They fluttered ceaselessly among the rocks, rising noisily, only to settle again.

These are the gleaming, baleful vultures of the North, and often they attain a considerable size and ferocity.

The men gazed at them with apathy. Was it worth while to spend the steps to see what drew them? By following their course they would pass far to the right.

"I hate the dam' things," said Crowley, crossly. "I seen 'em, oncet, hangin' to a caribou calf with a broken leg, tryin' to pick his eyes out. Let's see what it is."

He veered to the left, scrambling up among the boulders. The birds rose fretfully, perching nearby, but the men saw nothing. As they rested momentarily, the birds again swooped downward, reassured.

Then, partly hidden among the detritus, they spied that which made Crowley cry out in horror, while the sound of Buck's voice was like the choking of a woman. As they started, one of the ebony scavengers dipped fiercely, picking at a ragged object. A human arm slowly arose and blindly beat it off, but the raven's mate settled also, and, sinking its beak into the object, tore hungrily.

With a shout they stumbled forward, lacerated by the jagged slide rock, only to pause aghast and shaking.

Sully lay crouched against a boulder where he had crawled for the sun heat. Rags of clothing hung upon his gaunt frame, through which the sharp bones strove to pierce; also at sight of his hands and feet they shuddered. With the former he had covered his eyes from the ravens, but his cheeks and head were bloody and shredded. He muttered constantly, like the thick whirring of machinery run down.

"Oh, my God!" Buck whispered.

Crowley had mastered himself and knelt beside the figure. He looked up and tears lay on his cheeks.

"Look at them hands and feet! That was done by fire and frost together. He must have fell in his own camp fires after he went crazy."

The garments were burned off to elbow and knee, while the flesh was black and raw.

Tenderly they carried the gabbing creature down to the timber and laid him on a bed of boughs. His condition told the grim tale of his wanderings, crazed with hunger and hardship.

Heating water, they poured it into him, dressing his wounds with strips from their underclothes. Of stimulants they had none, but fed him the last pinch of flour, together with the final rasher of salt pork, although they knew that these things are not good for starving men. For many days they had traveled on less than quarter rations themselves.

"What will we do?"

"It ain't over twenty miles to the niggers'. He'll die before we can get help back. D'ye reckon we can carry him?"

It was not sympathy which prompted Crowley, for he sympathized with his boyish companion, whose sufferings it hurt him sorely to augment. It was not pity; he pitied himself, and his own deplorable condition; nor did mercy enter into his processes, for the man had mercilessly planned to kill him, and he likewise had nursed a bitter hatred against him, which misfortune could only dim. It was not these things which moved him, but a vaguer, wilder quality; an elemental, unspoken, indefinable feeling of brotherhood throughout the length of the North, teaching subtly, yet absolutely and without appeal, that no man shall be left in his extremity to the cruel harshness of this forbidding land.

"Carry him?" Buck cried. "No! You're crazy! What's the use? He'll die, anyhow—and so'll we if we don't get grub soon." Buck was new to the country, and he was a boy.

"No, he won't. He lived hard and he'll die hard, for he's a hellion—he is. We've got to pack him in!"

"By God! I won't risk *my* life for a corpse—'specially one like him." The lad broke out in hysterical panic, for he had lived on the raggedest edge of his nerve these many days. Now his every muscle was dead and numbed with pain. Only his mind was clear, caused by the effort to force movement into his limbs. When he stopped walking, he fell into a half slumber, which was acutely painful. When he arose to redrive his weary body, it became freakish, so that he fell or collided with trees. He was bloody and bruised and cut. Carry a dead man? It was madness, and, besides, he felt an utter giving away at every joint.

He was too tired to make his reasoning plain; his tongue was thick, and Crowley's brain too calloused to grasp argument, therefore he squatted beside the muttering creature and wept impotently. He was asleep, with tears in his stubbly beard, when his partner finished the rude litter, yet he took up his end of the burden, as Crowley knew he would.

"You'll kill us both, damn ye!" he groaned.

"Probably so, but we can't leave him to them things." The other nodded at the vampires perched observantly in the surrounding firs.

Then began their great trial and temptation. For hours on end the birds fluttered from tree to tree, always in sight and hoarsely complaining till the sick fancies of the men distorted them into foul, gibing creatures of the Pit screaming with devilish glee at their anguish. Blindly they staggered through the forest while the limbs reached forth to block them, thrusting sharp needles into their eyes or whipping back viciously. Vines writhed up their legs, straining to delay their march, and the dank moss curled ankle-deep, slyly tripping their dragging, swollen feet. Nature hindered them sullenly, with all her heartbreaking implacability. They reeled constantly under their burden and grew to hate the ragged-barked trees that smote them so cruelly and so roughly tore their flesh. Ofttimes they fell, rolling the maniac limply from his couch, but they dragged him back and strained forward to the hideous racket of his mumblings, which grew louder as his delirium increased. They were forced to tie him to the poles, but could not stop his ghastly shriekings. At every pause the dismal ravens croaked and leered evilly from the shadows, till Buck shuddered and hid his face while Crowley gnashed his teeth. From time to time other birds joined them in anticipation of the feast, till they were ringed about, and the sight of this ever-growing, grisly, clamorous flock of watchers became awful to the men. They felt the horny talons searching their flesh and the hungry beaks tearing at their eyeballs.

A dogsled and birchbark practice covering both banks of the Yukon for two hundred miles yielded Doc Lewis sufficient revenue to grubstake a Swede. Thus he slept warm, kept his feet dry, and was still a miner. He did not believe in hardship, and eschewed stampedes. Yet when he had seen the last able-bodied man vanish from camp on the Skookum run, he grew restless. He scoffed at fake excitements to Jarvis, the faro dealer, who also forebore the trail by virtue of his calling, but he got no satisfaction. A fortnight later he rolled his blankets and journeyed toilsomely up the river valley.

"Better late than never," he thought.

Arriving at the empty shack of the negroes, he camped, only to awaken during the night to the roar of the torrent at his door. Having seen other mountain streams in the breakup, he waited philosophically, hunting ptarmigan among the firs back of the cabin.

He had lost track of the days when, down the gulch in the morning light, he descried a strange party approaching.

Two men bore between them a stretcher made from their shirts. They crawled with dreadful slowness, resting every hundred feet. Moreover, they stumbled and staggered aimlessly through the niggerheads. As they drew near, he sighted their faces, from which the teeth grinned in a grimace of torture and through which the cheekbones seemed to penetrate.

He knew what the signs boded. For years he had ministered to these necessities, and no man had ever approached his success.

"It is the rape of the North they are doing," he sighed. "We ravage her stores, but she takes grim toll from all of us." He moved the hot water forward on the stove, cleared off the rude table, and laid out his instrument case.

Born in London, Victor Rousseau Emanuel (1879–1960) emigrated to the U.S. during the First World War. From 1916 until the outbreak of World War II he contributed hundreds of stories to a wide range of fantasy, science fiction, Western, and adventure pulp magazines. His knowledge of the people and places of the Far North was considerable, as evidenced by his numerous appearances in North-West Stories *and by "Captives of the Arctic Wastelands," a rousing saga of action and adventure on the Labrador coast. Several of his Northern serials were published in book form in England in the 1930s; they include* The Big Muskeg *and* Wooden Spoil.

Captives of the Arctic Wastelands

★★★★★★★★★★★★★★★★

Victor Rousseau

THE little trading schooner deposited Dan Tennant upon the ice-battered quay at Nagatok about midday. The days of acute discomfort while the boat ran the gauntlet of the Labrador coast were over. Dan picked up his suit-case and wondered what the rest of the year was like, if this was a specimen of June.

Besides the *Mary Binns*, the only other craft of any size in the "tickle," or arm of water that led to Nagatok, the most northerly charted harbor of Labrador, was a large, trim yacht that lay off-shore.

Across the stretch of mud that performed the functions of a street, Dan saw the postmaster watching him as he essayed the difficult transit. The postmaster, elsewhere called a factor, was standing at the entrance of his store, a huge log building. Over the door Dan read:

HERBERT MACAULAY, POSTMASTER
AGENT FOR LIPPMANN BROS., NEW YORK

And that sign was unspeakably galling to Dan, because there was a photograph of that same store in the family album, in the house on Long Island, and in that photograph the sign read:

HERBERT MACAULAY, POSTMASTER
AGENT FOR SAMUEL TENNANT, NEW YORK

And for an instant Dan's eyes filmed slightly at the memory of the stubborn, irascible, whimsical, hardfisted old man who had quarreled so bitterly with him—a quarrel that had been cut short by his father's death before a reconciliation could be effected.

Sam Tennant had died in Labrador, and Dan's visit has been inspired in part by the desire to see the place where he had been buried.

Dan negotiated the last ruts of the road and stood before the postmaster, a short, thick, burly Scotchman.

"Mr. MacAulay," he began, "my name's Dan Tennant, and Sam Tennant was my father."

"I've heerd of you."

"I've just arrived by the *Mary Binns*."

"I've been expecting you."

Dan was nonplussed. He had confided to nobody his intention of visiting Labrador.

"Then you know what I've come for, I suppose?" he asked.

"Aye," responded MacAulay, "ye've come to see if there's not some pickings I've been holding back."

"You have no cause to suggest—" began Dan hotly.

"And ye've come to see your father. We're burying him this week."

"What's that?" cried Dan. "You mean—my father's—not buried yet?"

"There's nae burying in the Labrador between November and June. Your father's at the back."

Unnerved, Dan followed the surly postmaster toward the outhouse in the rear. MacAulay unlocked the door. It was an icehouse, and the huge blocks filled the greater part of the interior.

By the light that came in through the door and a tiny window, Dan could see the coffin resting on a pair of trestles. He steadied himself with one hand against the wall. It was incredible, it was abominable, that all of Sam Tennant's mortal being should be resting between those four coffin-boards.

"My father had a stroke, I understand," he said, trying to pull himself together.

"A stroke it was. He'd come into Nagatok to take the steamship out. If he'd taken her, he'd have found a grave beneath the waves, like Captain Fairleigh. But it was a stroke.

"He was standing in the store, talking to me, and he went down like a forest tree and never spoke again. He died next day. That was two days after the warehouse burned, and he knew he was a ruined man. Maybe it was the best way. It's not for me to say."

"No, it's not for you to say," Dan muttered. "And you've kept him there ever since?"

"Aye, and where else should he have been put? I was telling you there's no burying in the Labrador except in the summer months."

"I—I'd like to see him."

"I was waiting for ye to say that," muttered MacAulay, scowling at Dan. "I wouldn't advise it."

"Why not?"

"He was disfeegured. He went down on some iron anchors in the store. And he was a heavy man."

Dan, still overcome by the realization that his father lay inside that shell of pine, was in no state of mind to oppose MacAulay's attitude. He permitted the postmaster to usher him back into the store.

The interior of the log building was stacked high with furs and trade goods. Behind the long counter a Livyere breed was sorting out trade tokens of various values. MacAulay led the way into his office, which was partitioned off at one end of the warehouse. He gave Dan a chair and placed some books before him. "You'll find a full statement of your father's affairs there, Mr. Tennant," he said. "I understand from what your father let drop that you hadna seen each other for a year or two."

Dan nodded. No need to tell MacAulay the details of the quarrel. Sam Tennant had wanted his son to take over the business after he passed on, but Dan had refused to countenance methods that the hardhanded old man had proposed to use against the Lippmanns, who had broken down his fur monopoly in northern Labrador. He had left and enlisted in the Royal Mounted; while serving there he learned of his father's death, but it was three months before he could get his discharge.

"I understand," said Dan, "that everything is lost—the warehouse burned down, and the steamship sunk."

"Aye," said MacAulay.

"I had an offer from the Lippmanns of five thousand dollars for the goodwill of the business."

"And ye refused it, and threw away that much guid money. There's nothing of your father's left, except a few old traps."

"What I don't understand," said Dan, "is how my father's business could have been wiped out so completely."

"It had been running downhill for years. Your father's methods were antiquated. He expected his trappers to take all their trade in goods, and when the Lippmanns came in with modern methods and cash payments they drove him out. He wadna take advice.

"He stored his furs and shipped them when the ice went oot. That was all there was to it. When his warehouse burned, and the ship was lost, that was the end. His trappers are all working for the Lippmanns. They asked me to represent them, and I had to agree. I had to look oot for myself. I'd advise ye to go back."

"I understand my father had some rare furs in the warehouse, which he released as the market warranted. Are they all gone?"

"Everything went, I'm telling ye."

"And Captain Fairleigh?"

"Lies fifty fathoms deep off Tungalok. He sailed too late, and the ice pack caught him and his daughter.

"Molly Fairleigh was with him?" cried Dan in horror.

"Aye, she persuaded him to bring her up for the season. He was a fool to yield to a girl's whim."

Dan rose and strode up and down, while the postmaster watched him silently.

"Whose yacht is that in the harbor?" asked Dan abruptly.

" 'Tis a sportsman's, and he's looking for bears in the mountains. A domed fool of an Englishman."

"I thought it might be the Lippmanns'."

"Ye thought wrang. They willna be here till next month. I'd advise ye to go back on the *Mary Binns*."

"I've been thinking of going north and looking over my father's territory."

The postmaster, who had risen, advanced and gripped Dan's shoulder with a hand of steel, turning him around, so that he looked through the little window. Dan saw the barren foreshore, the tangle of dead bake-apple shrubs, the flats, the cliffs behind them.

"Noo ye see all there is to see," he said. "Ye could go hundreds of miles and see na mair. There's nothing north of Nagatok."

He released Dan's shoulder and stood glowering at him.

"Maybe," said Dan. "Anyway, I'll see the burned warehouse first. Where is it?"

The postmaster pointed westward. "A mile along the tickle,"

he answered. "Ye canna miss it. But it'll do no good to see it. Oot of this window ye can see everything. There's nothing north of Nagatok."

II

DAN left his suitcase in one of the three so-called bedrooms which, with a dining room, formed an annex at the rear of the postmaster's store and served to accommodate infrequent visitors. The room, which was divided from the one on either side by the thinnest of pine planking, contained a stretcher cot and a pitcher and a basin on a washstand—nothing more.

Declining MacAulay's surly offer of a meal, on the plea that he had already dined, Dan left the store and started along the muddy road, conscious that the postmaster was watching him from his door the while. Where the so-called road ended, a comparatively hard trail ran along the shore of the tickle, and Dan, glad to have left Nagatok behind him, gave himself up to the consideration of his problem.

The discovery that his father's body still remained unburied had shocked him to such an extent that he felt he had been unable to meet MacAulay on his own ground, had probably given him the impression that he was a weakling in will. Certainly MacAulay, hectoring Dan and laying his hand upon his shoulder in a contemptuous manner, could not have guessed that during his two years in the Royal Mounted, Dan had made a name for himself as an efficient and fearless constable.

Should he insist on seeing his father's face again before the remains were committed to the ground? It did not seem a matter requiring prolonged deliberation, and yet Dan's indecision left him miserable.

And then there was the news that Molly Fairleigh had gone down with her father off Tungalok, in fifty fathoms of icy water.

Dan had never met Molly, but he had met old Captain Fairleigh three or four times, since the old man always came to dine with Sam Tennant at Manhasset, after bringing the *Hope* south in the fall.

Fairleigh had been superlatively proud of that daughter of his and was educating her at a private school on the St. Lawrence. Dan had seen Molly's photograph and had heard a good deal about her. She had seemed to have her father under her thumb.

But how could Fairleigh have been mad enough to take her with him into Labrador?

And how could Fairleigh, with thirty years' experience of the sea and knowing the Labrador coast like a book, have got caught in the ice off Tungalok?

Besides these two items for reflection, Dan had to consider the situation as it concerned the business.

Sam Tennant had gone to Labrador when a young man and had slowly established what was practically a monopoly in the fur trade. When the modern demand for furs sent prices sky-rocketing, he had seen the possibilities of fabulous profits in a land almost unexploited.

It was on one of his infrequent trips south that he met and married the girl who became Dan's mother. After her death, Sam Tennant lived only for his ideal. Before his death he was nearly a millionaire, and the owner of a country home on Long Island, and Dan had gone through Princeton.

Then the Lippmanns had invaded the Labrador with a policy of ruthless price-cutting and had begun to eat into Sam Tennant's profits. It was over the methods to be adopted against them that Dan had quarreled with his father.

Though he knew that the old man had been badly hit, he had been astounded to learn that the whole business had been wiped out. He knew that his father had had something like a quarter of a million dollars' worth of the rarer furs stored in his ware-house at Nagatok. If the warehouse had been destroyed by fire, it had been an incendiary fire, and Dan suspected that the Lippmanns had been responsible for it.

Dan's plan had been to go to Tungalok, a coastal district about a hundred and fifty miles north of Nagatok. He knew that a number of his father's trappers had cabins in that region. And there was a man named McAndrew of whom Sam Tennant had often spoken as one of his best employees. Dan had planned to seek out McAndrew and discuss the situation with him, learn what he could learn.

Since the interview with MacAulay, for some reason his suspicions had been growing stronger.

As he left the settlement behind, the fog of despondency began to lift from Dan's mind. He inhaled the salt air from the sea and threw back his shoulders. After all, suppose MacAulay's story was true, and there was nothing left, why should he not remain in Labrador and fight the Lippmanns on his father's ground?

Greenhorn though he was, his experience in the Northwest would stand him in good stead. And he felt that in that way he would be atoning for the foolish quarrel that had separated him from the father whom he had always admired and loved.

In the clear air of the afternoon the distances seemed foreshortened. Dan could see the bend of the tickle to the end of the humpbacked island and the open sea beyond. In the middle of the bend he could make out a cluster of Eskimo skin tents near the water. Some distance back, on a rising knoll, surrounded by a patch of dwarf willows, was what looked like a ruin.

Dan knew that this was his father's warehouse, and, leaving the trail, he struck out a course through the dead bake-apple shrubs, at whose base the green of new shoots was just beginning to appear. The half-frozen marsh made progress difficult at first, and Dan found himself floundering ankle-deep in the viscous mud; then, as the ground began to slope upward, he was able to make his way more easily. At last he reached the ruined structure.

The devastation had been complete. The large warehouse consisted of nothing more than a crisscross of charred logs. The roof was gone, and half-burned beams filled the interior, together with a miscellaneous debris of what had once been trade goods, but was now simply a mass decomposition.

Looking closely, Dan could distinguish fibers of cloth in this amorphous substance, and here and there tin cans, fused by the heat into shapeless lumps of metal. The hole lay a foot deep in the ground, half buried under the snow that still covered the greater part of the interior.

Dan did not know what he was looking for, or what incited him to his more or less aimless examination of this debris. Certainly he did not expect to find any clue that would assist him in his problem. Nevertheless, he went idly about the inside of the ruined structure, poking here and there with a stick, but uncovering only fragments of trade cloth, scraps of fur, coated with mud, bits of wood, broken glass, scraps of metal.

He was about to turn away when he saw what looked like an iron bar lying in a corner of the place, under a fragment of roof that had left that particular corner free from snow and mud. He stooped and picked it up idly, without any particular purpose.

Then of a sudden he saw something on the end of it—something that made him spring back and drop the bar in horror.

After a moment he stooped and picked it up again. It was a round bar of iron, about two feet long, such as might have been used to protect a door or window. But on the end of it, as if stuck to the metal, was a little bunch of graying hair.

And it was human hair!

In that moment all Dan's suspicions leaped into the light of consciousness. That tuft of hair was so terribly like his father's. It was human hair, beyond a doubt, and not that of an animal. Dan stared at it, touched it with thumb and finger, and suddenly the pent-up sorrow of the past three years overwhelmed him.

If this was Sam Tennant's hair, and if his father had been foully murdered, he vowed then and there that he would never rest until he had brought the murderers to justice.

For a few minutes he lost his self-control. It would have gone ill with MacAulay if he had happened into the ruined warehouse during that first outburst of Dan's grief and anger. At length, however, Dan grew calm again. All his doubts were resolved now. He would go on to Tungalok, see the trapper, McAndrew, and learn whatever he had to tell him. He had no longer any doubt but that his father had been the victim of a huge conspiracy.

But Dan knew that he must keep himself in control until the time arrived for striking. With this resolution in mind, he turned back again toward Nagatok, and by the time he reached the postmaster's store, no one who saw him could have imagined that he was the same man who had given way to that fearful outburst of grief and anger a little while before.

MacAulay was standing in the entrance, a burly, sinister figure, and with him were two other men, looking like breeds, but not Livyeres. They were French breeds, as could be seen immediately, the lowest type of wandering *habitant*. The trio favored him with scowls as he came up to them.

"Well, Mr. Tennant, and have ye made up your mind to go back on the *Mary Binns*?" inquired MacAulay, with a sneer that he hardly took the trouble to conceal.

"I'll let you know my decision after my father's burial, MacAulay," answered Dan tersely. "I should like it to take place tomorrow."

"Aye, we'll see to it tomorrow," replied the postmaster. "Ye were fortunate in getting here in time. We were thinking of burying him tomorrow."

"I thought I saw a church here," said Dan.

"Aye, there's a church?"

"How about a minister?"

"The meenster's due to arrive next month. He doesn't stay here the winter. If ye want releegion, ye'll have to read the service yourself. Did ye find the warehouse?"

"I found it," answered Dan.

"Ye saw 'tis a ruin. We tried to save it, but it couldna be done. Weel, there's no helping it. We'll see about the burial in the morning then." He turned to go.

Dan nodded. He couldn't trust himself to speak. Old Sam Tennant had not been what might be called a religious man, and Dan felt instinctively that the love and pity he felt for him would hallow the burial as much as the presence of a strange minister.

"Koononok's cooking your supper," MacAulay called after him as he turned away.

Dan entered the store. At the end farthest from the office a table had been placed, and the breed assistant was removing the tin plates and cups which MacAulay and his companions had evidently been using. Dan sat down and began to make a meal of the stewed canned beef and vegetables that Koononok dished out of a caldron. He found that he was hungry in spite of the terrific discovery that he had made that day. He noticed that Koononok seemed nervous, and that his hands shook.

After the meal Dan went into his room. Lying on the bed, he gave himself up to the consideration of the matter once more. He saw the paramount necessity of acting cautiously, so that MacAulay should have no inkling of his suspicions. That was the hardest part of all, but it had to be done.

Until he had seen McAndrew, everything would have to remain in suspense.

He lay on the bed a long time. His watch showed that it was nine o'clock, but the sun was still high above the horizon. Probably there would be no more than an hour or two of darkness at that time of year. Dan had scarcely slept the night before, and again and again he dropped into a doze, from which he would awake to find that it was still sunlight. But at last he started up to discover that the sun had set. The room was half-dark. And someone was at the door. The handle was turning softly.

Dan reached out cautiously and opened his bag, which he had

placed upon the floor beside the bed. Inside was his Police Colt, though he had not expected to have any use for it in Labrador. He closed his fingers on the butt and waited. The door was opening a little more. Now Dan could see the round face of the Livyere in that opening.

"Come in, Koononok," said Dan softly, drawing out the weapon and covering him.

III

A little, choking sound came from the Livyere's lips. The man remained motionless, apparently paralyzed with terror.

"Come right in," Dan repeated. "Don't try to run, or I shall fire."

Koononok shuffled into the room, letting the door swing back behind him. He threw out his arms with a convulsive movement.

"No shoot," he whispered. "Me your friend, Mr. Tennant. Me your father's friend. Me come to tell you something important."

Dan studied the Livyere's face in the fading twilight. Koononok had already impressed him not unfavorably; he came to the conclusion that the man had not come there on any murderous mission. He let his hand fall.

"Well, Koononok, what's the trouble?" he asked.

The Livyere laid his finger across his lips, glancing fearfully toward the door. He seemed to be in a state of deathly fear. "You be careful, Mr. Tennant," he whispered. "You watch um MacAulay all the time you here. Tonight Mr. MacAulay send um Livyere boy to the Lippmanns to ask what um do with you if you no go back on the *Mary Binns*."

"The Lippmanns? Then that is their yacht in the tickle?"

"Lippmanns have um yacht, yes. But Lippmanns not on yacht. They go on to Tungalok with party, to find your father's furs."

"You mean—my father's furs are at Tungalok?" demanded Dan.

Again the Livyere made that gesture for silence. "No can tell you now," he said. "MacAulay got drunk and go to sleep; bimeby he wake up and find me here. MacAulay like wolverine, walk all night, find out everything. Me want to help you. Me your father's friend. If you no go back by the *Mary Binns*, they kill you. What you want to do?"

Dan hesitated. Was it possible that this was a trap of Mac-Aulay's? He decided that it was unlikely that that was the case. MacAulay's whole interest lay in getting Dan back by the *Mary Binns*. He would certainly not have told him that Alexis and Kuno Lippmann were on their way to Tungalok.

Dan had never seen the Lippmann brothers, but he knew that they were Russian refugees who had forced their way to the front in the most unscrupulous trade in the world by sheer daring and villainy. During the three seasons that Alexis Lippmann had spent in the Labrador, he had introduced methods previously unknown in that country.

With a gang of French breeds, and gangsters recruited from the slums of Montreal, he had established what was veritably a reign of terror among the northern Livyeres. Old Sam Tennant had considered making an application to the Newfoundland Government to intervene, but had been deterred by the belief that his complaint would be regarded as a matter of trade rivalry.

And Sam Tennant, with his years of two-fisted action behind him, could hardly have been called squeamish. But he had balked at some of the stories about Alexis Lippmann that had filtered down from the Cape Childley region.

Now it appeared that Kuno had come up from New York to join his brother, and the two were on their way to Tungalok! No, Dan was convinced that Koononok was not attempting to trap him.

"What you want to do?" repeated the Livyere anxiously.

"I'm going to Tungalok," Dan answered. "But that's between you and me."

"Me understand. Me go with you. MacAulay very bad man. He say he kill me. Beat me much. Look!"

The Livyere bared his shoulder, and in the gloom Dan could see a half-healed gash six inches long, apparently extending down to the bone.

"MacAulay do that with edge of frying pan. Beat me all time. Afraid me know something. You go to Tungalok and Koononok follow you, work for you. You understand?"

"I understand," said Dan, looking at Koononok thoughtfully. "Is that what you came here to speak to me about?"

The Livyere bent toward him.

"You want to see your father?" he asked in a whisper. "Me can show him to you before MacAulay um wake up. Today when you gone to see warehouse, MacAulay very much afraid. He call um French Indian mans and ask what um do. They say for to kill you, and he say no, not till um *Mary Binns* gone, because Captain Sims would hear about it. Then he send um Livyere boy to follow Lippmanns and ask them what to do if you no go back on boat. Lippmanns start for Tungalok three days ago.''

"I understand," said Dan.

"Tonight MacAulay unscrewed coffin to hide wound in head, in case you say you must see your father's face before they bury him. You come with me, me show you um.''

It had grown quite dark at last. The radium dial of Dan's watch showed that it was eleven o'clock. The only sounds were the distant splashing of the waves against the beach, and now and then, far away, the yapping of a husky in the Eskimo camp.

Laying his finger across his lips once more, Koononok crept through the doorway, and Dan, thrusting his revolver into his belt, followed him.

There was no moon, and the clouds, obscuring the stars, made the night completely black. As the two left the rear of the building, Dan stopped suddenly at a raucous sound that broke in upon his consciousness.

For a moment he did not know what it was. Then he realized that it was MacAulay breathing in his drunken sleep. He was not snoring, but drawing in great bubbling breaths of air, of incredible volume and duration, as if the man's chest contained a large fire bellows instead of lungs.

Dan followed the Livyere to the outhouse, and Koononok unlocked the door. Again Dan stood before the coffin on the trestles. The chill of the interior gripped him like a great, icy hand closing upon his body.

In the almost total darkness within the outhouse Dan heard the Livyere removing the lid of the coffin, which had evidently remained unscrewed. Probably MacAulay had intended to fasten it down in the morning.

There came a sudden finger of light from a torch in the Livyere's hand. For a moment Dan stood still, his eyes averted. He could not bring himself to look upon his father's face.

But then, controlling himself with a strong effort, he looked.

He had expected to see his father's face horribly disfigured, as MacAulay had suggested that it was. Instead, Sam Tennant lay within the shell, looking not very different from the way he had looked in life. The skin, waxen and shrunken, only brought into clearer relief the fine, prominent jaws and chin, and the strong nose and rugged contours.

Sam Tennant had been an uneducated man, and not entirely
scrupulous in his business dealings, but he had been essentially
a big man. His faults had been due to his early experiences.
Nothing petty or mean had ever come within his cognizance. A
product of his age and environment, he had been made for bigger things than he had accomplished, big though those undoubtedly had been.

A rush of emotion came over Dan as he saw his father, on
whose face he had never expected to look again, lying there,
peaceful in death. For a few moments the face disappeared, and
Dan was living over again episodes of his youth and childhood.
His father had loved him. He had disappointed the old man, but
Dan was sure now of what he had only surmised before, that
with death there comes the healing of wounds and the forgive-
ness of past injuries.

"You see? You see?" Koononok was whispering.

The mists disappeared. Again Dan was looking into his father's dead face, with the closed eyelids and the grim lines about
the mouth.

"You wantum see where kill him?" asked Koononok.

He beckoned Dan to his side, and, putting an arm beneath
the neck, attempted to raise the head. This was, of course,
impossible, for the whole form was rigid; nevertheless, by the
light of the flash, Dan could now see the hideous wound at the
back of the head, over which MacAulay had tried to comb
the long gray hair.

Dan looked fixedly at the wound. He knew that he would see it
to his dying day, photographically portrayed in his mind's eye.
But the mad wrath that had consumed him in the warehouse was
wholly lacking. It had been replaced by a resolution of steel.

At last he turned away, and Koononok let the body fall back
into position.

"Who killed him?" asked Dan in quiet tones. "Was it
MacAulay?"

"Me don't know. Me don't think so."

"Who?" Dan repeated.

"Me don't know. Mr. Tennant um starting for Tungalok last
fall to meet um Captain Fairleigh and him girl there and sail
home with furs. Somebody killed um in warehouse. Then they
burn warehouse. That's all Koononok knows."

"Was Alexis Lippmann here at the time this happened?"
asked Dan.

"Alexis Lippmann come into Nagatok next day from down north. Mr. Tennant had been very mad at Alexis Lippmann because of something he'd done. Him say um shoot him. Then somebody hit Mr. Tennant over head in warehouse and kill him, and bring um body here. MacAulay say um die of a fit. That night big frost begins, and no can bury.

"They look in warehouse before burn, but only cheap furs there. Fine million dollar furs all gone to Tungalok. Mr. Sam Tennant him fool um all. They never find um fine furs um look for. Search all winter at Tungalok and never find. Now Alexis and Kuno Lippmann come from New York and go again to Tungalok to find um furs. That's all me know."

Dan saw that Koononok was speaking the truth. The Livyere seemed almost crazed with fear. Only some powerful motive, either attachment to the dead man or hate for MacAulay, had given him the courage to take Dan into that mortuary.

Dan understood what the man had been trying to tell him. During the preceding autumn the ill feeling between his father and the Lippmanns must have reached its height. Sam Tennant had threatened to kill Alexis Lippmann, and Alexis had taken the initiative. Afterward the warehouse had been ransacked, but the collection of priceless furs had already been removed to Tungalok for shipment. The Lippmanns had burned down the warehouse to hide all evidences of their crime, but they had not found the furs that winter.

Had Captain Fairleigh removed them aboard his ship, and were they lying fifty fathoms deep of Tungalok?

That would seem the natural deduction, but, in that case, why had the two Lippmanns come to the Labrador to renew the search for the furs at Tungalok?

Again Dan realized that he must see the trapper McAndrew before he could go further.

"All right, Koononok," he said to the Livyere. "I'm going to start for Tungalok tomorrow, and you can catch up with me on the trail. You understand?"

"Me understand," said Koononok.

Dan went quietly out of the outhouse, while the Livyere replaced the lid upon the coffin. It had been, in the end, a struggle to turn away without trying to get another last glimpse of his father's features. But all Dan's resolution was firmly set to play the game that he had mapped out for himself—first, vengeance upon the man who had killed his father; then the restoration of the business that Sam Tennant had built up in Labrador.

It had been a struggle to turn away, but now a tenser struggle confronted him, for as soon as he stepped out of the house, Dan again heard the horrible breathing of the postmaster filling the night. Blindly he made his way toward the source of that sound, until he reached the little room that MacAulay occupied at one end of the building.

Looking through the window, he saw, or imagined he saw MacAulay, lying on his cot, a huddled heap. And Dan already held his revolver in his hand. To throw up the sash quickly, to riddle that inert mass beneath the blankets would be a matter of seconds.

At the last moment Dan pulled himself together and turned away. And that was the greatest act of self-conquest that he had ever accomplished.

IV

DAN slept soundly, in spite of the events of the night, slept so soundly that, when he was awakened by the sun shining into the little bedroom, they seemed for the moment like a chaotic, jumbled dream.

It was only for a moment, however. Then his mind tuned itself to his resolution. He went out of the room and into the store. MacAulay was behind the counter, trading with a Livyere who had brought in a bundle of furs. He looked up at Dan and snickered.

"Hey, ye keep late hours. This isna New York," he grinned. "A fellow's got to be up early if he's going to win back the fur monopoly of the Labrador."

He pointed to the table, snickering again. It was clear that MacAulay and his breed of companions had finished their meal some time before. Dan said nothing, but sat down, and MacAulay called Koononok and cursed him roundly for being slow in coming.

"Get Mr. Tennant his breakfast, ye squint-eyed devil!" he commanded. "It isna what you've been accustomed to in New York, Mr. Tennant, but we won't starve ye."

He seemed in fairly good humor, and Dan could see he had no suspicion of his activities of the night. Dan sat down at the table without responding. In a few minutes he was eating a meal of bannock and fried bacon, washed down with coffee. Mac-

Aulay addressed one or two jocular remarks to him, finished his trade, and then went into the office.

Dan had just risen when he saw four men pass the front of the store, grunting as they carried something. He went to the door and saw that it was the coffin.

For a moment he saw red again at the thought of his father's body being borne by such a crew. Two of them were the ill-favored French breeds whom he had seen the night before; the two others might have been anything, with a strong dash of Indian in them.

MacAulay came out. The snicker on his lips died away as he read Dan's face.

"Well, Mr. Tennant, we're ready to pay our last respects to your father," he said. "The grave's been dug in the burying ground behind the church. As soon as you're ready, we'll proceed."

"I'm ready," said Dan, trying to keep his voice steady.

"I've brought a prayer book," said MacAulay, handing Dan a tattered copy of the Church of England services.

The coffin was loaded onto a cart. After Dan had waited about fifteen minutes longer, a pony was led down the muddy street and attached. The procession started.

"What are you doing here?" bawled MacAulay, as the Livyere, Koononok, appeared.

"Me go see um bury Mr. Tennant," said Koononok, cringing nevertheless before the postmaster's upraised fist.

"I want this man to go, if he wishes," said Dan quietly.

MacAulay sneered. "Oh well, if you wish it, Mr. Tennant," he answered.

The burying ground was a dilapidated half acre behind the small frame structure used as a church. A score or more of graves, some few with toppling stones, rudely chiseled, marked the places of interment of Nagatok's dead. A shallow grave had been dug in the half-frozen soil. Dan motioned to the bearers to set down the coffin, and, opening the prayer book, found the burial service.

He read it, unashamed of the mist that blurred his vision and of the choking in his throat. He closed the book and made a sign to the breeds, who lowered the coffin with ropes into the ground. The earth was shoveled in and the place leveled. Dan signed to Koononok, and the two men picked up a large stone and rolled it to the site of the grave, to mark it. Some day Dan meant to erect a memorial there.

And that was the end of old Sam Tennant, who had fought and won and suffered, had taken and given hard blows, but had always fought fair.

"He fought fair," Dan was thinking. He meant to have that engraved on old Sam Tennant's monument.

Now came the time for action. Dan walked back beside Koononok. "I shall start this afternoon," he said. "I'll expect you tomorrow."

"Me come," said Koononok.

MacAulay, who had not gone to the burial, was lounging at the door of his store. "Weel, Mr. Tennant, so that's feenished," he said. "It's sad. Your father was a fine fighting man, but circumstances were too strong for him. Cap'n Sims tells me the *Mary Binns* will sail in the morning. Ye'll be going back by her?"

"I'll not be going," answered Dan. "I'm starting north this afternoon."

MacAulay glowered at him. "Aye? So that's the decision?" he inquired. "And where will ye be going? There's nothing north of Nagatok, as I've been telling ye all along."

"I'm going to look over the country," answered Dan. "I'm going to find out just how my father happened to lose everything."

"I've told ye—"

"I want you to put me up a pack."

"Aye, I'll put ye up a pack," growled the postmaster. "But it's all ye'll have to live on. There's no game north of Nagatok—nothing but a howling wilderness. And ye can't take a sleigh and dogs now the snow's melted."

"I understand that," answered Dan, "I'm going to mush."

"Ye'll find nothing, Mr. Tennant, and I doubt if the Lippmanns will renew that offer they made ye."

"I'll do the worrying about the Lippmanns—when they arrive." Dan shot a keen glance at the postmaster, whose eyes fell. "I'll give you that list of the things I'll want."

Sullenly the postmaster accompanied Dan inside the store. Dan wrote out the list of supplies that he would need: flour, bacon, tea, sugar, lime juice—he had had his experience of scurvy in the Northwest—and a few odds and ends. He added a heavy blanket and a waterproof sheet. With it all, he would be traveling light. MacAulay put the things together in a pack, and in another half hour Dan was ready to start.

He transferred to the pack the few things he had in his suit-case, which he left in MacAulay's keeping. He stood at the door of the store, looking north. It seemed queer to him that, beyond his intention of seeing McAndrew at Tungalok, he had very little idea how he was going to work. The two French breeds, who had been loafing outside the store while the pack was made up, looked on, muttering and scowling.

"If ye're taking the north road, there's an empty hut ten miles beyond Nagatok," vouchsafed MacAulay sullenly. "Ye could sleep there the night. But there's nothing beyond."

He offered Dan his hand, but even the necessity of trying to lull MacAulay's suspicions could not induce Dan to take it. With the pack between his shoulders, Dan started.

When he was nearly abreast of the ruined warehouse again, he looked back and saw an Eskimo or Indian loping along the shore road, parallel with him. He knew the man was a messenger, sent on in advance of him to warn the Lippmanns, who must evidently have started for Tungalok only lately. He could still see MacAulay and the breeds standing in front of the store, watching him.

But the sun was high in the sky, and, with Nagatok behind him, Dan felt a new sense of freedom. He shook off the de-spondency caused by his father's burial and the discovery that he had been murdered. And he felt renewed confidence that he would be successful in his determination to bring his father's murderers to justice.

Dan struck the shore road two or three miles beyond Nagatok, and mushed forward steadily. It could hardly have been called a road, however, for it was merely a rough trail among the rocks that littered the foreshore.

Still, it was free of snow, and Dan felt that he was making progress. Also, since the cliffs here came down almost to the sea and presented a vertical barrier of unbroken rock, Dan was sure that the runner who had preceded him was still upon the same trail as himself—hence he need fear no ambush.

He reckoned that he could cover the distance to Tungalok in six days. But he must wait for Koononok, and when he reached the camp of which MacAulay had spoken, he decided to camp in the neighborhood overnight.

The hut was a fisherman's and had long been falling into decay; the weight of the winter's snow had broken down a cor-ner of the roof, and the interior was empty. Nevertheless, Dan collected some driftwood, managed to kindle a fire in the rusting sheet-iron stove, and prepared himself a meal.

After which he scouted along the base of the cliff till he found a convenient cave, in which he ensconced himself for the night, taking the precaution to roll a heavy stone into the opening, so as to prevent being taken by surprise.

He slept light, but he was not molested, and in the morning, going to the hut, he satisfied himself, from the absence of any footprints except his own, that an ambush so near to Nagatok had not been a part of MacAulay's plans. Presumably MacAulay would do nothing until he had word from the Lippmanns. There was now nothing to do but wait for Koononok.

Dan waited all that day, but the Livyere did not put in an appearance. By the middle of the afternoon Dan's gorge had risen. He was convinced that Koononok had repented of his good intentions, probably through fear of MacAulay.

He did not consider that the presence of the Livyere would have been any particular asset. It had been Koononok's own proposition to accompany him. Dan's resentment was chiefly because he had lost a day—and given the Lippmanns an extra day to take measures against him.

Among his things Dan had a map of northern Labrador. It had been prepared by a cartographer from material supplied by his father and was much better than the official maps of the country.

Tungalok was shown here at the mouth of a small stream debouching from the interior plateau. There was a rough shore trail all the way, but Dan meant to take the road above the cliffs that had been stamped out by the Montagni Indians from time immemorial—if only because MacAulay expected him to take the other.

He camped that night in the same place, and, satisfied that it was useless to wait any longer for Koononok, set off at dawn on the second day. He traveled till noon before he found a possible ascent and spent the remainder of the day climbing the thousand-foot elevation, hanging on literally by his fingernails and eyelashes at times before he surmounted the outjutting rocks and crags.

Reaching the top at last, there was still an ascent of some five hundred feet before he found the trail marked on the map and stood on the summit of the interior plateau of Labrador.

Here a new difficulty presented itself. On the seashore the

temperature had been a few degrees above the freezing point;
here it was still winter. Arctic blasts cut through his mackinaw,
and the snow was still a foot deep. Dan had brought no snowshoes, and every step was labored.

The map showed a trapper's hut at some indefinite distance
from the point where Dan had ascended, and he pressed on as
fast as possible, in the hope of making it by nightfall. This place
was the headquarters of one of his father's original employees,
a Livyere with an unpronounceable name, and from him Dan
hoped to obtain useful information.

It was actually dark when the place loomed up suddenly on
the edge of the bare plateau—and Dan discovered that it was
even more of a ruin than the hut on the shore.

It afforded shelter, nevertheless, from the biting blasts that
swept across the plateau, and Dan was glad of its four walls and
broken roof, though there was not even a stove inside. He could
find no wood in the darkness. There was nothing to do but curl
himself up in his blankets after a meal of stale bannock, and try
to sleep.

He did sleep, shivering the while, until the roaring of the wind
awoke him. He started up to find that it was a little after midnight, and that the gale had brought a snowstorm with it. Attempting to leave the hut, he was almost swept off his feet by
the force of the wind, and the snow lay two feet deep about him.

He was about to turn back into the hut and make the best of
a bad situation when he thought he heard voices coming out of
the storm not far away.

He stopped in the entrance, supporting himself against the
wind, and listened. Then there was no mistaking it: a woman's
scream, piercing and terrified, was borne upon the gale toward
him.

He shouted, and heard the scream again. He waited, trying
to peer out through the impenetrable darkness. He called once
more—and of a sudden the figure of the woman emerged out of
that darkness, and came running toward him, groping with outstretched hands.

A woman, wearing a long *kossak*, or sealskin coat, and snowshoes, and so close to him that she almost collided with him at
the instant that she became visible through the storm. She stumbled and Dan caught her. She wrested herself free, looked back
again, and screamed in terror.

Then out of the night appeared the figure of the man. At the sight of him the girl caught at Dan's mackinaw, twisting her fingers in it tightly.

"Save me! Don't let him take me back!" she cried in clear English. "Don't let him take me!"

V

THE girl had almost collided with Dan as she ran forward, but the stronger impact of the man hurled him against the hut, and the two went sprawling in the snow together. Dan managed to find his feet first; he reached out, grabbed the other, and yanked him to his feet. Then the force of the wind caught them and sent them staggering into the hut, as if some giant had shoved them with the palm of a mighty hand.

Dan could see only the dimmest outlines of his captive, but he held him tightly, and the two wrestled together for about a minute.

"*Sacré*, let go, you fool! I'm Monsieur Lippmann's man!" snarled Dan's captive.

"I'm not surprised," Dan panted. "The Lippmanns are no friends of mine."

"Watch him! He's got a knife! Oh, take care!" came the girl's voice above the tempest.

The warning came in the nick of time. Dan could see nothing, but subconsciously he was aware of the weapon held in his captive's palm. He leaped back at the vicious thrust, which slit the skin of his forearm.

So sudden was the attack that, had there been light enough to see by, the breed could have carried home his attack to victory. In the dark the second thrust missed, and the breed overbalanced and fell against Dan, who, by the sheerest luck, succeeded in grasping the man's knife arm.

They fought from side to side of the interior, Dan clinging to his hold for dear life, while the breed battered at his face with his free hand, and let a continual torrent of vile imprecations pour from his lips. Snarling, kicking, and gouging, he directed all his efforts toward plunging the murderous weapon into Dan's body.

More than once the edge of the blade hit Dan's fingers, but in spite of the breed's strength Dan didn't let go.

He couldn't let go, not for the instant that he required in order to draw his revolver. The howling of the storm, the cries of the girl, the blasts of snow that whirled in on them added to the fury of the struggle, and the confusion. Minutes went by—three or four.

Suddenly the breed changed his tactics. With his left hand, which had been hammering Dan's face, he compressed his throat in a strangle hold, gripping the windpipe and digging into the flesh on either side.

A cry of agony broke from Dan's lips. He choked; he put all his strength into a desperate effort which wrenched the breed's arm backward, and half turned him around. The two slipped and rolled to the earth floor of the hut again. Dan's throat was free; but so was the breed's arm. Dan rolled upon his adversary, groping for the hand again and expecting every instant to feel the knife between his ribs.

But suddenly a strangled cry broke from the breed's throat. His hold of Dan relaxed, and his heels began to drum a devil's tattoo upon the floor, while his horrible, whistling inspiration sounded above the whine of the wind.

Dan leaped back. He drew his revolver.

"I've got you covered now!" he shouted. "Don't move, or I'll fire!"

But no answer came—only that whistling sound, going on and on, in more and more labored fashion, and the sound of the girl's quick breathing close at hand. Then came a choking gasp from the man on the ground; another drumming of the heels— a sigh; silence.

Dan stepped back, found the door, which was being held open against the building by the force of the wind, and succeeded in getting it shut. Even so, the wind filled the hut. Dan got out his matchbox, and, after several failures, succeeded in getting a match to stay lighted long enough to assure him that he was not mistaken in his interpretation of what had happened.

The breed lay dead on his face, pierced through the heart or lungs by the knife. He had fallen upon it in the struggle and impaled himself. The face was contorted in ghastly fashion, the eyes staring.

Dan looked up. "He's dead," he said to the girl, who had come up beside him.

"Fell on his own knife."

Looking at her, he saw her face for the first time in the last flickering light of the match. Fair hair, escaping under the hood of the *kossak*, two gray eyes, wide with terror, and fixed on his—youth . . . that was Dan's momentary impression before the match went out.

"No need to keep him in here," Dan said and, bending down, he gathered up the body. He hurled himself against the door and forced it open in the teeth of the wind. He managed to get it shut again, and then, dragging the dead man through the snow, he began to make his way cautiously, step by step, toward the precipice.

It would be six steps, he estimated, and, halting at the seventh, knee-deep in the snow, he hurled the breed's body from him. The movement of his arms almost flung him over the precipice in its wake. He slipped, caught at the rocks, and saved himself. He made his way back to the hut.

The girl was standing in the doorway, clinging to the doorposts, in the face of the furious blasts of wind. Dan saw her dimly, vaguely outlined against the night. He stumbled toward her and drew her inside the hut.

"You're safe. There's nothing more to be afraid of," he told her.

He got the door shut and turned to her again. She was crouching against the interior wall, so quiet and motionless that for a moment or two he could not find her. Then he saw her and went up to her.

"You're safe," he said again. "You can trust me."

"Who—who are you?" she whispered, in a voice broken by terror.

"I'm a friend. I was on my way to Tungalok on—on business. I'm going to protect you. I'll take you to your friends. You're safe. Nobody shall harm you."

"Tungalok? You're going to Tungalok? I—I've come from Tungalok. If you're going to Tungalok you must be one of them—one of the Lippmanns' men."

"I'm not one of the Lippmanns' men," Dan answered. "I'm on the trail of the Lippmanns, fighting the Lippmanns. My name's Tennant. My father was Sam Tennant, who owned almost everything in these parts until a year or two ago. You must have heard of him. You'll know that he wasn't friendly with the Lippmanns."

"What's that you say?" Dan was startled at the wild cry that broke from the girl's lips. "You're Dan Tennant? Dan Tennant? Swear that you're telling me the truth!"

She sprang forward and seized him by the shoulders, trying to peer into his face, though in the darkness they could see nothing of each other. "Do you swear that you're Dan Tennant—Sam Tennant's son?"

"Yes, I swear it. But you—who are you, then, and why—?"

But suddenly Dan began to understand, though the explanation seemed impossible to believe. He stepped forward in turn, trying to read the girl's face.

"You're Molly Fairleigh!" he cried.

"Yes," she whispered. "I'm Molly Fairleigh."

And she relaxed suddenly, and lay, a dead weight against his breast.

It seemed hours before Dan succeeded in bringing the girl back to consciousness. Hours during which he kneeled over her in the lonely hut, while the blizzard howled and raged furiously outside, roaring through the chinks in the log walls and twisting away the blanket that Dan tried to keep about her.

Dan rubbed the girl's hands and feet, the latter icy cold beneath the mukluks, though the circulation did not seem to have stopped. At last a deep respiration indicated that she had become once more aware of her surroundings.

A long interval passed, and then she whispered Dan's name again.

He wouldn't let her talk. "You must try to get some rest," he told her. "We'll talk in the morning." And after that there was unbroken silence through the remainder of the night.

And all that night Dan crouched beside her. But, even though the girl did not speak again, he knew from her irregular breathing that she was lying awake. He tried to adjust his mind to the understanding of her presence there, while the laggard hours crept by. How could this be Molly Fairleigh, when she had gone down with her father fifty fathoms deep off Tungalok?

Slowly the hours went by. Everything ends at last. The night began to wane. The force of the storm had lessened though the wind still blew a gale. At length the faint light of day began to creep through the chinks between the logs, and little by little Dan began to see the girl and the interior of the hut.

She had fallen asleep at last, and lay huddled beneath the snow-covered blanket. Dan was horrified at the sight of her. This was Molly Fairleigh, whose photograph he had seen, but changed almost beyond recognition. Her fair hair straggled about her face and hung down in ragged ends, her *kossak* was a mere Eskimo garment, her mukluks were torn, and there was a stain of blood on one of them. Her eyes were closed, but on her thin face was stamped lines of terror, lines that no woman's face should show.

It was impossible to make tea for her. There was no fuel in the hut, not even a scrap of moss between two logs. Dan could only wait until, about the time that a dim effulgence outside indicated that the sun had risen, the girl opened her eyes.

Dan was at her side in a moment, ready to assuage her fears, but she knew and remembered everything. She sat up, pushing him away when he tried to restrain her.

"You're Dan Tennant," she whispered, fixing her eyes on his. "And you killed that breed last night, and saved me. But what brought you to the Labrador?"

"My father was murdered. I didn't know it until the other night. I came up to see if I could retrieve anything out of the wreck of his fortunes."

"Murdered? Sam Tennant murdered?" cried the girl.

"Struck down in his warehouse, killed instantly by a blow from an iron bar. They kept his body all the winter. I was at the burying. You didn't know that?"

"They told us he was dead," said Molly, "but we thought they might be lying. We couldn't know—"

" 'Us!'—'We?' "

"My father and I!"

"You mean to say that Captain Fairleigh—is he alive, too?" cried Dan.

"Alive? Did you think he was dead?"

"MacAulay told me that you were both dead, and had gone down with the ship in fifty fathoms of water off Tungalok."

"You believed that? I don't understand, except that it's been a dreadful nightmare all through the winter."

"Will you tell me just what happened since the time when you sailed for the Labrador with your father?" Dan suggested.

She was incoherent for a little while; then seemed to pull herself together. Her voice grew calm and stronger.

"I'd always wanted to see the Labrador," she said. "I worried Dad until he agreed to let me sail with him last summer, when he went north to get Mr. Tennant and some of the choice furs that he meant to dispose of in New York that season. We stopped at Nagatok and saw Mr. Tennant, and arranged to go on to Tungalok and wait for him there. He was going to make the journey overland, to visit some of his trappers on the way.

"Your father told Captain Fairleigh that he believed the

Lippmanns were plotting to get some of the choice furs—black-and-silver fox, and sable—that he had stored in the warehouse at Nagatok. There was half a million dollars' worth, and he wanted him to take them to Tungalok, ship some for New York, and conceal the rest in a certain place that had been selected for just that purpose. My father got the furs on board without letting MacAulay know.''

"If MacAulay had known," Dan was thinking, "my father might not have died."

"We got to Tungalok, and at once our troubles began," Molly continued. "Mr. McAndrew, one of your father's most trusted men, told us that all his lines had been robbed systematically the preceding winter. He had lost everything, and was in despair. Then one night our two sailors, poor John Greggs and Tom Jarvis, who had sailed with Dad for years, were murdered. We'd been living on board, but they had gone ashore to make some purchases at the little store McAndrew was running. They were shot down from ambush in the forest—riddled with bullets by their cowardly murderers.

"We learned about it next day from a frightened Livyere boy who had worked for Mr. McAndrew. Dad went ashore at once; he was afraid to take me, and afraid to leave me on the boat, but in the end he decided to leave me, and told me he'd be back within two hours. He didn't come back all day, and at night three horrible-looking French breeds rowed out and told me he had met with a bad accident, and I was to go with them at once.

"I didn't believe them; I didn't know what to do, but they forced me to accompany them. They took me to Mr. McAndrew's store, and there I found Dad and Mr. McAndrew roped tightly, and Alexis Lippmann.

"He told us that Mr. Sam Tennant had died suddenly, and was bankrupt, and owed him a large sum of money, and he demanded the furs, promising to let us go and give us a good sum of money if we'd tell him. They were hidden in a rock cave in the cliff, which your father had had constructed, but neither my father nor Mr. McAndrew nor I would tell Lippmann where the place was.

"They kept us tied for days, using all sorts of horrible threats to make us reveal the hiding place, but it was useless. Dad's a Newfoundlander of the old kind, and you know what those men were. He told Alexis Lippmann that he wouldn't betray his trust if he tore me to pieces before his yes. And he wouldn't have done so, nor would I.

"And they didn't know that Mr. McAndrew knew.

"Alexis Lippmann threatened to torture Dad, but he changed his mind in the end. It was getting late, and he had to sail for New York, and when he saw he couldn't get the secret, he decided to leave us there through the winter and come back this summer, hoping that we'd have changed our minds after a winter of captivity.

"He left us in charge of his gang of French breeds. That man you killed, Paul Tessier, was the chief of them, and obeyed his instructions implicitly. They kept us prisoners in Mr. McAndrew's house, and only gave us just enough fire to keep us from freezing, and only just enough food to live. All the time Tessier kept telling us that if we'd only reveal the hiding place of the furs, we could go free, but Dad refused. Besides, he knew that the moment he did so he and Mr. McAndrew would be killed, and as for me—"

She shuddered violently and turned her face away. "I'd rather have been imprisoned like that forever than have seen Alexis Lippmann again," she cried. "He'd threatened me—when he came back this summer—I knew what he meant—"

For the first time during the girl's narrative, Dan let an oath escape his lips.

"I wasn't guarded as closely as the others. They thought I couldn't get away alone. But I did, in the worst part of the winter, hoping to reach Nagatok and get help, though I might have known that there was no one who would help me there. I was crazed by what we had all gone through.

"I got nearly halfway when Paul Tessier overtook me and brought me back. He abused me and struck me. After that we were more closely guarded than ever. But a week ago I managed to secure some food, and got away again. I'd heard that the Lippmanns were expected, and I was frantic for myself and dad, and poor Mr. McAndrew.

"You know the rest. Paul Tessier caught me in this hut, and began to take me back. I broke away from him in the storm, and he caught me again—was just about to catch me when . . . you were here, and you—killed him!"

She broke down, and Dan just put his arms about her and held her, feeling that she derived strength and comfort from him. This was no strange girl, but Molly Fairleigh, whom he had always known, though he had never met her before that night.

"What can we do?" she whispered, looking up at him, and that terror on her face filled Dan's heart with infinite pity. "The Lippmanns will be there any day, perhaps they are at Tungalok already. Dad will refuse to tell them where the furs are, and they'll kill him—"

"Not till they've got you, too, Molly. They wouldn't dare. That leaves the captain safe for the present. We'll save him, and Mr. McAndrew—and the furs, too."

He opened the door of the cabin. The wind had dropped considerably since dawn, the snow had stopped, and in the east a hazy glow denoted the presence of the sun.

Molly Fairleigh came to Dan's side. "I believe you will," she said. "I believe it's Providence that sent you here. Try to trust me. I was unstrung last night, but I'm no coward. I've got myself in hand now, and I'll fight with you as if I was a man. Think of me as a man, Dan Tennant."

VI

By a tacit agreement they put their memories behind them for the time. Dan saw that the girl was half starved. Food and hot tea was their immediate need. But there was no wood visible anywhere in the waste of snow, in which Dan stood knee-deep, though Molly, who had put on her snowshoes, was on top of the drift and towered a full head over him.

Dan told the girl what he wanted. "There's sure to be driftwood along the beach, if I can get down," he said.

He went to the edge of the precipice. There was a way down, which probably accounted for the fact that the cabin had been built in that particular spot. It was a steep descent among the rocks, but owing to its precipitous character, it was fairly free of snow.

"I'm going down," said Dan. "You're not afraid of my leaving you for a little?"

"I'm not afraid," said Molly. She took the revolver that Dan handed her, however. "Be careful, won't you!" she pleaded, as he lowered himself over the edge.

Dan found the descent easier than he had expected. He climbed from rock to rock and at last found himself on the snow-covered shingle at the bottom. The tide was coming in, and the great Atlantic combers dashed themselves upon the rocks in showers of foam. The first thing Dan saw was the body of the dead man.

Paul Tessier, fearfully mangled by the fall, lay huddled at the very base of the cliffs, but life had been extinct before he fell, and Dan was glad that he had not deliberately taken that life. His training as a policeman had perhaps made him over-scrupulous in that regard.

As Dan looked at the body, it occurred to him that Tessier might have carried a revolver, though, with the instinct of his kind, he had pulled his knife. A quick search confirmed his suspicion. In the pocket of the mackinaw worn by the dead man was an old model Colts, and a further search produced about a dozen cartridges. There was nothing else, neither letter nor papers of any kind.

But there was one thing more, and this was the happiest discovery Dan could have made. Not far away, sticking up out of the snow, was one of Tessier's *raquettes*. And without snowshoes Dan could not have proceeded a hundred yards through the snow.

He searched a long time for the other, but failed to find it and reluctantly had to abandon the search. He did not know how a single snowshoe would carry him, but he would have to make the attempt. Not far away was driftwood, and Dan gathered enough of it to make a fire, and, carrying it with the snowshoe under one arm, began to make the ascent again.

He reached the top to find Molly waiting there, with the other snowshoe in her hand. "Look what I've found, Dan," she said. "You must have dropped it last night, and it was nearly buried in the snow."

"Yes, I've found the other one," answered Dan. He felt that it was better not to let her know he meant to wear Tessier's *raquettes*.

He cleared a space and soon had the fire blazing and the kettle boiling. He sliced bacon, made cakes in the ashes, and forced Molly to eat a big breakfast, and to wash it down with copious draughts of tea. By this time the gale had blown itself out, the sun was shining fitfully through the clouds, and already it was beginning to grow warm. The snow was covered with a film of ice.

"We should be able to make Tungalok in five days," said Dan when they had both eaten. "Four possibly, but that's doubtful, with this snow on the ground. How many men are guarding your father and McAndrew?''

"There were six of them, including Tessier," said Molly.

"Will you give me some description of the place? Where are they living?''

"Dad and Mr. McAndrew are in the store, and there are always two or three armed guards there, watching them. They tied us up at night. The rest of the men are living aboard the *Good Hope*.''

"My father's ship," said Dan. "Well if they're split into two parties, that makes it easier.''

"But there are a number of Livyeres there, too," said Molly. "They built *igloos* there last winter, and they've been trapping and working for the others.''

"Which side would they take?''

"Neither," said Molly promptly. "They're too much afraid. Paul Tessier and his brother, Caribou, have been making slaves of them. And they took their women—it has been like a hideous nightmare, and I think we were best off in being shut up in the store. They were drunk nearly all the time, and they behaved vilely to us. I don't know what they'd have done, if they hadn't been afraid of Alexis Lippmann.''

"That's the chief point," said Dan. "I imagine he must have reached Tungalok by now. The question is whether he took this trail or the shore trail, and by which trail he'll be coming back to find you. Also how many men he has with him.''

Molly shook her head. "I don't know at all," she said. "But I know that I met no one coming south from Tungalok, until Paul Tessier caught me.''

"We'll take this trail, then," Dan decided.

They started, striking out a path toward the summit of the elevated land behind the cliffs, from which they felt that they could obtain a wide view of the country. By mid-afternoon they were some considerable distance from the hut and out of sight of the sea.

It was still bitterly cold on the high plateau, and they made quick time over the frozen snow. They lit a big fire that night, in a little depression where it would not be visible at any distance, and Dan watched over Molly, sleeping, till he, too, slept, waking as the sun rose over the hills.

And that was the beginning of six days together which were to remain forever in Dan's memory as a time of perfect comradeship. It was amazing that a girl brought up as Molly had been should be able to endure what she had endured, and yet to walk beside him, covering the miles without faltering. And Molly was even growing stronger. There was a faint color in her cheeks. Despite her anxiety over her father, her trust in Dan had given her new hope and courage.

Also it was, in a way, like coming into touch with his father again. Molly had spent a week with Captain Fairleigh at Sam Tennant's place on Long Island the summer before, and Dan heard from her lips how much his father had cared for him, and how bitterly he had regretted the quarrel that had divided them.

Well, all that was past now, and there remained only the duty of avenging him. Dan's first burst of fury against his father's murderers had changed to a steely resolution, and that resolution grew even harder as he measured off the miles to Tungalok with Molly at his side.

On the afternoon of the sixth day Molly halted Dan as they reached the summit of a high hill, and pointed.

Far in the distance Dan could see the sea again. A broad stream ran down into it, and in the stream, careening over at an angle that showed it was still frozen in the ice, was a stoutly built ship—the *Good Hope*, her strong greenheart timbers intact still after all her adventurous voyages.

"Mr. McAndrew's house is on the other side of the river," said Molly, pointing to a high bluff, fringed with dwarf willow scrub. "What are you going to do?" she continued, with an indrawn breath.

"Free your father and McAndrew." He had given Molly the dead man's revolver, and now she pulled it out from beneath her *kossak*.

"Yes, we two can do it," she answered.

Dan looked at her face, and saw in her eyes a look that forbade him to oppose her. So he said nothing, though he did not mean to let Molly jeopardize her life if he was able to prevent it.

They took a circuitous route toward the harbor, to avoid being seen by anyone from Tungalok, but the sun was still a good way above the horizon when they stopped, about a mile from the river.

They had agreed to try to raid the store during the hour or two of darkness, but it seemed as if the sun would never set. It was traveling round and round the sky, a ball of lurid flame.

It touched the horizon at last, dipped slowly, and still that half circle of fire seemed to swing its way through a long arc before it disappeared. Then, for what seemed an hour, the twilight lingered. With the first tinge of red in the western clouds lights sprang up aboard the *Good Hope*, and presently another light began to shine upon the bluffs beyond.

"Let's go," said Molly, rising from the clump of dwarf growth in which they had been hiding.

They went down to the river shore. Presently they began to hear the sound of voices from aboard the vessel; the sounds grew louder, bellows of laughter were heard, and once the high-pitched shriek of a woman.

Dan stopped and seemed to grow rigid.

"It's one of those Livyere girls," Molly explained. "I don't think they're harming them—more than—"

Dan quickened his stride, so that Molly had some difficulty in keeping up with him. If that scream had been repeated, he might have turned aside; it was not, and he concentrated himself upon the task at hand.

They reached the river shore about a quarter of a mile from the ship, which was here hidden from view by a bend of the banks. The ice was firm and piled up in hummocks, the accretions from the upper reaches of the water, which had thawed and floated down, without disturbing the solid ice bridge in the lower harbor.

They were across the river now and scrambling up the bluffs beyond. From the ship they could still faintly hear the drunken shouts of the revelers, and now they began to hear other voices through the willow scrub in front of them, sounds of men quarreling and shouting at one another. Then they had reached the top of the ascent and saw McAndrew's store a little distance away, beyond the tangle of brush.

It was still light enough to distinguish the long, low log building. In one end of it an oil lamp burned, and it was from this end that the shouts had come. Dan felt Molly press his arm convulsively, and he took her hand and pressed it.

"Stay here," he said in a low voice. "It will be only a minute or two before your father is free. Remember, I've been a policeman. I'm used to this sort of job."

"I'm going with you," answered the girl. "Don't send me from you, Dan. I'm not afraid; and I can shoot. You may need me."

Again Dan could make no answer. He went forward softly,

till he was abreast of the small pane of glass set into the end of the store.

Through this he could see four men sitting around a table under the light, playing cards. Each had a bottle at his elbow, and they snarled and cursed each other as they slapped down the cards. No sound came from beyond them at the other end of the store, which was in darkness. Dan felt Molly trembling.

He gestured her back, then stepped to the door and flung it wide. He was inside the store before the four men at the table were aware of his presence.

"Reach high!" he commanded curtly, as he covered them.

A moment of stupefied silence; then the four leaped up from their chairs. French breeds, all of them, and more villainous-looking than the breeds at MacAulay's store. The nearest of them Dan recognized as Paul Tessier's brother, Caribou, both from his resemblance to the dead man and from his likeness to the beast from which he had acquired his nickname.

Quick as a flash Caribou's hand went to his belt. Quicker rang out the discharge of Dan's weapon, and Caribou began to scream and dance, wringing his nipped finger.

There was no wavering on the part of the others. Their hands went up. Dan put them in line and quickly relieved them of their knives and revolvers.

"Keep facing that wall," he ordered. "The first man who looks around gets his." The breeds, snarling, obeyed.

Dan backed away, still covering them. Behind him he had heard Molly's cry of gladness, movements, voices—then the girl was coming into the glare of the oil lamp on the wall, supporting the man whom Dan had imagined deep down under the waves.

"Dan—Dan!" she cried, stretching out her hands to him.

Dan half turned, and that quarter second was the undoing of their plans. One of the breeds dropped silently beneath the table and pulled the revolver that was hidden in a sling beneath his arm, a trick Dan had supposed to be unknown in the Eastern snowland. There followed the roar of the discharge. The shot shattered the lamp chimney, which fell to the floor in a shower of tinkling splinters. The flame leaped up, then almost died away, throwing the long room into momentary darkness.

Before it had sprung up again, the four men were running for the door, the breed with the revolver turning to fire, and Dan answering him, shot for shot all the way.

One of the four dropped, howling and cursing upon the threshold, a second stumbled but regained his feet; the breed who had fired turned in the doorway to empty his revolver. Dan was not hit, though he felt the wind of one of the bullets, but his own efforts had failed. Three of the breeds were already outside the store and racing through the night, shouting the alarm, while the fourth man, howling with the pain of his wound, was wriggling away like a great worm; his bawling growing fainter as the sound was cut off by the front of the building.

VII

FOR a moment or two the three men and the girl looked at one another in consternation. Then Dan stepped forward.

"We must follow them," he said. "We can reach the ship almost as soon as they can. We can as good as take the Lippmanns by surprise. It's our only chance."

"There's ten men with the Lippmanns," said McAndrew, in broadest Scotch.

Dan looked at McAndrew for the first time. To his astonishment he saw that McAndrew was apparently a full-blooded Eskimo. Not more than an inch of five feet, he stood, a squat and sturdy figure, with copper skin, high cheekbones, and little, oblique eyes.

Dan also saw that the man was gaunt with hunger. He looked at Captain Fairleigh, and saw that he, too, was apparently in the last stage of emaciation. Molly was supporting him. It dawned upon him that, after their experiences, neither man was in any condition to take part in such a plan as he had proposed.

"I'm weeling," McAndrews continued, "But there's a better way. We've got to get Molly out of these parts, and likewise her father. If we try to make for the south, they'll follow our tracks in the snaw. There's no escapin' that way."

"Then—" Dan began.

"He means the fur cave," said Captain Fairleigh. "And we've got to start at once. Lippmann and his crew will be here in a few minutes."

"Lippmann's here, then?" Dan shot at him.

"Both the Lippmanns arrived yesterday. They arrived dead drunk, and that was all that saved us. We'll hide up in the cave where your father stored his furs, Dan. They've never found it. We'll be safe there, and get a breathing spell."

"And I've got food in the pack—enough to last us a day, at any rate," said Dan. The pack had grown very light, but neither

Dan nor Molly had eaten much, and Dan had ordered considerably more supplies than he had actually needed.

"Let's start then," said McAndrew.

The left the store, McAndrew leading, Molly supporting her father, and Dan bringing up the rear. The Eskimo led the way along the top of the bluff toward sea, which could be heard lashing the cliffs not far away.

Suddenly out of the darkness there emerged a cluster of Eskimo *igloos*. They were round houses of stone, constructed during the preceding winter, and still unaffected by the partial thaws of that spring; seven or eight in number, they stood at the edge of the bluff like ghostly sentinels. For a moment it seemed to Dan that he could see faces peering at him out of the holes, level with the ground, that took the place of doorways.

Then all was still and silent, and nothing was to be seen except the squat contours of the houses, and Dan concluded that the faces had been a figment of his imagination.

The four passed the line of *igloos* and hurried toward the ridge of cliffs fronting the sea, whose roaring was becoming louder. Now they could hear the clash and grinding of the ice floes where ice and water met, the sound premonitory of the breakup. They reached the end of the harbor, and the full blast of the sea gale caught them.

Then behind them, from the shore, there broke out suddenly the yelling of the breeds. It was evident that they had come with reinforcements from the ship, probably with the Lippmanns, and had found their quarry gone. Dan caught the captain by the other arm and hurried him along. Behind them the yells and shouts were redoubling.

Then of a sudden Captain Fairleigh disappeared, and Dan found himself descending the face of the cliff by a narrow path so steep that they were forced to cling to rocks to keep from falling. The cliff above them deadened the sound of the shouting.

They reached the beach and went on in single file, along a strip of shingle and rocks, so narrow that the spray from the waves drenched them. For fifteen minutes or so they continued on their way. Then Fairleigh turned into a tiny cleft among the rocks, just large enough to admit one at a time. There came a short ascent of a rocky path, and Fairleigh disappeared apparently into the face of the cliff.

* * *

Dan saw a hold not more than four feet high in the straight escarpment. He followed the rest inside.

"Ye havena a candle in that pack of yours, Tennant?" came the voice of McAndrew.

"I believe I've got one. Is it safe to light it?" asked Dan.

"It's absolutely safe, laddie. There'll be nae reflection ootside this cave, and none to see it if there was."

Dan opened his pack, found the candle, and lit it. The light showed a commodious interior, about as large as the two ground-floor rooms in a modern house. The cave seemed to resemble such a ground-floor, for it was of two approximately equal parts, separated by a low-hung roof of stone.

McAndrew, who was already in the rear portion, looked back and chuckled.

"Weel, they havena found the furs. There're here, safe, sound and dry," he said.

Dan, following him, saw that the interior was packed with bales of furs, carefully wrapped in caribou hide, with the skin inside. Holding up the candle, he could see, too, the gleaming skin of a silver fox protruding from one of the bundles.

It was, of course, impossible to attempt to estimate the value of the stored furs, but from what his father had told him, he knew that there must be at least half a million dollars' worth, the selected skins of many seasons, and all cured on the spot by Livyere and Eskimo labor.

McAndrew took the candle from him and set it down in a niche in the wall. "Weel, we're here," he remarked dryly, "and we owe it to you, laddie. What we're goin' to do next I dinna ken, but it's sure that scum of the Lippmanns ar'na on our track."

He help up his hand for silence, and they listened, but nothing was audible above the crashing of the breakers on the rocks.

But suddenly Dan seemed to see, framed, in the narrow entrance to the cave and silhouetted against the sky, a human face and shoulders!

Without a word he leaped forward and gained the entrance, revolver in hand. Nothing was visible but the rocks and the sea.

"What's the matter, laddie?" McAndrew was at his side. "What did ye think ye saw?"

"It looked like a face," said Dan.

"It couldna be. There's nane can ken the way to this cave. Your father and me saw to it that nane should ken. And whaur could he have gone?"

They looked down the path that led up to the cave, trying to search the approach through the darkness; nothing stirred.

"It couldna be. It was imageenation, laddie," said old McAndrew, laying his hand upon Dan's shoulder.

Inside the cave they discussed their situation. McAndrew told the story much as Molly had told it. He had been surprised in the store, threatened with torture, and he and Captain Fairleigh had been kept in bondage all the winter. Apparently Alexis Lippmann had given orders that the two were to be treated with the utmost harshness short of destroying life, for they had been starved and frozen. The old Eskimo, with his queer Scotch accent and sturdy frame, had resisted better than Fairleigh, who was in bad plight.

McAndrew said that the two Lippmanns had arrived with an escort of breeds, and he estimated, from what he had heard the guards say, that there were at least ten men with them, apart from those who had been left at Tungalok during the winter.

His proposal was that he and Dan should try to establish a reign of terror by lying in ambush and firing into any parties that showed themselves.

"It's their lives against ours, and Molly's," he said. "And we canna escape, and they canna afford to let us escape. We've got to pick them off, ane by ane, till they're all gone to hell and damnation."

Dan saw the point, but it went against the grain to shoot at men from ambush. Still, as McAndrew had said, it was their lives against those of the others.

"We've got to have food," he said.

"There's food in the store, laddie," answered McAndrew. "And there's rifles, and I misdoubt the breeds hae taken them, because they've got rifles of their ain. I had aboot a score of condemned army rifles shipped up for trade. And there's ammuneetion."

After a good deal of discussion, it was agreed that Molly and her father should remain in the cave, while Dan and McAndrew raided the store on the following night to obtain food and firearms. Dan had the four guns that he had taken from the breeds, and he gave one to McAndrew and another to Captain Fairleigh. They built a little fire of driftwood near the entrance to the cave and baked cakes with the last of Dan's supply of flour.

Morning found the four in high spirits. The sun shone warmly, they could hear the cracking and grinding of the ice at the mouth

of the harbor, and they guessed that the Lippmanns were fran-
tically combing the country for them.

"If they canna get the furs in time to sail when the ice goes
oot, they'll miss the auctions and hae made their trip in vain,
laddie," chuckled McAndrew. "We'll best them ane way or
ither, or ye're no your father's son."

And Dan began to understand that day how strong a hold on
the imaginations of these men his father had. He learned that
Sam Tennant had taken McAndrew, a savage Eskimo of thirty
years, and put him through the mission school under old Angus
Fraser. He felt an irrepressible pride in his father and a determination to be worthy of him.

"We'll come back safe," he told Molly that evening, as they
prepared to start.

He shook hands with Fairleigh, and he and McAndrew
started.

They did not return by the course that they had taken before,
but ascended the cliffs along the shore and began working back
in the direction of the store through patches of scrubby willow
and the dead stalks of last summer's sugar herts plants.

It was rough going over the snow, which the day's thaw had
converted into a succession of miniature ice hummocks, and
nearly an hour had passed before they reached the top of an
elevation and saw the store before them in the faint light of the
stars. It was dark, and a cautious reconnaissance showed that it
was empty.

"Noo, laddie, we'll just mak free with the goods we need,"
said McAndrew, with his inimitable chuckle, "and then we'll
be prepared to stand a siege all summer, if need by, or till we've
worn the scoundrels down to their last man."

The door was unbolted. Working by the light of matches, lit in
succession, Dan and McAndrew soon collected a supply of food.
A sack of flour, a great side of bacon, and some tinned stuffs
were wrapped about with three heavy trade blankets. In spite of
Dan's protests, the old Eskimo insisted on the bundle's being
hoisted upon his broad shoulders. Weak as he must have been
after his ill-treatment of the preceding winter, he seemed to bear
his burden as if it had been featherweight.

"Na, na, laddie, I'll be the beastie, and you'll gang beside
me to protect me," chuckled the Eskimo.

There was, however, one disappointment. The rifles that
McAndrew had hoped to secure were not to be found, and it

was evident that they had been removed by the breeds, probably long before.

Dan cursed vehemently.

"Weel, it canna be helpit," said McAndrew philosophically. "We'll have to conseeder that matter later. At present we'll call it a guid night's work."

"Wait a minute," said Dan, as McAndrew was about to leave the store.

"Eh, laddie?"

"I want to try to put some of these things back where they were," said Dan, "so that gang won't suspect we've paid the store a visit. We'll probably find it necessary to return."

"Eh, that's a braw idea!" exclaimed McAndrew in admiration. "It's plain that ye're a chip of the old block, laddie. I was no mistaken in ye."

The somewhat slow-witted Eskimo seemed lost in admiration at Dan's forethought. As well as he could, by the light of an occasional match, Dan replaced the pile of blankets on the shelf, and the goods that the two had dislodged. But the delay, slight though it had been, was productive of unforeseen consequences.

As Dan turned, he heard a cry from McAndrew, and saw the old man struggling to draw his gun from under his pack. At the same moment shouts sounded outside, and a volley of bullets came smashing into the door.

McAndrew managed to leap back, uninjured. Dan ran forward. Four men were standing in the starlight not more than fifty yards away, yelling to one another, and apparently as much taken by surprise as McAndrew had been.

Dan leaped forward, firing as he ran. There came an irregular, straggling volley, and the four turned and fled. One dropped, and then McAndrew, pack on back, loosed his revolver, and a long shot brought a second man yelling to the ground, while the two surviving members of the party quickly vanished into the. darkness.

McAndrew turned to Dan and chuckled. "Two mair of them oot of action, laddie," he said. "There willna be mair than ten of them left, including the Lippmann brothers. A guid beginnin'—a verra guid beginnin'."

VIII

"Eh, laddie, and we forgot the matches!" exclaimed Mc-Andrew.

There was momentary consternation. The party were down to their last box.

"Weel, we'll just hae to pay anither veesit and bring back some mair," chuckled the Eskimo. "And maybe we'll hae the luck to meet up with anither party," he grinned.

Good luck or bad, it was clear that they would have to go back to the store the following night. A preliminary reconnaissance showed that it was empty, and McAndrew speedily found the matches.

They were about to leave when Dan saw something white on the inside of the door that had escaped his notice. He struck a match and saw that it was a scrap of paper, with writing on it, and pinned to the wood.

"Yon looks like a message!" exclaimed McAndrew.

They read:

"No need to fight like fools. We want to talk turkey with you and arrange terms. Fire four shots at sundown as a signal and I will meet you alone at the edge of the ice bridge.
                                        HERBERT MACAULAY."

"So MacAulay's here!" Dan exclaimed. "Well, I won't accept!" He was thinking of his father, and a flame of mad rage burned in him.

McAndrew laid a hand on his arm. "Laddie, there's naething to lose by listenin' to what that skunk wants to say," he said, "so long as they dinna find our hangoot. I'd listen to the deil himself, which doesna mean I'd accept his proposeetions."

That was the opinion of the rest. Accordingly, the next afternoon McAndrew and Dan made their way to the edge of the ice field by a circuitous course, and fired the four shots required. Presently a solitary figure appeared, rounding the bend.

A short distance away MacAulay stopped. Dan and Mc-Andrew went forward.

"Well, Mr. Tennant, ye're your father's son all right," grinned MacAulay, "and I was a fool na to ken it. Tennant, I was in a hell of a poseetion. I'd served your father faithful for years, almost since I was a boy. When the Lippmanns came in, with their modern methods, I saw your father was up against a losing game.

"I did my best to change him, but he was too old to be changed. I saw that the Lippmanns were getting mair and mair of a foothold in the Labrador, and when they asked me to represent them, I couldna do anything else than agree."

Dan was silent; so was McAndrew. Evidently MacAulay did not like their silence, for he went on:

"After your father died, I kenned that the Lippmanns were on the track of his furs, and that he'd removed them. And I guessed something of what was doing up here. Weel, I couldna do anything. Mr. McAndrew and me have always been the best of friends, hey, Mac?"

MacAulay was growing flustered by the utter failure of response. And Dan knew that there could be no truck with MacAulay. Had he confessed the facts about his father's murder, he would have listened. But MacAulay evidently did not guess that Dan knew Sam Tennant had been murdered, and he was still shielding the Lippmanns.

"Weel, noo, there's been some fighting up here," MacAulay went on, "and lives taken, but there's no reason why things shouldna rest where they are. Ye're in the Lippmann's power, Tennant, however lang ye manage to hide up in the cliffs, or wherever ye are. Ye canna get away, none of ye, and sooner or later they'll get ye. But they're proposin' to go fifty-fifty wi' ye on the furs, if ye'll hand them over, and they'll pay ye fifty thousand for all rights in the Labrador that your father held.

"They'll draw up an agreement, and I'll bring it here wi' their signature on it, and ye can go back to wherever ye're hidin' and watch them sail awa' when the ice goes oot. Ye can see them on the deck—and they'll send ye a pair of opera glasses, so ye can be sure there's nane left in the Labrador."

"That's your proposal?" asked Dan in a choking voice.

"Aye, that's the proposal. Is it no reasonable?"

"You ask me to acquiesce in the theft of half my father's furs?" Dan shouted. Before his vision came again, the face of his father, grim in death. The landscape faded out. His father's face faded and was replaced by the surly, peering face of MacAulay. Dan did not afterward remember the next moment, but he found old McAndrew holding him by both arms, while he raved and struggled.

"Na, na, Mister Tennant, the man's an envoy," the Eskimo

said. "Ye canna offer violence to an envoy. Ye'd better gang,"
he added to MacAulay. "Ye see, the offer's refused."

"And the fool will lose everything, his life included,"
sneered MacAulay, turning and beginning to shamble away.

Dan came back to himself. "I'm sorry, McAndrew," he said
shamefacedly. "But I wouldn't have accepted such terms on any
account. They were too dishonorable. And I don't believe either
Molly or her father would have wished me to do anything else.

"Perhaps I did wrong," he added, "but that man was privy
to my father's murder, and I saw my father's body before he was
buried. MacAulay had had it in his icehouse all the winter."

McAndrew uttered a cluck that sounded like a reversion to
the Eskimo.

"Ye saw him? And ye say he was murdered? Molly was tellin' me and her faither that, but it didna seem possible."

"I mean to find the man who did it and make him pay for it
with his life. I guess it all got the better of me when I saw
MacAulay."

"Ye needna worry." There was a peculiar ring in the old
Eskimo's voice.

"What do you mean?"

"Ye needna worry aboot havin' rejected MacAulay's terms.
He didna mean them for to be accepted. If he had, he'd had
made better ones and bargained some. He was just trying to
keep you here for a spell."

"While they ambushed us?"

"I'm hopin' it was only that."

"What else—?" Dan began, realizing that some ominous
thought lay behind old McAndrew's words.

"We'd best be gettin' back," answered McAndrew, and
jerked his thumb toward the distant figure of MacAulay. "He's
oot of range noo, and the conference is suspended."

He turned away without another word, and began to scramble
up the bluffs. The sun had set, and the pale twilight of that
northern latitude held sway over the land.

Dan followed quickly in McAndrew's wake. As he climbed,
he drew his gun, fully expecting to be greeted at the top of the
bluff by a shower of lead from hidden marksmen; but none
came, and the desolate summit of the cliffs lay before them,
stretching into the infinite distance and relieved only by an occasional clup of willow or bake-apple bushes.

Dan was still wondering what had been in McAndrew's mind.

A feeling of undefined fear was growing in his own as he followed the Eskimo along the cliffs and down the trail to the beach. McAndrew quickened his pace. There was no one on the shore. There was no possibility that any pursuer could come up in time to see them enter the cave. Nevertheless that fear was still growing in Dan's heart, as if it had been communicated from McAndrew to himself by some telepathic process.

They were almost at the entrance of the cave when McAndrew stopped and stiffened, pointing to a patch of snow near the mouth, which, twilight though it was, Dan could see was trampled and scuffed up.

Just what happened next Dan never knew. Of a sudden he knew that the ambuscade was in the mouth of the cave itself; instinctively he dropped, and his gun roared its answer to the challenge of spurting lead.

Three of the 'breeds confronted them, and had McAndrew's warning come an instant later the two would simply have been targets for their bullets.

Dan emptied his gun and leaped to his feet. One of the 'breeds lay writhing in the snow; a second fired point blank, and the impact of the slug against his shoulder bone swung Dan around. That was what saved him from the 'breed's last shot, which grazed his cheek. He regained his stance, heard the 'breed's hammer snap on a spent cartridge, and was upon him in another moment.

The 'breed was a powerful man, but he was a child to Dan in that moment of frenzy. Dan's revolver butt crashed on the man's head, his knees sagged, his arms dropped, and Dan seized him about the middle and hurled him down the cliff to the rocks below.

He turned to see the third 'breed drop under old McAndrew's deliberately aimed shot. He rushed into the cave, calling.

It was almost dark within, but light enough for Dan to see that the cave and the rear compartment were both empty.

He ran back like a madman. The 'breed whom McAndrew had shot was already dead, the other was in the last throes. Nevertheless Dan grasped him by the throat.

"Where are they?" he shouted.

The Frenchman looked at him, his eyes already glazing, and the death rattle beginning in his throat.

"At the ship," he gasped.

"How did you find this place?"

"It was—the Eskimos. They—followed you one night. We knew that you were here."

"Who sent you?"

"The Lippmanns. Five of us. Two took them away, and we three—waited for you."

The breath rattled in his throat, he turned his face away and entered the last agony.

IX

DAN turned to McAndrew, unconscious of the blood that was streaming from his wounded shoulder. "You heard that? We've got to get Molly and her father," he cried. "We may be able to intercept them before they are taken aboard. How long ago—?" He turned to the dying man. "How long ago did your gang kidnap them?" he demanded.

But the 'breed had already passed beyond all understanding. Dan turned to McAndrew again, stretched out his hand to grasp him, and saw that the old man's face was covered with blood.

"You're hit! You stay here! I'll go—"

"Na, la, laddie.'Tis but a scratch," answered the old Eskimo, brushing away the blood that oozed from a flesh wound across the forehead. "Let me see that wound of yours."

Dan became conscious of his injured shoulder then. But he shook McAndrew off. "There's no time to be lost," he answered. "Come, McAndrew!" And he started down the trail again at top speed.

McAndrew followed him. Neither thought of anything but Captain Fairleigh and Molly as they sped across the tundra in the gathering darkness. It seemed only a matter of a few minutes before they had once more descended the bluff and were upon the groaning ice bridge. Here progress was slower. They went slipping and tumbling over the glazed ice.

Dan's shoulder was throbbing painfully, and a fiery thirst had begun to torment him, but he would not stop, even to assuage it with snow. McAndrew seemed keyed up to the same height of red-hot rage. They passed the bend, and the *Good Hope*, lying with the packed ice almost as high as her deck, a blaze of lights in the cabin at the stern.

McAndrew stretched out his arm and caught Dan's sleeve. "What are ye aimin' to do, Dan?" he demanded.

"Rush them," Dan answered briefly. "Maybe they're sure

we fell into that trap, and aren't expecting us. Rush them and
shoot—shoot and kill. They're mad dogs. No mercy!''

"I'm w' ye, laddie," McAndrew panted.

It was almost dark now. The harbor narrowed suddenly above
the bend, and the two were able to approach almost to the side
of the vessel unobserved, by edging along the growth of last
year's willow tangles along the shore. Now they could hear
voices from aboard, shouts and laughter, coming from the
lighted cabins. But the deck smelled abominably and seemed
to be littered with something. . .

Dan and McAndrew scrambled up the packed ice floes,
grasped the rail, and leaped aboard. The deck was a pigpen of
cluttered shacks, built by the Eskimos who had wintered there.

In the darkness the two men could see the squat forms and
gleaming eyes of the natives, who seemed to be huddled everywhere. There must have been more than a score of them, muttering and whispering together. But none of them made any
attempt to intercept either McAndrew or Dan, who ran past
them and darted down the stern companion.

The cabin door stood open, and the cabin was filled with
men. There were the two Lippmanns, Caribou Tessier, and three
or four more of the 'breeds. Dan was hardly conscious of them.
His eyes were riveted upon Molly, bound and gagged, and fastened to a chair, and Captain Fairleigh, lying roped upon the
floor. And one of the 'breeds was in the act of withdrawing a
bar of white-hot iron from the sheet-iron stove in the middle of
the saloon.

Gun in hand, Dan rushed into the room. But of a sudden a
strange silence seemed to descend about him. He was vaguely
conscious of the grinning face of Caribou Tessier, looking into
his own, but he was unaware that he had been struck on the
head with the butt end of a revolver as he ran by. He groped
forward and slumped inertly to the floor.

Dan opened his eyes and came shuddering back to consciousness under the shock of the ice-cold water that drenched him.
His head ached violently, his shoulder and whole arm were
numb. He looked at the circle gathering about him without understanding for a few moments.

Then slowly consciousness began to link up the associations.
He knew where he was now. That was Alexis Lippmann, with
the sallow, evil face and underhung lip; that was his brother,
Kuno; there was MacAulay at Kuno's side. Caribou Tessier was

still holding the empty pail, whose contents he had flung over Dan. Molly was still seated in the chair, though the gag had been removed from her mouth; on the floor beside Captain Fairleigh was old McAndrew, roped, and glaring defiantly around him.

"Well, Tennant, you're coming around at last!" sneered Kuno Lippmann. "That will be enough, Caribou," he addressed the 'breed. "Put that poker back in the stove; it's got cold while we've been fiddling with Tennant here."

Dan saw Tessier thrust back the bar of iron. He tried to collect his wits. What was it all about? Why hadn't they finished him while they were about it?

"Well, Tennant, we've got you," began Kuno. "I guess you know what we want. . . . Your father's furs. These people are still obstinate, and I was about to try the effects of a little red-hot iron upon them when you blundered in your customary way. You've played a good hand, Tennant, but the game's up now, and if you want to save your life, and the lives of the rest here, you'll come through with the information we want. Where are the furs hidden?"

Dan saw Captain Fairleigh's eyes fixed upon his own. And suddenly it came to him that the Lippmanns had been guilty of the crowning piece of stupidity of their career.

They had discovered the cave, but knew it only as the fugitives' hiding place. In the darkness their men had failed to discover the furs hidden in the part of the cave behind the living quarters. They had never guessed that the furs were there, or even thought to look!

As if reading Dan's answer in his face, and wishing to anticipate it, Kuno turned to Fairleigh again.

"You'd better come through now, you old fool," he snarled. "Sam Tennant's dead, and that trust you prated about last autumn doesn't exist any longer. Give up those furs, and we'll all make terms. If you don't, do you know what I'm going to do?"

He bent forward, leering, and Dan saw the spirit of degenerate cruelty leap into his eyes.

"I'm going to torture—not you, but Molly. I'm going to kill her bit by bit with fire. I'm going to burn her flesh from her bones in shreds. What's it going to be, Fairleigh? Still stubborn, eh? Wait till I begin. How about it, McAndrew? And you, Tennant? Sweet on the girl, aren't you? Get him, Caribou!" he yelled, as Dan hurled himself forward from his position on the floor.

Dan's leap was stopped by the fist of the 'breed, which sent him back in an inert heap.

"Tie him up, Caribou!" Kuno Lippmann commanded. Dan was quickly trussed, in spite of his struggles, and fastened to one of the cabin beams.

"How's the iron, Caribou?"

Grinning, the 'breed withdrew the iron from the stove, cherry-red, and white-hot at the tip. He handed it to Kuno, who advanced toward the helpless girl.

At that moment, as Molly, gagged and hardly able to move a muscle, fixed her eyes fearlessly upon the degenerates, Kuno flinched. Some power that seemed to emanate from her left him temporarily incapable of executing his fiendish plan.

"Stop!" shouted McAndrew. "I'm goin' to tell him, Fairleigh. Flesh and blood canna stand for that de'il's doin's. Dan, I'm goin' to tell him."

"That's my job," said Dan quietly. "I'll tell you where the furs are, Lippmann—one hour after Miss Fairleigh and her father and Mr. McAndrew have sailed on board this boat."

Kuno grinned from ear to ear. "You'll tell me now, Tennant," he answered.

Dan looked into the faces of those about him and saw no pity there. "You win, Lippmann," he said quietly. "The furs are in the rear of that cave that we were living in. Your men weren't smart enough to find them."

"You're lying!" burst out Alexis.

"Go and see," answered Dan.

Alexis peered into his face and knew that he was speaking the truth.

"And now how about your terms?" demanded McAndrew.

A roar of laughter answered him. "Don't worry about terms, McAndrew," shouted Alexis. "You'll know the terms fast enough. We'll make sure that the furs are there first."

He stepped across to Molly, wrenched the gag out of her mouth, and slashed her bonds. "Kuno bluffed them!" he shouted exultantly. "I'd never have let him burn you, Molly. You're mine!" He clasped her in his arms and bent his face to hers.

Dan all but broke free in his struggles. McAndrew cursed and raved. Only Fairleigh, exhausted by his ordeal of the winter, remained passive, a look of unutterable despair frozen upon his features.

"What's that row on deck? Keep those damned Eskimos quiet!" bawled MacAulay.

Two of the 'breeds ran out of the cabin and up the companion. There was the sound of a scuffle, and they came tumbling back. The foremost, running into the room, displayed a hideous gash across the check that extended from his mouth almost to the ear.

Yells and frenzied bawling suddenly filled the night. And down the companion, and into the saloon, there burst a mob of drink-maddened Eskimos, waving their long knives. At the head of them was Koononok!

X

DAN lay stupidly watching the sudden transformation, not sure that he was not dreaming. How could Koononok, who had failed to accompany him on the road from Nagatok, because he was afraid of MacAulay, be here?

And was this Koononok, or was it actually an illusion, this man transformed into a veritable savage? This man with the murder-maddened face and hanging jaw, from which the tongue protruded like a dog's, who, knife in hand, was leading the mob of maddened natives?

So sudden was the interruption of the Eskimos that the group within the cabin had no time to organize against them. In a moment each man was beset by two or three. The cracking of revolvers was drowned in the long, swelling death cries of the Arctic savages as they hurled themselves upon their prey. Each knife thrust had its echo in the death cry of a victim.

Probably the natives would have been unable to discriminate between Lippmann's followers and his prisoners, and it was the fact that the three men and Molly were bound and incapable of offering resistance that saved their lives. Over them surged the savages, driving the Lippmanns and their men back against the wall. The saloon was a shambles of dying men, struggling in their last agony.

Dan saw Alexis Lippmann fall, transfixed through the heart by Koononok's knife, and the yell that broke from the Livyere's lips as he thrust was like the shriek of a Fury. Kuno, dragged down by three or four pairs of hands, was being literally hacked to pieces. Last to fall was Caribou Tessier, his long, bovine face

convulsed with terror, while the great ox jaws clamped the air
and peal after peal of frenzied terror broke from him.

No, not the last! Through the swarm of marauders MacAulay
broke like a battering ram, gained the door, and disappeared,
and after him surged the maddened mob, leaving the cabin filled
with the moaning, writhing victims of the attack, and Fairleigh,
Dan, and McAndrew, huddled about Molly in one corner.

McAndrew reached out his hand and picked up a knife that
was lying near him. He quickly slashed the ropes that fastened
himself and his companions. The three men formed a wedge
and got Molly into the middle of it. The girl had fainted and
seemed to know nothing, though her limbs seemed to move
automatically as the three got her to the stern companion.

Down the companion Koononok came leaping. Dan, who
was in the lead, struck at him, but the the Livyere parried the
blow and held up his hand. He seemed in his right mind again.
Out on the ice Dan could hear the yells of the pursuing mob.
Overhead the stars shone clear and bright.

"Me save you. Me bring Eskimos to save you because me
know that Lippmanns plan to kill you all. Me follow MacAulay.
Me no go with you because me hear MacAulay telling of plans
to kill you, and me stay and listen."

Koononok grinned, and Dan's hand shot out and grasped his.

"Me tell Eskimo mans must kill Lippmanns and all party
tonight," Koononok went on. "They all very mad at Lippmanns
long time because they take um women away. Plan to kill um
all long ago, but too much afraid. I tell um no to be afraid,
because law um say may kill when white mans kill first and take
um womans away.

"When Eskimos look in and see that Lippmanns make hot
um stick to burn you all up, me tell um that now is the time to
kill. Me tell um not to get so mad that they kill you and your
friends, too. They understand. You tell um law no hang Eskimos on gallows because they kill."

"I'll see to that," said Dan. "But you just come with me at
once and see if we can stop them killing MacAulay,"

"MacAulay bad man, bad as Lippmanns," said Koononok.

"That may be so," said Dan, "but the law doesn't permit
killing except in self-defense. I'll attend to MacAulay. He'll
hang all right, if we can get evidence enough against him."

"Not stop kill um," said Koononok.

Dan grasped him by the arm. "You're coming with me at
once," he reiterated.

"Me go, but no stop kill um MacAulay," said the Livyere obstinately. "Maybe you kill um yourself when you know about all."

"Know what?" demanded Dan.

"Maybe you want to kill MacAulay yourself when you know MacAulay kill your father."

"What's that you say?" Red rage was burning in Dan's heart; he saw the Livyere through a fog of red. "He—killed—my father?"

"Sure MacAulay he kill um. You ask me who kill um, and me afraid to tell you. Me see it all."

"Your father go into warehouse with MacAulay and they talk together for a while. Then MacAulay send me back to the store to get something, but me stay and hide and watch because me afraid for Mr. Tennant. They talk a long time and Mr. Tennant get angrier and angrier. He tell MacAulay him a thief, and MacAulay say him no thief. Then Mr. Tennant go into corner of store to look at a bale of furs, and me see MacAulay stoop down and pick up long stick that he got hidden under blankets.

"MacAulay creep up soft behind Mr. Tennant. He raise um stick so!" Koononok made a dramatic gesture. "Then your father look up suddenly and see. He put up um hand, and MacAulay bring stick down on your father's head. Your father drop, never move again. Me see MacAulay strike um again, and then me run. If MacAulay know me see, he kill me."

Dan looked at him steadily. Far out across the ice he could hear the yells of the Eskimos, which seemed to indicate that their quarry had still succeeded in eluding them. The stars were still bright overhead, but even while Koononok was speaking, there had seemed to come an imperceptible change.

Dawn was at hand; the short midsummer night was over. And Dan knew that before the sun rose his father would be avenged.

All the instincts of the policeman, all the arguments that Dan had used to Koononok had been swept away in that terrific desire for vengeance.

Yet it was something more than the desire for vengeance. It was the feeling of fatality, the sense that everything which had transpired had been so guided that in the end he and the man who had killed his father should stand face-to-face.

Without a word Dan turned toward the companion. But McAndrew put his hand upon his arm, and Dan became aware of the old Eskimo's presence at his side.

"I'm gangin' wi' ye."

"Stay and take care of Molly," answered Dan. "Get her off this ship quick. I can manage this affair alone. No, it's my business."

Outside, upon the ice, the evidences of the approaching dawn were plainer. The stars had lost their luster, and in the east, above the dun line of the sea, a faint pink had begun to tinge the horizon. It was getting light. A warm wind was blowing.

The Eskimos were visible now, gathered along the side of the ice bridge, yelling and baiting the tiny, isolated figure that came into view, almost at the edge of the breakers. It was evident that their hearts had failed them after their first burst of frenzied anger, for none of them ventured to rush upon MacAulay, hopelessly trapped and cut off though he appeared to be.

And Dan's heart was singing a primal paean of joy and thanksgiving. MacAulay had been spared that they two might meet face-to-face. He was unarmed, and MacAulay no doubt had his revolver. Dan was glad of that. He knew that, come what might, MacAulay would not live to see the sunrise in the east that morning—that east that was already deepening from pink to rosy red.

It was growing light fast. The ice was groaning and cracking with reverberations like pistol shots. A day or two more, and it must go out. It must have thawed all night, for the surface was covered with a film of water, through which Dan splashed steadily as he trudged toward MacAulay.

He could see him more plainly now. He was abreast of the jeering Eskimos, who, lining the side of the bridge, were shaking their fists at MacAulay and hailing him with taunting gibes.

Dan went on. He was seen now, and the Eskimos began to shout to him, as if in warning. Dan paid no heed. MacAulay had seen him and was standing in the spray of the breakers, looking toward him. He began to shout, too.

Then Dan understood. MacAulay was trapped even more hopelessly than he had supposed. The ice bridge had already broken. Great floes were swirling down into the sea through a gap in what was a solid wall of ice, twenty feet high, and on the very edge of this ice wall, cut off from escape, MacAulay stood, with the breakers booming at his feet and showering him with spray, and the whole mass quivering under the impact of the floes that were hurling themselves against its base.

It was death to leap back into that cannonade of enormous,

jagged floes that were bombarding the ice bridge like cannon-balls. And between Dan and MacAulay was a widening rift of ten or a dozen feet, through which the torrent poured.

Dan came straight on with the mechanical gait of one who has himself become a machine; he saw only MacAulay, material obstacles did not exist for him. A yell went up from the throats of the watchers as they saw him poise himself upon the edge of the grinding floes and leap.

He landed at the extremity of one of the floes that composed the ice bridge, and scrambled up. High above the torrent that seethed past them, upon an ice platform ten feet square, Dan and MacAulay stood face-to-face.

With a shriek of craven fear MacAulay dropped to his knees and clutched at Dan's hands, howling for mercy.

And with that the fog cleared from Dan's brain. He knew he could not kill, knew that his training as a policeman held good to the end.

MacAulay read the change in him; he struggled up, babbling, hands clasped in desperate appeal.

Suddenly the whole bridge vibrated under a mighty shock that swept Dan from his feet. He tried to struggle up, grasped at emptiness; with a roar like that of thunder the fragments of the bridge dissolved.

Dan fought as he had never fought before to rise from beneath the waves, gained the surface, gasping and battered, and saw MacAulay almost at his side.

As Dan reached for MacAulay, he saw to his horror a block of ice rise up and batter the man's head as if an invisible hand had wielded it. MacAulay sank.

Dan dived beneath the floe, grasped him, and brought him to the surface. Clutching him, he began striking out toward the shore.

How he reached that shore he never knew. Again and again a jagged tongue of ice would reach out at him, with a slow momentum capable, nevertheless, of battering him to pieces. Huge pinnacles came toppling down around him.

Weakened by the dead weight of the man he held, Dan fought for life. He was nearing the shore now, he saw the Eskimos that lined it, gaping at the sight of such a struggle as they had never seen before. Then Dan felt ground beneath his feet.

He rose up and, with a last effort, dragged MacAulay's body to the land. There was no need to look at him to know that the man was dead.

He dropped, and for a moment consciousness went out. Then, feeling his head raised, he opened his eyes, to find it pillowed on Molly's knees.

Near her were Fairleigh and McAndrew, but Dan had only eyes for her. They had won through—great as the struggle had been, they had won through.

A shaft of light from the risen sun turned the sea into gold.

Samuel Alexander White was often referred to, with some justification, as the "Jack London of Canada." White, who was born in a Canadian pioneer village toward the end of the last century, wrote prolifically about all areas of his native country and its history—notably about northern Ontario and the activities of the Hudson's Bay Company in the vicinity of James Bay. His writing career spanned some forty years, beginning in 1910 with the novel Stampeder. *His other novels include* Law of the North, North of the Border, Morgan of the Mounted, *and* Northwest Crossing. *"The Bear Trap," a tale of the North Woods, is a good example of his skill with the short story.*

The Bear Trap

★★★★★★★★★★★★★★★

Samuel Alexander White

MIDNIGHT struck in the Dawson Road at Lake Superior Landing and lights all over the place began to wink out. Cabin lamps went first, then those of the smaller roadhouses.

In George Rodney's place, the Superior House, big and pretentious, the glare did not dim. Most of the games had died, but at a rough pine table sat McArthur, the manager of the Lake Shebandowan Station of the Dawson Road, and Whitewater Reynolds, head of the rival North-West Transportation Company; holding up the house.

Back of them, on top of another table, reclined Randall Cherriman, boss of the Dawson Road, his attention divided between watching the play and trying to keep the oil lamp from smoking in the bracket over his head.

The reflector of the lamp cast the light down upon the faces of McArthur and Reynolds. McArthur's was a florid Scot countenance, genial and whimsical, with a droll twist to the mouth. Whitewater's was keen, swarthy, belligerent, embellished by his yellow mustache.

From the expression of those faces a casual onlooker would have picked the N. W. T. C. man for the loser, but it was not so. White-water Reynolds seldom lost at cards, while McArthur played in proverbial hard luck. Now McArthur was very near his limit; so near, in fact, that Randall Cherriman reached over a lazy leg and touched him upon the shoulder with his moccasined toe.

"Better give it up, McArthur," he advised.

"By the good St. George, now, Randall," McArthur beamed as he lifted his broad, florid features from his hand, "and I'll be having just one more try. Don't faint, mon, it's the very last. Whistle Cock o' the North awhile, Randall, and see if the good old tune will scare the evil spirits that are backing Whitewater. Reynolds, you rascal, and have you the cards bewitched?"

Whitewater's tobacco-stained teeth showed through his drooping yellow mustache.

"It's sure nothing but a run of luck," he avowed.

"Run of luck, you son of the N. W. T. C.! It doesn't work for me. The de'il's worst luck never camped with me so long. It's a spell you've got on me, Whitewater, with your swift hands and dark looks. A wizard you are tonight. But I'll call your bluff on this hand. Show me!"

Whitewater spread his cards. It was his third full house. McArthur leaped up from the table with a curse.

"It's gone, Randall," he mourned, half-whimsically, half-lugubriously. "My last stake, I am saying. My summer's wages on the Dawson Road thrown to the de'il, and the roll you lent me besides, Randall, and—and—"

"Never mind the roll," Cherriman cut in. "But I will say that you're a stubborn fool to go to the limit. Why don't you quit when you strike a streak of losses?"

McArthur shook his head. Whitewater gathered his winnings off the pine boards with rapacious hands and turned to the onlookers with a triumphant grin.

"Come on, boys," he invited. "The treat's on me."

They lined up. The bar, like the tables, was of rough pine. A loose sliver jabbed McArthur's elbow as he slid his arm along. He exclaimed softly, then a smile came over his florid face as he stopped and thoughtfully thrummed a tune upon the sliver. In his preoccupation he did not notice that Cherriman and Reynolds had wormed into their fur coats. Suddenly the door opened, letting in the frost with a smokelike vapor. When McArthur turned at its closing bang, the N. W. T. C. man was gone.

"I'm next," announced Cherriman, turning up the collar of his heavy coat and staring apprehensively at the door, through which the cold bored in spite of its double cleating. He had quite a distance to go before he reached his own warm cabin, where he lived in company with his head stage driver, Leatherpuller Davis.

After moments of contemplation of the front rime on the hinges, Cherriman pulled the door open.

"Night, Arthur," he called back. "Night, Rodney." Through the cracks of the barrier as the cold stabbed him, they heard this: "Wouf! Curse such gimlet weather, anyway! It shuts down all transportation west."

Cherriman gone, McArthur turned to his sliver and thrummed it once more with renewed vigor. It was singing a comforting song and revealing to the Shebandowan Station manager things that were hidden.

"What's making you smile?" asked George Rodney. "You're a thundering good loser, if I know anything."

The two were alone in the place. McArthur continued to smile across at the proprietor.

"Slivers," McArthur answered enigmatically. "Slivers, I am saying. Where's my old mackinaw reefer, mon?"

Rodney took it off the hook and gave it to him. McArthur threw it across the table upon which he had been playing cards and pretended to hunt through its pockets for his neck cloth.

Instead of searching there, his fingers were feeling deftly the underside of the table, where Whitewater Reynolds had been sitting.

He found what he sought and hid it swiftly in his pocket. His back was to the yawning Rodney, and the latter could not see the light of satisfaction on McArthur's face as he swung through the door.

That day on the North Shore of Lake Superior had been a demon of wind and cold. Through the pine trees the blast slashed like a knife. All day their tops had swayed and met, had parted and reeled, till the Laurentian ridges were cloaked in gloom. A three-hour fall of snow had come with the night, but by this time the fall had ceased and the prowlers of the Northern night were abroad.

From his lair in the spruce-crowned ridges overlooking the Landing stirred one of the few grizzlies of the section. He had the human instinct of comfort and his lair was warm, but hunger, the slave driver, forced him out.

All fall he had been a sort of Nemesis to the men of the Dawson Road, and not without reason. They had blotched his range with way stations and roadhouses, and ripped up his best hunting grounds with the twists of their road and their eternal bridges. He retaliated by padding their camp with his tremendous tracks in the night and carrying off the moose quarters slung to the ridge poles of their cabin.

He knew nothing of the struggle between the N.W.T.C. and the Dawson Road for the transportation of the West. He went where his muscle-corded limbs and wilderness cunning took him in his midnight wanderings, and he marked his way with mighty teeth and claws, so that crimson smudges blazed as a record on the morning snows. The Dawson Road men had trailed him, dogged him, attempted to poison him, and reared deadfalls for his destruction, but still he was very much alive. He had a way of vanishing in the ridges that baffled men and dogs alike.

His lair had never been found. Charlie Beauchene, the trader of Isle Beauchene, had chased him a dozen times with a pack of huskies. The dogs could follow until they struck the bare ridges sheering up from the Grande Portage shore, but farther they could not trail. The scent disappeared upon the windswept rock, and no effort could find it.

Of course night watches were set to get him when he came to the cabins, but on the occasions of these vigils he never appeared. His visit was always the night after, the night before, or in the space of a few days.

Upon this night the grizzly had crawled out earlier than usual, approached the D.R. camp, and made a round of the closed buildings on the outskirts, where there was hope of food.

Disappointment met him everywhere he sniffed. The wave-shaped windrows of snow seemed aware of his discomfiture, for they spat scornfully in his face with every shift of the wind. Grown used to his depredations, the Dawson Road men had left nothing outside.

He wondered if there was anything in the middle of the camp. There was no glare of light to deter him. Midnight had struck, and the lamps were out. He lumbered swiftly and silently up the rough macadam which Randall Cherriman had spread upon his Western trail to make the way smooth for Leatherpuller Davis's wheels.

The grizzly was now half buried in the drifts, now sprawling upon the clean, iced places where the bite of the frost made him cringe. The cabins were black splashes, black as ink against the pallid snow. Above, the cold stars hung like sparkling stalactites, dripping from the floor of heaven. The moon was a round, frosted mirror. In the north the fountain-like aurora sprayed its glowing silver flame.

The grizzly reached the shelter of a silent cabin and lurched along to the next, and to the next. On the edge of the Dawson Road were sunken holes and stumps and boulders. As he floundered along, the voices of men sounded up the trail.

He crouched in a dark angle between two clapboard buildings. While he waited, a snappy report split the frost, a report that woodcraft had taught him carried unseen death. The missile whizzed past his hiding place, glanced, and sang shrilly through space.

With a growl of rage the grizzly sprang out and launched fair upon a bulky figure standing in the middle of the Dawson Road. The figure turned quickly. A second shot spat out.

The unseen missile seared the grizzly's shoulder with a hot pain and spoiled his spring. His head struck the pistol in the outstretched hand, knocking it into the snow. Then the big beast, his balance upset, fell clumsily past the man.

Instantly a new weapon flashed in the man's hand, a great knife a foot long. It struck the grizzly in the neck, just at the base of the head and, his mighty limbs paralyzed for a second, the animal sagged upon the crust.

His helplessness lasted only a minute, but it gave the man who had struck the blow time enough to leap aside and off the road. A cabin door banged after him, and the Northern night settled once more into frosty stillness.

The grizzly's inactivity did not last long, but when he arose again he was bewildered. There was a second manshape in the trail which in his charge he had not seen before. He pushed the shape with his nose. It was still as the night. His instinct telling him that death lay there, the big animal backed away.

He continued to back away, the long knife sticking in his neck and wabbling fantastic shadows on the snow, until he struck the outskirts of the camp. Then he dropped on all fours and headed for the Laurentian ridges, the blood speckling the trail he left behind.

In the morning the Dawson Road men read a tale on the Western trail through the camp. There they found McArthur's body.

The bullet hole in his breast, and the two discharged cartridges in the pistol he still gripped in a badly sprained wrist explained it all. The sprained wrist was jammed in tight against McArthur's chest. It was Cherriman who pointed out the singed spot where the flaming muzzle had touched.

"Mac sure got one ball into the brute before it smothered him, boys," he pointed out. "Then the grizzly's body jammed the weapon back into Mac's chest as he pulled the trigger again, and poor Mac got the second missile himself. Yonder's the grizzly's track going off, all staggery and showing blood.''

A bold thing the men declared, for the grizzly to prowl in the center of the Landing before all were asleep, but they attributed it to his hunger and the unprecedented cold. Also, it was just McArthur's luck again, his eternal losing luck, to walk out of George Rodney's Superior House and meet him on the way home.

They burned a hole in the ground to receive the body of McArthur. As Randall Cherriman looked on the face of his faithful Shebandowan manager for the last time, he swore a vow that he would get the beast that killed him. George Rodney came to Cherriman after the funeral ceremony, and gave him McArthur's mackinaw coat, his watch, and a few trinkets.

"You'd better keep them, Randall,'' he suggested. "It's all he had left. He ain't got any relations here, and you were his boss and friend. I thought you'd like to have them.''

"Sure, George,'' nodded Cherriman, "I'd like to have them. And I'll tell you something. I'll tan that grizzly's hide and put it with them. Savvy? I'll get him, or you boys'll never see me bossing the Dawson Road again.''

Cherriman went off to his Landing cabin with McArthur's old mackinaw across his arm. He put the trinkets in a safe place and turned the pockets of the coat inside out to see if they contained anything of further value. Two pockets were empty. From the third he drew two aces and a pine sliver.

"Wonder what Mac was doing with those?'' he asked his cabin companion, Leatherpuller Davis.

"Dunno,'' was Leatherpuller's answer. "Mebbe they're out of the pack he was using last. Lost everything, didn't he?''

"Yes,'' Cherriman agreed, "but he won't need any money over the Divide. Look here, Leatherpuller. I'm going to get that grizzly.''

Leatherpuller stood up suddenly, his wind-tanned, alkali-scarred face full of concern.

"Off your nut?'' he inquired dryly.

"Strictly on,'' Randall assured him, taking down his rifle from its pegs. "But I'm sure going on the warpath.''

"Well,'' sighed Leatherpuller, resignedly reaching for his own gun, "I'll just go with you. I don't want to see the Dawson Road lose its road boss. No sensible man goes alone stirring up a wounded grizzly!''

They struck the beast's trail where it left the Landing camp. In the snow it was easy tracking, but as they reached the spruce ridges that curved the lake edge for miles along the Grande Portage shore, the blood spots became faint, and on the rocky divide that looked down on the valley of the Pigeon River there was neither track nor blood.

"Wound's closed, I guess," hazarded Leatherpuller.

"Sure," nodded Cherriman.

All day they searched and searched, circled and circled, examined all the snow pockets of the gulches and the snow-plastered trunks and boughs of leaning trees, but there was not a trace. They had lost the chain of prints on a naked ledge, and progress seemed hopeless. Leatherpuller Davis sat down on a boulder and filled his pipe in disgust.

"We'll never get him," he prophesied.

"We've got to," declared Cherriman grimly. "He couldn't jump off this ledge without breaking his neck. Now, where in thunder did he go from here? That fallen pine is covered with snow, like the splintered rocks on either side. There isn't so much as a partridge track showing. Did a big brute like that go up in a balloon?"

"Monster pine. Isn't hollow, is it? Guess he couldn't make the squeeze if it was."

Randall got down on his stomach among the rocks.

"No, not hollow," he announced. "But, by thunder, there's something like a tunnel under it, and here's a clot of blood and a tuft of hair. We've run him down, Leatherpuller. He's sure trapped."

"Go easy," warned his companion. "I've known grizzlies all my life, and they don't hole in a place like that. If it's a tunnel, it runs into his real den. Stand back a piece."

Cautiously they observed the direction of the tunnel, which was a natural one made by the slide rock from above slipping down into the gulch. It extended in line with the pine trunk and almost directly beneath it. Soon Cherriman found the other opening, which came out among the mighty branches of the prostrate trunk. He put an eye to it. There was light filtering through from the farther orifice.

"Nothing in it!" he snorted with chagrin.

On sudden thought he looked up. The branches of the pine arched toward the rock wall, and a black slit showed in the granite three feet from the topmost bough.

Randall gave a low whistle. He gazed at Leatherpuller, and back again at the cliff-like rock.

"Dead, skinned, quartered, and the bear steak in the pan!" he exulted.

He was clambering over the branches of the fallen pine as he spoke.

"You be thundering careful, Randall," cautioned Leatherpuller, gazing apprehensively up after him.

Cherriman nodded confidently. With all his speed he was observing needful caution. A grizzly has more fight to its inches than any claw-armed beast upon earth, and Randall knew it. He paused once in his ascent and fed a new cartridge into the chamber of his rifle. Also he eased the knife in his belt before starting on.

Slowly and warily at the top he came on a level with the hole. He raised himself gingerly upon his insecure footing. When his head came in line with the opening in the rock wall, he caught the glitter of eyes. Instantly his chin dropped upon his rifle stock.

The grizzly's leaping body blurred the mouth of the den, but Cherriman's bullet met it fairly between the flashing eyes. The huge beast went limp in midair and crashed to the slide rock below.

Leatherpuller Davis gave a quick jump, thrusting his rifle muzzle back off the shoulder against the heart, but there was no occasion to shoot. There was no motion, no pulse, in the huddled mass of hair.

"You're some sharpshooter, Randall!" grinned Leatherpuller appreciatively as the Road boss came down.

"I had to get him, Leatherpuller," Cherriman returned.

He pushed the grizzly's head around with his foot. The action brought to view a long knife sticking in its neck.

"Thunder!" Randall exclaimed. "McArthur was sure game, wasn't he? Must have used the knife before he pulled his gun."

Leatherpuller nodded solemnly as he pulled out the knife and wiped the blood off it.

"But it ain't McArthur's knife!" he cried, scratching at the nameplate on the hilt.

"What's that?" blurted Cherriman. "Whose is it?"

The Road boss snatched the knife from Leatherpuller's hand and read the owner's name.

In silver letters it ran: *Whitewater Reynolds*.

George Rodney's Superior House was ablaze with the light of freshly filled oil lamps.

Inside a great clamor broke out, as the door opened to admit Leatherpuller and the Road boss.

"Here's Randall Cherriman."

"You got the grizzly's hide, eh?"

"Bully for you, Randall."

"Must have got him, or he wouldn't show face in the Dawson Road camp again."

These and a score more greetings fell upon the ears of Cherriman and Leatherpuller as they crossed the floor. Randall heeded none of the greetings. Stalking straight to where Whitewater Reynolds sat at a gaming table, he threw upon the board a knife, a pine sliver, and two aces.

Whitewater drew back, a snarl on his swarthy face. His hand went into the pocket of his mackinaw coat.

Leatherpuller jerked the hand out again. Cherriman shoved his rifle muzzle into Whitewater's ribs.

"Don't you so much as shiver," he warned the N.W.T.C. man.

"What's the row here?" demanded Rodney, shouldering through. "What you two fellows mean by starting a roughhouse?"

"Wait, Rodney," requested Randall. "Wait till I explain. That sliver used to stick under the pine table, there on Whitewater's side, before McArthur found it last night, with these handy aces in it. No wonder Reynolds could win, eh?"

"Turn up that table," commanded George Rodney.

A dozen hands flipped it. The sliver fitted exactly. A nasty silence fell in the room.

"That's enough," observed Randall solemnly. "The knife tells the rest. It was stuck in the grizzly's neck. That was the grizzly's medicine for butting into the argument when McArthur and Whitewater quarreled outside on the trail, and Whitewater shot my Station manager down. Now, what are you Dawson Road men going to do about Whitewater?"

"Hang him!" rose an ominous, reverberating roar.

An ardent conservationist, James Oliver Curwood (1878–1927) wrote passionately of such Northern locales as the vast Peace River country, the arctic plains, and the Hudson Bay wilderness. His robust, evocative novels include Kazan, *a dog-wolf story that many critics feel is only a cut below Jack London's classic* The Call of the Wild; Son of Kazan, Baree, The River's End, The Valley of Silent Men, *and* Steele of the Royal Mounted. *Lesser known but no less stirring are his short stories, such as those in such collections as* Back to God's Country, *and the narrative of cowardice and courage which follows.*

The Yellow-back

★★★★★★★★★★★★★★★

James Oliver Curwood

ABOVE God's Lake, where the Bent Arrow runs red as pale blood under its crust of ice, Reese Beaudin heard of the dog auction that was to take place at Post Lac Bain three days later. It was in the cabin of Joe Delesse, a trapper, who lived at Lac Bain during the summer, and trapped the fox and the lynx sixty miles farther north in this month of February.

"Diantre, but I tell you it is to be the greatest sale of dogs that has ever happened at Lac Bain!" said Delesse. "To this Wakao they are coming from all the four directions. There will be a hundred dogs, huskies, and malamutes, and Mackenzie hounds, and mongrels from the south, and I should not wonder if some of the little Eskimo devils were brought from the north to be sold as breeders. Surely you will not miss it, my friend?"

"I am going by way of Post Lac Bain," replied Reese Beaudin equivocally.

But his mind was not on the sale of dogs. From his pipe he puffed out thick clouds of smoke, and his eyes narrowed until they seemed like coals peering out of cracks; and he said, in his quiet, soft voice:

"Do you know of a man named Jacques Dupont, m'sieu'?"

102

Joe Delesse tried to peer through the cloud of smoke at Reese Beaudin's face.

"Yes, I know him. Does he happen to be a friend of yours?"

Reese laughed softly.

"I have heard of him. They say that he is a devil. To the west I was told that he can whip any man between Hudson's Bay and the Great Bear, that he is a beast in man-shape, and that he will surely be at the big sale at Lac Bain."

On his knees the huge hands of Joe Delesse clenched slowly, gripping in their imaginary clutch a hated thing.

"*Oui*, I know him," he said. "I know also—Elise—his wife. See!"

He thrust suddenly his two huge knotted hands through the smoke that drifted between him and the stranger who had sought the shelter of his cabin that night.

"See—I am a man full-grown, m'sieu—a man—and yet I am afraid of him! That is how much of a devil and a beast in man-shape he is."

Again Reese Beaudin laughed in his low, soft voice.

"And his wife, *mon ami*? Is she afraid of him?"

He had stopped smoking. Joe Delesse saw his face. The stranger's eyes made him look twice and think twice.

"You have known her—sometime?"

"Yes, a long time ago. We were children together. And I have heard all has not gone well with her. Is it so?"

"Does it go well when a dove is mated to a vulture, m'sieu'?"

"I have also heard that she grew up to be very beautiful," said Reese Beaudin, "and that Jacques Dupont killed a man for her. If that is so—"

"It is not so," interrupted Delesse. "He drove another man away—no, not a man, but a yellow-livered coward who had no more fight in him than a porcupine without quills! And yet she says he was not a coward. She has always said, even to Dupont, that it was the way *le Bon Dieu* made him, and that because he was made that way, he was greater than all other men in the North Country. How do I know? Because, m'sieu', I am Elise Dupont's cousin."

Delesse wondered why Reese Beaudin's eyes were glowing like living coals.

"And yet—again, it is only rumor I have heard—they say this man, whoever he was, did actually run away, like a dog that had been whipped and was afraid to return to its kennel."

"Pst!" Joe Delesse flung his great arms wide. "Like that—he was gone. And no one ever saw him again, or heard of him again.

But I know that she knew—my cousin, Elise. What word it was he left for her at the last she has always kept in her own heart, *mon Dieu*, and what a wonderful thing he had to fight for! You knew the child. But the woman—*non*? She was like an angel. Her eyes, when you looked into them—what can I say, m'sieu'? They made you forget. And I have seen her hair, unbound, black and glossy as the velvet side of a sable, covering her to the hips. And two years ago I saw Jacques Dupont's hands in that hair, and he was dragging her by it—"

Something snapped. It was a muscle in Reese Beaudin's arm. He had stiffened like iron.

"And you let him do that!"

Joe Delesse shrugged his shoulders. It was a shrug of hopelessness, of disgust.

"For the third time I interfered, and for the third time Jacques Dupont beat me until I was nearer dead than alive. And since then I have made it none of my business. It was, after all, the fault of the man who ran away. You see, m'sieu', it was like this: Dupont was mad for her, and this man who ran away—the Yellow-back—wanted her, and Elise loved the Yellow-back. This Yellow-back was twenty-three or four, and he read books, and played a fiddle and drew strange pictures—and was weak in the heart when it came to a fight. But Elise loved him. She loved him for those very things that made him a fool and a weakling, m'sieu', the books and the fiddle and the pictures; and she stood up with the courage for them both. And she would have married him, too, and would have fought for him with a club if it had come to that, when the thing happened that made him run away. It was at the midsummer carnival, when all the trappers and their wives and children were at Lac Bain. And Dupont followed the Yellow-back about like a dog. He taunted him, he insulted him, he got down on his knees and offered to fight him without getting on his feet; and there, before the very eyes of Elise, he washed the Yellow-back's face in the grease of one of the roasted caribou! And the Yellow-back was a man! Yes, a grown man! And it was then that Jacques Dupont shouted out his challenge to all that crowd. He would fight the Yellow-back. He would fight him with his right arm tied behind his back! And before Elise and the Yellow-back, and all that crowd, friends tied his arm so that it was like a piece of wood behind him, and it was his right arm, his fighting arm, the better half of him that was gone. And even then the Yellow-back was as white as the paper he drew pictures on. *Ventre saint gris*, but then was his chance to have killed Jacques Dupont! Half a man could have done it. Did he, m'sieu'? No, he did not. With his one arm and his one hand Jacques Dupont whipped that Yellow-back, and he would have killed him if Elise had not rushed in to save the Yellow-back's purple face from going dead black. And that night the Yellow-back slunk away. Shame? Yes. From that night he was ashamed to show his face ever again at Lac Bain. And no one knows where he went. No one—except Elise. And her secret is in her own breast.''

''And after that?'' questioned Reese Beaudin, in a voice that was scarcely above a whisper.

''I cannot understand,'' said Joe Delesse. ''It was strange, m'sieu', very strange. I know that Elise, even after that coward ran away, still loved him. And yet—well, something happened. I overheard a terrible quarrel one day between Jan Thiebout, father of Elise, and Jacques Dupont. After that Thiebout was very much afraid of Dupont. I have my own suspicion. Now that Thiebout is dead, it is not wrong for me to say what it is. I think Thiebout killed the half-breed Bedore, who was found dead on his trap-line five years ago. There was a feud between them. And Dupont, discovering Thiebout's secret—well, you can understand how easy it would be after that, m'sieu'. Thiebout's winter trapping was in that Burntwood country, fifty miles from neighbor to neighbor, and very soon after Bedore's death Jacques Dupont became Thiebout's partner. I know that Elise was forced to marry him. That was four years ago. The next year old Thiebout died, and in all that time not once has Elise been to Post Lac Bain!''

''Like the Yellow-back—she never returned,'' breathed Reese Beaudin.

''Never. And now—it is strange—''

''What is strange, Joe Delesse?''

''That for the first time in all these years she is going to Lac Bain—to the dog sale.''

Reese Beaudin's face was again hidden in the smoke of his pipe. Through it his voice came.

''It is a cold night, M'sieu' Delesse. Hear the wind howl!''

''Yes, it is cold—so cold the foxes will not run. My traps and poison-baits will need no tending tomorrow.''

''Unless you dig them out of the drifts.''

''I will stay in the cabin.''

''What! You are not going to Lac Bain?''

''I doubt it.''

''Even though Elise, your cousin, is to be there?''

''I have no stomach for it, m'sieu'. Nor would you were you in my boots, and did you know why she is going. *Par les mille cornes du diable*, I cannot whip him but I can kill him—and if I went—and the thing happens which I guess is going to happen—"

"*Qui?* Surely you will tell me—"

"Yes, I will tell you. Jacques Dupont knows that Elise has never stopped loving the Yellow-back. I do not believe she has ever tried to hide it from him. Why should she? And there is a rumor, m'sieu', that the Yellow-back will be at the Lac Bain dog sale."

Reese Beaudin rose slowly to his feet and yawned in that smoke-filled cabin.

"And if the Yellow-back should turn the tables, Joe Delesse, think of what a fine thing you will miss," he said.

Joe Delesse also rose, with a contemptuous laugh.

"That fiddler, that picture drawer, that book reader—Pouff! You are tired, m'sieu', that is your bunk."

Reese Beaudin held out a hand. The bulk of the two stood out in the lamp glow, and Joe Delesse was so much the bigger man that his hand was half again the size of Reese Beaudin's. They gripped. And then a strange look went over the face of Joe Delesse. A cry came from out of his beard. His mouth grew twisted. His knees doubled slowly under him, and in the space of ten seconds his huge bulk was kneeling on the floor, while Reese Beaudin looked at him, smiling.

"Has Jacques Dupont a greater grip than that, Joe Delesse?" he asked in a voice that was so soft it was almost a woman's.

"*Mon Dieu!*" gasped Delesse. He staggered to his feet, clutching his crushed hand. "M'sieu'—"

Reese Beaudin put his hands to the other's shoulders, smiling, friendly.

"I will apologize, I will explain, *mon ami*," he said. "But first, you must tell me the name of that Yellow-back who ran away years ago. Do you remember it?"

"*Oui*, but what has that to do with my crushed hand? The Yellow-back's name was Reese Beaudin—"

"And I am Reese Beaudin," laughed the other gently.

On that day—the day of Wakao, the dog sale—seven fat caribou were roasting on great spits at Post Lac Bain, and under them were seven fires burning red and hot of seasoned birch, and around the seven fires were seven groups of men who slowly turned the roasting carcasses.

It was the big day of the midwinter festival, and Post Lac Bain, with a population of twenty in times of quiet, was a seething wilderness metropolis of two hundred excited souls and twice as many dogs. From all directions they had come, from north and south and east and west; from near and from far, from the Barrens, from the swamps, from the farther forests, from river and lake and hidden trail—a few white men, mostly French; half-breeds and 'breeds, Chippewans, and Crees, and here and there a strange, dark-visaged little interloper from the north with his strain of Eskimo blood. Forgathered were all the breeds and creeds and fashions of the wilderness.

Over all this, pervading the air like an incense, stirring the desire of man and beast, floated the aroma of the roasting caribou. The feast hour was at hand. With cries that rose above the last words of a wild song, the seven groups of men rushed to seven pairs of props and tore them away. The great carcasses swayed in midair, bent slowly over their spits, and then crashed into the snow fifteen feet from the fire. About each carcass five men with razor-sharp knives ripped off hunks of the roasted flesh and passed them into eager hands of the hungry multitude. First came the women and children, and last the men.

On this there peered forth from a window in the factor's house the darkly bearded, smiling face of Reese Beaudin.

"I have seen him three times, wandering about in the crowd, seeking someone," he said. "*Bien*, he shall find that someone very soon!"

In the face of McDougall, the factor, was a strange look. For he had listened to a strange story, and there was still something of shock and amazement and disbelief in his eyes.

"Reese Beaudin, it is hard for me to believe."

"And yet you shall find that it is true," smiled Reese.

"He will kill you. He is a monster—a giant!"

"I shall die hard," replied Reese.

He turned from the window again and took from the table a violin wrapped in buckskin, and softly he played one of their old love songs. It was not much more than a whisper, and yet it was filled with a joyous exultation. He laid the violin down when he was finished, and laughed, and filled his pipe, and lighted it.

"It is good for a man's soul to know that a woman loves him, and has been true," he said. "*Mon pere*, will you tell me again what she said? It is strength for me—and I must soon be going."

McDougall repeated, as if under a strain from which he could not free himself:

"She came to me late last night, unknown to Dupont. She had received your message, and knew you were coming. And I tell you again that I saw something in her eyes which makes me afraid! She told me, then, that her father killed Bedore in a quarrel, and that she married Dupont to save him from the law—and kneeling there, with her hand on the cross at her breast, she swore that each day of her life she has let Dupont know that she hates him, and that she loves you, and that some day Reese Beaudin would return to avenge her. Yes, she told him that—I know it by what I saw in her eyes. With that cross clutched in her fingers, she swore that she had suffered torture and shame, and that never a word of it has she whispered to a living soul, that she might turn the passion of Jacques Dupont's black heart into a great hatred. And today—Jacques Dupont will kill you!''

''I shall die hard,'' Reese repeated again.

He tucked the violin in its buckskin covering under his arm. From the table he took his cap and placed it on his head.

In a last effort McDougall sprang from his chair and caught the other's arm.

''Reese Beaudin—you are going to your death! As factor of Lac Bain—agent of justice under power of the police—I forbid it!''

''So-o-o-o,'' spoke Reese Beaudin gently. *''Mon pere—''*

He unbuttoned his coat, which had remained buttoned. Under the coat was a heavy shirt; and the shirt he opened, smiling into the factor's eyes, and McDougall's face froze, and the breath was cut short on his lips.

''That!'' he gasped.

Reese Beaudin nodded.

Then he opened the door and went out.

Joe Delesse had been watching the factor's house, and he worked his way slowly along the edge of the feasters so that he might casually come into the path of Reese Beaudin. And there was one other man who also had watched, and who came in the same direction. He was a stranger, tall, closely hooded, his mustached face an Indian bronze. No one had ever seen him at Lac Bain before, yet in the excitement of the carnival the fact passed without conjecture or significance. And from the cabin of Henri Paquette another pair of eyes saw Reese Beaudin, and Mother Paquette heard a sob that in itself was a prayer.

In and out among the devourers of caribou flesh, scanning the groups and the ones and the twos and the threes, passed Jacques Dupont, and with him walked his friend, one-eyed Layonne. Layonne was a big man, but Dupont was taller by half a head. The brutishness of his face was hidden under a coarse red beard; but the devil in him glowered from his deep-set, inhuman eyes; it walked in his gait, in the hulk of his great shoulders, in the gorilla-like slouch of his hips. His huge hands hung partly clenched at his sides.

His breath was heavy with whiskey that Layonne himself had smuggled in, and in his heart was black murder.

"He has not come!" he cried for the twentieth time. "He has not come!"

He moved on, and Reese Beaudin—ten feet away—turned and smiled at Joe Delesse with triumph in his eyes. He moved nearer.

"Did I not tell you he would not find in me that narrow-shouldered, smooth-faced stripling of five years ago?" he asked. "*N'est-ce pas*, friend Delesse?"

The face of Joe Delesse was heavy with a somber fear.

"His fist is like a wood-sledge, m'sieu'."

"So it was years ago."

"His forearm is as big as the calf of your leg."

"*Oui*, friend Delesse, it is the forearm of a giant."

"He is half again your weight."

"Or more, friend Delesse."

"He will kill you! As the great God lives, he will kill you!"

"I shall die hard," repeated Reese Beaudin for the third time that day.

Joe Delesse turned slowly, doggedly. His voice rumbled.

"The sale is about to begin, m'sieu'. See!"

A man had mounted the log platform raised to the height of a man's shoulders at the far end of the clearing. It was Henri Paquette, master of the day's ceremonies, and appointed auctioneer of the great Wakao. A man of many tongues was Paquette. To his lips he raised a great megaphone of birch bark, and sonorously his call rang out—in French, in Cree, in Chippewan, and the packed throng about the caribou fires heaved like a living billow, and to a man and a woman and a child it moved toward the appointed place.

"The time has come," said Reese Beaudin. "And all Lac Bain shall see!"

Behind them—watching, always watching—followed the bronze-faced stranger in his close-drawn hood.

For an hour the men of Lac Bain gathered close-wedged about the log platform on which stood Henri Paquette and his Indian helper. Behind the men were the women and children, and through the cordon there ran a babiche-roped pathway along which the dogs were brought.

The platform was twenty feet square, with the floor side of the logs hewn flat, and there was no lack of space for the gesticulation and wild pantomime of Paquette. In one hand he held a notebook, and in the other a pencil. In the notebook the sales of twenty dogs were already tabulated, and the prices paid.

Anxiously Reese Beaudin was waiting. Each time that a new dog came up, he looked at Joe Delesse, but as yet Joe had failed to give the signal.

On the platform the Indian was holding two malamutes in leash now and Paquette was crying, in a well-simulated fit of great fury:

"What, you cheap *kimootisks*, will you let this pair of malamutes go for seven mink and a cross fox. Are you men? Are you poverty-stricken? Are you blind? A breed dog and a male giant for seven mink and a cross fox? *Non*, I will buy them myself first, and kill them, and use their flesh for dog feed, and their hides for fools' caps! I will—"

"Twelve mink and a Number Two Cross," came a voice out of the crowd.

"Twelve mink and a Number One," shouted another.

"A little better—a little better!" wailed Paquette. "You are waking up, but slowly—*mon Dieu*, so slowly! Twelve mink and—"

A voice rose in Cree:

"Nesi-tu-now-unisk!"

Paquette gave a triumphant yell.

"The Indian beats you! The Indian from Little Neck Lake—an Indian beats the white man! He offers twenty beaver—prime skins! And beaver are wanted in Paris now. They're wanted in London. Beaver and gold—they are the same! But they are the price of one dog alone. Shall they both go at that? Shall the Indian have them for twenty beaver—twenty beaver that may be taken from a single house in a day—while it has taken these malamutes two and a half years to grow? I say, you cheap *kimootisks*—"

And then an amazing thing happened. It was like a bomb falling in that crowded throng of wondering and amazed forest people.

It was the closely hooded stranger who spoke.

"I will give a hundred dollars cash," he said.

A look of annoyance crossed Reese Beaudin's face. He was close to the bronze-faced stranger and edged nearer.

"Let the Indian have them," he said in a low voice. "It is Meewe. I knew him years ago. He has carried me on his back. He taught me first to draw pictures."

"But they are powerful dogs," objected the stranger. "My team needs them."

The Cree had risen higher out of the crowd. One arm rose above his head. He was an Indian who had seen fifty years of the forests, and his face was the face of an Egyptian.

"Nesi-tu-now Nesoo-sap umisk!" he proclaimed.

Henri Paquette hopped excitedly and faced the stranger.

"Twenty-two beaver," he challenged. "Twenty-two—"

"Let Meewe have them," replied the hooded stranger.

Three minutes later a single dog was pulled up on the log platform. He was a magnificent beast, and a rumble of approval ran through the crowd.

The face of Joe Delesse was gray. He wet his lips. Reese Beaudin, watching him, knew that the time had come. And Joe Delesse, seeing no way of escape, whispered:

"It is her dog, m'sieu'. It is Parka—and Dupont sells him today to show her that he is master."

Already Paquette was advertising the virtues of Parka when Reese Beaudin, in a single leap, mounted the log platform, and stood beside him.

"Wait!" he cried.

There fell a silence, and Reese said, loud enough for all to hear:

"M'sieu' Paquette, I ask the privilege of examining this dog that I want to buy."

At last he straightened, and all who faced him saw the smiling sneer on his lips.

"Who is it that offers this worthless cur for sale?" Lac Bain heard him say. "P-s-s-st—it is a woman's dog! It is not worth bidding for!"

"You lie!" Dupont's voice rose in a savage roar. His huge shoulders bulked over those about him. He crowded to the edge of the platform. "You lie!"

"He is a woman's dog," repeated Reese Beaudin without excitement, yet so clearly that every ear heard. "He is a woman's pet, and M'sieu' Dupont most surely does lie if he denies it!"

So far as memory went back, no man at Lac Bain that day had ever heard another man give Jacques Dupont the lie. A thrill swept those who heard and understood. There was a great silence, in that silence men near him heard the choking rage in Dupont's great chest. He was staring up—straight up into the smiling face of Reese Beaudin; and in that moment he saw beyond the glossy black beard, and amazement and unbelief held him still. In the next, Reese Beaudin had the violin in his hands. He flung off the buckskin, and in a flash the instrument was at his shoulder.

"See! I will play, and the woman's pet shall sing!"

And once more, after five years, Lac Bain listened to the magic of Reese Beaudin's violin. And it was Elise's old love song that he played. He played it, smiling down into the eyes of a monster whose face was turning from red to black; yet he did not play it to the end, nor a quarter of it, for suddenly a voice shouted:

"It is Reese Beaudin—come back!"

Joe Delesse, paralyzed, speechless, could have sworn it was the hooded stranger who shouted; and then he remembered, and flung up his great arms, and bellowed:

"*Oui*—by the saints. It is Reese Beaudin—Reese Beaudin come back!"

Suddenly as it had begun, the playing ceased and Henri Paquette found himself with the violin in his hands. Reese Beaudin turned, facing them all, the wintry sun glowing in his beard, his eyes smiling, his head high—unfraid now, more fearless than any other man that had ever set foot in Lac Bain. And McDougall, with his arm touching Elise's hair, felt the wild and throbbing pulse of her body. This day—this hour—this minute in which she stood still, unbreathing—had confirmed her belief in Reese Beaudin. As she had dreamed, so had he risen. First of all the men in the world he stood there now, just as he had been first in the days when she had loved his dreams, his music, and his pictures. To her he was the old god, more splendid—for he had risen above fear, and he was facing Dupont now with that strange quiet smile on his lips. And then, all at once, her soul broke its fetters, and over the women's heads she reached out her arms, and all there heard her voice in its triumph, its joy, its fear.

"Reese! Reese—my *sakeakun*!"

Over the heads of all the forest people she called him beloved! Like the fang of an adder the word stung Dupont's brain. And like fire touched to powder, swiftly as lightning illumines the sky, the glory of it blazed in Reese Beaudin's face.

And all that were there heard him clearly:

"I am Reese Beaudin. I am the Yellow-back. I have returned to meet a man you all know—Jacques Dupont. He is a monkey-man— a whipper of boys, a stealer of women, a cheat, a coward, a thing so foul the crows will not touch him when he dies—"

There was a roar. It was not the roar of a man, but of a beast— and Jacques Dupont was on the platform!

Quick as Dupont's movement had been, it was no swifter than that of the closely hooded stranger. He was as tall as Dupont, and about him there was an air of authority and command.

"Wait," he said, and placed a hand on Dupont's heaving chest. His smile was cold as ice. Never had Dupont seen eyes so like the pale blue of steel. "M'sieu' Dupont, you are about to avenge a great insult. It must be done fairly. If you have weapons, throw them away. I will search this—this Reese Beaudin, as he calls himself! And if there is to be a fight, let it be a good one. Strip yourself to that great garment you have on, friend Dupont. See, our friend—this Reese Beaudin—is already stripping!''

He was unbuttoning the giant's heavy Hudson's Bay coat. He pulled it off, and drew Dupont's knife from its sheath. Paquette, like a stunned cat that had recovered its ninth life, was scrambling from the platform. The Indian was already gone. And Reese Beaudin had tossed his coat to Joe Delesse, and with it his cap. His heavy shirt was closely buttoned; and not only was it buttoned, Delesse observed, but also was it carefully pinned. And even now, facing that monster who would soon be at him, Reese Beaudin was smiling.

For a moment the closely hooded stranger stood between them, and Jacques Dupont crouched himself for his vengeance. Never to the people of Lac Bain had he looked more terrible. He was the gorilla-fighter, the beast fighter, the fighter who fights as the wolf, the bear and the cat—crushing out life, breaking bones, twisting, snapping, inundating and destroying with his great weight and his monstrous strength. He was a hundred pounds heavier than Reese Beaudin. On his stooping shoulders he could carry a tree. With his giant hands he could snap a two-inch sapling. With one hand alone he had set a bear trap. And with that mighty strength he fought as the caveman fought. It was his boast there was no trick of the Chippewan, the Cree, the Eskimo, or the forest man that he did not know. And yet Reese Beaudin stood calmly, waiting for him, and smiling!

In another moment the hooded stranger was gone, and there was none between them.

"A long time I have waited for this, m'sieu'," said Reese, for Dupont's ears alone. "Five years is a long time. And my Elise still loves me."

Still more like a gorilla Jacques Dupont crept upon him. His face was twisted by a rage to which he could no longer give voice. Hatred and jealousy robbed his eyes of the last spark of the thing that was human. His great hands were hooked, like an eagle's talons. His lips were drawn back, like a beast's. Through his red beard yellow fangs were bared.

And Reese Beaudin no longer smiled. He laughed!

"Until I went away and met real men, I never knew what a pig of a man you were, M'sieu' Dupont," he taunted amiably, as though speaking in jest to a friend. "You remind me of an aged and over-fat porcupine with his big paunch and crooked arms. What horror must it have been for my Elise to have lived in sight of such a beast as you!''

With a bellow Dupont was at him. And swifter than eyes had ever seen man move at Lac Bain before, Reese Beaudin was out of his way and behind him; and then, as the giant caught himself at the edge of the platform, and turned, he received a blow that sounded like the broadside of a paddle striking water. Reese Beaudin had struck him with the flat of his unclenched hand!

A murmur of incredulity rose out of the crowd. To the forest man such a blow was the deadliest of insults. It was calling him an *Iskwao*—a woman—a weakling—a thing too contemptible to harden one's fist against. But the murmur died in an instant. For Reese Beaudin, making as if to step back, shot suddenly forward—straight through the giant's crooked arms—and it was his fist this time that landed squarely between the eyes of Dupont. The monster's head went back, his great body wavered, and then suddenly he plunged backward off the platform and fell with a crash to the ground.

A yell went up from the hooded stranger. Joe Delesse split his throat. The crowd drowned Reese Beaudin's voice. But above it all rose a woman's voice shrieking forth a name.

And then Jacques Dupont was on the platform again. In the moments that followed, one could almost hear his neighbor's heartbeat. Nearer and still nearer to each other drew the two men. And now Dupont crouched still more, and Joe Delesse held his breath. He noticed that Reese Beaudin was standing almost on the tips of his toes—that each instant he seemed prepared, like a runner, for sudden flight. Five feet—four—and Dupont leaped in, his huge arms swinging like the limb of a tree, and his weight following with crushing force behind his blow. For an instant it seemed as though Reese Beaudin had stood to meet that fatal rush, but in that same instant—so swiftly that only the hooded stranger knew what had happened—he was out of the way, and his left arm seemed to shoot downward, and then up, and then his right straight out, and then again his left arm downward, and up—and it was the third blow, all swift as lightning, that brought a yell from the hooded stranger. For though none but the stranger had seen it, Jacques Dupont's head snapped back—and all saw the fourth blow that sent him reeling like a man struck by a club.

There was no sound now. A mental and a vocal paralysis seized upon the inhabitants of Lac Bain. Never had they seen fighting like this fighting of Reese Beaudin. Until now had they lived to see the science of the sawdust ring pitted against the brute force of Brobdingnagian, of Antæus and Goliath. For Reese Beaudin's fighting was a fighting without tricks that they could see. He used his fists, and his fists alone. He was like a dancing man. And suddenly, in the midst of the miracle, they saw Jacques Dupont go down. And the second miracle was that Reese Beaudin did not leap on him when he had fallen. He stood back a little, balancing himself in that queer fashion on the balls and toes of his feet. But no sooner was Dupont up than Reese Beaudin was in again, with the swiftness of a cat, and they could hear the blows, like solid shots, and Dupont's arms waved like treetops, and a second time he was off the platform.

He was staggering when he rose. The blood ran in streams from his mouth and nose. His beard dripped with it. His yellow teeth were caved in.

This time he did not leap upon the platform—he clambered back to it, and the hooded stranger gave him a lift which a few minutes before Dupont would have resented as an insult.

"Ah, it has come," said the stranger to Delesse. "He is the best close-in fighter in all—"

He did not finish.

"I could kill you now—kill you with a single blow," said Reese Beaudin in a moment when the giant stood swaying. "But there is a greater punishment in store for you, and so I shall let you live!"

And now Reese Beaudin was facing that part of the crowd where the woman he loved was standing. He was breathing deeply. But he was not winded. His eyes were black as night, his hair windblown. He looked straight over the heads between him and she whom Dupont had stolen from him.

Reese Beaudin raised his arms, and where there had been a murmur of voices, there was now silence.

For the first time the stranger threw back his hood. He was unbuttoning his heavy coat.

And Joe Delesse, looking up, saw that Reese Beaudin was making a mighty effort to quiet a strange excitement within his breast. And then there was a rending of cloth and of buttons and of pins as in one swift movement he tore the shirt from his own breast— exposing to the eyes of Lac Bain, bloodred in the glow of the winter sun, the crimson badge of the Royal Northwest Mounted Police!

And above the gasp that swept the multitude, above the strange cry of the woman, his voice rose:

"I am Reese Beaudin, the Yellow-back. I am Reese Beaudin, who ran away. I am Reese Beaudin—Sergeant in His Majesty's Royal Northwest Mounted Police, and in the name of the law I arrest Jacques Dupont for the murder of Francois Bedore, who was killed on his trap-line five years ago! Fitzgerald—"

The hooded stranger leaped upon the platform. His heavy coat fell off. Tall and grim he stood in the scarlet jacket of the Police. Steel clinked in his hands. And Jacques Dupont, terror in his heart, was trying to see as he groped to his knees. The steel snapped over his wrists.

And then he heard a voice close over him. It was the voice of Reese Beaudin.

"And this is your final punishment, Jacques Dupont—to be hanged by the neck until you are dead. For Bedore was not dead when Elise's father left him after their fight on the trap-line. It was you who saw the fight, and finished the killing, and laid the crime on Elise's father. Mukoki, the Indian, saw you. It is my day, Dupont, and I have waited long—"

The rest Dupont did not hear. For up from the crowd there went a mighty roar. And through it a woman was making her way with outreaching arms—and behind her followed the factor of Lac Bain.

*James B. Hendryx (1880–1963) was one of the most successful and consistently entertaining of the writers who specialized in Northern fiction. Between 1915 and 1954 he published thirty-six novels set in the Yukon and Alaska, many featuring such sterling officers of the RCMP as Corporal Downey (*Downey of the Mounted, Blood on the Yukon Trail, The Yukon Kid*). But by far his most popular character was Black John Smith, leader of an outlaw community on Halfaday Creek not far from the Alaska line, who dispenses his own brand of swift justice to those less scrupulous than he. Black John and his compadres appeared in dozens of pulp novelettes, the bulk of which were collected under such titles as* Outlaws of Halfaday Creek, Law and Order on Halfaday Creek, *and* Skullduggery on Halfaday Creek. *"Black John Gives a Tip," like all of the bearded giant's adventures, is as much a crime story as a frontier Northern and is flavored with a generous measure of wry and salty humor.*

Black John Gives a Tip

★★★★★★★★★★★★★★★★

James B. Hendryx

I

BLACK John trailed his paddle and sniffed at the warm air as his canoe carried him swiftly down Halfaday Creek a short distance above its confluence with White River. The faint odor of spruce smoke reached his nostrils and his eyes scanned the banks for sign of a camp. Five minutes later the light craft shot out into the swift current of the river and he saw a canoe drawn up on a strip of shingle just below the mouth of the creek. At the edge of a thicket a man sat beside a small fire above which a tea pail was suspended.

The man rose to his feet as, with a twist of the paddle, Black John beached his canoe beside the other and stepped ashore. He said, "Hello!"

"Overlookin' the triteness of yer observation, I'll return it," Black John replied, as he joined the man at the fire, his glance taking in the shifty eyes, wide spaced below a bulging forehead, the buck teeth, and the receding chin that gave the man's face a beaver-like appearance.

"How?" The bulging brow wrinkled as though the man were trying to grasp the meaning of the reply.

"Jest another way of sayin' 'hello'."

The man stared into the bearded face. "You might be Black John Smith," he said.

"Damn if I mightn't."

"How?"

"How! The simple accident of birth coupled with a certain ingenuity of misnomer produced the result."

"By God, you be him! Cuter Malone claimed you looked like a pirate an' talked like some damn lawyer. It was him told us about Halfaday Crick an' the gang of outlaws you run up there."

"Us? Is there more than one of you?"

"Not here there ain't. The other boys is down to Dawson. I come on up ahead to sort of look the ground over an' kind of get acquainted with you. Ever hear tell of Simcoe Sam?"

"No. The name seems strangely onfamiliar."

"That's me. I guess you don't read the papers much."

"Livin' quite a ways back like we do, it's kind of hard to keep right up to the minute on news. Has the papers, perchanct, be'n mentionin' some exploit of yours?"

"The Montreal, an' Winnipeg, an' Toronto papers, an' most of the ones in the States has be'n printin' pieces about the C.P.R. holdup, east of Winnipeg. I had bad luck on account the mail clerk on the train was Walt Kimmon, which I an' him used to go to school together, an' he seen me an' squarked. Sence I quit school I'd be'n guidin' tourists till I lost my license on account some rich guy claimed I stole four hundred dollars off'n him on a trip up in the Nippigon country."

"Did you get the four hundred?"

"Sure I got it! What I claim, if a guy takes four hundred dollars back in the bush, he deserves to lose it."

"Was the C.P.R. venture a financial success?"

"How?"

"I say, did you make a cleanup on that train robbery?"

"No. That was some more hard luck. After I lost my license I hung around Winnipeg pickin' up a few dollars peddlin' dope. That's how I met up with the boys from the States. An' believe me, they're okay! They'll tackle anything from a bank to a train. They're good.

"I'd got acquainted with a bank messenger, an' he tipped me off about this here shipment of money to Montreal. Only the damn cuss either lied, or he got balled up, because the night he claimed this eighty thousan' would be in the mail car, it wasn't. An' all we got was four thousan' that was shipped to some branch bank. So when Walt Kimmon seen me an' squarked, the papers claimed how I was one of the train robbers, an' they printed my pitcher, only it didn't look nothin' like me, on account it was some other guy's pitcher they printed an' claimed it was me. After that we figgered we better get to hell outa the country. So we split the four thousan' an' come to Dawson."

Black John nodded. "Misfortune seems to dog yer footsteps, Sam," he said. "What was yer object in headin' fer Halfaday to get acquainted with me?"

"We've got a job on, an' we aim to hit fer Halfaday Crick when we pull it. So the boys figgered I better go on up ahead an' get acquainted with you, an' find some place to stay, an' fix it so we can join up with your gang. Fact is, I ain't so good when it comes right down to the rough stuff, like the other boys is. I'm all right in the bush with a rifle, but I never had no use fer a pistol. I'm a better hand at kind of chummin' up with folks, an' findin' out things, like when shipments is goin' to be made, an' then tippin' the boys off."

"Sort of a smoothie, eh?"

"Yeah, that's right. It was me that found out about this here gold shipment. We be'n hangin' around Cuter Malone's sence we hit Dawson, an' Cuter he tipped me off to a guy that works fer the Consolidated Dredge Company, an' I get acquainted with this guy, an' he tips me off that the Consolidated is makin' this shipment on the *Helen* the first of the month. He tips me off about the shipment fer a cut, on account he's be'n losin' heavy lately playin' the wheel an' the faro layout in Cuter's place, an' it would give him a chanct to get even, an' some more along with it."

"Did he say how much gold was bein' shipped?"

"He claimed it was a hundred thousan' dollars. Right around four hundred pound. An' it would be in four heavy wooden boxes."

"The amount is worth contemplatin'," Black John admitted. "How many of you boys is there? An' how do you figger on pullin' this robbery off?"

"There's three besides me. There's the Chicago Kid, an' Lefty Horowitz, an' the Parson."

"The Parson!"

"Yeah. He ain't no reg'lar preacher. We call him the Parson on account when he gets drunk he likes to sing church pieces, like "Rocky Ages," and "Nearer By God to Thee," an' pieces like them. He can beller 'em out good an' loud, so it sounds almost like a guy would be in a church, 'specially if he can get some perfesser to whang along on the pyanner at the same time he's singin'. One night he had a couple of them girls in the Klondike Palace bawlin'. An' I claim, if a man can sing good enough to make them bawl, he's goin' some!"

"It was ondoubtless a touchin' scene," the big man observed. "But about this robbery? Was you aimin' to pull it off in Dawson?"

"Cripes, no! The police is there. The boys will be on the *Helen*, an' when she gets somewheres around the mouth of the White, they'll make the captain pull over to shore, an' they'll load the gold on one of her boats, an' bury it somewhere, an' then pole the boat on up to Halfaday Crick. We ain't no dumb clucks. We figger everything out ahead. That's why I come on up to get acquainted with you an' fix it so we can join up with your gang."

"H-u-u-m. They wasn't aimin' to fetch the gold up to Halfaday, eh?"

The man grinned. "I told you we wasn't no dumb clucks. Why would we fetch a hundred thousan' in gold up to a crick where forty er fifty outlaws hangs out? No, sir! We aim to bury that gold where no one but us knows where it is. Twenty-five thousan' apiece is a damn good ace in the hole."

Black John nodded. "The plan has its merits. But when does this Consolidated man that tipped off the shipment get his cut?"

The other laughed. "What you doin'—kiddin' me? That damn sap don't get no cut. All he gets is a promise—an' he's had that."

"Suppose he'd squawk when he finds out he's been double-crossed?"

"He won't dast to squark. He couldn't do it without he got hisself in bad."

"Well, there's that angle, too," Black John admitted. "It looks like you boys has figgered everything out."

"You bet we have! Cuter said we'd ort to fit right in with your gang. He claims that you're the damndest crook that ever kep' out of jail. We'll sure be proud to join up with you."

Black John nodded. "An' fer my part I can state, without the peradventure of a doubt, that never within my recollection has Halfaday be'n menaced with sech a dubious acquisition to her population."

The man looked pleased. "Oh, that's all right, John. I know'd you'd be glad to get us, when you found out about us. It's just like Cuter claimed—you sure can talk like a damn lawyer. Maybe that's how you've kep' out of jail."

"Well, there's other reasons, too. I've got to be goin', now. I'm shore glad I met up with you. You better shove on up Halfaday. Tell Cush I said to let you move into One Eyed John's shack till I get back, when we'll ondoubtless call a miners' meetin' an' abruptly terminate yer mundane sojourn."

"How?"

"In the usual manner, I hope."

"I mean, I don't get you. I ain't onto all them big words."

"It don't make no difference—neither is Cush. So long."

"Where you goin'?"

"Dawson."

"Dawson, eh? Well then, you stop in to the Klondike Palace an' tell Cuter Malone I said to make you acquainted with the boys. They'll be proud to know you."

"Okay. Any friend of Cuter's is an enemy of mine, too."

"How?"

"When a man strives for obfuscation rather than clarity, the postulate becomes too involved in application to—"

"Gawda 'mighty!" the man cried, a look of awe on his face. "A man would have to be a Chinee to figger out what you're talkin' about!"

II

AFTER a couple of drinks in the Tivoli Saloon, Black John proceeded to the office of the Consolidated Dredge Company and inquired for the manager. After a short wait he was shown into an inner office to be greeted by a pompous individual with a cold eye and muttonchop whiskers, who was seated behind a flat-topped desk. The man glanced at him over the top of a pair of rimless nose glasses. Black John noted that he was dressed in store clothes—evidently a rank cheechako.

The official cleared his throat with a show of importance, opened a drawer in his desk, took out two cigars, tendered one to Black John, and bit the end off the other. Black John took the cigar, sniffed at it, and laying it on the desk, produced pipe and tobacco.

The other frowned, lighted his cigar, and spoke in short,

clipped sentences: "Come, come, my good man—speak up! My time is valuable. I presume you have a property to dispose of?"

Black John held a match to the tobacco, and when his pipe was going, drew up a chair and seated himself. "Nope," he replied, and blew a cloud of gray smoke from his lungs.

The manager's frown became a scowl. "If you come to seek employment, you should have applied to the superintendent, or to one of the various foremen, I can't be bothered with trivial matters."

"Can't, eh? You ought to correct the habit of goin' off half cocked."

"What's that!"

"When you've be'n in the country longer, you'll learn to find out what yer talkin' about before you start talkin'."

The manager's face flushed with anger. "What do you mean?" he demanded.

"Meanin' that I ain't huntin' a job. I wouldn't work fer yer damn outfit if you'd give me half of it. I come here to give you a tip."

"A tip?"

"Yeah. It's about that hundred thousan' dollar gold shipment yer figgerin' on sendin' out on the *Helen*, on the first of the month."

The color drained from the man's face, his eyes widened, and he leaned forward in his chair. "What's that? What do you know about a gold shipment? How could you possibly know?"

"You've got a leak in yer dike."

"What?"

"A trickle of information has reached the ears of the wrong parties. There's a plot afoot to knock off that hundred thousan'."

"Who passed out that information?"

Black John shrugged. "I don't know. An' I wouldn't tell you if I did."

"But—who is planning this robbery?"

"There's four in the gang."

"Who are they? Are they here in Dawson?"

"I understand that three of 'em is. I never seen 'em."

"How do you know of this plot, then?"

"There's a leak in their dike, too."

"Who are you?"

"John Smith. More er less favorably known as Black John, on account of my whiskers resemblin' that color."

"Black John Smith! You mean that you are the—the notorious—ah—er—outlaw? The leader of the band of criminals that infests Halfaday Creek, on the Alaska border?"

"Well, I've heard rumors to that effect."

"And knowing your reputation, do you expect me to sit here and give heed to any tip you might give me?"

Black John shrugged. "You know whether you're contemplatin' shippin' out that gold, er not. I don't. I was only tellin' you what I heard. If you'd ruther yer tip come from someone with a different reputation, there's half a dozen preachers in Dawson— you might see what you can get out of them."

"But it doesn't make sense! Why should you, an outlaw, come to me and warn me of an impending robbery?"

"Well, it ain't on account of no inherent sense of rectitude I've got in my soul. Nor neither it ain't because I'd hate to see the Consolidated lose that shipment. I wouldn't give a damn if someone would steal one of yer million dollar dredges. I might even help 'em hide it—if they kep' it off'n Halfaday. An' it shore as hell ain't on account of any personal regard I've got fer you. The reason is simple, bein' merely that these robbers aim to hit fer Halfaday after they pull off the job. An' I don't want no sech depraved characters on the crick."

"But why not? What difference would it make, if you're all outlaws, up there?"

"If you claim the boys on Halfaday is all outlaws, you know a damn sight more about 'em than I do. I wouldn't neither admit, nor deny that somewheres in their past some of the boys might have committed some slight infringement of the law. What they done before they come to Halfaday ain't none of my business. But onct they locate there, every damn one of 'em has got to be a pillar of rectitude, er get hung. Halfaday is the moralest crick in the Yukon—bar none."

The man seemed unconvinced. "Extraordinary!" he exclaimed, and slanted a shrewd glance at the speaker. "Would you be willing to wait here while I send for Corporal Downey? He is the officer in command of the Northwest Mounted Police," he added, eyeing Black John as though he expected him to bolt from the room.

The big man knocked the dottle from his pipe on a corner of the desk and refilled it. "Shore, I'll wait. They say a man is known by the company he keeps. I hate to have Downey find me in here. But I guess he'll overlook it, if I don't let it happen again.''

When Corporal Downey stepped into the room a few minutes later, the manager of Consolidated pointed at the big man who had elevated his heels to the desktop, tilted back against the wall, and was calmly smoking his pipe.

"This person brazenly admits that he is Black John Smith, of Halfaday Creek," he announced.

Downey grinned. "Well—what of it?" He turned to the other. "What you doin' here, John?"

"Merely consortin' with a doubtful character," the big man replied. "I feel safer, now you're here."

The manager flushed angrily. "Do you stand there and permit a citizen to be insulted in his own office?"

"I ain't heard no insult," Downey replied. "An' even if I had, insultin' ain't a crime, in the Yukon. Is that what you sent fer me for?"

"This man came here and warned me that there is a plot afoot to steal a shipment of gold that we are supposed to be sending outside on the *Helen*, on the first of the month. He says there are four men implicated."

"Well? I'd say he done you a favor."

"But—the man is a notorious outlaw! Why should he warn me of this impending robbery?"

Black John's grin widened. "He can't seem to get it through his skull, Downey, that I'm doin' it because I don't want them damn cusses pilin' in on us on Halfaday. Me an' Cush has trouble enough as it is tryin' to keep the crick moral, without a lot of cheap crooks pilin' in on us.''

"Who are these crooks?"

"I wouldn't know, Downey. An' I wouldn't tell you if I did."

"That is the second time he has had the effrontery to boast of the morality of Halfaday Creek," exclaimed the manager, in disgust.

"I shore wish every crick in the Yukon was as free of crime as Halfaday is," Downey said. "It would make our work a lot easier."

"Do you mean to say that you would give credence to this man's warning?"

"I shore would," the officer replied. "If Black John tipped me off that a robbery was planned, I'd give heed to it, you bet!

There's be'n plenty of times when information he's slipped me has proved correct.''

"Then I demand a police guard for this shipment. I demand that an adequate detail of police be placed aboard the *Helen*."

Downey shook his head. "I'm sorry, sir—but it ain't in the cards. I've got just one constable at detachment to police Dawson with. All the others are down to Fortymile workin' on a murder an' robbery on Coal Crick. Any other time I'd be glad to accommodate you.''

The manager thumped the desktop with his fist. "Do you mean that this shipment—a hundred thousand dollars' worth of gold, must go out on the *Helen* unprotected? What kind of police cooperation do you call that? It's an outrage!''

Corporal Downey held his voice level. "You could hold the shipment over a few days. The *Hannah's* due upriver on the fourth, an' the *Sarah's* due the seventh. I expect my men back by that time—part of 'em, anyway. I could detail a man, then.''

"But I've made arrangements to ship this gold on the *Helen*!''

Black John grinned. "You don't look like no Mede, er no Persian. You could change them arrangements, couldn't you?''

"I suppose I'll have to," the man admitted grudgingly. "But it is a deuced nuisance! It is a fine state of affairs when police inefficiency is allowed to disarrange the due course of business!''

"Ain't it hell!'' Black John exclaimed, with a covert wink at Downey. "But at that, if I was you, I'd rig up a dummy shipment an' send it out on the *Helen*. Accordin' to the tip I got, there's three of these robbers here in Dawson, an' they'll shore be watchin' fer that shipment to go aboard. An' if it don't go, neither will they.''

"What do you mean—a dummy shipment?''

"Well, lead's heavy—an' it's cheap. Box up some lead an' ship it out on the *Helen*, jest as you'd have shipped the gold. If the robbers get it, you ain't out much—an' if they don't, the boat can fetch the lead back on her down trip.''

"That looks like a good bet,'' Downey agreed. "Anyway, it'll take these damn cusses out of Dawson till I get some men back.''

Black John rose, placed his pipe in his pocket, and turned toward the door. "I got to be goin'. It's about time the sourdoughs will be showin' up at the Tivoli fer a game of stud.''

When the door closed behind him, the manager frowned.

"Despite your indorsement of that man, I can't help but believe that there is some deep ulterior motive behind his action. The idea of allowing a known outlaw to come in and suggest a method of averting a robbery is as preposterous as it is bizarre! I'd be willing to wager that the *Helen* will make her trip with the dummy shipment aboard unmolested. And that the boat with the gold on it will be the scene of an attempted robbery—and that this Black John will be mixed up in it."

"I'll take that bet, fer a box of cigars," Downey said.

"But the man is an avowed outlaw!"

"That's what they say," Downey admitted. "But you ain't be'n in the country long enough to know that there's a damn sight of difference in outlaws."

III

BLACK John played stud that night, and next morning he stepped into his canoe and headed up the Yukon.

Early in the evening of the first day of the month, he lay in the bush at the mouth of the White River and grinned to himself as he watched a smudge of smoke resolve itself into a steamboat forging steadily against the current. "This ort to be good," he muttered, "watchin three hard guys stick up a steamboat fer a shipment of lead!"

The boat held well toward the middle of the river, and just as the big man began to think that there had been some hitch in the plan—that the dummy shipment had not been made, or that the three robbers had not boarded her—the boat swerved toward shore. As it neared the bank, Black John could clearly make out the name *Helen*, could see also that there were two men in the pilothouse, and that a dozen or more persons, evidently passengers and crew, were huddled into the bow on the upper deck where a man kept them covered with a revolver. On the lower or freight deck, a boat was ready for launching, and two other men, evidently roustabouts, stood beside four stout, flattish wooden boxes piled near the boat. These men were also covered with a revolver held in the hand of a large man, and as the boat nosed into the bank, Black John saw that the pilot was also covered.

A bell jangled and the wheel slowed to a churning just sufficient to hold her against the bank. The large man barked an order and the two roustabouts slipped the rowboat into the water, and stowed the four wooden boxes, together with three packsacks, into her. The man on the upper deck kept the group in the bow covered until the man in the pilothouse came down and stepped into the rowboat. Then he joined the two others.

Again the bell jangled and the steamboat backed away from the bank, swung her bow into the stream, and continued up-river. Two of the men in the rowboat manned the oars and rowed into the mouth of the White. Shifting his position, Black John watched them land a short distance above. The three stepped ashore, taking their packsacks with them, but leaving the boxes in the boat which they drew part way onto the sandy beach and secured her painter to a tree.

The sound of chopping was soon followed by the appearance of a thin column of smoke. The men were camping for the night, evidently intending to cache the boxes under cover of darkness.

As the daylight faded, Black John devoured a cold lunch, then made his way stealthily to a spot where, screened by a scrub spruce, he could see and hear all that went on in the camp on the sandbar at the edge of the bush.

While the other two prepared supper, the large man sat with a bottle in his hand from which he drank from time to time, occasionally passing it to the others. Presently he broke into song, waving the bottle in the manner of a baton. His bull-throated voice, booming out on the still air, sounded startlingly loud:

> "Touch not the cup, it is death to thy soul,
> Touch not the cup, touch it not!
> Beware of the demon that lurks in the bowl,
> Touch not the cup, touch it not!"

He paused and tendered the bottle to the others. "C'm on, boys, join in the singin'! Hell, a man don't like to sing all alone!"

"Grub's ready," one of them replied. "You better throw something into you besides that rotgut, Parson. Accordin' to Cuter Malone, we've got better'n a hundred miles of upriver shovin' before we hit Halfaday Crick, an' he claims part of it is damn tough goin'. You ain't goin' to be worth a damn tomorrow if you've got a hangover."

The large man returned the cork to the bottle and rummaged in his pack for cup and plate. "I ain't goin' to have no hang-over," he said, a bit thickly. "I'll do as much work as both of you half-pints. We'll eat, an' then we'll sing. By God, I like to sing, an' I'm goin' to sing, an' no one's goin' to stop me!''

One of the men filled his plate and frowned across the fire. "I wish to hell we had Simcoe Sam along. He's the only one of us that knows how to handle a boat—an' you send him on up ahead, an' leave us to do all the work.''

The Parson blinked owlishly. "Lefty, I'll have you to know who's runnin' this job. Simcoe Sam ain't worth a damn with a gat, an' he ain't got no guts, besides. I wanted him to kind of fix it up with this here Black John, an' sort of get the lay of the land before we got up there. What we've got to do is get in with him—not buck him. Accordin' to Cuter's tell, there's forty, fifty of them outlaws, an' they're damn bad actors.''

"Will Simcoe tell 'em about this job?" asked the Chicago Kid.

"Sure he will. How else would Black John know we was any good?''

Lefty frowned. "Cuter claims they've hung plenty men, up there. Suppose they grab us an' offer to hang us unless we give 'em a cut on this gold—or maybe give 'em all of it?''

"They won't hang us. They might make a play like that—but it would only be a bluff. If we kep' our mouth shut, they'd let up. It wouldn't get 'em nothin' to go through with it—an' it would give us a swell chanct to show 'em we've got guts. The main thing is to get in good with this Black John. Once we get in, I've got plans. He's pretty good—but he ain't be'n around none. Cuter claims there's a hundred cricks with prospectors on 'em just waitin' to be took—an' Black John don't make no play for 'em. He's got the gang, an' the setup—but he ain't got what it takes to go out an' get the stuff.''

"What you goin' to do about it?''

"Listen—I ain't be'n there a month till I'm runnin' that gang—see? We'll watch our chance, an' when the time's right, we rub this Black John out. Hell, with a setup like that there's millions in it!''

"Why didn't you go up to Halfaday yourself an' leave Simcoe to help us with this damn boat?''

"Like I said, Simcoe wouldn't have be'n worth a damn there on the *Helen*. An' besides, he's be'n a guide, an' he's used to gettin' around in a country like this. Hell, I couldn't never have found Halfaday Crick! I'd got lost. On top of that, Simcoe's good at gettin' in with folks. You boys know that. He'll be damn

handy for us in a country like this. None of us is worth a damn
outside of a city.''

"You said it—an' I wish I was back in one, right now!" the
Chicago Kid growled. "To hell with this country! It's too big,
an' too damn still. Listen—you can't hear nothin' but a lot of
damn mosquitoes!''

"We'll get used to it," the Parson said. "An' what with all
the gold that's layin' around to be lifted, it won't be no time at
all till we're headin' back with a million." He finished his meal
and tossed his plate aside. "I'm like you. I think it's too still,
so I'm goin' to sing a hymn. Come on, boys, join in. Let's wake
the damn place up a little." He picked up the bottle, took a
long pull, and broke forth in song:

> "Oh come, we'll gather at the river,
> The beautiful, the beautiful a-river.
> Oh come let us gather at the river
> That flows by the throne of—

"Well, I'll be damned! Who the hell are you?" The song
broke off abruptly, the bottle dropped from his hand, and the
firelight flickered on a blue-black six-gun that covered the big
man who had stepped suddenly from the bush. Guns appeared
also in the hands of the other two.

White teeth flashed behind the black beard as Black John stepped
into the firelight. "Put up yer artillery, gents. I'm jest a lone
traveler in the Northland. I was driftin' down the river in my
canoe an' I heard the singin' an' thought there was a camp
meetin' goin' on, like the missionaries sometimes holds fer the
Siwashes. I never miss a camp meetin' if I can get to one.
They're very beneficial to a man's soul."

The Parson scowled. "Well, now you've found out this ain't
a camp meetin', the best thing you can do is climb back in your
canoe an' get to hell out of here. I was just singin' for our own
amusement."

The smile died from Black John's lips. "You ain't a very
hospitable bunch," he said. "I'd like to stay awhile. I take
amusement in singin', too. 'Specially songs like that last one. It
sort of sets me to wonderin' if a man can hang onto what he
gathers at a river."

"What! Hey—what do you mean by that?"

"Merely that, as an abstract proposition, it is interestin' to contemplate the ability—"

"Say—who the hell are you, anyway?" the Chicago Kid demanded, abruptly.

Again the smile flashed behind the black beard. "Me? I'm Black John Smith."

"Black John!" cried the man known as Lefty.

The Parson pocketed his gun and thrust out his hand. "By God, it's him, all right! Cuter claimed he talked like a damn lawyer, or a preacher, or someone like that! Did you see Simcoe Sam?"

"Oh shore. Sam, he's up on Halfaday. He told me about you boys aimin' to take that shipment of gold the Consolidated was sendin' out on the *Helen*. How'd you make out? Did you get it?"

For an instant the Parson hesitated, then jerked his thumb toward the boat drawn onto the sand. "Take a look, an' see what *you* think."

Black John stepped to the boat and glanced down at the four wooden boxes. "Damned if you didn't!" he exclaimed. "You boys must be good!"

The Parson tendered his bottle. "I'll say we're good!" he agreed. "Have a snort of licker. Nothin' like a little licker amongst friends."

Black John took a drink and the Parson passed the bottle to the others. "Kill it, boys," he said. "I've got a couple of more in my packsack."

"What you doin' down here?" the Chicago Kid asked, with a glance toward the boat. "Cuter Malone claimed it's better than a hundred miles from here to Halfaday Crick."

"Sam claimed you boys was city fellas, an' I figgered you might have trouble shovin' the boat up the river, so I come on down to give you a hand. There's quite a bit of white water between here an' Halfaday."

"Did Simcoe fix it up for us to join up with your gang?" the Parson asked.

"Yeah, he claimed you'd like to j'ine up. Fer as Sam goes, he's all right. He's a good hand with a rifle an' a canoe, an' he can find his way around in any country. But I don't know—with city fellas, it's different."

"What do you mean—different?" the Parson asked, as he

produced another bottle from his packsack and drew the cork. "Them boxes of gold says we can deliver the goods, don't they?"

"Oh shore. That part's all right. But—did you have to do any shootin' to get 'em?"

"Hell, no!" the Parson exclaimed. "We had it all worked out. We watched 'em load the stuff, an' seen that they sent a couple of guards along with it. Yesterday, Chicago an' Lefty, here, makin' out like they was a couple of cheechako prospectors, got acquainted with the guards. An' this evenin', just before we got to the White River, they slipped 'em a couple of drinks out of a bottle that was loaded with enough chloral to kill a horse. Believe me, them two will be lucky if they ever wake up!

"In the meantime, I'd chummed up with the deckhands, an' when one of 'em pointed out the mouth of the White River, I give Chicago an' Lefty the office, an' Chicago slipped into the pilothouse an' covered the pilot, an' Lefty herded the passengers up in the bow an' kept them covered, an' I covered the deckhands, an' made 'em shove the boat in the water an' load the boxes of gold, after Chicago had made the pilot run the *Helen* to the bank. It worked slick as grease—just like we figured it would. It takes brains to pull off a job like that."

Black John nodded. "That's right. But the brains has got to be backed up with a certain amount of skill. What if the pilot, er one of the passengers, er a deckhand had put up a fight—draw'd a gun on you. What would have happened then?"

"Why—we'd have blasted 'em down—that's what!"

Again Black John nodded. "That's what I'm gettin' at. Take my gang, up on Halfaday, every man has got to be good. Some are good at one thing, an' some at another. But they're all good in their line. It ain't brains I'm after—it's skill. I've got brains enough fer the whole outfit. What I'm gettin' at is, how do I know you boys would have had the skill to blast anyone down? Take it with a six-gun, a man's not only got to be a good shot, but he's got to be fast."

The Parson laughed. "I guess you don't need to worry about us," he said. "We'll show you in the morning."

Black John's face became grave, and he slowly shook his head. "Jest what I was afraid of," he said, speaking more to himself than the others. "Daylight shooters."

"What do you mean—daylight shooters?"

"Most anyone can shoot pretty good in daylight. But the fact is, from the nature of our enterprises, most of 'em is pulled off in the night. Take it like now, with what little starlight there is on the water there, if I was to toss a chunk of this firewood into the river, there ain't a man in my gang that couldn't empty his gun into it as it floats past without a damn miss—some with a rifle, an' some with a six-gun."

"There ain't a damn one of us that couldn't, neither," the Parson said.

Black John smiled. "Well, as the fella says, I'm from Missouri. You've got to show me."

"Toss out your chunk! Come on, boys, we'll show him!"

Selecting a sizable firewood chunk, Black John stepped to the water's edge. "Now you boys line up below me, here, an' have yer guns ready. When this chunk hits the water, I want the man nearest to me to shoot, then the next man, an' then the next. I want them shots to foller one another without no break in the rotation. An' I want 'em to foller fast, an' straight. That'll not only show me how good you are, but whether you can carry out an order without gettin' balled up an' shootin' out of turn. All right—here goes—an' keep them shots a rollin' til yer guns is empty!"

He tossed the chunk into the river and a barrage of shots rang out as the chunk rolled and bobbed from the impact of bullets, as water splashed up all about it. The noise ceased abruptly.

"An' now yer guns is empty, toss 'em in the river!" Black John commanded, his voice gone suddenly hard.

Lefty and the Chicago Kid, the two nearest, turned to face him, sudden terror depicted on their faces in the bright starlight. Beyond them there was a swift movement, and Black John leaped aside as a shot roared out. An agonizing pain shot through him, and his left arm dangled helplessly at his side.

"You ain't got all the brains!" cried the Parson, "or you'd have counted them shots. I saved one shell—just in case!"

Black John's right hand flashed beneath his shirt and came out grasping a .45 six-gun whose muzzle covered the three. "If you'd be'n twict as smart you'd have saved two," he retorted. "Toss them guns in the river—an' be damn quick about it, er there'll be a row of corpses follerin' that chunk downstream!"

Three guns splashed into the water, and three pairs of hands reached skyward.

"What the hell is this—a stickup?" the Parson asked.

"What do you think?" Black John asked, grinning despite the pain in his arm. "I'm free to admit that you boys displayed a modicum of skill. But skill without brains won't get a man very far. An' I'll further admit that the Parson, there, displayed a certain amount of craftiness in holdin' back that last shell. If he'd had jest a little more skill, he'd have rubbed me out—like he claimed he would, awhile back. You see, I was layin' there in the scrub listen' to what you planned to do onct you got to Halfaday.

"I'd ort to shoot every damn one of you rats right where you stand. Or better yet, take you up to Halfaday an' hang you. But instead, I'm givin' you a break. Keep together, an' pick up yer packsacks an' walk on ahead of me to the big river, jest below where the *Helen* landed."

"What are you goin' to do to us?" the Parson asked, a note of fear in his voice.

"I'm goin' to load you into my canoe, an' start you on yer way. An' if you've got any sense at all, you'll keep on upriver, an' go back out over the pass. This country don't need no sech onprincipled scum as you. Yer nothin' but common thieves!"

"How about you—liftin' that gold off'n us?"

"That is neither here nor there. You men have your own sins to answer for. I'm not takin' this property through any desire to profit by the transaction, but merely to teach you men that crime don't pay. Get goin'!"

As the three, under Black John's direction, slipped the light craft into the water, the Parson eyed it dubiously. "We can't ride in that damn thing! We'll get drowned. We don't know nothin' about canoes."

"You'll know quite a bit about 'em by the time you get to the Chilcoot. Keep on up the Yukon, an' up through the lakes. Don't try to go to Halfaday, or the boys will hang you like we hang Simcoe Sam."

"Hung Simcoe!" cried Lefty. "What did you hang him for?"

"We hung him because, after he'd outlined this nefarious plot to rob the Consolidated, we deemed him to be a man of questionable repute. We can't afford to have no sech onprincipled characters on Halfaday. An' don't try to go back to Dawson. I'm headin' fer there, right now, to get my arm patched up. An' the first thing I'll do when I get there will be to furnish the police with a detailed description of all three of you, an' tell 'em about you bein' wanted fer that Manitoba train robbery. An' if them Consolidated guards imbibed as much chloral as you figger they did, there'll be a little item of murder agin you, to boot. Git goin' now—an' remember that the closter you hold

to the shore, the less chanct you've got of gettin' drowned.
You'll get the hang of it after the first few tip overs. So long.''

IV

WHEN the canoe, with one man seated amidships, and two paddling, disappeared upstream, Black John returned to the fire,
slit the sleeve of his shirt, and examined his wounded arm.
Blood oozed from the holes made by the Parson's bullet, but
not in sufficient quantity to indicate damage to any important
artery or vein. The bone, however, was undoubtedly broken at
a point three inches above the elbow. Picking up the Parson's
bottle, he took a stiff drink, and sloshing the remainder onto his
wounds, bound a clean handkerchief about the arm and rigged
a sling out of an extra shirt he took from his packsack.

''The quicker I get to a doctor, the better,'' he muttered. ''It
shore is a good thing that Dawson is downriver from here, er
I'd be in a hell of a fix with a busted arm, an' this heavy boat.''
He untied the painter, and after some difficulty, and no little
pain, succeeded in shoving the boat from the sand and climbing
in.

As it shot swiftly out into the Yukon, he eyed the four wooden
boxes with a scowl. ''Blood pizen ain't apt to set in,'' he said
aloud, ''but if it does—well, a left arm is a hell of a price to pay
fer a little fun, an' four hundred pounds of lead! Anyway, I
headed them damn cusses off'n Halfaday. We shore don't want
no one like them gummin' up the crick. It would have be'n jest
like that damn psalm singin' bum to try to rub me out like he
claimed he would. I didn't like the look in his eyes.''

The hours passed slowly as the heavy rowboat floated down
the Yukon, turning aimlessly as the current carried it along.
Black John dozed fitfully, the throbbing pain in his arm waking
him at frequent intervals. With the coming of early dawn he
managed, by using an oar, to work the craft ashore on a point,
cook his breakfast, and down a half-dozen cups of strong black
coffee. He scowled at the four wooden boxes in the bottom of
the boat. ''At the rate I'm driftin', it'll be midnight before I hit
Dawson,'' he figured aloud. ''But with this south wind, the boat
would drift a damn sight faster without all that lead. I'll dump
the damn stuff in the river an' shorten the trip a mile an' hour,
er more.'' Suiting the action to the word, he stepped into the
boat, and with much cursing under his breath, finally succeeded

in dumping the boxes overboard, despite the pain which every movement cost him. When the task was accomplished, he grinned. "There—I'll make better time, now. An' I won't be caught with any incriminatin' evidence when I get to Dawson. That manager would think I was out of my head—knockin' off that cargo of lead!"

It was early evening when he managed, handicapped as he was, to beach the boat a short distance below the sawmill. Stepping ashore, he shoved the boat out into the current and proceeded at once to the hospital.

"Gunshot wound, eh?" the young intern observed, as he removed the bandage and examined the arm.

"Yeah. Don't amount to no hell of a lot. Jest a prank."

"A prank! Say, you're Black John Smith of Halfaday Crick, aren't you? I've seen you several times in the Tivoli."

"Yeah, that was ondoubtless me. It's a habit of mine, when in town, to frequent places of doubtful repute, an' consort with evil companions."

The doctor laughed. "From what I hear, you've got evil companions enough on Halfaday Crick to consort with. According to all reports, that must be a mighty rough bunch, up there."

"Oh, I don't know. We've be'n more er less maligned. Fact is, we ain't so rough. We're about like any other crick. We dig our gold, an' have our fun, in our own quiet way."

"But—this wound? You say it is the result of a prank?"

"Yeah. Me'n Cush got tired of shakin' dice, the other day, so we got to playin' hit er miss."

"Hit or miss? I never heard of it."

"Oh, it's jest a little game we invented, up there, to pass the time away. We each lay a six-gun on the bar an' then watch the clock, an' when the minute hand gets to an agreed p'int, we grab fer our guns an' shoot. It's fun when four er five games gets to goin' at once acrost the bar."

The young doctor's eyes widened. "You mean, you grab up these guns and shoot at each other!"

"Oh shore. It's all in fun. Jest fer the drinks. We try to jest nick the other fella. Cush, he held jest a might too far to the right, this time. He claimed it was on account öf his glasses bein' gummed up on him. Anyhow, the drinks was on me."

"So they brought you down to get fixed up, eh?"

"Brought—hell! I come down alone. It ain't but a little ways—

couple hundred miles. You'd ort to come up an visit us some-time. It gets kind of dull on the crick, an' we like to have a friend er two drop in on us, now an' then. We'll try to stir up a little excitement fer you."

"Thanks for the invitation," the doctor said, dryly. "I may do that—sometime when I feel the need of excitement." A few minutes later, he looked up. "You're lucky," he announced. "The bullet just chipped the bone and broke it clean. It isn't shattered. You'll be as good as ever in a few weeks."

The following morning Black John, his arm in a sling, strolled into police detachment to find Corporal Downey busy at his desk. The officer looked up.

"Hello, John! I thought you'd pulled out. What the hell! What happened to your arm?"

"Broke it."

"How'd that happen?"

"I was paddlin' upriver, day before yesterday. The mosqui-toes was kinda bad an', goin' agin the current like I was, I didn't dast to stop paddlin', so I tried to scratch my ear with my el-bow—an' it didn't work."

Downey laughed, and before he could reply, the door flew open and the manager of the Consolidated Dredge Company burst into the room.

"We've been robbed," he cried. "It's a damned outrage! I demanded police protection for that shipment—and you re-fused. And now we've been robbed. I just got word from White-horse!"

"What shipment are you talkin' about?" Downey asked. "The one that went out on the *Helen*?"

"Certainly, the one that went on the *Helen*!"

Black John grinned. "What you all het up about? Hell, there wasn't nothing but lead in them boxes!"

"Lead—your grandmother! It was gold. One hundred thou-sand dollars' worth."

Corporal Downey frowned. "But—I thought it was agreed that you would make up a dummy shipment for the *Helen* and hold the gold over for shipment on one of the later boats, when I could furnish you with a guard."

The manager's muttonchop whiskers fairly quivered with rage, as he pointed a shaking finger at Black John. "The plan was his! I'll admit that, at the moment, it sounded reasonable. But afterward I got to thinking—"

"That was a mistake," grinned the big man.

The other ignored the interruption. "This man, a notorious outlaw, was the one who suggested the plan to outwit the robbers. The thing looked strange to me—mighty fishy. I smelled a plot within a plot! I realized that here was some deep laid scheme of this outlaw to force me to somehow play into his hand. I was determined to outwit him. So apparently carrying out his suggestion, I had dummy packages made up so that, if any information was leaking out, it would reach his ears that the plan was being carried out as agreed. But unknown to anyone but myself and a single trusted employee, we switched the packages. And it was the gold that went out on the *Helen*! I also armed a couple of my own men and placed them aboard as guards, just in case these robbers he mentioned should really exist and make a play for the gold. These men are now at death's door in the hospital at Whitehorse, apparently the victims of some drug."

Black John's grin widened slowly. Then, suddenly, he threw back his head and roared with laughter.

"What's so damn funny?" asked Corporal Downey glumly.

"Hell, Downey!" the big man replied. "Ain't you got no sense of humor? This man's master-mindin' has cost the consolidated a hundred thousan' dollars! It serves 'em right fer hirin' anyone to run their outfit who thinks he can think."

"But that don't get the gold back," retorted the officer sourly.

"That's right. An' what's more—I'm bettin' you never will locate it. Them damn criminals is smart. What with the start they've got—an' you shorthanded, I'd say you ain't got a chanct in the world." He turned to the irate manager. "An' now, my good man, my advice to you is that the next time someone slips you a friendly tip—you take it. Better jest leave the thinkin' to someone else." He rose, stretched his good arm high above his head, and yawned prodigiously. "Heigh-ho! Well, I've got to be goin'. It'll prob-ly be a hell of a job tryin' to play stud one-handed—but I'll make her, somehow."

As he made his way toward the Tivoli, Black John chuckled to himself. "When this arm gets well, I'll do a little quiet divin'. The water off that p'int ain't no more'n six, seven foot deep. I guess this busted arm wasn't sech a bad investment after all. Luck shore moves in a mysterious way, sometimes. A man can't never tell."

While Samuel Alexander White was known as the "Jack London of Canada," William Byron Mowery (1899–1957) was often referred to as the "Zane Grey of the Canadian Northwest." From 1929 to 1938 he published fifteen first-rate novels—outstanding among them The Girl from God's Mercie, Resurrection River, The Phantom Canoe, *and* The Black Automatic—*and numerous short stories set in the towns, villages, and wilderness areas of Western Canada. Much of his fiction deals realistically with the men of the Northwest Mounted Police. Among the best of his shorter works about the Mounties is "The Long Shadow," a tale of one of Canada's little-known gold rushes; others were collected in* The Long Arm of the Mounted *(1948) and* Sagas of the Mounted Police *(1953).*

The Long Shadow

★★★★★★★★★★★★★★★★

William Byron Mowery

FOR hours that August afternoon Sergeant David Kirke had been lying on the buffalo grass behind the Mounted Police barracks, his gray eyes troubled as he gazed at the Rockies a hundred miles westward. Under the evening sun the prairie and wild Alberta foothills were bluish hazy, as though from the camp smoke of Indian bands, and the dust of the great shaggy herds that were vanishing out of sight to north and south stood out stark and clear.

Kirke's eyes were on those massive giants, but his thoughts went on beyond them—to the wilderness of mountains, valleys, and placer rivers west of the Great Divide. With the low-slanting sun inching down behind them, the lofty peaks of the Rockies were flinging long shadows far out across the rolling plains and making queer, darkish shapes in the summer-evening clouds. Now the shadows would seem like covered wagons lumbering across the prairie; now like Piegan warriors on their ponies, sullenly watching the caravan of the pioneers; now like the lone sentinel figure of a Mounted horseman, watching both the red hunter and the homesteading white man.

Abruptly a voice broke into Kirke's thought. "Sergeant Kirke! Sergeant David of the Dalhousie Kirkes! Where in consternation are you, Dave?"

As Constable "Dusty" Goff came breezing around the corner of the barracks, David closed the book that had lain in front of him unread and got up slowly, his face hard with determination. In the past hour his troubled thought had crystallized into plans for action.

The constable's joking mood grated on him, but he made himself smile at Goff. "Looking for me, Dusty?"

"Inspector Haley wants to see you, Sarge. In his cabin. At your ad libitum, he said—whatever that means. I think he's got your furlough papers and your *chickamin* ready." The constable sobered a little. "Where're you spending your leave, Dave—back East? Been a long time since you've been home to see your folks."

"Thanks for rousting me," David said. "No, Dusty, it won't be back East, I'm afraid."

Goff looked at him, puzzled; then he hurried back to the police quadrangle where he and another off-duty constable had been tossing turnips in the air and practicing dry-shooting with their revolvers.

For a moment longer David stood looking at the Great Divide. Yes, it had been a long time, a long and pleasureless time, since he had seen the Eastern cities. It seemed endless years that he'd been watching over Indian bands, shepherding homesteaders, keeping track of prospectors and trappers, and being the long arm of the law in that frontier country. He had wanted desperately to get home that summer, before it was too late; to see his mother and dad once again. But this other business came first. It came ahead of anything else on earth.

As he started for Inspector Haley's cabin, he came upon a middle-aged Blood Indian squatting on his heels at the side door of the barracks. It was Itai-Po, the Moon-Shadow, whom the police detachment had been using as a scout for patrols into the mountain fastnesses to the west.

Clad in breechclout and moccasins, Itai-Po was no reservation "Smoky" but thoroughly an Indian. For weapons he carried only a knife and a short ram's-horn bow, wound with a rattlesnake skin. The blanket across his shoulders was a Stikine River *narhkin*, woven of big-horn wool and decorated with the Snake and Magic Crane of the North Fox totem.

As the Indian rose up facing him, David said, "You remember yesterday I said you'n me might pitch off together again? On a *hiyu* big scout this time."

Itai-Po's black eyes lit up with the adventure of spruce-shadow trails and man-hunting with the lean, quiet sergeant.

David went on, "Good. This evening we pitch off. We leave *hyas* quick—in half a pipe. You ready, huh?"

"I been wait," Itai-Po answered."Where go, mebbe? Peace River? Sikanni River? What work, mebbe? Patrol?"

David jerked his thumb to the northwest. "We go there. No patrol. We go *stoh lepee neiska*—on our own hook. You wait here two-three minutes for me, Itai-Po."

He went on to Inspector Haley's cabin, knocked, and went in. The officer, elbow-deep in paperwork at his desk, answered David's salute and reached for two envelopes.

"Here's your furlough, Kirke," he said, holding out the larger envelope. "And here"—the smaller envelope, with the dull jingle of gold coins—"is your means of enjoying it. I sincerely hope you have the fine, refreshing leave you deserve."

David folded the furlough papers carefully into his money belt and dropped the gold coins into his pocket. "This leave," he remarked, "is only for a month, sir—"

Inspector Haley looked at him blankly. *"Only?"* he echoed. "Why, Division Headquarters issued an order that no officer or man is to get more than two weeks, Kirke. I nearly perjured myself to get an 'only a month.' I felt you've been working too hard. You've done two terms out here on the Plains without one free day."

"I'm grateful to you, sir," David said. "And ordinarily I'd be ashamed to ask for still more time, but I simply can't get back here by the fifth of September."

"Why not?"

David looked out the window. "I'd just as soon not say, now. It might seem like a wild-goose chase."

"But you're visiting your home in the East, aren't you?"

"I've given that up."

Haley looked at him narrowly. "Are you sure you can't tell me where you're going and what you'll be doing? If not as your superior officer, then as your friend. You know how serious the penalties are for overstay."

David slowly nodded."I know. I'll take what comes."

Haley thrummed on the desk a moment. "Well, I'll do what I can for you. If you simply can't get back by the fifth of September, and any question comes up, I'll state that you're on a secret patrol to the Okanagan."

David shook his head. "That's mighty fine of you, sir, but I won't let you risk a marred record for my sake."

"That's my concern. There's just one thing I'm asking of you—to get back here and wipe the McPherson killing off our slate before winter sets in. Headquarters has been riding me to get that murder cleaned up. The case has been all yours so far, so you're the one to finish it off."

"What if it can never be finished?" David asked quietly.

Haley cleared his throat uneasily. "Kirke, I want to ask you a frank question. Do you think Esther Shannon and her brother had any connection with the murder? I know that you—uh, saw Esther Shannon pretty steady this summer. You are better acquainted at their place than anybody else, so your opinion ought to be authentic."

"Esther and Paul were given a jury trial and acquitted for lack of proof, weren't they, sir?"

"That trial," Haley said impatiently, "didn't prove anything. The court had no facts except what you presented, and that's why I want your own personal opinion. Do you think—yes or no—that the Shannons had some connection with this murder?"

"No! The very idea is absurd."

"Then why under heaven did you recommend that they be arrested and given a public trial? They told a flimsy story, I know, and the evidence against them was strong, but—why that trial?"

"That's hard to answer, sir," Kirke said slowly. In the days since the trial, he himself had more than once doubted if he had done the right thing. It was no clear-cut issue one way or the other. But always he had come back doggedly to the conviction that he had acted wisely.

Haley went on, "It's true that the Shannons were acquitted, Kirke, but you dragged them into that trial and you ought to feel responsible for getting back here as soon as possible and finding the killer. Acquittal or no, they'll be under a cloud until you do. Will you have a mailing address where I can reach you if anything new comes to light?"

David smiled a little grimly. "A mailing address, where I'm going—hardly!" He noticed Haley's puzzled frown and added, "I'm not hiding anything willfully, sir. The truth is, I don't know myself where this business will take me, or what I'll be doing."

"Hmmph! Well, can I help you in any way? Extra money? Personal backing?"

David turned to leave. "You might keep an eye on the Shannons, sir. Paul isn't strong, you know, and Esther—well, she just doesn't belong in a raw country like this.''

"I'll watch out for them both," Haley promised. He reached out his hand. "Good luck and Godspeed—wherever you're going."

David shook hands, saluted, then turned and walked out of the cabin.

A few steps from the door Itai-Po was waiting for him.

"You got our canoe ready, Itai-Po?" David asked.

The Blood pointed to a clump of whitewoods along the bank of Bear River, a quarter mile west of the post. "Canoe tied up there. My light birch rind."

"Good. How about your camping outfit?"

The Indian tapped a small pack he carried which was not much larger than a folded blanket. "*Hiyu* many portages," he explained. He pointed at a long-tailed magpie that was flying over the barracks and having an awkward time in the evening breeze. "Fool bird carry heap big tail and go *flap-flap*; hummer bird tote little tail and go *zip*."

David smiled. "Right. Now listen, Itai-Po. You go put canoe to water and paddle up Bear River to landing at Shannon place. I go there by horse. We meet there at dusk and pitch off. You *kumtux*?"

Itai-Po nodded and started toward the whitewoods. David went into the barracks and crossed to the boarded-off corner that was his room.

His preparations were brief. He took off his uniform, laid it away in the locker, and put on civilian khaki. Into his pack went a light fishing outfit, a few articles of clothing, two pairs of moccasins, his Service binoculars, extra ammunition for his belt-gun and Enfield rifle, and two tight-woven blankets to wrap it all in.

Dusty Goff sauntered in and stood watching. "Not wasting any time getting away, I see, Dave. Where are you heading? Looks like a bush trip of some sort."

"Might be," David evaded.

"If it wasn't that I ain't seen you spending any evenings at the Shannon place lately. I'd guess you might be pitching off on your honeymoon."

The remark cut David like a knife. But he said nothing, and went on with his preparations. From his locker he took a battered felt hat and a patched old corduroy coat, and stowed them carefully in his pack.

"Snakes," Goff remarked, "them ain't no duds for a honeymoon, if you *are* off on a honeymoon. But with quiet fellers like yourself, you never cain tell what they're up to. The hours you used to keep when you went off to the Shannon place was something scand'lous—''

David whirled around, an angry order on his lips. But he managed to fight it back. "Dusty," he said quietly, "go out and saddle a horse for me, will you? I'll be riding for a few miles on this trip. Then I'll send the horse back. Keep an eye out for it after supper."

"Surelee will, if you say so," Dusty agreed. "But you know it brings bad luck to send your horse home with the saddle on. When that happens, the Crees say, it means you won't ever come back from that trip."

"That's not the worst thing I can imagine," Kirke said cryptically. "No, not the worst . . ."

II

In the first hush of evening, David left the police post on the chestnut gelding that Dusty had saddled for him and headed northwest over the park-prairie country, cutting across a bend of the Bear River. The region was at the far northern wash of the homesteader wave, and it looked as lone and deserted as when it had been a battleground between the Bloods and Assiniboins, not so many years ago. Three miles from the post he rode past a small nester place in a creek bottom—the only settler sign in his hour's ride.

Four miles beyond the nester place he struck the bank of the Bear River, just below the great bend where the stream swung abruptly west and headed straight for the distant foothill wilderness. Through the riverbank whitewoods and birches he rode out into a small clearing where a gravel creek flowed into the Bear.

In the middle of the clearing stood a rambling, split-log building of several rooms, with a small, empty stable at the woods edge, a fur-cache dugout, a springhouse, and canoe landing. Built by Esther Shannon's uncle in the year when David had first come to this region, the place had been intended as trading post and overnight lodging for trappers, homesteaders, and prospectors. But the homesteader wave had failed to come, travelers were few, and the tiny post had never panned out.

The twilight river, the creeping prairie roses around the clearing, the piny tang drifting down from the low hills up the creek brought David poignant memories of the evenings he had gone walking in the whippoorwill dusk with Esther Shannon. He hated to think of the long weeks when he would be away and she would be by herself there. The spot was lonely for human habitation. Lonely, wild, and isolated.

He took his rifle from the saddle bucket, lifted off his pack, and turned the horse around. At his sharp command to "home," the police mount started back toward the post at a brisk canter. Leaving his rifle and pack near the canoe landing, David walked up the path toward the split-log building.

In the small garden near the springhouse Esther Shannon was gathering an apronful of peas for the evening meal. As David drew near, she heard him coming, turned, and he was face-to-face with her, for the first time since the murder trial at Bear River Settlement.

A graceful, medium-tall girl of twenty-three, with soft brown hair and warm brown eyes, Esther Shannon had come from the East, like David, and the East still clung to her. It was always a marvel to him that this girl should be living in that raw, pioneer region. Her parents, homesteaders in the Moose Jaw district, had died in a prairie blizzard; and she had been thrown entirely on her own, with a younger brother to look after. For two years she had taught at a mission school in Saskatchewan, then at the half-breed school at Bear River Settlement. On the death of her uncle, who had homesteaded this tract along the Bear River and staked a float-gold claim up the tributary creek, she had come here to live out the two remaining years of the fief and nurse her brother Paul back to health.

It had been a bad mistake. The gold claim had proved to be worth little; the expected settler tide had kept far to the south; the life here had been dreadfully lonesome and bleak for her. In his quiet way David had tried to watch over the Shannon place and buoy her up through the bad times. But then, as the last and worst of all her troubles, the McPherson incident—

As David confronted her now, he was shocked at the deep weariness on her sweet young face. Uncertain how she would receive him, he touched his hat and said awkwardly, "I meant to call around sooner, Esther, but I had extra work to clean up before my furlough."

She did not answer. David noticed the coldness in her manner. She was looking at him as though he were a stranger. Or worse—an enemy.

He picked up the wooden pail of vegetables she had gathered and said, "I'll carry it for you," and they went along the gravel path to the kitchen door. Esther stopped there, not inviting him inside. David set the pail just over the threshold and stood fumbling his hat.

"I'm going away on furlough, Esther," he finally blurted out. "For several weeks. I came past to say good-bye—and to see you." Then he remembered her book that he had and took it out of his jacket pocket. "And to return this, too."

Still, Esther said nothing. In the silence he heard her brother Paul down on the creek-bank trail, evidently coming home.

He tried again to probe into what she was thinking and feeling toward him. "When I get back—sometime in September—would you lend me that book again, Esther? I thought to finish it this afternoon, but—"

She interrupted him. "If you really want to finish the book, Sergeant Kirke, you'd better keep it now. I won't need it anymore."

David was jarred by her words. As plain as daylight, she was saying that she did not intend ever to let him see her again.

He scuffed at the gravel with his boot and plunged into the subject that lay between them. "Lord knows you've reason to be bitter about that trial, Esther. But I was hoping you'd withhold judgment till I could talk with you and explain—"

Again she cut him short. "I think that the trial spoke for itself, Sergeant Kirke. Nothing that can be said now would recall one word or one moment of that dreadful experience. I wish you wouldn't bring the subject up again."

"But don't you see, Esther, that I acted under compulsion? I had reasons for causing the arrest and the trial."

Esther tossed her head angrily. "Of course you had. Good reasons, to your way of thinking. When some silly clue pointed to this place, you felt it was your duty to follow that clue. You'd been welcomed here as a friend, and because of that, you were able to unearth other alleged evidence against us. That also, I suppose, was your duty. And then, as an officer of the law, you were simply compelled to drag us into the glare and shame of a trial for murder!"

"That open trial, Esther, was safer than to let rumor and dangerous talk go on till it got out of hand. You and Paul were suspected by everyone in this district—"

"Including yourself!" Esther interrupted, her low tones passionate with anger. "Otherwise, you'd have had the courage to stand between us and arrest. And you probably still have your suspicions. And now you're going away on a pleasure trip—now, of all times!—leaving Paul and me to bear this odium."

Under her bitter indictment, David stood silent and miserable, realizing the hopelessness of any explanation. Yet he felt that no man could let charges like hers go unchallenged.

"Whether you believe me or not, Esther," he said, "I did *not* use my welcome here to spy on you and Paul. You mustn't say things like that—things which can never be unsaid."

Instead of answering him, Esther turned and went into the cabin, closing the door in his face.

As David slowly turned away and went down the path, he met Paul Shannon coming up from the creek trail.

The nesters and half-breeds thereabouts pitied Paul Shannon because he was a "lunger," but their pity was mixed with contempt—a young man of twenty who could not chop down a tree or ride a bronc or hold a plow in the prairie sod. But Kirke had early realized that Paul Shannon had been born for other things. There were times when he felt a little in awe of the lad's dreaming, visionary nature. And he knew that Esther, too, understood the quality of genius in her young, stricken brother, and this had made her fight for him all the fiercer.

David noticed the boy's muddied trousers. "You've been tom-rocking up on that claim, Paul," he said. "That's too hard for you. Didn't you and I have a private agreement that when you needed a bit of money to tide you over, you'd let me lend it to you?"

"I didn't think an hour or two at the claim would hurt any," Paul said, in his dreamy way. He put down his shovel and mattock as a spell of coughing came on, and leaned weakly against a sapling. "But I guess—it did—hurt, David."

David put a steadying hand on the boy's shoulder. "Paul," he said, when the worst of the coughing was over, "I'm going away for a few weeks, and while I'm gone I'll want to know that you're not tom-rocking, or doing any other work you shouldn't. Here"—he reached into his pocket for the gold coins of his furlough pay and put them into Paul's hand—"this'll tide you over. Just don't let on about it to Esther, for heaven's sake. She doesn't understand about that trial. I hope you do."

"I knew you were trying somehow to be our friend," Paul said. "It was like walking through a dark woods at night, with you guiding us and fighting off dangers." He looked at the gold in his hand and slowly shook his head. "But I can't accept this, David. No, I can't."

"Why not? It's just a loan. You've taken other little loans from me."

"That was when I felt sure I could pay you back."

David thought that the boy was losing his courage and giving up his dogged fight for life. "Nonsense, Paul!" he argued. "You're starting to pick up. After a winter here in these pine hills, you'll be hard as nails. You mustn't be discouraged. That's letting Esther down. Of course you'll pay me back."

"It's not that I'm discouraged," Paul explained. "It's that—well, we won't be here, David."

"*What?*"

"We're leaving," Paul added. "Esther has started to pack already. We're going back East. It's too hard a fight to hang on till the land becomes ours."

It seemed to David that all his plans came crashing about his ears. A little dazed, he stood there fighting to think; fighting down a rebellion against the role he had been forced to play and the raw injustice to himself. What was the use, he asked, of going ahead with the long, dangerous trip he had planned? When he got back, Esther would be half a continent away.

Out of the deepening twilight he saw Itai-Po's slender birchbark come gliding silently in toward the canoe landing. The sight of it reminded him again of his plans, his duty, and his long, spruce-shadows trail ahead. He shook Paul's hand and said good-bye, and went out the path for his pack and rifle.

At the landing he stepped into the canoe and shoved it off. They swung out into the current and headed west, toward the foothills and the mountains on beyond.

III

THE days that followed were long and each alike. Dawn broke at three in the morning, and at ten at night there was still paddling light on the bosom of lake or river. At the earliest gray of morning, when the solitaire was singing his "*Leve! Leve!* Come alive," David was out of his blankets and whipping a pool for trout. By the time he returned with four or five, Itai-Po would have his cone of fire built and camp ready to be broken. In twenty minutes they were through with breakfast, into the canoe and gone.

Every two hours they stopped for a pipe, and three times during the long day for a mug-up. They carried no food, but relied on fish, berries, waterfowl, and occasionally a blacktailed deer or woodland caribou at a lake edge. At each camp

Itai-Po produced a gum pot and smeared cracks in his birch-bark.

The foothills themselves ran through cycles that were as regular as the days. First it was silent river, winding through forests of columnar spruce; then a river-widening or valley lake, aflutter with teal, ducks, geese, and the sonorous trumpeter swan; then a gushing, white-water creek at the upper end, leading to a tiny watershed over some hill range; then portage, white-water creek, lake, and the spruce-buried river again.

The two of them had silence in common, and they passed hours without so much as grunting at each other. Itai-Po's expertness at canoe work and David's strength and white-man stamina made a unique water-dogging combination. Their swift pace was a reassurance to David, whose furlough days were precious, and it brought a keen satisfaction to the wilderness-loping Itai-Po. Their "pipes," the Blood said, were the longest he had ever known in canoe travel. When they covered in two days a distance which the swiftest Assiniboin runner had never covered in less than three, Itai-Po's swarthy face cracked in a derisive grin at besting the ancient enemies of his tribe.

For the sake of speed they were constantly taking white-water *sautes* which looked like suicide and scudding straight across windswept lakes instead of following the shoreline. They poled up rapids, towed through gorges, and shortcut over the padded trails of moose and bear.

When Bear River shallowed into a foothill brook, they portaged through six heartbreaking miles of new windfall to the nearest canoe water, and sped on, range after range, till they dropped down into the broad valley of Mountain River, a snow-fed stream that wound between the foothills and the Rockies.

So far, they had followed the centuries-old trade route between the Coastal Siwash and the Indians of the Great Plains; but at Mountain River the route bent south a hundred miles to an easy pass across the Great Divide.

"Too slow, that trade route; we waste days," David said. On a sandbar he sketched a map and indicated a point on the far side of the Divide. "We want to go there, Itai-Po. You get us there quickest quick can."

For half an hour the Indian squatted on his heels and studied the map. Finally he said, "No man ever go straight through. But *we* go straight through. It five sleeps quicker than follow trade path."

That evening they laid their canoe away in a cave, and the

next morning they lifted their packs and began the climb up the eastern slope of the Divide.

For nearly half the distance there they followed an old moccasin trail which the Chilcoots had used on their raids against the Blackfeet. It took them steadily higher and higher, with few dips into the canyons. The trail dimmed to nothingness, but Itai-Po pushed boldly ahead, with a surety that amazed David. They made lean-tos of limber pine branches at night, and put moss into their moccasins against the jagged stones and increasing cold; and David kept his rifle free to guard against the huge, lumbering silvertips.

They climbed out of the hardwoods into the big conifers, where the gray crow was at home; out of these into the storm-gnarled tamarack and ground pines; then up, across the heather terraces, which were vivid splashes of red-and-yellow flowers, with innumerable butterflies playing over the heather. Above these terraces they came abruptly into the high snow lands, where the wind was keen as a whiplash; where they walked through clouds and watched storms sweeping through the valleys a mile below them.

Finally they came to a level boulder field, half a mile across, with an acre-sized lake of steel gray water in the middle of it. A small brook flowed out of the lake toward the east, and on the other side a brook flowed toward the west, and they knew they were standing on the Great Divide itself. It was a wild, elemental scene, with white ptarmigan chortling among the boulders, and the plaintive whistle of Picas drifting to them ventriloquially. In every direction they looked out across an immense sweep of ranges, *neves*, and endless miles of ever-green forestry.

As they dropped down the west slope, they seemed to be entering a different country altogether—a warm, moist, luxuriant land. Different songsters flitted in the bushes, the trout had different markings, the stag fern and maidenhair were strange and exotic. The winds no longer carried the chill of the Mackenzie Barrens, but were mild, soft Chinooks, charged with the moist warmth of the Kuro Siwo.

It was David's first trip into the country of the Western slope, and his days were filled with new experiences. The weather seemed perpetually on the verge of rain, and a cloud as big as a thumbnail would bring a heavy shower. Just below timberline they ran into slender spruce no bigger around than a saucer, but which reached up a hundred and fifty feet. From a cave shelter, where a storm drove them, they saw stances of these spruces whipping in the gale like fields of tall grain. As they dropped down and down, they passed through timber belts where the trees towered two hundred and fifty feet high. Still lower, they came to giant cedar and yellow spruce which made saplings of the timber above.

At the first sizable creek they struck, they saw a grizzly scooping out salmon that were spent and bruised raw by their long run from the Pacific.

"He fool, that bear," Itai-Po remarked. "Scoop out too many fish. Watch 'em flip-flop; grin. Plenty fish bring fish hawks circling. Fish hawks bring Indian. Indian shoot bear. Ha!"

"Bears and men, too," David observed. "Prospector tom-rocks gold. *Hiyu* gold. Throws hat in air. Yells 'Hi-yippety yip!' Bush-sneak hears. Bellies up close. Shoots man."

Itai-Po looked at him. "Mebbe prospector—this McPherson man, huh?"

David shrugged. "Mebbe so. Mebbe so. We wait-see."

They followed down the headwaters creek to a small river. There the Blood struck a fresh moccasin trail, backtracked it, and found a canoe cached under some riverbank ferns. After setting the canoe to water, he tied some knots in a strip of babiche and put the string on a flat rock, along with a fine hunting knife and a pound of trade tobacco.

"Canoe belong Caribou Indian," he explained to David. "String knots tell him we took canoe. Pay him with knife and tobac'. You *kumtux*?"

They placed a hollow rock in the canoe prow, laid in some live coals, and put damp moss on these, to make a smudge and keep the mosquito clouds away. Then they shoved off, down the unknown western river.

Forty miles downstream they came to a triple fork and here struck the old trade trail which they had followed through the foothills. Turning north on the trail, they pushed ahead all one day and night and the next day; and that evening, just fourteen days from the time they had left the Mounted post, they came to their journey's end—the point which Kirke had indicated on his sandbar map across the mountain.

At the mouth of a little creek, whose silty water whispered of gold alluvium upstream, a larch tree had been stripped of its branches and at the top of this lobstick an old shirt fluttered conspicuously. It was a lonely prospector's way of drawing the attention of any travelers and making sure they would not go by without visiting him.

David motioned at the lobstick. "Here we find prospector called Sock-Eye Sullivan, Itai-Po. Here we find out if our trip is fool chase or not."

IV

AT Sullivan's diggings, a hundred yards up the creek, they lifted out their canoe and David looked around at the prospector's camp in the little birch glen. It was a typical sourdough's place, with only the raw necessities of a wilderness existence: a lopsided tent, a clothesline strung between two trees, ore specimens tossed here and there, a litter of broken tools, a homemade stone stove under the flap front of the tent, a pet marmot that scurried under a log at the sight of strangers, and a freshly killed deer hanging in a bent-over birch.

At the diggings just up the creek, a burly, red-whiskered man was tom-rocking away, talking to himself as he worked. Presently he paused to rest, looked around and saw the two visitors. The shovel dropped from his hands and he came splashing down to greet them.

"Gosh a'mighty!" he spluttered, drop-jawed in surprise. "Comp'ny! Sock-Eye Sullivan, you're a born lucky malamute! Hello, strangers! Where might you be a-goin', and who might you—Why, I'm a pigeon-toed coyote if it ain't Davy Kirke! Davy, you ornery dog, is't really you or just your spook? What the blazes are you a-doin' way over here acrost the Rockies from where you belong? My blessed eyes—hand me your front hoof, Davy, for an honest-to-goodness shake."

His joy was pathetic. He shook hands with both of them several times over and then set about rustling up a meal, all the while keeping up a spate of talk.

"You got any t'baccy, son? I'm run out. And what time of the year is't, anyway?"

"Yes, I'll give you a couple pounds of tobacco. As for the date, this is the eighteenth."

"August, I s'pose?"

"Yes," David replied, himself amazed.

Over their early supper he eased the talk around to the matter which had brought him across the mountains. "Still trying to find that mother lode, are you, Sock-Eye? This makes your

fourth year. You didn't come across to Bear River post for supplies this summer, and I took a long chance on your still being
here. You must have stuck close this season.''

Sullivan nodded to the last question. "Mighty close. Didn't
leave at all. No, I ain't found the lode yet, but the tom-rockin'
here is purty rich."

"I suppose you have company often?"

"Comp'ny!" Sullivan snorted. "They ain't half a dozen people in two hundred miles. I seen one pusson in three months, I
have.''

"Who was he?" David asked casually.

" 'Nother sourdough. He struck a durn nice lode over in this
country last spring. Was goin' out, he was, and get help. He hit
acrost the mountains from here."

"So he'd struck it, had he? What made him tell you about
that?''

"Why, us prospectors don't keep mum to each other about
our strikes. It's the hatchet-and-pencil gentry that we don't dass
allow to get wind of any good lode or placer we find. In gold
country they's always bush-sneaks around that 'ud ax a man for
a goose quill of dust.''

"Why didn't this sourdough drop down west to Siwash Fork,
instead of crossing the mountains?"

"Wull, he was a-carryin' a nice poke out, and the Siwash
Fork route has got a bad name. He was by hisself, and he didn't
have no weapons 'cept a grouse gun."

Very casually David asked, "You didn't know him, did you,
Sock-Eye? What was his name?"

"I knowed him well, Davy. He and me worked right alongside each other once, on a pair of fractions down in Kootenay.
Sort of a foot-loose, homeless feller, he was. Rough-lookin',
but gentle as they come. Some people they call him 'Sumdum'
and others they call him 'Red.' His last name it was McPherson.''

David jerked a little. But he refused to jump to conclusions.

"What sort of a man was this McPherson, Sock-Eye?" he
asked, "Can you describe him for me?"

"Wull, he was big and bony, and about forty year old. Harmless sort of pusson, he was, like I said."

Still, David would not let himself take anything for granted.
In the length and breadth of British Columbia there might well
be a dozen big, bony McPhersons. The man whom Sock-Eye

had known and the man who'd been murdered at the Shannon place across the Rockies might not be the same person at all.

He reached into his pack and pulled out the old felt hat and corduroy coat which he had brought along. "Take a look at these, Sock-Eye. Do they mean anything to you?"

Sullivan looked at the clothes, blinked his eyes, and swore. "Why, them's the identical duds that Sumdum was a-wearin'."

Itai-Po grunted. Slowly David put the hat and coat back into his pack. Sock-Eye looked from one to the other, puzzled and frowning.

"What's up, Davy? What've you been pokin' all them questions at me for?"

David lit his pipe and said quietly, "McPherson was murdered, Sock-Eye. This summer. Across in my country. Just ten miles from the Mounted post."

Sullivan jumped to his feet excitedly. "You're lyin', Davy. You can't mean that. Sumdum McPherson dead—killed—Why, there wa'n't a dog that'd bite him, or a man alive that didn't take to him like a brother. I don't believe it!"

"But it's true, Sock-Eye," David said. "I tell you, McPherson was murdered. Those holes in his coat are bullet holes. He was shot in the back, along a riverbank, one Sunday, and his body was thrown into Bear River. The party that did it is somewhere on this green earth, and I'm out to get that party."

"I'd kill him bare-handed, I would," Sullivan snarled.

"I had only two clues," David went on. "I learned his name from an old Telegraph Creek grub list in his hatband; and I found a gun near where he was shot—the weapon that was used to kill him. I myself had given that gun to a family there on Bear River, the Shannons. They're cheechakos, from the East; Esther Shannon and her younger brother.

"They told me that McPherson had spent the night, his last night on earth, at their place. They also told me that they had in their possession McPherson's eight thousand dollars in dust and nuggets. They said McPherson had left the gold with them because he felt he was being followed; and also that he had borrowed their rifle for that same reason. They said they hadn't heard of his getting shot, or they would have reported at once about the gold."

"Sounds like a flimsy yarn to me," Sullivan interrupted. "A 'mighty flimsy, I'd say."

David nodded. "That's how people over there thought. When

young Paul Shannon innocently gave it away about their having the gold, the rumors began flying, and tempers started to get ugly. So I recommended that the Shannons be arrested and given trial. The evidence for a murder case was not sufficient, and they were acquitted."

"I'd have hung 'em!" Sock-Eye asserted flatly.

David said nothing to that. Across his mind jigged the bitter memory of Esther Shannon closing the door in his face; and the anguishing thought that they would be gone, she and Paul, before he could possibly get back from this wilderness trip.

"Let's suppose," he went on, "that the Shannons told the truth. Then somebody else killed McPherson. For what? A grudge? He didn't look to me like a man who would make enemies. For his gold? I didn't quite believe so. A simple robbery, without the danger and hullabaloo of a murder, would have been more credible. So I asked myself, 'Exactly why was McPherson being shadowed and why was he killed?'

"His poke of gold gave me an idea. It wasn't flour gold or smooth nuggets. It was rough nuggets—which meant that it hadn't been washed along very far from the mother lode. It might well be lode gold itself. I reasoned that maybe McPherson had made a strike and had picked up what gold was handy, and then started out for help. According to what you've just told me, McPherson really did make a strike. So we're on solid ground so far.

"Now, let's do a little more supposing, Sock-Eye. Suppose you were McPherson, and you'd just made a good strike. What would you have done?"

"I'd have busted in to a land office and had it registered. Then I'd have got me three-four good partners and hotfooted it right back here."

David nodded. "That's what any sourdough would have done. But in country this wild, with so many creeks and canyons all looking alike, how would you make sure that you'd know the way back to your Discovery claim?"

"Why, I'd make me a map," Sock-Eye said. "I'd make me a birch bark map that'd take me right back to the—" He broke off, staring open-mouthed at David. Finally he burst out, "Why, Davy, that's it! That's why they killed Sumdum! He had a map. They did't hanker for his poke so much; it was the map they wanted!"

"That's what I suspected. And when I examined his coat and saw where he'd sewed a secret pocket into the lining and somebody had ripped it open, I felt pretty sure of my guess. Furthermore, this would account for their killing him. You see, they couldn't take over the Discovery unless he was safely out of the way.''

''That's abs'lutely so. But how did you know that Sumdum made his strike over in these parts?''

''Some more figuring,'' David said. ''There's very little nugget gold on the east side of the Rockies, and besides, McPherson was a stranger over there. I reasoned that he'd come from somewhere across the Divide, on the old trade trail, thinking it was safer than the Siwash Fork route. So I decided to come over here with Itai-Po and look around. I counted heavy on you being acquainted with him. And you were!''

Sock-Eye helped himself to more of David's tobacco. ''You figger this was a one-man job?''

''No. Certain features about it make me believe it was two or three men. I also believe they came back over here and are working that lode now.''

Sock-Eye pushed his hat back and scratched at his tousled hair. ''But dang it, Davy, I don't know where Sumdum's strike is at. He didn't tell me and I didn't want him to. All I know is it was somewhere up in the Left-Over.''

''Where and what is that?'' David asked.

Sock-Eye jerked a thumb to the north. ''It's a country up yon; a jumble of rivers and hills and every whichnot, between two big ranges. Somebody said that when the Lord got finished creatin' the earth, He hadda lot of cricks and broken mountains and wild timber left over, so He just chucked it all into that region to get shut of it, and that's why it's called the Left-Over.''

''How does a person get there?''

''You just follow up this river and over the watershed, and you drop down into it. But if you're thinkin' of ferretin' out them killers in that country—'' He shook his head sadly. ''You'd not have a Chinyman's chance, Davy. It's the dangedest mullock of cricks, canyons, moraines, mountains, deep woods, windfall, and rocks you ever saw. Not even the Goat-Eater Ind'uns go in there. A needle in a haystack 'ud be easy huntin' compared with findin' the party as killed Sumdum.''

David thought unpleasantly of how swiftly his furlough was draining away, but he said doggedly, ''Itai-Po and I'll find those killers. We've got to, if it takes all winter.''

'' 'Nother thing,'' Sock-Eye added. ''They's something wrong with that country up yon. Fellows that go into the Left-

Over come out shakin' hands with the willows. The Left-Over breaks 'em. Sumdum was a bush-loper all his life and he wasn't in there long, but he was half batty when he got out to here. Me, I wouldn't go in there for all the gold you could shake a stick at. People say it's full of h'ants and queer doin's . . .''

V

Two full weeks later David made a lonely camp one night at a fork where two canyons led back into the eastern mountains. He cooked supper for two, then sat down to wait.

Itai-Po should have returned to the rendezvous. He had gone up the north canyon two days before, to clean up a maze of creeks leading out of a big moraine. David had taken the south canyon and ferreted it out to his complete satisfaction—and disappointment.

The two weeks had passed without yielding one sign of any recent party in the Left-Over. Working northwest up the trunk river, David and the Blood scout had turned into every branch stream and followed them back to the first portage, where a party would have left signs for Itai-Po to read. But they had found nothing.

They had paddled from twilight to twilight, with only two or three hours of sleep at night. They had chopped their way through the piled-up, tangled windfall of centuries, and fought white waters, and felt seeping into them the loneliness and nameless fears of a country wilder and more elemental than anything they had ever imagined.

Again and again in the lonely hours of those weeks, David had thought of the bitter charges that Esther had flung at him. When he had planned this long wilderness trip, it had been with the hope that he would return with evidence which would completely free her and Paul from suspicion, and that she would then understand about the trial. But now he could have no hope of any such end to the trip. She would be gone. All that would remain would be the barren satisfaction of clearing up the murder of Sumdum McPherson. And even that was beginning to look like a fool's hope.

Itai-Po did not return at dark. In an hour the moon rose, and still no Itai-Po. David ate a solitary supper and sat beside the fire, smoking. Sometime after midnight a shadow glided out of the canyon silently, and Itai-Po crouched down across the dying fire.

David looked sharply at the Indian's swarthy face, and his heart leaped. *"You've found 'em!"*

Itai-Po nodded. "Struck trail at dusk time. Didn't follow the camp. We find that tomorrow. Easy. Tonight—sleep."

At dawn they hid their canoe, smoothed out all signs of their camp, and hurried up the north canyon to Itai-Po's first "find." It was a shoe track, so faint and rain-obliterated that David himself would never have noticed it. At a swift pace the Indian led him on up the canyon, pointing casually to signs where David saw nothing.

Four miles above the forks the canyon opened out into a dark, oval valley, five miles long and a half-mile wide. They went cautiously now, knowing that the camp was close. A mile farther on, Itai-Po stopped suddenly, with a warning gesture.

Through the buckbrush David caught a glimmer of white, the dirty white of a canvas tent. He started forward to get a better look, but Itai-Po clutched his arm.

"Mole-eye! Look!" he ejaculated in his own tongue. "A papoose could see a trap so clumsy!"

Two juniper bushes leaned almost together across the path. Between them a green cord was stretched, so that an unwary intruder would run into and break it. Cautiously Kirke and Itai-Po followed the string. It led over a rock ledge. They looked over, and then at each other.

"Huh!" the Blood snorted. "Warning! You run into string, rattle-pan drop on rock, make *hiyu* noise, warn 'em!"

"That settles another thing," David thought to himself. "No decent prospector wants to be warned *against* company. He hangs out his shirt so that folk won't miss him. That green cord means we're at the end of our trail!"

They crept away from the path and bellied through the undergrowth toward the camp. It was newfound, on a little spot thirty steps above the stream. The tent was large—a three-man affair. No one was about, but on up the valley they heard the ring of pickax against rock.

"We go see," Kirke directed.

They backed off, circled, and from a jumble of boulders and juniper, looked down upon the diggings. The Discovery was a quartz vein at the foot of an eroded bank, which showed ten foot of gray gravel on top, then a stratum of serpentine rock, then a layer of black rock which carried the quartz. The gravel bar in the streambed was rich with free gold that had trickled out, but an eighteen-foot tunnel had been thrust into the hillside to follow the richer quartz vein.

Three men were working in and about the tunnel. Through his Service glasses David scrutinized them closely.

One of the trio was a *métis*, an Assiniboin half-breed. While he worked, he kept glancing sharply into the timber and rock tangles all around. His movements were furtive and sinuous, like those of a woods animal. The other two men were whites. One of them, rather small, with spindly legs and long arms, had features that suggested Chinese blood. The third was a big, bushy-whiskered man somewhat resembling Sock-Eye Sulli-van—except that Sock-Eye's honesty and simple human kind-ness were no part of his makeup.

All three were strangers to David. He handed the glasses to Itai-Po, and said, "D'you know 'em?"

The Indian studied the three a little while, then lowered the binoculars. " 'Un't know two whites," he said. "But the *métis*, him Charlo Daoust. People say he once kill man over at Mc-Murray Landing. He woods-loper, sharp as mountain cat. Twig broken, leaf upset, he see."

David nodded. The makeup of the party was clear enough. The whites were city outcasts; the 'breed was their reliance in the wilderness. His cunning was the reason no signs had been left on the trunk-river portages.

"Look, Itai-Po," he cautioned, "this bush-wise Charlo Daoust, he mebbe find out somebody's around. That bad dan-ger. You're bush-wise, too. You got to keep him from finding out. Got to show that a Blood is a better bush-shadow than an Assiniboin 'breed. You *kumtux*?"

Itai-Po nodded to the challenge.

David went on, "You and me see green cord. We know what that means. We know these men guilty. But white-man's court don't know. Court won't take our yes-word. You *kumtux* what court-sure evidence means? Good. We got to get court-sure evidence. Then we arrest. Not before."

Itai-Po chewed thoughtfully on a birch twig. "How get this court-sure evidence?"

It was a question easier asked than answered.

That afternoon, while Itai-Po lay watching the three men at the lode, David slipped into their camp and gave it a thorough searching. He found no map, no writing, no clues of any sort. He knew then that they had carefully destroyed every bit of evidence connecting them with their crime. They had surely burned McPherson's map and made one of their own, leaving nothing whatever to link them with that brutal killing across the mountains last summer.

That evening, while the three were eating supper at their camp, Itai-Po slipped up to within a dozen steps and listened to their talk. It was David's hope that they would talk about McPherson and betray themselves out of their own mouths. But evidently that subject was taboo. When Itai-Po came back at the end of an hour, he reported that they had not once mentioned the killing or the prospector.

In a side canyon that evening, at the cave camp which he and Itai-Po had established, David sat up most of the night, a dead pipe in his teeth, trying to plan how he could get sure evidence against three killers who had left *no* evidence. He had run them down; he knew within himself that they had murdered Sumdum McPherson for this rich lode they were working; but bringing them to justice and clearing the Shannon name—that was something else again.

As he sat there, the appalling loneliness and savagery of the Left-Over weighed on him. The eerie wail of wind through the rock fissures and the black spruce tops, the play of moon-shadows on the needle-carpeted moss, the distant, ghostly cries of night animals—all these made him understand why the Left-Over had so frightening a name. Could he somehow make use of the uncanny spirit of that wild, lonely valley? he wondered. Could he somehow use it to strike terror into the hearts of men whose consciences were already burdened with a murder?

VI

ONE morning Murph Mecklin straightened up from his work and leaned for a moment on his pick handle. He looked at Chink Greever and Charlo Daoust, who were shoveling behind him. He looked at the leaden sky and held out his hand to feel for rain.

On the north slope something cracked sharply. Mecklin whirled around to look. As his glance went up the slope, his throat split in a yelp of warning. Daoust and Greever jerked upright and would have run for their rifles but Mecklin's frenzied gesture stopped them. They looked.

Down the north slope a ten-ton boulder came careening

straight toward them, gathering speed and lesser boulders as it rolled. For a split-wink none of the three could stir. Daoust recovered first. With the agility of a big cat he sprang toward the tunnel mouth, out of the path of the boulder. Mecklin, with Greever on his heels, hurled himself into the buckbrush and went crashing through it like a panicky bull moose.

A few seconds afterward, with a roar that shook the ground and filled the gorge with the dust of splintered rock, the boulder slide swept over the place where the three men had been working and piled up in the streambed below.

When the last trickle of gravel had subsided, the men approached the spot gingerly and eyed the destruction.

Mecklin shuddered and swore. "That was by the skin of our teeth, Greever. I heard a noise up there like a stick breakin' and looked up and there come that roll. If I hadn't heard that crack, we'd all be dead right now! Mashed flatter'n a bodewash chip!"

"Dry up!" Greever snapped. "You blow off too much. Let's find out what started that boulder rollin'. It was a balancer; I seen it up there several times, but it always looked solid enough to me."

They climbed up the slope to where the big boulder had "balanced" on a pedestal of slate. The immediate cause of its toppling was plain enough; it had been hit by a smaller rock, which had bounded down the slope in ten-foot jumps and broken into fragments at the impact. But what had started that smaller one?

"Likely a grizzly huntin' for mice," Mecklin rasped. "Daoust, get busy and find his tracks, and we'll shoot him."

With Daoust leading, they tracked the smaller boulder up into a thicket of salmon berries and found where it had lain. Daoust looked for signs through the thicket; he circled; he came back to the boulder site, dropped on hands and knees, and searched all around.

"Well," Greever demanded impatiently, "where's the grizzly's tracks? Let's trail him; we don't want a hunnert tons of boulders a-pilin' down on us ever' time a blasted bear gets hungry."

Daoust stood wide-legged, puzzled. "No bear signs. No bear. No signs a-tall. Nothing! I don't *kumtux*."

"Mebbe it just started rollin' natural," Mecklin concluded. "Let's get to work cleanin' away that rock mess. We'd better cut a channel through it, or the crick'll back up into our tunnel and flood us out."

Dismissing the incident as just some freak happenchance,

they went back to the lode. But all that morning and afternoon their nerves were taut and jumpy over their hairbreadth escape.

That night, as they were going down the creek to camp, a footlog across a forty-foot chasm gave way just as Charlo Daoust, leading, stepped upon it. By a great leap backward he caught an overhanging bush and saved himself from an ugly fall down on the jagged, water-lashed rocks below.

"You built that footlog yourself," Greever snarled at the 'breed accusingly. "You ought to've done a safe job, 'stead of makin' a mantrap like that. If you'd broke your dirty neck, 'twould have served you right."

"I fix footlog good," the 'breed retorted angrily. "Good and strong. We use it two-three weeks now, and it didn't fall."

"Strong—blazes! Didn't you just see it break?"

A hot quarrel sprang up between the two. Mecklin finally stepped between them and ordered them to shut up.

"Mebbe these rains started the footlog slippin'," he suggested. "Let's get on to camp and eat. Mebbe that'll make us feel better."

In the dead quiet of one o'clock that night, with no rain falling or whisper of breeze blowing, a dead spruce snag thirty feet from their tent suddenly crashed full length to the ground, missing their tent by a scant eight feet. They sprang up, lit the lantern, and looked at the wreckage.

"Darned funny about that tree fallin' down on a still night like this," Mecklin remarked, his voice low and shaky. "Don't look natural-like to me. We've had high wind, and we've had rain, and we've had 'em both together, but that snag stood there solid as the brass gatepost of hades!"

Chink Greever jerked out, "We're hoodooed, that's what. They's a hoodoo a-workin' on us. Three times now—"

"Shut up that hoodoo stuff!" Mecklin cut him short. "That sort of talk'll give us all the willywams in mighty short order. This spruce a-fallin' down was just another accident. Go to bed, you big, whiskered baby. What're you shiverin' about? I thought you had guts!"

They crawled into their blankets again and tried to sleep.

When morning came and the gray shadows lifted from the spruces, the three ate breakfast and went up the gorge to their digging. As they cut a channel through the rock debris, one of them was on the lookout all the time, watching for they knew not what.

It happened late that afternoon. They had cut the channel

through and gone back to the tunnel, to work inside of it. Just before twilight, when they were all three in the tunnel, Mecklin set a tiny powder blast under a stubborn rock. They backed up to the tunnel mouth and awaited the explosion nonchalantly—they had shot off a dozen similar charges.

It was Murph Mecklin again who yelled the warning, a second after the little charge went off. In the center of the tunnel, a staunch cedar upright, the key prop of their timbering, started skidding to one side at its base. It stopped against a rock, but the roofing timber no longer had solid support. It gave way slowly, writhing like a tortured thing, and the tunnel began caving in. Mecklin leaped outside into the buckbrush, and, like a flash, Daoust dived after him. But Greever, whose brain was as slow as a turtle's, did not entirely escape; his legs and hips were caught by the falling gravel and he lay pinioned there, yelling and thrashing.

Mecklin pulled him out, and the three of them stood speechless, dazed, looking at the ruined tunnel. Mecklin finally found his tongue.

"If I hadn't seen that upright slippin', we'd be buried alive in that hole. Greever, if you'd left that prop like I fixed it in the first place, 'stead of tamperin'—"

"I didn't tamper!" Greever snarled. "I never touched it. I suppose I tampered with that boulder, heh? And that footlog. And that dead spruce, heh? Tamper, nothing—we're hoodooed on this job."

Mecklin no longer tried to bolster up his two confederates. He needed bolstering up himself.

As they walked back to camp, they kept close to one another, glancing into the underbrush around them and clutching at their belt-guns when shadows flickered under the dark spruces. A subtle dread was weaving itself around them. The "accidents," one after another, were driving them toward panic.

At camp that evening another blow fell, a blow which could not possibly be set down as accident but had to be interpreted as the work of some hand, whether ghostly or human.

Mecklin was cooking supper and Daoust was cleaning their tools. Greever had just gone into the tent to stow away a couple of good-sized nuggets he had picked up at the lode. The two men outside heard him bellow suddenly, as if he had been struck a blow, and they leaped into the tent to see what had happened.

Frozen in his tracks, Greever stood holding the can in which they had put their dust and nuggets. "Look't!" he gasped hoarsely, thrusting the can at them. "Look't what our dust and nuggets have changed into."

Mecklin snatched the can from him and looked. Daoust looked—

The gold dust had changed to yellow sand, the nuggets to bits of heavy yellow gravel.

For an hour they sat in the darkness of their tent, rifles across their knees, and talked in whispers. It was Mecklin who first got hold of his jumping nerves and could think clearly. Gradually he managed to quiet Greever's panic and the half-breed's superstitious terror.

"Them accidents," he kept saying, "didn't just happen. They was staged. We ought to've seen that. Now this can business proves it. Somebody robbed us, the low-down carcajou. They's somebody around here, a-tryin' to get our lode."

They began laying plans. Courage came back to them with the thought that they were dealing with an enemy of flesh and blood. After supper, they put out the fire and lantern and rolled up in their blankets.

Half an hour later Daoust slipped out of his poke, crept noiselessly away from the tent, and faded into the blackness of the spruces. Greever and Mecklin lay listening.

"That 'breed'll get 'em," Greever whispered. "There ain't a white man, 'breed, or Ind'un alive that's his match in a woods. Daoust'll spot the sneaky devil out there and give him a knife between the ribs."

But in the gray of morning Daoust slipped back into camp and reported that during his all-night vigil, prowling and circling through the surrounding woods, he had not heard or seen one sign or whisper of an enemy.

"Then, we'll go after 'em and hunt 'em down," Mecklin rapped. "We're bound to strike their trail somewheres, and we'll hang onto it till we see the color of their bloody insides."

After breakfast they stuck their belts full of cartridges and started combing down the valley, swinging back and forth from rimrock to rimrock, and beating thoroughly through the thick woods. Daoust, ranging ahead, covered the ground like a dog coursing for a cold trail.

They combed the narrow valley to a point eight miles below their camp and found nothing. The next day they hunted up valley, but found no sign of their unknown, shadowy enemy. When they tramped home at nightfall, they were morose and quarrelsome, their nerves at the breaking point. Mecklin alone still kept a grip on himself.

"A whoop your hunch was worth!" Greever snarled at him. "Exceptin' ourselves, there ain't been a live person in this gorge since McPher—I mean, exceptin' ourselves. Daoust would've seen signs. We're hoodooed, Murph Mecklin, I tell you. Hoodooed *and worse!*"

That night, at the same hour that the dead spruce had fallen, Daoust awakened his two partners and bade them listen.

A faraway, hollow noise came echoing down the gorge. It rose high-pitched, died to a whisper, and rose again—weird, mysterious, and hair-raising.

"Wolf," Mecklin grunted, and tried to shrug his shoulders unconcernedly.

"No wolf!" Daoust flatly contradicted.

"Then what in blazes is it, if you know so much?"

" 'Un't know. Never heard animal or bird cry like that."

Greever sat shivering as the call rose and fell in its weird cadence. His teeth chattered; his courage melted into nerveless terror. A whir of night wings in a thicket made him shudder. A white owl brushing over his head brought him to his feet with an oath.

"That's the cry of a speerit!" he burst out, as the call started again. "Hear it! It's his ghost! McPherson's! He yelled identical like that when I up with the goose gun and killed—"

Mecklin's hand dropped to his belt and dragged out his heavy, snub-nosed revolver. "Shut up! You ever open your mouth ag'in about that doin's, you crybaby—just one word about it—and I'll make a ghost of *you*. That call is some kind of an animal, and the gorge is playin' tricks with the sound, that's all."

The next morning they stayed in camp, haggard and sleepy-eyed. Greever and the 'breed wanted to leave. They were for throwing everything away but their rifles and enough grub to get them out of the Left-Over. Mecklin alone kept his nerve. He laughed at their terror, though his laugh was hollow in his own ears. At sunny noonday he drove them up the valley to the Discovery, and set them to hard work to distract their minds.

Twilight came unexpectedly, as a pall of clouds whipped over the mountains and filled the deep valley with shadows. A few heavy drops of rain fell as they threw down their tools and started for camp.

Halfway there Daoust suddenly stopped. His quick ears had caught a noise in the purple spruce shadows up the right-hand slope. As they listened, breath bated, they heard a sound as of something running—parallel with them.

Greever jerked his rifle to his cheek and fired. With one accord, they raced up the slope through the buckbrush in the direction of the noise, shooting again and again into the bushes. The queer sound retreated, came nearer, played with them, led them on and on toward their camp, and then vanished.

They stumbled to the tent and lit the lantern. As the flame rose up and the glow of light widened till it lightened up the nearest trees, Greever pointed suddenly at an object at the edge of the light, a shadow-wrapped object that looked like the head and torso of a man.

Mecklin emptied his belt-gun at it. The object quivered and fell. They went over to it, fearfully, and saw that it was a battered felt hat and a coat riddled with bullet holes.

"Gosh a'mighty, it's McPherson's coat and hat!" Greever stammered hoarsely. "He's been here, he has. He's been h'antin' us. *He* caused them accidents. Only a speerit could've changed that gold to w'uthless sand!"

From the torn lining of McPherson's coat something white fell out and fluttered to the ground. Mecklin grabbed it up, glanced at it.

"Why—uh," he gulped, his iron nerve deserting him at last, "it's a n-n-note—f-from McPherson."

Greever snatched the note away and stared at it. "Writ in his blood!" he cried brokenly. "Look't—in his own blood! Says we killed him without warnin'. Shot him in the back. And worst of all, we killed him on a Sabbath!"

"It was you killed him!" Daoust cried at Greever. "Let his h'ant keep 'way from me. I didn't—"

Greever whirled on him. "You was there, too! You was a part of it all—You're as guilty as me—"

"Oh no, we ain't," Mecklin put in. "It was you as shot him, Greever, and it's you he's h'antin'. He's a-want-in' your life for his own, and he'll never rest or let us be till you're dead, Chink Greever."

Snarling like an animal in a trap, Greever dragged out his belt-gun. "If you're thinkin' on shootin' me to get rid of his h'ant, I'll blow your brains out—"

There was a movement at the edge of the fire glow. A man's figure stepped out. A cool, level voice said, *"Gentlemen!"*

The three whirled around. Hardly ten steps away a tall, lean man stood looking at them, his rifle leveled; behind him was the half-naked figure of a Blood scout.

"Put your hands up!" the tall man ordered. "Drop that gun, Greever."

For a moment the three were too stupefied to obey. It took them a little time to realize that they were face-to-face with living men.

"I said, put up your hands!" David Kirke repeated, sharply. "One—two—"

With a yell, Charlo Daoust crouched and kicked at the lantern. Greever whipped up his gun and shot point-blank, in wild haste. A bullet from David's rifle tore through his heart before he could shoot again. As the lantern rolled on the moss and went out, Greever toppled backward, dead before he sprawled on the ground.

In the next second the camp was plunged into darkness. And in the next it was filled with the cries and oaths of a hand-to-hand fight.

David saw Itai-Po leap toward where Daoust had crouched. With an oath at his wrecked plans, he himself sprang forward, swinging a clubbed rifle at the dim form of Mecklin. The stock struck only a glancing blow, and then Mecklin locked with him, clutching his gun hand. They crashed against a tree, and the rifle fell. Locked in a wrestle, they pitched into the buckbrush, hands at each other's throats. They rolled over and over, clutching each other, smashing at each other's faces in blind fury. In the darkness they broke loose, sprang to their feet, and grappled; but they tripped over a mat of roots and fell again, still locked in a wrestle, and started rolling and slipping down the steep hillside.

At the creek edge they brought up against a boulder. David tore free and sprang to his feet. Mecklin scrambled out onto the gravel bar, leaped up, and David closed with him again. In the wan moonlight of the streambed they smashed at each other. David lunged at Mecklin, wrapped arms around him, picked him up bodily, and slammed him back against the boulder.

It was a jarring, paralyzing fall. Before Mecklin could shake off his daze, David was on top of him, pressing his face down into the gravel and bending his arms behind his back.

A shadow-silent figure moved out upon the gravel bar toward him. For a second David thought it was the Assiniboin half-breed Daoust, but then he saw that it was Itai-Po. He saw the glint of a long knife in the Indian's hand and saw the Indian wipe the blade on the leg of his deerskin trousers, and he knew that Charlo Daoust was dead. In that savage knife fight with the half-breed in the blackness, Itai-Po had killed his enemy.

"*Don't*, Itai-Po!" he ordered, as the Indian bent over Mecklin. "We don't put a man away unless we're forced to. We need this one alive anyhow—to take back with us, across the Divide. Help me tie him up."

VII

NEAR sundown of a brooding September day, a battered canoe nosed in to the landing in the whitewood clump on Bear River. David, Itai-Po, and their prisoner got out and trudged up the path to the Mounted post.

All three of them were weary and travel worn from the long, fast trip across the Divide. In the last two days and nights they had come a hundred and fifty miles without sleep or rest.

As they passed the Police stables, they heard a shout of astonishment, and Constable Dusty Goff came rushing out, a currycomb and brush in his hand, his eyes bulging.

"Great Jumping Jeerusalem!" he gasped. "Where'n consternation have you been, Sarge? And who's this mother's son with his hands tied?"

"Take him up to the butter-tub and lock him up safe, Dusty," David said. "See that he gets something to eat and a chance to sleep. Itai-Po will answer your questions. I want to report to Inspector Haley."

As he went on to the officer's cabin, he was remembering the deserted Shannon place that he had passed a little while ago and wondering where Esther and Paul were.

When he knocked at the cabin and went in, Inspector Haley looked at him in amazement—at his torn, muddy clothes, his unshaven face, and the other visible marks of his long wilderness trip.

"Good heavens!" Haley breathed. "I don't yet know where you've been, Kirke, but it surely was *somewhere*. Sit down. Was it the wild-goose chase you were afraid it might be?"

"I was lucky and I did all I set out to do," David said. "I cleared up the McPherson murder and brought back one of the killers."

Briefly he told the story of his and Itai-Po's patrol across the Rockies and into the unknown Left-Over. Of his original suspicions. Of the trip across and Sock-Eye Sullivan. Of the lode and the three murderers he'd found there, working it, without the slightest fear that the long arm of the Mounted would ever reach across a thousand miles of mountainous wilderness and bring them to justice.

"That's about all, sir," he finished. "Sullivan is in charge of that lode. If we can locate any of McPherson's people, Sullivan will get a quarter and they the rest. Otherwise, he can file for himself. Legally the gold that McPherson left with the Shannons belongs to them; he said it was to be theirs if he didn't happen to come back. It can be sent to them now, since their innocence has been proved."

Inspector Haley drew a deep breath. "It's all an astounding story, Kirke. As remarkable a patrol as the force ever turned in. I'll get off my report to headquarters at once." He was silent a moment, thrumming on the desk. "As for the gold that McPherson left with the Shannons, we won't have to send it to them. Just after you went away, Paul came down sick, and I had him brought in here to the post, where Dr. Whittier could look after him. He seems to be picking up a bit, but it's still touch and go."

David started a little. "You mean that Esther—Is she here?"

"Yes. We fixed up one of the *métis* cabins for them." He looked at David thoughtfully for a long moment. "I think I understand this whole sorry business, Kirke, except for one point. You say that all along you suspected that some bush-sneak gentry killed McPherson for his map. Why, then, did you have the Shannons arrested and brought to trial?"

"For their own safety, sir," David answered. "You know that everybody considered their story a flimsy one. Feeling against them was running pretty high, and it finally got so ugly that I had to do something. There's always an element that wants to take things into their own hands. I had to guard the Shannon cabin every night for a week. It seemed to me that an open arrest, trial, and acquittal was the only way to head off something dreadful."

"But why didn't you tell Esther this?"

"Before the trial she had troubles enough, sir, without my letting her know that on two different nights I stopped parties that were going to 'visit' her and Paul. And after the trial, she was so bitter that she wouldn't listen."

Haley thrummed on the desk. Finally he said, "I think I'll go down and talk to Esther, Kirke. I'm going to tell her myself all that you've told me. I don't think you're very good at tooting your own horn. I'm sure she'll want to see you and thank you. If you'll stay here, I'll send her up."

"Good heavens, not now, sir," David objected hastily. "Look how I look. I want to shave and dress—"

"That's something else you don't know about women," Haley remarked. "She's not interested in you as a fancy Dan. For her sake you went through two thousand miles of hardship and danger, and that's how you look, and that's how she ought to see you."

From the window David watched the inspector cross the police quadrangle and knock at one of the *métis* cabins by the freight-wagon trail. He was fagged out and sleepless, but he forgot all that as he watched the cabin. The slow minutes of his waiting seemed endless. He was shaken with the uncertainty and suspense, and when he saw Esther come out at last, he went across to meet her.

Faraway westward the sun was just inching down behind the massive ranges, and a sharp evening chill was creeping into the air. In the scattered clouds overhead, the long, strange shadows of the Rockies were shifting and weaving, like a slow panorama of the Western Prairies.

When he met Esther on the path beyond the barracks, she stood stock-still and looked at him, her brown eyes seeing and understanding the signs of the long patrol that he had made for her sake.

Presently she laid her hand on his arm and said, "Can you forgive me, David?"

He gulped a little at that and scuffed awkwardly at the gravel. "It was—uh, pretty bad for everybody concerned, but it's all past," he managed. The afterglow of the sun was tangled in her hair. He drew her arm through his. "Let's walk a little. There's so much I've got to tell you, Esther. It couldn't be said before, but I can say it now—if you'll listen."

During the twenties and thirties, George Marsh was a leading writer of tales set in the Hudson's Bay district of Canada. His most popular novel, Flash, the Lead Dog, *is highly regarded by aficionados of animal stories. Notable among his other novels are* Whelps of the Wolf, Valley of Voices, River of Skulls, *and* Vanished Men. *Marsh was also adept at capturing the mystery and grandeur of the Northern wilderness in his short stories. "The Valley of the Windigo," a chilling tale (in more ways than one) of an outlaw's encounter with the dreaded Windigo in the haunted valley of the Crees, is one example of his prowess; others can be found in his 1921 collection of stories,* Toilers of the Trail.

The Valley of the Windigo

George Marsh

FRANÇOIS Hertel, outlaw, grounded his canoe on the sand beach at Ptarmigan Lake House, leaped into the water, and swung the woman in the bow to the shore. Leaving her to hold off with a whip, the threatening post huskies from his own two dogs snarling defiance from the canoe, he went up to the trade house. Entering the whitewashed log store, the tall Frenchman found Campbell, the factor, alone.

"Bonjour!" said Hertel, shaking hands.

"Good day!" coldly returned the Scotchman, eyeing the stranger with frankly curious gaze, for French trappers were rare so far north as the Ptarmigan Lake country. When Hertel offered Canadian paper money in payment for tea, sugar, and flour, the factor's interest was further aroused.

"You've come far," suggested Campbell, fingering the bill Hertel handed him.

"Yes, we travel sence June."

"Where are you headin'?"

"I t'ink I traverse dees countree for trappin' groun'."

"Oh!" The thick eyebrows of Campbell rose.

"Ever travel this country before?"

"No, I alway' hunt de Height-of-Land countree, Saint M'rees water."

"What brought you so far north, then?" the factor quickly demanded, believing that he knew why this stranger had journeyed to the James Bay watershed, for in his desk lay a letter six months old warning the northern posts to keep a lookout for one François Hertel, wanted for murder at Coocoocache, on the Saint Maurice.

François Hertel shrugged his wide shoulders, looking Campbell fair in the eyes.

"I keel a man las' year at Coocoocache," he said quietly.

"You are François Hertel?" asked the factor, amazed at the admission.

"Yes, I keel de man who burn de cabane and tak' ma wife. Dey hunt me tru de long snow from de Saint M'rees to Grand Lac, but dey not tak' François Hertel. Dees spring I fin' her. She ees out dere wid de canoe."

Hertel pointed through the door to the shore, then turned fiercely upon the factor.

"De man I keel cum lak' de wolf in de night to tak' ma wife. W'at would you do?"

The frankness of the voyageur carried with it the aroma of truth. The factor knew men in the rough, and this one shaped up square; or else he was playing a game too subtle for the Scotchman's understanding. Still, the orders from Ottawa received in the Christmas mail were not to be lightly ignored.

"Hertel, if what you say is so, I don't blame you for getting your man and taking to the bush. But if it leaks out to Ottawa that you are trading here, I'm in a pretty mess."

"At Ottawa I am dead man," and Hertel handed the factor a soiled envelope. Campbell took from the envelope two folded sheets of paper. On the first was written:

"On March last it was reported to the authorities at Ottawa that the body of François Hertel had been found frozen on the Abitibi Trail, by Harricanaw Crees. Pierre, the trapper, who was at Flying Post, on Grand Lac, in January, must trap his fur in the James Bay country for a year or two.

"A FRIEND OF PIERRE."

Campbell was plainly mystified. Then he opened the other note. It was dated at Coocoocache on a letterhead of the Hudson's Bay Company, and ran as follows:

"To any Company man—

"The bearer, François Hertel, has long been a faithful employee of the Company on the Saint Maurice. One night, a year ago, in June, his house on the island at Coocoocache was burned down. At the same time Walker, a railroad contractor with a bad record, was seen paddling from the island to the construction camp. Failing to find the body of Hertel's wife in the ruins, we believed her thrown into the river to cover the crime. Hertel returned and obtaining proof of Walker's guilt, killed him and took to the bush. Last winter Hertel met two of the Government Police, who were on his trail, starving in a blizzard on Grand Lac, and at the risk of arrest brought them in to Flying Post. Out of gratitude, they reported at Ottawa that he had been found frozen on the Abitibi Trail, and wrote to Hertel at Coocoocache to that effect. Returning this spring to Coocoocache, Hertel found his wife, who had escaped from Walker in a canoe and been picked up by Vermilion River Crees. He leaves here for the north until the matter blows over, and carries an order on Company posts issued to Pierre Chapleau, to amount of $300.00. Please honor this order, against Coocoocache, and give him any help you can, as he is the best canoe man and hunter on the Saint Maurice. We think a good deal of him and believe him justified in what he did.

"ANDREW SCOTT, *H. B. C. Coocoocache.*
"J. MCCREADY, *H. B. C. Lost Lake.*"

"Well, if Jock McCready says you're all right, Hertel, it's good enough for me," said Campbell, returning the envelope. "I've put in some good years with old Jock at Fort Chimo and the Fading Waters. But you'll have to pass as Pierre Chapleau at the post here and keep away when the Crees are in for the trade. It won't do to have it leak out to Rupert House that you're here."

"T'anks, Meester Cameel, I understan'," and the Frenchman gripped the factor's hand.

"Now, you'll have to hurry to cruise out good trappin' grounds and net whitefish for your dogs."

"De free fur countree ees far from here?"

"The best of it is; some of my Crees trap clear over on Nottaway waters. You'll have to move lively to get your shack built before the freeze up. And mind you keep off trapped grounds. The Crees will wipe you out if you don't."

Hertel smiled good-naturedly at the warning. He knew only too well the law of the fur country that there shall be no trespass in another's valleys.

"Oh, by the way!" continued Campbell, "If you're not afraid of Windigo, Injun-devils, and such nonsense, there's a country over west that old Joe, my head man, can tell you about. You won't be running into any of the Crees over there; they won't go near it; they say it's full of evil spirits."

Hertel's keen face lighted with interest.

"W'ere ees dees countree?"

"It lies four or five days' travel straight west, on Harricanaw waters. The Cree name for this branch is Devil's River. I'll call Tom; he started to trap it once, but was almost scared to death and quit."

Presently a wrinkled Cree, aged in the Company's service, was smoking a pipe with Hertel and the factor.

"You know the trail to the valley of the Windigo, Tom?"

The Indian looked suspiciously at the two men, then nodded gravely.

"Good huntin' ground? No Injun trap that valley?"

The Cree shook his head. "No Injun hunt dere for long tam; too much devil. Plentee game dere, I t'ink."

"How far is it from here?"

"Four, five sleep."

"You make a map of the trail to the Windigo valley on this paper. Pierre is going to trap it this winter."

The Cree's small eyes widened in wonder at the daring of the stranger who would winter in the dread land of evil spirits, shunned by the Ptarmigan Lake Indians for years as they would shun the pestilence. He turned to Hertel in protest.

"De Windigo, he live in dis valley; he rob trap; kill you; eat you' squaw. It is ver' bad place." Closing his eyes, the Cree shook his head and shoulders as if to blot out the evil memory of the valley of the Windigo.

"Never mind, Tom, Pierre takes the risk. He's a medicine man in his country and has a charm for the devils. You show him how to get into the valley with this pencil and paper."

So, much against his will, old Tom proceeded to trace a crude map of the waterways through which ran the trail to the haunted valley of the Crees.

Hertel wished to lose himself—to disappear from the ken even of the fur posts. Campbell he could trust, but to the Crees, trading at the post, must be given a wide berth. How better, he thought, than to build his shack and run his trap-lines in the forbidden country, the land no Indian would enter? As for the Windigo and devils, he had a charm for the worst of them in the bark of his 30–30. That the evil spirits of the Crees traveled on four padded feet, and their pelts would bring good prices over Campbell's counter at Ptarmigan Lake he had little doubt. Hertel had spent his life in the Indian country and knew the Cree makeup—his superstition and childlike belief in the supernatural. The hardy Frenchman had smiled as the old Cree gravely pictured the fate that awaited him and his Marie in the far-off valley. He had more than once heard a lynx or a wolverine, called Injun-devil, fill the forest with demoniacal caterwauling that would have frozen the blood of a superstitious Indian, and later, when he found the vocalist in his trap, had terminated the nocturnal voice culture by knocking the brute on the head with a club. For him the land of evil spirits held no terror.

The next day Hertel shoved his heavily loaded canoe from the beach at Ptarmigan Lake House, called a last *bonjour* to the factor, and with Marie handling the bow paddle, headed west. Day after day the voyageurs, following the Cree's map, toiled by river and lake and portage toward the Harricanaw headwaters, until at last their canoe floated on the Devil's River of the Crees. Then Hertel poled up the swift stream to its headwater lakes, where they were to net the whitefish needed for winter food for the dogs.

As they pushed upstream between timbered hills that rolled away to the blue horizon, the woman in the bow exclaimed with delight at the beauty of the valley vistas which every turn of the river opened to their eyes. And each outburst of admiration brought a low chuckle from the stern man toiling at his pole, as he thought how little Marie might appreciate the beauty of this land had she but known that these forests bathed in the August sun held in their silent depths terrors unspeakable; that this soft valley, asleep in the spell of the northern summer, was the lair of demons insatiable and pitiless. But François Hertel was a wise man and no baiter of women, so held his tongue.

While they netted and dried whitefish at the lakes, Hertel cruised the country for a good central location for his cabin. Everywhere he found signs of game. The shores of dead water and pond were trampled by moose which came to feed on lily roots and water grasses at sundown. The round-toed hoofprints of caribou trails networked the mud and moss of the muskeg beyond the valley. Along the streams mink and otter had left numberless tracks. Doubtless the hurrying feet of marauding marten, fox, and fisher would mark the first snow on the ridges. Truly the Cree trappers had given the country a wide berth, for never had the Frenchman seen such evidence of game.

Creeping south from the great bay the first September frosts roamed the valley, edging the river with the red of the willows, leaving a wake of birch ridges aflame against the somber green of the spruce. The rising sun lifting shrouds of river mist, rolled them back to vanish on the ridges, and later died on western hills, hung with haze.

Long before the first snowfall the Hertels moved from their tent to a cabin of spruce logs, chinked with moss, flanked by a mud-mortared stone chimney. Beside it a pile of birch logs and split wood was heaped high against the withering cold of the coming long snows.

Night after night through the October moon the geese honked south, racing the nipping winds which, following hard on the end of the Indian summer, swept the last leaves from poplar and birch. Then suddenly, between one sunset and dawn, narrows and dead water closed tight, an icy film crept out from the lake shores, and the subarctic winter shut in upon the lone cabin in the valley of demons.

By December the snow stood three feet deep in the forest levels, and for twenty miles the traps of Hertel lay set on the ridges and along the streams. Never had he reaped such a harvest of fur. Black-and-silver fox, marten, otter, and mink, all had found his traps; and the pelts of two gray wolves hung on his cabin walls.

The early dusk of one December day overtook Hertel at the far end of his lines down the valley, where at a lean-to, thrown together in the fall, he passed the night once or twice a week. Already that buccaneer of the forests, the wolverine, had discovered some of his traps and robbed him of valuable fur. So with the most hated enemy of the trapper loose in the valley, only constant patrolling of his lines could save him the loss of many a prized fox and marten.

Hertel cut his wood for the night, shoveled away the new snow with a shoe, and built a hot fire at the open end of the lean-to. He threw two whitefish to the husky which drew his small sled, boiled his tea and moose meat, then rolled himself in his warm rabbit skin blankets and slept.

It was a windless night, when the relentless fingers of the frost grip the timber till it snaps; when the shell of river and lake, con-tracting, splits with the boom of cannon, and the stars, glittering like myriad jewels, swarm the heavens. Above the black silhouette of far hills the aurora alternately glowed and died, then, in snakelike ribbons of light, streamed across the north.

Suddenly the husky, curled beside the blanketed figure by the fire, straightened, lifted his head, and sniffed the stinging air. Then, with hair bristling from ears to tail, he stood up while his shaggy throat swelled in a low rumble of warning to the one who slept.

Hertel stirred and thrust his head from the blankets.

"*Qu'avez-vous?* What's the matter with you?" he grumbled.

For reply the dog lifted his nose to the stars in a long howl. Thinking the husky had scented game, Hertel was again adjusting his blankets, when across the hushed valley floated a long cry, half howl, rising to a shrill scream, then dying slowly away.

Again the excited dog flung back the wolfish challenge of the husky to the unknown foe. Quieting the animal, Hertel, now thoroughly aroused, sat up in his blankets, listening intently for a repetition of the wail. Presently it was repeated, but this time farther up the valley.

The warning of the old Cree at Ptarmigan Lake flashed across his memory.

"De Windigo, he leeve een dees valley. He rob trap; kill you; eat you' squaw."

"*Bonsoir!* M'sieu' Weendigo!" called the imperturbable Frenchman as he reached for his Winchester in its skin case, and, drawing out the rifle, threw a shell into the barrel. Hertel had little fear of the thing that waked the white valley with its unearthly cries. For if it had lungs to howl, it had lungs and heart and stomach to stop his rifle bullet, or bleed at the thrust of his knife, and from the Roberval to the white Gatineau men knew how sure was the eye and what power lay in the right arm, of François Hertel. But, as he sat listening with straining ears, he cudgeled his brain to identify this prowler of the night. Lynx he had heard screaming like a child or a woman in agony; the wolverine, or Injun-devil, he had known to terrify superstitious French and Indian trappers by his maniacal caterwauling, and the howl of timber wolves on a fresh trail was familiar to his ears; but this was neither lynx, wolf, nor wolverine. What could it be? Then the Cree's flouted tale of the demons of the valley returned to mock him.

For one thing he was deeply thankful—Marie, in the shack with the dog, far up the river, had not been wakened. Now, moreover, she must never know the Cree tradition of the valley or he could not leave her again alone, with this yowling thing, beast or devil, to terrify her.

Hugging his replenished fire, Hertel smoked a pipe, wrestling with the mystery, as his dog whined and fretted beside him, then turned into his blankets.

The next morning he was swinging up the hard-packed river trail behind his sled thinking of the hot dinner awaiting him at the shack, when the dog stopped, sniffed in the snow, then turned sharply off the trail, upsetting the sled. Running up, Hertel found the husky nosing huge tracks which crossed the sled trail at right angles.

"Ah-hah! De Weendigo travel here, eh?" he exclaimed, studying the footprints. They were shaped somewhat like bear tracks, with deep indentations of long claws, but larger than any bear tracks he had ever seen, and, besides, bear were holed up for the winter. What beast, then, could have made that trail?

In the mental makeup of Hertel there was no trace of superstition. But the emotional Marie was keenly susceptible to the supernatural, and it was of her that he thought as he examined this strange trail in the snow. This thing must be kept from his wife if he wished to finish the winter in the valley.

As he shuffled through the soft snow beside the trail, one characteristic of the footprints was at once marked by his trained eyes—their shallowness. Despite his tracks, the beast was not heavy or he would have sunk deeper into the snow. Then, from the looks of the trail, he did not pick up his feet; he was a slow and lumbering traveler. The impulse to follow the tracks, run the beast down on snowshoes with his dog, and have it out with his 30–30 was strong in the hunter; but it meant another night away from Marie, and he was anxious to learn how it had gone with her at the shack. The unknown, beast or demon, would feel the sting of his 30–30 in good time. He would now hurry home.

The husky at the shack howled a welcome to the sled team, but when Marie opened the door Hertel knew from the look in her eyes that she, too, had heard the cries in the night.

"Oh, François!" she said weakly, and fell to sobbing in his arms.

It had been as he feared. Toward morning the whining dog had roused her. Opening the door, she heard the wail back on the ridge. The dog rushed savagely into the spruce, but was soon scratching at the door, badly frightened. Not until daylight, when the cries ceased, would the husky again leave the shack.

"Oh, *ma chérie*, she don' get scare' at one leetle lucivee dat shout lak de grand beeg somet'ing? I hear heem seeng down riviere. Eet ees not'ing."

In the end, Hertel convinced his wife that she had heard merely the customary shrieking of that great northern cat with tufted ears, the lynx.

But at heart the Frenchman was worried, for the length of his trap-lines compelled his frequent absence at night from the shack, and another shock like the last would reduce Marie to a state of mind forbidding his leaving her. It was clear that the brute must be hunted down and wiped out at once. No beast, Windigo, or devil should drive François Hertel out of free fur country like a craven Cree. This valley belonged to the one who could hold it by fair fight or foul. The wild blood of the *coureurs-de-bois* which coursed the veins of the Frenchman was up.

Next morning Hertel started under the stars, promising to return before sunset. He was following the shoulder of a long ridge on which were set *cabane* traps for fisher and marten. In a few of these the bait, as usual, had lured foraging moose-birds or squirrel interlopers to their doom. Resetting the traps, he continued on until a shattered *cabane* with the silent witnesses in the snow about it told a story which brought from his throat a cry of rage.

The jaws of the steel trap gripped the severed forefoot of a marten, while, strewn with tufts of fur, the blood-stained snow in the vicinity was trampled by the same tracks which had crossed the sled trail on the river.

Quickly freeing the excited husky from his harness, Hertel, fierce for revenge, abandoned his sled and took up the trail. With this plunderer loose on his trapping grounds, his long days of toil would be thrown away. He must either kill his enemy at once or drive him from the valley. Over ridges and horsebacks, down along frozen watercourses, the pursuing trapper followed the tracks in the snow. For a space the eager husky led, but at length the long snowshoe swing wore down the plunging dog, who sank deep at every leap, and he was content to follow in the better going of the packed trail of his master. On through the hours of the short December day toiled man and dog. If his quarry had not too long a start on him, Hertel knew he would overhaul it in the deep snow before the dusk, for, from the spacing and the depth of the tracks, the animal was traveling slowly. Twice it had stopped to rest, leaving an impression that baffled the woodcraft of the Frenchman. If he could only, for an instant, line up his rifle sights on this robber, he, François Hertel, would give him a *"bonjour"* of lead that would sicken him—evil spirit, Windigo, or furry thief—of the game of ruining the trapping of a Saint Maurice man.

Finally, in the afternoon, the trail led over the watershed ridges into a muskeg country to the south. The masked sun dipped behind western hills and dusk already hung in the thick timber, when the tracks brought weary man and dog to the edge of a wide barren.

Shortly the swift northern night would close in, and he was already
three hours' hard snowshoeing from the shack.

With hood thrown back from his unbelted capote, while, even
in the freezing air, the sweat coursed down the bold features, Hertel
searched with narrowed eyes the silent reaches of the white barren,
but in vain. He would have followed the trail deep into the moonlit
night, camped on it, and taken it up at daylight, but he had promised
to return to a woman who waited alone back in the valley. With a
sigh he turned homeward with his dog.

In the days following he found his mink and otter traps on the
streams around the headwater lakes unmolested, and reached the
shack without again crossing the strange trail.

On the night of his return Hertel was pulling at his after-supper
pipe, watching a piece of smoke-tanned moose hide take the shape
of a moccasin in the capable hands of Marie, when one of the dogs
stood up with a low growl, hair bristling like a mad porcupine's
quills. Then both huskies made for the door. Hertel sprang to the
low entrance of the shack, while his wife's dark face went white
with dread. Outside, the light from a frozen moon flooded the clearing in the forest. Hertel hushed the dogs, blocking the open door
with his body, then waited, tense as a bowstring. Shortly, from the
ridge back of the shack, drifted out over the still valley a wail, half
human, rising to a catlike scream piercing in intensity, then slowly
dying away.

The trapper closed the door, pushed aside the clamoring huskies,
and seized his caribou-skin coat and fur mittens.

"*Mon Dieu*, eet ees le diable! Eet ees le diable!" moaned the
terrified woman. "Don' leeve me, François!"

"Eet ees only de lucivee!" the man insisted as she clung to him.
"He shout beeg, dees lynx, but he seeng 'noder song w'en he feel
de bullet."

With such talk he strove to hearten the horror-stricken woman,
but Hertel knew that the dread cry that chilled the blood of all living
things that heard it was the howl of no lynx. What it was he was
going up into the black spruce to find out.

"I leeve de husky and shotgun. You safe wid dem." And em-
bracing the hysterical girl, he closed the door against the dogs, who
were useless in a still hunt, stepped into the thongs of his snowshoes, and started up the ridge.

The muscles of Hertel's face set stone hard as he hurried in the
direction from which had come the cry. Tonight his enemy should
not escape him. The beast was not more than a mile or two back in
the "bush," and in the deep snow the trapper knew that he could

give any four-footed creature in the North that much start and run
him down before dawn, for no dog runner from Lake Saint John to
Flying Post on the Ottawa headwaters could take the trail and hold
it from François Hertel. Beast or devil, whatever he was, he left
tracks in the snow to follow. Beast or devil—and there had been
enough in the last few days to sway a mind less balanced, to shake
nerves less steady, than Hertel's—if it made tracks in the snow and
howled at night, there was flesh and blood for his bullet and knife
to find. If neither lead nor steel could tear its vitals, then Hertel was
beaten. It was Windigo or demon, as the Cree had said, and he
would slink out of the valley like a whipped husky. So ran the
thoughts of the desperate Frenchman as he mounted the ridge.

At length he stood on the crest of the hill overlooking the frozen
river valley lit by the low moon, when the eerie wail lifted from
the black forest in a creek bottom below him.

Hertel glanced at the action of his rifle and broke into a run. As
he swung swiftly through the soundless forest, ghostly shapes of
snowshoe rabbits faded before him into the white waste; a snowy
owl, disturbed in his hunting, floated off like a wraith.

He had traveled some distance when suddenly he ran into the
familiar trail of the beast at the edge of a spruce swamp.

"Now," muttered the hunter, "you run lak snowshoe rabbit,
M'sieu' Weendigo, or dees tam François Hertel get you."

Fear of the hated thing was not in him. The raw lust for battle
made his blood hot as he plunged forward on the trail. Again rose
the cry, this time nearer. His quarry had neither scented nor heard
him, for plainly he was not traveling. But already the wind had
shifted and, to the chagrin of the trapper, the moon now traversed
a thickening sky where the stars grew dim. Hertel cursed under his
breath, for without light the tracks would be lost in the gloom of
the spruce. He was following stealthily now, lifting his feet to
muffle the click of his shoes, his muscles tense as springs for the
swift action which sight of the beast would loose.

Finally, from the top of a hardwood knoll, his keen eyes swept
a beaver meadow some distance below, to make out, entering the
thick scrub at its edge, a dark shape. The rifle flew to his shoulder.
Once, twice, three times the silence was shattered; then the trapper
ran as only one born in the North can run on snowshoes. At the
spot where the beast had disappeared there was no blood sign on
the snow, but the lopped branch of a fir told by how little the snap
shot in the dim light of the forest had missed its mark.

Plunging ahead, he took up the trail, less distinct now, in the
masked light of the moon and stars. If he were to see his game

again, he had no time to lose. The trail now doubled back toward the swamp, and the moon and stars were soon gone. The frenzied hunter was forced to bend low to distinguish the tracks which zigzagged through low cedar and spruce. Time and again he tripped and fell as he forced his way headlong through the brush on the flank of the swamp. Then he ran into a network of tracks leading in all directions, utterly obliterating the fresh trail he followed. The wily brute had doubled back to his starting point that night, where his trail would be lost. The game was up.

Soon even his own back tracks were indistinguishable, so with a wide circle through the swamp the disappointed trapper turned homeward. But in his defeat there was ground for hope. He had seen the thing in the life, unmistakably; shot at it, and learned that it feared the man on its trail. Instead of raging at him with teeth and claws, or loosing upon its helpless victim the black terrors of the old Cree's tale, this Windigo, devil, or what you will, had traveled like a bull caribou for the safety of the swamp. Elated at the thought, the Frenchman laughed loudly; beast or evil spirit, it had no magic for the rifle bullet of François Hertel. Someday luck would turn, someday a wail should rise in the valley that would wake even the sleeping bears in their dens. It would be the death cry of M'sieu' Weendigo.

At the shack he found his wife keeping sleepless vigil for his return. The agony of fear she had endured was plainly written on the drawn face.

"You see de Weendigo?" she gasped.

"Oua, I see heem," laughed the hardy Frenchman, taking her in his arms. "I shoot, and he run lak snowshoe rabbit for de swamp. I mak' bad shot for de light. Eet ees only beeg lucivee. I get heem someday in de trap." And he patted her shoulders reassuringly.

Marie's travels took her no farther than her rabbit and ptarmigan snares in the neighboring forest, so she did not know that in size the tracks of the beast dwarfed those of a lynx, and he did not intend she should.

The day following Hertel beat through the swamp, but so many tracks led out of it over the watershed that he gave up all idea of immediate pursuit. Returning to the shack, he overhauled two bear traps, the steel jaws of which bristled with vicious teeth, harnessed a husky to the sled, and started for his marten *cabanes* across the river. There, before two of the stick houses, he buried in the snow the traps with their log clogs in the manner that he hid lynx traps to take the pilfering wolverines that had already harassed his lines. If the night-wailer followed down this trap-line again, he would not escape the hidden steel jaws gaping under the snow. Then on a line of fisher traps Hertel erected three log deadfalls, which would crush the life from a three-hundred-pound bear.

"Eef he got bone to break, dees weel break dem," chuckled the trapper as he turned homeward.

For a week Hertel patrolled the sleeping forests of the white valley, but neither heard his enemy nor found fresh signs. Twice he climbed the big ridge and traversed the swamp beyond, where he had lost the trail the night the moon failed him, but evidently the beast had abandoned his former haunts, for the new snow lay unmarked. Over the river the logs in the deadfalls still menaced the doomed creature that should trip them, but the yawning jaws of one of the bear traps had closed on a young wolverine rashly entering the house of sticks which his cunning elders first would have torn to pieces gingerly from the rear, then ferreted out the bait, or eaten the animal in the sprung trap inside.

Another week of waiting passed and Hertel began to wonder if the beast had quit the country. Then, one bitter night on his return under the stars from the lakes, the familiar challenge floated faintly up the valley.

"Ah-hah! Eet ees you, *mon ami*?" he muttered, and quickened his stride. He had traveled for some time when the cry was repeated. The thought of Marie alone in the shack with the cowed huskies, while the skulking thing was loose in the neighboring forest, spurred him into a run. He was nearly home when again the windless night was filled with the horror of the lingering wail echoing from the hills. Now the runner on the river trail was close enough to locate his enemy. The beast was on the ridge the trapper had prepared for him.

"By Gar!" Hertel exclaimed, in his joy at the discovery. "I get you dees tam, M'sieu' Weendigo, for sure."

Shaking a mittened fist at the black hill across the valley, he turned up to his cabin, where he found Marie and the dogs with nerves on edge over the return of the dreaded prowler of the night.

While the Frenchman wished to give his traps and deadfalls a fair chance to catch the plunderer, the fear that the beast might avoid them and again escape hurried him through supper. Heartening the trembling Marie as best he could, he oiled the action of his Winchester and was off. With the approach of January the nights were growing increasingly bitter. Entering the stinging air, Hertel drew the fur-lined hood of his capote over his face, where his hot breath turned to ice on his mustache, and reknotted the sash at his waist. The inexorable grip of the frost was tightening on the ice-locked valley.

He climbed the ridge and waited, for the beast might leave the trap-line if he discovered that he was followed. Once Hertel heard the cry hardly a mile away, then he went to his first fisher trap. The thief had done his work well. The trap was sprung and the bait gone. The second had been treated in the same way. At the next trap was a deadfall, and the Frenchman's heart pounded with hope as he approached. The drop log had been tripped and lay in the snow in front of the *cabane*, which was torn to pieces.

The trapper cursed out loud. The cunning of the beast was uncanny. Through the brain of Hertel there flashed a flicker of doubt. Could this after all be the work of a devil in brute shape? But the Frenchman's head was hard, and grasping his rifle he continued on.

For some time the night had been free from the voice, when, as he approached his second deadfall, the wail again rose from the lower shoulder of the ridge down the valley. But, as it lifted in volume to the maniacal scream, it ceased abruptly, as if choked off by some giant hand.

Hertel found the remaining deadfalls in similar condition to the first. The tracks on the snow told the same story. The ponderous engines of destruction had been rendered harmless from the outside by the crafty thief.

There was one hope left—the toothed jaws of steel hidden in the snow at the end of the marten line. He would go to them at once and take up the trail from there.

The cold was increasing. Deeper and deeper bit the fangs of the frost. His eyebrows and mustache were a mass of ice. Time and again all feeling left his toes under the thongs of his shoes, and he swung his gun from mittened hand to hand to keep up circulation. The boom of the river ice and the snap of the timber alone violated the white silence under the star-incrusted sky.

The lone runner in the forest approached the first of his bear traps at the marten *cabanes*. If the hairy thief had escaped these, little hope remained of running him down that night in this withering air which cut the lungs like thrusts of a knife. Rounding a thicket of low spruce, Hertel sighted the trap. Like a flash the hunter dropped to his knees, cocked rifle at his shoulder. One, two, three seconds his eye held his sights lined on a black shape by the *cabane*. But the mass on the snow was motionless. Then, rising, Hertel stealthily moved forward, rifle ready. Suspicious, he stopped a hundred feet from the trap, peering long at the spectacle before him, then slowly shook his head. With rifle thrust forward and every nerve tense, Hertel approached the trap. Was his enemy in his power at last, or was he being lured into some fiendish ambuscade? He glanced quickly to the side and rear. There was nothing there. The shape in the snow did not stir. Then he walked deliberately to the trap.

"By Gar!"

The Frenchman stared at the hairy bulk crushed in the grip of the merciless steel jaws.

He touched the thing with his snowshoe. It was frozen stiff.

With a wrench he turned the heavy trap and its victim over—to stare into the swart face, hideous in its grimace of death, of a Cree Indian.

Ryerson Johnson's first story, "The Squeeze," was published in Adventure *in 1926; he has been writing professionally ever since, in a remarkable sixty-year career that has seen him produce almost every imaginable type of fiction and nonfiction. He was a regular contributor of both Westerns and Northerns to all the major pulp titles, including* North-West Stories/Northwest Romances, *and was especially adept at capturing the lusty flavor of life in the Canadian Barrens, an area in which he spent some time during a widely traveled youth. "Webs for One" is not only one of his best Northern stories, but has the added distinction of having been one of the very few pieces of fiction to first appear in the* Reader's Digest-*type non-fiction magazine,* Coronet.

Webs For One

★★★★★★★★★★★★★★★

Ryerson Johnson

GOLD bowed the little man's back—60 pounds of gold.

The weight forced his bear-paw racquets deep into powdery snow and made the going excruciatingly hard. Let the pack straps gall! It was a good hurt. At first Alf Newberry had only wished it would hurt more. More hurt would mean more weight of gold. And the more gold a man had, the bigger twist he could take on the world's tail when he got outside.

Of course, he wasn't going to get outside. The Canadian barren grounds, this great lone land that sprawled in frozen silence across the top of a continent, would never let him go. He could read his death warrant clearly in his empty food pack, the 40-below cold, and the two days' travel yet required to put him on Bent Willow Creek at timberline.

Not any one thing, but a lot of little things had tipped the balance the wrong way. That roving Yellowknife Indian with whom he had shared his scant food supply . . . But what else could a fellow do? The Indian was starving. No way to have predicted he would repay by stealing most of the rifle cartridges.

Right to the end, the little things had kept bunching up to spell northern death. His last bullet, fired at a snowshoe rabbit . . . and that streak of white lightning in the shape of an Arctic fox detaching itself from the snow hummock. The fox had been stalking, too. And it was the fox that got the rabbit.

Alf had thrown away the rifle to lighten his load. Now it was time to throw away his gold.

He made the decision calmly, after falling twice within the same five minutes. On this rolling rock-ribbed tundra, every snow-pillowed half acre looked like every other half acre. It had been a six-year job to trace the gold through the cracks and crannies of frost-split granite to its ultimate hiding place.

Six years—and he could lose it all in six minutes! But life alone was the stake now.

After his last fall, he stayed down while he groped stiff-handed in the snow to loosen his pack straps. He didn't make much head-way, and a small panic touched him. A man with his strength too far run out could die in the North, anchored to his gold!

But Alf Newberry, being a little man, had long since learned the rashness of butting into things full tilt, whether it was a bigger man who opposed him, or simply the waiting hostile North. There were things fully as potent as force. There was timing and there was headwork. He quit his exhausting struggle with the incubus that rode his back; and he wriggled his wool-gloved hand from its huge covering mitt of moose hide, and from an inner recess of his parka, brought out a pint whiskey bottle. Only about enough whiskey left for one good jolt. But it was north-country liquor, supercharged stuff with an alcoholic content so high that the coldest weather couldn't freeze it.

Alf knew how to take it. In nips. That way it would feed through his jaded body with a reviving fire. He'd get out from under this gold all right, and he'd go a long way yet on his feet. When he flopped on his face for the last time—well, that would be something else again. He'd save the last swallow for then. Cold, whiskey, and fatigue would anesthetize him. He'd die just like going to sleep.

Not that that made it easier to get used to the idea. Why, he'd hardly begun to live! Tramping the world's shrinking gold frontiers ever since he'd been old enough to carry a pack and an ore hammer, he'd been lonely, with the good things always beckoning from over the hump of the next hill. So lonely that sometimes over his fire, in the drag of the night wind, he'd hear laughter. Soft laughter from the woman never loved because never known; shrill gay laughter from children, shadow-born; gusty laughter from mellowed friends that in his will-o'-the-wisp wandering over the back trails he'd never stopped long enough to meet.

And now, just when it had given golden promise of arriving somewhere, his trail had run out—

Or had it?

His eyes, gray-dull and expressionless, took quick fire. His head on its scrawny neck poked ludicrously from his parka hood, and his nostrils flared. Thin and acrid in the cold air, a trace of coal smoke had wafted to him. Coal smoke? Why not! There was coal in this country as well as gold. The trick was to find it . . .

The low shale cliff was plastered ten feet deep with snow. But Alf Newberry found it. Trembling in near exhaustion, he had only to push aside the wolf-hide coverings in order to enter the cave and embrace life instead of death. But he held back. The assurance of life had made the gold of prime importance again. A little man, Alf Newberry had early bought into a game where bone and muscle held blue chip values. The pushing around he'd had to take from bigger men had made him wary. Six years scrounging the top bleak quarter of the globe for gold . . . He didn't propose to lose it now in a single unguarded moment.

With concentrated effort, he wrung his shoulders free from the rucksack loops, let the burden of gold plump deep in a drift. Only then did he move to poke his head beyond those wolf-hide coverings.

He stood silently at first, peering inside the cave. Rime was white and heavy on his parka hood where it fringed his gnome-like face. He appeared, perhaps, not quite real.

At least the man who sat on the shale ledge, staring back at him through the haze of coal smoke, seemed to have doubts. The man was a giant. Compared to Alf he was. His pale eyes stared with a curious burning from under a tangle of bushy brows, shaggy hair. A six-months' beard inundated the rest of his face. Alf surmised that under its dirt and soot the shrubbery might be blond.

The giant stirred.

"Where the hell'd you come from?"

His voice from the back of the cave was a hollow booming. It sounded as though he were trying hard to believe what he saw.

Alf lifted his hand in a weak sweep toward the North. Words pushed through his frost-scabbed lips: "Headin' for timberline. Got a grub cache on Bent Willow Creek." He shook his head. "I'd never made it. Don't mind tellin' you, brother—runnin' onto you has saved my life."

The big man kept staring while Alf moved deeper inside the

cave, shaking off his mitts and blinking his eyes to accustom himself to the smoky gloom. A tiny coal fire flickered on the floor. He hunkered close to it.

"Make yourself at home," the brooding giant said, and laughed. It wasn't an insane laugh. But there was a flat mirthlessness about it that put Alf on his guard.

"What are you, man or boy?" the big one spoke again. "Pound for pound, inch for inch, I'd make two of you."

"You wouldn't miss it much," Alf conceded.

"You're all beat in, ain't you?"

"It's been tough goin'," Alf further conceded.

"Ain't you got a gun?"

"Threw it away to lighten my pack."

"What pack?"

"Unloaded that, too."

There was a taut eagerness in the big fellow's voice when he put the next question.

"Snowshoes?"

"I kicked the webs off outside here."

Something like a satisfied animal grunt sounded faintly from the big man's throat.

Alf said wearily, "Let me ask you one, brother. How long's it till dinner time?"

"Hungry?"

"Starved."

"Makes it tough," the big man said. "I only got enough for myself."

He hadn't changed his tone. But the words were as damning to Alf Newberry's hopes of living as though a black-garbed judge had resounded sentence: ". . . hanged by the neck until dead."

Alf blew on his fingers. "Like that, huh?"

"Like that," the big man said. Surprisingly, then, he made a wheedling attempt at self-justification. "I been sittin' here myself waitin' to die. Run across this coal ledge last summer, so I based out of here. When the snow clamped down, I holed in. Coal outcrops right in my parlor, like you can see. Lucky thing for me. I lost my gun and my snowshoes right after freeze-up when I went through the ice."

Alf could understand the other's special interest now in the matter of snowshoes. And the laugh—sardonic, as well it might be, because in both their cases the North had rendered its judgment, and it was the same judgment: Death for Alf Newberry because he had no food. Death for the big fellow here because he had no snowshoes.

There was, of course, a corollary to that. Each man was only half a man; together they were whole.

The big man heaved to his feet. Even with his shoulders humped, his bushy head scraped the roof. "Think I'll have a look at them snowshoes of yours," he said.

"Wait a minute," Alf jerked. All his life pushed around by bigger men—but one certain result of it had been to sharpen his wits. He made a stab at breaking up decision before it might crystallize. He said earnestly, "You're not seein' it all the way through, brother. We can both live."

"Yeah?"

"Easy," Alf pressed. "Divvy a little of your grub with me, just enough for a two-day trip to the creek where my food cache is. I'll lug enough stuff back for you to last out the winter here if you want."

"Yeah?" The dangling arms swung slowly. "How do I know you'd come back?"

"You'd have to take my word for it, brother."

"I don't take nobody's word for nothin'."

It had been a pass at something; that was all. The big grizzly, the way Alf sized him up, ran his life by hard and fast rules, with greed—and consequently suspicion—high among the motive powers. Solid beef had always been enough to get him by, so he'd never felt prodded to develop much imagination. Hard to reach a man like that.

"We'll gamble," Alf said desperately. "How about it? Your grub sack against my snowshoes."

Agreement came readily. Too readily, was Alf's uneasy thought. It was as though the big man knew he had nothing to lose.

"We can toss a coin," the big man said. "I got one. United States dollar I always kept for luck."

He went ahead and made the toss, caught the twirling dollar in the chunky palm of one hand, and spanked his other hand down flat across it.

"Call it."

"Heads."

The big man opened his dirt-slick hands. The dollar was showing heads all right.

"I win," Alf said, but without elation. That was because he was more than half primed for what happened next.

The big man pulled a long skinning knife from his belt. The

firelight glinted on the blade in the same dim way it had on the dollar. Cold decision flared in the pale eyes, and the big man moved in on Alf.

Alf fumbled his own knife out and brandished it. But he was backing away. What else could he do? His nerves screamed the question. Weak as a rabbit, and showing only half the other's size—

The big man kept moving in, crouched low, stumping his feet down wide apart for balance, his tree trunk body weaving as he took his inches-short steps. The knife in his blocky first kept fanning slowing in front of him as he came. Alf, feinting desperately, gave ground as he had to. When he felt his shoulder brushing the wolf-hide flaps at the cave opening, he went all out on another gamble.

This big grizzly, he reasoned, wasn't a natural killer. He would kill now, but only because of his stubborn belief that his life depended on it. That was why, undoubtedly, he had agreed to gamble in the first place. A win would have quieted his conscience, settled everything for him without the need for violence.

Alf reached back through the door flaps and threw his knife as far as he could into the snow. He showed his hands, flat out, and empty.

"I quit!" he shouted.

The big man quit, too. He straightened up. He seemed vaguely pleased. "Glad you got some sense," he said. "I didn't want to kill you."

"What do you think you're doin' by leavin' me here to starve?"

"That's only your hard luck."

Alf stared bitterly. "The twists a man can put on his reasonin'!"

The big man clumped about, pulled a small canvas bag from a wall cranny, and sat down with it on the ledge. He untied the knot at the loose end of the bag and took out a piece of caribou jerky. With his knife he hacked off a little of the hard dry meat. He crammed it in his mouth and chewed with relish.

Alf's own gnawing hunger put a weakening tremor over him, and he could feel the saliva jet from under his tongue.

"Never like to start a long trip on an empty stomick," the big man offered, talking thickly through the raw meat that swelled, with mastication, to fill his mouth. "Figure I got a week's hard trek to the closest caribou hunters' camp below timberline."

When he finished, he put the remainder of the jerky away and retied the knot in the bag's loose end.

"Better tie it tighter," Alf told him. "I might make a grab and open it."

The big man didn't read any sarcasm in Alf's scraping voice. He reacted literally; gave the knot another yank. Then he put the food bag down beside his gold pan that was full of melted snow water, and keeping one eye on Alf, he lowered his face to drink. After that he stood up, carefully wiped off his beard, moved about and pulled on a mackinaw, and over that a fur parka.

Alf rummaged inside his own parka and brought out his bottle. He held it out.

"What's that?"

"Whiskey."

"What you handin' it to me for?"

"You're the one who's got somethin' to celebrate."

The big man came over and took the bottle. He shook it skeptically, held it to the light and watched the bubbles chase to the top and disappear. He opened the bottle, smelled it, tilted it cautiously to his lips.

He whipped it down. "It's got the old sting," he said. "It's whiskey, all right." Then his voice turned whiney mean with suspicion. "I get it—you think you're goin' to soften me up. Makin' me presents. Yeah. Well, that's out, see? I'm strong, and not only in my muscles. My willpower. If I have to let somebody die to save my own life—well, that's how it is, see?"

He lifted the bottle, disposed of half the liquor with one big noisy swallow.

Alf said doubtfully, "You think you ought to drink the rest? You're goin' out in the cold, and you know what that can do to a drunk man."

"To a runt like you maybe," the big man said. "Not to me. When that much whiskey makes me drunk, I'll sign the pledge." He drained the rest of the whiskey and let his breath out in a noisy *wo-oo-oo-sh.*

Alf sighed, and went over and dropped down on the ledge on the side of the water pan that was away from the food bag. He lowered his face and drank deliberately, tipping the shallow pan a little, the better to get at the water.

"Sure," the big man said, "I'll drink the whiskey; you take the chaser. Just don't get inside of monkey range with my food bag, that's all." He laughed in that flat short way. "Them scrawny fingers of yours. They couldn't untie the bag anyhow. When I tie somethin', it stays tied."

He made a roll of his eiderdown sleeping bag, then picked up a small rucksack from the corner. He hefted it as though he liked to feel its solid weight, and the greed was naked in his pale eyes. "I got thirty pounds here. Figures around sixteen thousand. I did all right, huh?''

Alf lifted his mouth from the pan. Water dripped from the point of his thin nose and from his lightly stubbled chin. ''Fair,'' he said. ''But I beat the North for twice that much.''

''Yeah—to hear you tell it.''

''I'll show you.''

Alf got up and ducked outside. The big man came and watched narrowly from the cave opening. Alf dug his rucksack from the drift and dragged it back through the snow to the cave. He opened it up on the floor, revealing the tightly packed skin pokes. He loosened the babiche strings on one of them. Raw, new gold in dust and nuggets of cornmeal yellow glowed softly in the firelight.

''Thirty thousand, easy,'' Alf said.

The big man was breathing hard, his pale eyes squeezed half shut and staring. Alf dipped up a handful of the gold, let it stream back through his fingers. Six years to accumulate it, grain by grain, speck by speck. Now he dusted his hands prodigally against his sides.

''Don't do that!'' the big man jabbed.

''Why not? Mine, ain't it, to waste if I want?'' Alf looked up with sly malice. ''You know what I got a notion to do? Take this whole sixty pounds of gold and scatter it on the snow. I'd have me one high minute that way.''

The big man pushed threateningly close, and Alf stood up and moved back. His frost-cracked lips were bent in a crooked grin, and a slow fire pierced the dull gray of his eyes. ''Don't worry,'' he said. ''I give you the gold. I give it to you before you have to bash my skull in and take it away from me. I'll make it easy for your conscience, brother.''

The big man looked relieved in about the same degree as when Alf had thrown away the knife. ''Go bring those snowshoes in,'' he ordered.

Alf brought them in and the big man tried them on in the middle of the floor. Right after that he set about loading the gold on his back. The straps on Alf's pack were too tight. They bunched the parka fur at the neck, bound the shoulders.

''Here, I'll fix it for you,'' Alf said.

Like a mule being diamond hitched to a pack load, the big man stood, bowed over patiently, while Alf worked to center the load and adjust the straps. But as a precaution the big man had sheathed his knife on the outside of his parka, and as a further precaution he kept the knife in his hand while Alf worked over him.

His voice carried that self-justifying whine again when he said, "You're still figurin' you can get around me. But I told you when you gave me the whiskey, and I'm tellin' you now: I'm strong, see? Sixty pounds of gold, and it ain't buyin' you one mouthful to eat."

Alf stood back, said reflectively, "I donno; you think you ought to carry both these gold packs? You think you're strong enough? They'll add up ninety pounds. You're too heavy for these webs of mine anyhow, and the weight of the gold will push 'em even deeper in the snow. Liftin' 'em up and sockin' 'em down—they'll feel like boulders tied to your feet—"

"What the hell are you, my mother?" the big man flared. "I'm the one that's goin' to leave here and live. You're goin' to stay and die. Ain't that enough for you to worry about?"

"I died out there on the trail," Alf said. His voice was worn, his pinched face expressionless.

"Huh? You nuts or what?"

"I mean I had my mind all set for it. The worst was then. This is only a kind of tailin' off. I don't feel much now."

The big man said, "Huh!" and moved across the cave to the ledge where his food bag lay. The fire had gone down. In the smoky gloom he didn't see the puddle of water on the ledge until he put his hand in it. Then he swore.

"You splashed water all over the ledge," he said, accusingly.

"It was kind of dark," Alf said. "I couldn't see good. Must of tilted the pan too far when I was drinkin'."

The big man sheathed his knife and held the food bag away from him and wrung a drop or two of water from it.

Alf moved closer, peering. "It ain't wet but only on the loose end, is it? Water won't hurt the jerky none."

It was outside in the snow, with the big man loaded and standing on Alf's snowshoes and ready to go, that Alf resorted to downright appeal. His thin face puckered suddenly, and his words poured out in bursts:

"Before it's too late, think what you're doin', man! It doesn't have to be this way. Nobody has to die. We can both live. Just let me take the webs, like I said before, and enough grub to get me to my cache. I'll come back to you. We can both live—"

The big man broke savagely into his pleading. "I thought that iron nerve of yours was too good to last. Couldn't take it, huh? You had to get down and beg!"

Inside the parka Alf's thin shoulders were hunched against the gray cold. "Believe me," he chattered, "if I'm beggin', it's for you."

The big man snorted in derision. "You don't scare worth a damn, runt." But then he hedged the bet enough to ask sharply, "What you talkin' at anyhow?"

Alf's arms were swinging wide in an Eskimo slap against his sides. It was a good way to keep the circulation up. "Not any one thing," he said gently. "It's hardly ever any one thing, is it? Just a lot of little things workin' together."

"You're goin' nuts," the big man growled. "So long—and thanks for the gold." He lifted a snowshoe and leaned into the step.

That was when Alf made his play. "Just remember I gave you your chance." He mouthed the words as he lurched forward, with one of his swinging hands raking across the fur of the big man's parka to the place where his knife was sheathed.

Alf got the knife. The trouble was, he couldn't stay on his feet. The big man's elbow swerved around, striking and knocking him down. He kept himself tumbling and rolling through the snow until he was momentarily out of the other's reach. And he held on to the knife.

The big man waddled around on the webs and stood there, humped under the gold, watching warily while Alf floundered upright in the snow. Buried in whiskered stubble, the big man's lips pushed out words:

"Not any one thing, but a lot of little ones, huh? I'm gettin' it now. You gave me your whiskey. Yeah. And loaded me down with your gold and put me on your runt webs. Yeah. Then you stand there beggin', and with your teeth chatterin', and lookin' helpless, and throw me off my guard. Then you take my knife. . . . All right, you got my knife. Let's see you try to kill me with it."

He stood waiting on his tree-stump legs, his long arms dangling in their bulk of fur. His breath in the forty-below cold dropped past his knees in steamy feathers.

"Come on," he urged again. "You're goin' to find out I'm not drunk, and that I got what it takes to move around under ninety pounds of gold. It ain't goin' to anchor me down, like you thought. It'll only be like some armor plate instead. It'll help me. These runt webs of yours are sinkin' some under me, yeah, but not as far as them pipe-stem legs of yours are bogged down. Wallowin' in the snow, you'll never get that knife in me through all the clothes I got on, before I can knock it out of your hands and break your neck. But if you want to try it, come on."

Alf stood crouched in snow halfway to his hips, and as the heartbreak truth of what the big man said got through to him, his hand which held the knife began to sag.

The big man saw and snapped his clincher. "Drop the knife, or I'll move in on you. You won't get far without snowshoes. I'll kill you with my two hands."

A moment more Alf hesitated, his face in a tortured knot. Then his arm swung back and he threw the knife as far away as he could. It drove into a drift and disappeared.

"Go dive in that drift and bring me back my knife," said the big man.

"I'm through fetchin' for you, brother," Alf told him bleakly. "If you want that knife, you can unload the gold and dive for it yourself. If you want to kill me, that's all right too; one way or another, I won't be any longer dead."

The big man glowered, and seemed to be debating. At the last he said, "All right, have it your own way for once. Leave the knife stay. Only thing I'd need it for's to kill you with—and you ain't worth killin'. Like I always said, a good big man's better'n a good little man every time; and you ain't even a good little man. You got brains for plannin', but no nerve for pushin' things through to the finish. So long, runt. I'll be thinkin' about you when I spend your gold."

Alf watched the big man move away into the gray vastness of snow and sky. Oddly, there was no despair in his eyes as he watched; only serenity now. He turned aside and crab-clambered through the drifted snow to the place where he had thrown the knife. He fished around until he recovered it.

Inside the cave again he built up the fire, warmed himself, and rested. Then by the light of the smoky flames he poked around, exploring. He found two old discarded marrow bones and a few leaves of tea, which he picked up from the floor a leaf at a time. He cracked the bones, put them to boil with the tea in the shallow gold pan.

Then he went to work with the knife, taking one of the wolf-hide coverings from the door and cutting it into thin strips. He unearthed a fox skin which he had spotted the first time he had entered the cave. It was drying on a makeshift stretching board, a crude contraption of bent willow withes. He took the willow withes, along with a few more which had been laced into the wolf hides to hold the door coverings in place, and sat down with them near the fire.

He worked purposefully, but without haste, first steaming both the willow sticks and the stiff wolf hide to make them more pliable, then painstakingly using them in fashioning something which would pass for a little man's snowshoes. At intervals while he worked, he drank of the bone and tea broth. Before he left the cave on his patchwork snowshoes—with the knife ready at hand—he fortified himself against the outside cold by sucking out what remained of the marrow in the bones; and he ate the soaked tea leaves. Such scant nourishment, he knew, wouldn't get him much farther than the makeshift snowshoes would. But he nursed a hunch that that would be far enough.

He didn't miss it. The tracks he followed through the still sub-Arctic twilight played out at last, as he had been so confident they would, and he came upon the big man's stiff and frozen body. It was half buried in snow, the bearded face gray with hoar frost. Alf sank down, dog weary, to rest on the big one's body.

No elation showed on Alf's hunger-pinched face, deep in the parka hood. Elation would come later—down in the warm country where there was enough of everything to eat for everybody, where men and women laughed, touching each other trustingly with their eyes, their words, their hands . . .

The gold? He'd carry the small pack only, come back next summer and look for the other. Maybe he'd find it; there'd be a skeleton to mark the place. Right now it didn't matter.

Only the snowshoes were important. And food. He shucked his wool-gloved right hand from his mitt and took a firm grip on the handle of the long skinning knife.

For a last grim second, before using the knife, he contemplated the frozen hulk beneath him. Not any one thing, but a lot of little things all working together had brought the big one down. The whiskey which had exhilarated him enough so that for a while he hadn't felt the drain on his strength. It hadn't made him drunk. But it had made him much too scornful of the snow that clogged the deep-sinking webs and the weight that rode his back as he drove for his goal: life—and a place to spend ninety pounds of gold.

And when the stimulant had worn off and fatigue had knifed in, as had been clearly evidenced by the shortening and wabbling of his tracks in the snow, his own great greed had prodded him further to extend himself. He didn't want to abandon the gold on the snow, because he could never be sure of coming back and finding it again.

Finally he had sunk down here and tried to unharness himself from the packs. There was nothing about the lashings that a man under ordinary conditions couldn't have mastered. But maybe he had recalled that Alf had helped to secure the straps. He might have remembered, too, Alf's last words, "I gave you your chance . . ."

Fatigued and panicky, the big man had fought the pack, as was shown clearly by the snow.

Finally he had thought of his knife. He could cut the straps! But the knife, of course, wasn't there. Quite possibly then he had quieted down, determining to rest and eat, then with renewed strength make short work of unloading the gold. He had reached for his food bag. And then he must have gone stark raving wild.

His bare hands showed it—bare hands in the forty-below cold! He had jerked his hands free from moose hide and wool to claw with his nails at the tough canvas of the food bag. And there was blood crusted around his mouth to show how, futilely, he had torn at the bag with his teeth.

And all the time the cold needling in, petrifying his hands, and soon thereafter his whole great body.

Alf shifted his mordant glance to the unopened food bag still clutched in the dead hands. The bag was a formidable looking object all right, the opening guarded by a knot twice pulled by the big fellow and afterward wet with water by Alf himself.

The water had frozen, of course, glazing the knot with ice. Alf couldn't have untied it in a month of Sundays. But, of course, he didn't need to untie it. That was what he had the knife for.

Dan Cushman began writing for the pulp magazines shortly after the end of World War II, and was soon a prolific contributor to Northwest Romances, Action Stories, Jungle Stories, Adventure, and Frontier Stories. In 1951 he turned to the writing of Western and adventure novels, among them the Northerns Timberjack, which was made into a film with Sterling Hayden, and The Fabulous Finn. His 1953 novel, Stay Away, Joe, a hilarious and yet moving story of a group of American Indians, brought him his greatest success; it was a major book-club selection and a bestseller, and was later adapted into a play, Whoop-Up. Cushman's swiftly paced, rugged northland novelettes and short stories were popular with readers of Northwest Romances; "Mistress of the Midnight Sun" shows why.

Mistress of the Midnight Sun

★★★★★★★★★★★★★★★★

Dan Cushman

BLADE Crossen sat in the wickiup of Kakissa the Yellowknife and watched as three canoes approached on the choppy waters of Spirit Lake.

Kakissa peered over his shoulder and asked, "Mounted Police?"

Crossen lifted a finger indicating that one of them was. He looked like an Indian when he did it. He was a stolid man, burned very brown by sun and snow glare. He might have been thirty or thirty-five years old. He was tall, and lean, with the toughness of a babiche thong.

"Nine police," Kakissa said, counting them. "Munetoowa, who ever heard of nine police?"

Blade Crossen laughed and said, "Maybe they came to take me in."

"Eh-meyo! For no man do they need nine police."

Crossen reached for his Winchester, worked the lever enough to see the brassy shine of a cartridge in the chamber, and laid it across his thighs. Merely habit. He had no idea of needing it.

The canoes tied up one after another, and the men headed up through spotty timber toward the trading post. Only one of them was in police uniform. He was short and quick-stepping. Beside him was a rangy, big-boned man with blond hair.

A breed hurried from the post and ran the Union Jack up on the spruce pole, and when it was snapping in the breeze off the lake, Buchanan walked down from the company building to meet them.

Buchanan had changed to his white shirt and best plaid mackinaw pants. When a hundred yards separated them, he stopped and cried out a greeting, but Crossen knew he wasn't so pleased as he tried to sound. The arrival of white men, even a couple of white men, always irked him. Never to Crossen's knowledge had so many as nine come in one day, or even one season, to that remote post at Spirit Lake.

Buchanan shook hands, first with the policeman, then with the big blond man. He turned, walking between them, and took them inside. They'd all have one out of the company bottle. Two, maybe. Buchanan made the company bottle go a long way.

Kakissa said, "Hear me, O Koosia, have you every seen so many white men together at one time before?"

"Once in Montreal I saw nine times nine, and three besides."

"Eh Munetoowa! Eh watche!" Kakissa said, rocking to and fro, marveling at the thought of so many white men.

Crossen rubbed tobacco and red willow bark together, loaded his pipe, and smoked slowly. In less than five minutes, seven of the newcomers had reappeared and were grouped beneath the pale awning, dragging on ready-made cigarettes. Only the Mountie and the big blond man were still inside with Buchanan.

After a while Pete Whiterobe, Buchanan's half-breed clerk, came in sight, trotting toward the Indian camp. A hunch made Crossen move through the low door of the wickiup to meet him. Pete saw him and said in his French-Cree accent, "They lak to see you queek. Factor and le grand bourgeois from far south."

"What do they want?"

"How would I know what they want? You go damn-queek!"

Crossen was about to say they could come down to the wickiup damn quick, but he changed his mind and said, "Sure." He knocked out the heel of his pipe. "Where they from?"

"I said—from the south."

He laughed. There was nothing north of Spirit Lake except lake, tundra, and forest, a primitive country untouched by white men.

Crossen walked up the path. He'd long been used to moccasins, and even his step was like an Indian's. The newcomers had stopped talking and were watching him. He spoke and walked through the door without seeming to pay them more than the briefest attention, but the picture remained in his mind. They were not woodsmen. They were a picked group, too uniformly of a rough-tough type to come together by accident.

The trade room he entered was big, almost windowless, its walls smoked dark brown, filled with the mingled odors one associates with trading posts everywhere.

"Come in!" Buchanan called. "Here in the office, lad." Buchanan was there with Sergeant McCabe from Abitu post and the big stranger. "You already know Sergeant McCabe."

Crossen said, "Hello, Mack," and they shook hands. Then McCabe introduced the big blond man.

"This is Mr. Kordos. We wanted to see you about guiding us to the up-country."

Kordos moved over to shake hands. Light from the tiny, smoky window struck his face. He had an aggressive jaw, but aside from that his features were small and inconsequential, his eyes pale and too close together but intelligent. He was very large. Not thick, not muscle-bound. He was big in the way a moose is big, rangy and lean and tough.

"The up-country?" Crossen asked.

Kordos said, "Yes. We're looking for a half-breed Cree by the name of Matoos. Do you know him?"

Crossen thought a moment and said, "Sure, I know Matoos."

"Then you'll take us to him."

"I don't know if I will or not."

The answer irked Kordos, who stood powerful and spread-legged with the corners of his mouth twisted down. "Why wouldn't you?"

"Several reasons. One is that Matoos happens to be my friend."

"Oh, the police!" Kordos's booming laugh filled the low-ceilinged room. "So you think we came nine strong to arrest your half-breed. What an insult to the Mounted Police!" He stopped laughing and wiped moisture to the corners of his eyes. "No, we won't arrest Matoos. That's a promise, eh, Sergeant? Only a question we want to ask him."

"You travel a long way to ask a question of a half-breed."

Kordos nodded and said, "Yes. A long way."

Crossen said to McCabe, "What's it all about, Mack?"

"Why, just that. We want to ask him some questions. He's committed no crime I know of. It's just necessary to find him, and you're the only man I know of who could guide us in that country beyond the forks of the Beche.''

Crossen thought it over. He'd always liked McCabe, and if it hadn't been for Kordos and those hand-picked strangers outside, his answer might have been yes. Instead he lighted a pipe and said, ''It'd be a long trip, and I had it in mind to paddle down to Niksa Landing for a spot of nightlife.''

Kordos twisted his lips and said, ''Nightlife at Niksa Landing? There's nothing there but twenty shanties and one log saloon.''

''When you've spent ten solid months on the Deerpass, those twenty shacks look like Montreal. Sorry. Why don't you talk to the Yellowknives?''

McCabe said, ''They wouldn't take us up the Beche and you know it.''

Crossen shrugged and turned toward the door. Kordos suddenly realized he was leaving and moved over to block his path. He spoke to McCabe over Crossen's shoulder. ''You mean you would let him go without guiding us?''

''I can't force him to go!''

''You of the police can't force him to go?'' Kordos swore under his breath. Then he said, ''Wait,'' to Crossen in a conciliatory tone. He looked around and saw Buchanan's whiskey bottle. ''Wait, have a drink.'' The bottle was empty. He drew a crumpled five dollar bill from his pants pocket and tossed it on the table. Crossen shrugged and turned away from the door. In the north country it's an unforgivable insult to refuse to drink with a man. Pete Whiterobe brought the bottle, handed it to Kordos who pulled the cork, and handed it to Crossen. ''You say you were ten months at Deerpass Hills?''

Crossen had a drink and said, ''Yes.''

''Trap-line?''

''A short one.''

''Prospect for gold?''

''A little.''

''Struck it rich and now you're heading for Niksa Landing to toss a little color around. After ten months I don't know I blame you.'' Kordos was regarding him with his little pale eyes. He knew he hadn't struck it very rich. He was leading up to something. He drew a long, leather money folder from his pocket and commenced taking out twenty dollar bills and laying them on the table. Ten of them. He said, ''If you will find Matoos for us.''

''I'd still rather go to Niksa Landing.''

Kordos counted out ten more. ''Four hundred!''

"Try doubling it."

He showed his strong teeth and said, "Sure, I'll double it. I'll pay you this four hundred now, and the other four hundred after we've found the half-breed."

"All right," Crossen said, putting the money in his pocket. Actually, he'd have settled for half the amount. "Start tomorrow?"

"Tomorrow," Kordos agreed.

II

It was late, with the last twilight in the sky, when Crossen finished getting his outfit in shape and went to bed inside Kakissa's wickiup. He awoke suddenly at a low, Indian word spoken in the darkness.

He sat up and groped instinctively, his hand closing on the cold steel of his Winchester. Kakissa was a squat figure, hunched in the door of the wickiup.

"Ka-waya?" Crossen asked.

Kakissa said, "Bourgeois Buchanan. He come talk."

"It's all right." Crossen put the Winchester back against the wall. "Tell him to come in."

Kakissa backed away, out of sight in the shadow, and Buchanan's silhouette took his place in the door. He said, "Lad, it's dark in there. Hae ye no candle?"

Crossen struck a match and lighted the grease-dip. It filled the hut with smoky, yellow light. There was whiskey on Buchanan's breath, but he wasn't drunk.

Buchanan glanced over at the Indian and said, "I would speak wi' ye alone." He waited while Kakissa went silently outside and let the bearskin door drape swing shut behind him. Then he seated himself cross-legged on the floor.

"So you've decided to take them to Matoos? You're sure it's the right thing, lad?"

"Eight hundred dollars is the right thing."

"Aye, now, I've never been the man to turn up my nose at cash money, either. But are ye sure the big fellow will pay over the last four hundred like he said?"

"He'll pay me."

His tone made Buchanan chuckle and say, "Aye, you're the sort that collects."

Buchanan cleared his throat, uncertain how to say the thing he'd come to say. There was a half minute of silence as the flame rose and fell, making big distorted shadows against the caribou skins that covered the walls.

Finally Crossen said, "Who are they—Kordos and that bunch?"

"I don't know. That's the truth, I don't. They're from Montreal. So much I gathered. That, and that their mission is secret and regarded by the Mounted Police as verra important. But still, we that live here in the woods have to think of oursel'. Of our friends."

"Of Matoos?"

"Aye. What will happen to Matoos once you lead them to him?"

"I have McCabe's word on that. He promised not to arrest him. McCabe's a straight shooter. His word's good enough for me."

"Now, that's true. McCabe is a man of his word. But what about Kordos and the strong-armed lads he has with him? They are the real question."

"What do you want me to do?"

"You hae the four hundred. Your canoe is yonder. You can be ten miles down the lake before they miss ye."

"How about the other four hundred I have coming?"

Buchanan thought for a while. "Aye, the four hundred. If that's what's worrying ye, I'll give ye the money mysel'."

"You'll give it to me?"

"Aye. I'm Scotch, a herrin'-choker as they say, but not one to be stingy when it comes to helpin' a friend. I'll give ye the four hundred mysel'."

"Well, I'll be damned." Crossen decided to laugh. "I'll be damned!" he repeated.

Buchanan sat hunched forward, elbows on his knees. "What say ye to that, Blade?"

"No. I don't do business that way. I took his money and made a promise. I'll guide him upriver and find Matoos."

Buchanan went tight lipped, and his face looked hollow by the slanting lamplight, but he got hold of his anger, and when he spoke his voice was the same as before.

"All right. If that's your decision, I canna stop ye. But if you are a friend of Matoos as ye say, you could warn him to do no talking."

"About what?" Crossen made an exasperated gesture and lay back down on his spruce bough bed. "The hell with you,

Buchanan. You got some private deal with Matoos. If you want to warn him, jump in your canoe and do it yourself. Now get out of here and let me sleep.''

''If you knew the reason, then would you warn him?''

''Maybe.''

''For two hundred dollars would you warn him?''

''Four hundred seems to be the going price. For four hundred I'll warn him.''

''Aye, then. Four hundred it is.'' Buchanan reached in his hip pocket and brought out a knotted Hudson's Bay kerchief. Crossen thought he was getting ready to count out the money, but instead he untied a knot and took something between his stubby, blunt fingers. Light struck it and reflected in shafts of white fire. He was holding a diamond, square cut, broad across as the nail of his little finger.

''Where in the devil!'' Crossen breathed.

''From Matoos.''

''And where would he get a thing like that?''

''Found them beneath the floor of an old cabin, so he said.''

''Them? You mean he has more?''

''Perhaps. I dinna know. There hae been others before. I'll tell ye the truth. For ten or twelve years he has been bringing them in. I bought them and traded them in Winnipeg and Montreal.''

''At a profit.''

''Aye, at a good, solid profit, but I paid him enough. All that was good for him. Some red shirts, guns, knives, and now and then a bottle of hoochinoo.''

''Then that's why the big fellow is here—tracing the stones?''

''Aye.''

''They were stolen?''

''How would Matoos steal diamonds? Would he take them from these yellow-dog Indians? No, Matoos found them like he said. Look at this stone—they dinna cut them like this anymore. It is very old. Maybe as much as a hundred years. Probably they were hidden by some partner of the Northwest Company when they traveled like kings to the rendezvous, carried on litters, sleeping at night on brass beds, eating foods cooked by French chefs. Such a man could have hidden the jewels. If so, they belong to Matoos as much as anybody.''

''If they belong to Matoos, I'll bet beaver against rabbit that McCabe will see to it he keeps them.''

''McCabe! But McCabe is outnumbered one to eight.''

Crossen grinned and said, "You're not worried that McCabe might see to it he sells the rest of his diamonds for what they're really worth?"

"What would Matoos do with ten thousand dollars? Buy ten thousand dollars worth of knives? But it is true it might ruin my profit."

"All right, Buchanan. You put four hundred in my pocket and I'll warn him."

III

THEY set out at dawn, Blade Crossen in the bow of the lead canoe, Kordos taking the paddle just behind him. With a wind whipping the lake to whitecaps, they followed the long route, around its timbered shore.

"Been all your life in this country?" Kordos asked.

"Eleven years," Blade Crossen said without altering the regular sweep of his paddle.

"A man can wander over a lot of country in eleven years."

"There's enough here for a hundred years."

"Lived with the Indians?"

"Sometimes."

"Some of my men think you are an Indian." He laughed when he said it, afraid that Crossen would take offense. It wasn't natural for him. He was the sort who didn't give a damn whether someone took offense or not, but with Crossen he was trying to make friends.

"Man, I envy you," he said. "What a life, wandering up rivers that are marked by dotted lines even on the police maps, looking at country no white man has ever seen before."

They crossed a mile-wide arm of the lake where the polar wind got a good sweep at them. They kept turning the canoes, quartering into the rough water.

Kordos filled his great chest and said, "Ha! the forest! the limitless blue-green forest! It seems to go on forever. I have heard, Crossen, that there are unknown valleys in the North such as most white men never dream of. I have heard there are places where the ground is warmed by hot springs so that even in the winter it seldom freezes, and the trees grow big as the trees of southern Ontario."

"The Indians tell of it."

"But are there such places? Have you seen such places?" He

must have sensed the noncommittal answer that Crossen was about to give for he hurried to say, "If a man was willing to pay, could you take him to such a place?"

"I don't know." Crossen laughed and added, "It might depend on how much he offered."

"Then you could. So it is true!"

They camped where the Beche flowed swift and cold from the spruce forest. After supper, most of the men hunkered close around the camp fire, chain-smoking cigarettes against the swarming mosquitoes, but Kordos seemed immune to such petty nuisances and followed Crossen down to the canoe where he kept asking questions about the storied valleys of the North. He'd evidently made a study of them—not of the valleys themselves, for their actual existence was chiefly a matter of speculation, but the legends of Indians and fur traders.

He said, "In the year 1752, the fur trader Pierre Coville left Fort William for the last time and returned to Quebec, where five years later he died. In the University there is an unprinted manuscript in which he tells of the Vallon du Eden somewhere beyond Lac Spiritu, and a river he calls the Noire. As he describes it, the *vallon* is always warm because of the hot springs which everywhere flow from the ground; and the trees, he says, are often large in circumference as a Cree Indian's tepee. Do you know of such a place?"

"Those old Frenchmen were all alike. They liked to go home and spin yarns."

"But every other particular of his manuscript was faultlessly exact."

"Maybe I should ask you how to get there."

Kordos was watching him very intently, his eyes small and intelligent. "Perhaps if you had read the book, then you could find it. The place names were not in English, or French even. They were in an Indian tongue—an Indian tongue that has never been catalogued by scholars. An Athabascan tongue, perhaps the Yellowknife jargon you speak so well."

"You remember the words?"

"I have them in my notebook."

Crossen didn't ask to see them. At lodge fires in a hundred forest villages he'd heard stories like that repeated, the fabulous Edens of the North where the sharp fangs of Windigo were never bared. Of them all, maybe a couple existed. At least one of them existed, for Crossen had seen it.

Kordos went on talking. "He spoke of springs called the sulphur pots and the pitch pots, where hot sulphur and black bitumen rose from crevices in the earth. You've heard of such things?"

"The pitch pots? Of course. I've used the stuff to calk my canoe." He turned and met Kordos's eyes. "What do you plan on doing, barreling it and selling it down in Montreal? Do you think there's oil where you find pitch? Or are you looking for a diamond mine?"

He dropped his words unexpectedly, and watched Kordos for his reaction. Kordos's eyes barely narrowed, and his jaw looked a trifle harder than before, but he was good at controlling himself.

"Why do you think I would be looking for a diamond mine?" he asked in a velvet soft voice.

Crossen shrugged it off. "I never saw a white man come into this country who wasn't looking to line his nest. Gold, furs— that was the old story. Now it's just as likely to be uranium or oil. You tell me your secrets, Kordos, and maybe I'll tell you some of mine. After eleven years of the strong cold, it could be I'd like to line my nest, too."

"With eight hundred dollars."

"With eight hundred dollars, I can get good and drunk at Niksa Landing."

"How much money do you think I carry to the North with me?"

"How much do you expect to carry out?"

Kordos stood, spread-legged and massive, watching him. He looked ugly and predatory. Then he laughed with a hard twist of his lips. "You talk like a fool," he said, and stalked back to kick his bedroll out on the ground.

At that season there was a scant three hours of darkness, and they were up again with the first sun, fighting the river current with paddle and pike pole. The going was tough where the river cut its way through an area of little pointed hills, then the country flattened and it became broad and placid. There were swamps where the current was barely noticeable and waterfowl nested by millions.

Next morning they left the marshes behind, and late afternoon brought them to the fork of the Beche. Many Yellowknives had lived there once, but now only three of the wickiups were occupied.

Crossen found an ancient Indian by the name of Wolf Tail,

and after a pipeful in the smelly gloom of his wickiup, he learned
that Matoos was at Koo-wa village, still another day's travel to
the north.

A fine, cold rain was falling when they reached Koo-wa village. Fires burned in some of the wickiups, and smoke hung
like blue mist under the treetops. They'd been sighted downstream, and the entire village was at the water's edge to meet
them, men and squaws and children staring at the sight of nine
white men, more than most of them had seen in all the years of
their lives.

The chief, short and fat, garbed in caribou skins heavy with
beadwork, strode down with an old-time 45-90 rifle across his
arm and gave the sign of friendship. Crossen met him, and they
sat together beneath a spruce tree, smoking tobacco and willow
bark, passing the pipe back and forth without a word as Kordos
watched impatiently a dozen steps away.

"What does he say about Matoos?" Kordos finally shouted.

Neither of the men gave a sign of hearing him. When the pipe
was empty the Indian said:

"You look for Matoos?"

"Yes."

"He is wanted in the skookum house of the redcoats?"

"We do not come to arrest Matoos. It is the redcoat's promise. Where is he?"

"In his cabin, up the hill trail. He has a new squaw."

Crossen laughed and said, "Not another one!"

"Matoos is a great man," the chief said. "Never does he
trap, and yet each year he comes back from the trade store of
the white man his canoe heavy with knives and guns and red
silk shirts. And so he trades for a new squaw each time the
summer moons come."

The conversation was in the Athabascan dialect, half sign
language, but Kordos had been listening and he caught the repetition of Matoos's name and barked, "Well, what about him?"

Crossen's face, like the face of the chief, was perfectly composed, expressionless. He refilled the pipe, lighted it. Then he
said to the chief:

"I am Matoos's friend. Send someone to him. Tell him that
the redcoat is not here to arrest him. Tell him to talk, but to tell
nothing of the stones he trades to Buchanan."

The chief transmitted the message to a young Indian who set
off at a swift trot up the muddy pathway.

"Where's he going?" Kordos asked.

Crossen took his time in answering. "To Matoos. You don't want him to get scared and light out for the back country?"

He stood up, nodded to Kordos and McCabe, and the three of them walked up the path, through mud, across spruce needles spongy from rain. Trekell, a spare, predatory-looking man, Kordos's second-in-command, drifted along, far in the rear.

The path led them through solid, dripping forest. Then the spruce trees fell away and they caught sight of a cabin.

A man came to the door and lifted one hand in greeting. He was squat and powerful, broad faced, ugly, perhaps thirty-five. He wore gray wool trousers, beaded moccasins, and a silk shirt the hue of vermilion. He was unarmed except for a knife of Swedish manufacture that would have cost two prime skins at any trade store.

"Matoos!" Crossen said, "Wache! These men have traveled throughout the days of two moons from the great lodges of the white men to see you."

Kordos showed his strong teeth in a smile and strode forward with his hand thrust out. Matoos looked at him with a flat lack of interest. Finally he put out his hand, perfectly lifeless, for Kordos to shake.

"Come on inside and we'll smoke a pipe together," Kordos said.

McCabe started to follow, and reconsidered. It was obvious from his expression how little the mounted policeman trusted Kordos.

In a little while they heard Kordos shouting, trying to make the half-breed understand. Then he burst outside, looking flushed and angry. "Doesn't he understand English or French, either one?"

"Try him on Cree," Crossen said.

"You know well enough I don't speak Cree. Come on in."

Crossen found Matoos seated on a three-legged puncheon stool, hunched, with hands on knees, his eyes on Kordos.

Kordos took a position in front of him and thrust his clenched right hand out. "Look at it!" He opened his hand, revealing a diamond that shone like a crystal of white fire in the darkness. "Where did you get it? Crossen, tell him what I'm saying."

"Where'd you get it?" Crossen asked in Cree.

Matoos thought for a while, then he said, "Under old cabin on Beaver Fork."

"How many were there?"

"One stone. I found it under—"

"Buchanan says you've been trading them for years."

"Now all gone. All stones gone."

Kordos cried, "What are you talking about?"

Crossen told him, and Kordos bellowed, "He's lying. Tell the dirty breed I know he's lying."

Matoos understood English well enough, but Crossen went through the formality of translating. "He says you're a liar."

Matoos said, "Sure, all Crees liars."

Kordos asked, "What did he say then?"

"He says he's truthful, like all Crees."

"Where did you get it?" he shouted at Matoos. "Where did you get this diamond?"

"No savvy."

"You savvy me well enough. Where did you get it? A white man had it, didn't he? From white men you stole it. From white man who have hidden themselves in some valley of the north!"

Kordos had drawn himself to his full height. His two hands were lifted until the ceiling stopped them. Fury had turned his face purplish, veins stood out on his forehead. Then the half-breed's stony lack of response made his fury break its bonds, and he swung his right fist downward like a club. It struck Matoos high on the cheek and drove him backward to the floor.

Matoos was stunned only an instant. He rolled, came to a crouch with the hunting knife drawn. He lunged, but Kordos had snatched up the puncheon stool and smashed him to the floor.

Kordos did not hesitate. He sprang to drive his heavy boots to the side of the half-breed's head. Crossen tripped him, so that he stumbled and went face foremost across the slivery pole floor.

He rolled to his feet. For the instant he'd lost his sense of direction. He turned and saw Crossen silhouetted with the light of the doorway behind him. He roared out a curse and charged.

Crossen was carried back by the man's massive weight. The room was small. He knew instinctively he had no chance to escape. He flung himself back, struck the wall with both shoulders, his right foot braced. He rebounded, adding the power of driving leg muscles to the left hook he smashed to the point of Kordos's jaw.

Kordos took the blow. He fell back half a step. Crossen swung a right and another left. Kordos took them without blinking. He lunged in, seized Crossen, lifted him, and hurled him the length of the room.

Crossen was down with the rough pole floor under his hands. Unconsciousness was a black whirlpool threatening to engulf him. He knew that Kordos was a killer, charging to crush him under his boots. He got to hands and knees, ready to dive and clinch. Then through the spinning darkness he heard McCabe—

"Stand back, Kordos! Stand back, or I'll have to use it!"

McCabe was in the door with his Enfield revolver drawn and leveled. Kordos had drawn his own gun, but it was at arm's length, pointed at the floor. He stood and took a deep breath, getting control of himself.

Kordos said, "All right. As you say, Sergeant. You call the tune. This time, you call the tune."

IV

WHEN they got back to the village, it was misty twilight, and Crossen's right rib and shoulder pained after his collision with the cabin wall.

Kordos's men had erected their tents and tried to build a fire, but the damp wood only hissed and gave out volumes of smoke and steam.

Crossen gathered the lower dead branches of trees, built the fire up, and stood in front of its bright red warmth to dry his mackinaw. The tense antagonism of the camp was something a man could feel. Things were headed for a showdown.

Kordos decided to be conciliatory and said, "No hard feelings, Crossen? That breed just got me so damn mad."

"I didn't come because I liked you. I came because I wanted eight hundred dollars. So far you've paid me only half of it. How about the rest?"

"When you got it, what then?"

"I don't know. Maybe I'll head down for Niksa Landing. Maybe I'll find me a Yellowknife girl and stay here."

"You always do what you want?" Kordos mused.

Crossen grinned from one side of his mouth and said, "I try to."

"Why do you stay in this country? Why don't you make your stake and go outside? To Vancouver, or down to the States. Get yourself a white woman instead of these lousy squaws, a bed instead of a rabbit-skin blanket."

Crossen shrugged and looked at the fire. It was almost as though those little eyes of Kordos's were able to see beneath the surface and read a man's thoughts. He'd drifted North from Chipewayan eleven years ago with the idea of grabbing a quick stake and getting outside. There'd been a girl waiting for him back in the States. He thought of her now, trying to remember what she looked like. Probably she'd married someone else long ago. Given him up for dead.

"I've made a couple of little stakes," he said, more to himself than to Kordos. "But I blew them again."

"Gold?"

"Gold—furs—"

Kordos laid a heavy hand on his shoulder and said, "I like you, Crossen. You know why? Because you have none of the hypocrisy a man finds outside. Because if you hate a man you say so. You hate me, but that's all right. You're still my kind."

He pulled his shoulder free and said, "What you leading up to?"

"Why, about that stake you're looking for. That big stake. A stake so big you can say the hell with this rotten North Country forever."

"Diamonds?"

"Yes, diamonds. Rubies, and emeralds. You name it, and you'll probably be right."

"Maybe Matoos has traded them all away."

Kordos spat at the fire. "He can keep his diamonds. Trade them for his red silk shirts and hunting knives. Listen, on our way upriver I asked you about the hidden valleys of the North. Now I'll tell you something. Somewhere—" he cast a gesture outward, "out there, is a cache of diamonds, rubies, and emeralds that would make us millionaires."

Kordos had a way about him. He had power and conviction, and for a moment it almost seemed that he was speaking the truth. Then Crossen said, "You're offering me that instead of my four hundred dollars. Pay me my four hundred first, and we'll talk about the million afterward."

"Tomorrow I'll pay you your four hundred."

"I want it now!"

"No. Not tonight. I'll tell you why. Because I don't want to wake up tomorrow morning and find you've made a fool out of yourself and headed into the bush. I want you to think awhile before tossing a fortune away."

Crossen thought about it after supper as he lay inside the

darkness of the tent. It was raining, a drizzle fine as solidified mist that made a slight hissing noise on the damp-hardened canvas overhead. He could hear the breathing of men, the bark and snarl of malemutes in the Yellowknife village.

He went to sleep—a wary, hair-trigger sleep. Something snapped it. He sat up and listened. It was quiet. Even the rain had stopped. Just the occasional thud of a big drop that distilled and fell off a branch of a spruce tree. He reached, found his Winchester, laid it across his bed, and, still seated, dressed himself.

The bed beside him was empty. Odette had been sleeping there. He wondered how many of the others were gone.

He stood, hunched beneath the tent's slanting roof, and groped till he found the tent flap. Someone had tied it on the outside. He drew his H.B.C. knife, cut the strings, and went outside.

There was no sign of moon nor stars, but a slight grayness filtered through and larger objects were visible.

He stopped to button his mackinaw, his eyes on McCabe's tent. Something was wrong, but it took him a moment to decide what. The flap was hanging loose, and he knew that McCabe always fastened it on the inside. He started toward it, but a man moved from the shadow of the spruce tree with a rifle ready. It was stooped, heavy Paul Graves.

"Where you headed?" Graves asked.

Crossen stood back on the heels of his moccasins, the Winchester across his two arms, watching him. Instead of answering, he asked, "Where's McCabe?"

"In his tent!" He bristled as he said it. "What made you think he wasn't in his tent?"

"How do you know what I think?" He was about to go on.

"You stand where y' are."

"Why?"

"Kordos doesn't want anybody prowling camp. You better get back inside."

"Where's Kordos?"

Graves's lips twisted in a sour laugh and he said. "You're just filled up with questions, aren't you?"

"He started up to Matoos's cabin, didn't he? And then Mc-Cabe followed him."

"I told you McCabe was in his tent. Now get back inside

where it's nice and dry and nothing will happen to you. That's the way the boss wants it. He wants nothing to happen to you."

"Then you wouldn't dare put a 30-30 slug through me, would you?" He turned with his Winchester still across his arms as though to return to his tent. He stopped a quarter way around, and suddenly Graves realized the barrel was aimed at him.

"Anybody care what happens to you?" Crossen asked.

Graves took half a step back. He looked sick-scared. He opened his hands and let his rifle fall. It was still cocked, but the shock failed to make it explode. There was a Colt revolver strapped around his waist. Crossen plucked it from the holster and thrust it in his mackinaw pocket.

"Now tell me where they are."

Graves tried to say something, but the dryness of his mouth stopped him. On the third attempt he whispered, "They left an hour ago."

"McCabe followed him!"

"Yeah."

Crossen backed off toward the village street. "Don't try to get up there ahead of me. Stay where you are."

"Yeah!" Graves whispered.

When he reached the edge of the timber, Crossen stopped to look back. Graves was still there. He walked on, slowly, through the opaque, misty blackness of the forest. He groped his way. After long blindness he glimpsed a ragged bit of light through the trees. He walked on and it became a rectangle—candlelight shining from the open door of Matoos's shanty.

He stopped them. A man was inside, moving around. Only his shadow visible. Crossen left the path and threaded his way through brush and jack timber until he was behind the shanty, then he crossed and peered through a thin slot where moss chinking had fallen from between the logs. It was Kordos inside as he'd supposed. The man was leaning over, lifting the floor poles one after another, searching the ground beneath.

Crossen kept pulling the moss from between the logs, enlarging the chink. He could see the silhouette of a second man then. He seemed to be standing with arms outflung. Then Crossen realized he was limp, suspended by thongs that ran from his wrists to the rafters.

"Drop your gun, Crossen," someone said behind him.

He started around with his rifle and checked himself. It was Trekell, and he had the drop. The man edged forward warily, expecting a trick. "Don't you try nothin'."

"All right," Crossen said and let the Winchester fall.

"Get rid of the Colt, too. Take it out with two fingers."

He obeyed.

Kordos had heard them and came outside. "Trek?" he said, from around the corner. "What's wrong?"

"You were right about Crossen being a one-eyed sleeper. He followed us, and here he is."

Kordos cursed under his breath. He came in sight with his revolver drawn, stood for a while at the corner to make sure there were only the two of them, and rammed it back in its holster.

"What are you looking for?" he asked, watching Crossen's face.

"I guess just about what I found."

Kordos saw the unchinked logs then and knew he'd been peeping through. "All right, so I killed him."

"How about McCabe? Did you kill him, too?"

"Of course not."

"Where is he?"

"He's dead, but it was none of my doing."

Somehow, the admission that McCabe was dead failed to be a shock. "I suppose it was Matoos that killed him."

Kordos shouted, "Yes, it was Matoos!"

Crossen let his shoulders jerk in a hard laugh.

"You think I'm lying?"

"What difference does it make what I think?"

Trekell still had the rifle at his back, but Crossen ignored it and leaned to pick up his guns.

Trekell cried, "Leave 'em be!"

"The hell with you. You'll kill me if you want to anyway."

Kordos said, "Careful, Trek!", and Crossen knew he was safe enough. Safe for the moment anyway. He drew out a handkerchief, wiped mud off the guns, put the revolver in his pocket, and let the rifle hang in the crook of his arm. Kordos and Trekell remained one on each side of him, wary and alert.

He said, "Don't worry. I'll not start anything. Let's go inside."

He walked around the cabin and stopped in the door. From between the logs, he'd been able to see only Matoos's uncertain silhouette; now the candlelight struck him and he saw that he'd been stripped to the waist and beaten until his back was a mass of raw flesh. His head sagged sharply over and to one side, so his neck had been broken.

"Make a mistake and hit him too hard?" He said it carelessly, with no hint of the nausea that the sight gave him.

Kordos said, "Don't you think he deserved it after killing the policeman? Or do you still think I killed them both?"

"What the hell difference does it make what I believe? This is Koo-wa village, and it's a long way north of Edmonton. It's north of the law, and north of everything a white man calls civilization. Here you can do what you please. You can knife the mountie, and beat the breed to death; and if I don't like it, why you can kill me, too."

"You got guts," Kordos said in a musing voice. "I admire a man like you with guts. It is true I have no fear of you. Had I killed the policeman, which I did not, there would be no reason for me to lie about it. But McCabe was my friend. He came here to question the breed. I followed, and found him knifed. So I did that. I strung up the breed as you see and whipped him to find out why he had killed the policeman. No savvy! he said. But when I was through, he did savvy."

A babiche whip had been tossed in one corner. It was a cluster of wire-hard thongs drawn together and knotted in a handle weighted with a chunk of bullet lead.

Crossen said, "Good hunch you had, bringing the whip along."

Kordos laughed. "You will generally find me prepared." He was smug and satisfied with himself, and hatred of him was like something clawing at Crossen's guts. Still he kept it from showing on his face.

"He told you about the diamonds?" Crossen asked.

Kordos shrugged and said, "He told me a few things."

"Find his cache?"

"His few stones, they are nothing. Nothing compared with the cache waiting for us out there." It was significant the way he said us, with a tiny smile, a slight droop of one eyelid that Trekell, still in the doorway, couldn't see. He went on, slowly, "Wouldn't you like to help us look for them across the swamps of Nipphauk, beyond the sulphur water, in the valley watched over by the three sisters?"

Crossen had no choice. He'd serve as Kordos's guide, or end up like Matoos, suspended by his wrists and the flesh torn off his back.

"I'd like it," he said. "I'd like it fine."

V

ODETTE, a quarter-breed Blackfoot from the Belly River country, joined them on their way back to camp. He was a dark, taciturn man, the scout of Kordos's party. He walked with them silently for a few seconds and then said something about Matoos's squaw knowing what had happened.

"Where is she?" Kordos asked, and Odette shrugged, meaning he didn't know.

The Yellowknife village was filled with movement. From one of the wickiups came a chanting howl as women joined in a death chant.

"We won't wait until morning," Kordos said. "We'll get out now."

The tents were down in five minutes, rolled in bundles heavy from rain, tossed in the canoes. They looked to Crossen for directions, and he said, "Upriver!"

Dawn came through drifting layers of mist, but it was afternoon before the sun came through, a pale, white disc with no heat in it. They ate cold biscuits and kept going. The sun slipped behind a cloud bank and it was evening when they finally pulled in to shore.

When supper was finished, Crossen stripped to his underwear and dried his clothes at the fire. Kordos came up behind him, picked his teeth with the point of a hunting knife, and said,

"The swamps of Nipphauk, beyond the sulphur water, into the valley watched over by the three sisters. You know what he meant?"

"Matoos told you that?"

"Yes, and don't say I was tricked. Even a Cree-breed will tell the truth when he's blind from pain. Think you can take us to the place he was talking about?"

"What if I couldn't?"

Kordos took time to finish picking meat from his teeth. He put the knife away. "Why, in that case, you wouldn't be much use to me, would you?"

Crossen jerked out a short laugh and said he knew the way perfectly.

For three days they followed the river northward as it forked again and again. It dimished in size, became barely a creek, flowing between sharply cleft banks. They were forced to walk and propel the canoes by means of lines and pike poles. Then even that became impossible, and they portaged over a low bulge of country thickly studded with dwarf timber.

They reached a muskeg, level and apparently without limit. There were no trees, only brush that grew in stray patches. The footing was uncertain. It trembled under a man's weight, a vast island of moss floating on muck and water. Mosquitoes lay in the grass to rise in never-ending swarms. They became a major obstacle. No man could travel without the protection of netting, and at every stop a smudge fire had to be built before one could eat or rest.

It was impossible to pitch tents in the muskeg, and sleep without their protection was out of the question. So they kept going, afoot for many miles, then down a currentless waterway which, after long, apparently aimless wandering, led them to a chain of little lakes that they followed northeastward.

They were in forest again, with little hills breaking the country's level monotony. An odor, faintly unpleasant, hung in the air, and that night they reached the first of the sulphur springs.

The springs rose from rifts that broke irregularly across a mile-wide stretch of rock. Everywhere were little streams of warm water.

Crossen lay full length and drank. The water was only faintly unpleasant from dissolved hydrogen sulphide.

He sat up and wiped water from his nose and chin. Kordos was standing over him.

His face was puffed from mosquito poisoning, so it was scarcely recognizable.

"This is the sulphur springs?"

"Yes."

"I have to hand it to you, Crossen, you know the country. I thought we were lost back there in the muskegs. Our next stop should be the valley of the three sisters. Where is it?"

Crossen shrugged and said, "If I told you that, you'd have no further use of me."

They slept with their beds on clean swept rock within the smell of the sulphur water, but no one complained, for the air was clear of mosquitoes. Next day they traveled across one hot-spring terrace after another, and then along a river, through forest where trees grew larger than any they'd seen since leaving Spirit Lake. The air was clear again, filled with the pure scent of the forest. Game was plentiful, and that night they ate the flesh of a caribou calf siwashed over the coals. Late the next afternoon they sighted a cabin at the edge of a clearing.

Kordos signaled and went ashore, advancing warily on the cabin until he was sure it was abandoned. Then he examined it. Its logs were set upright after the manner of forts built by the early French fur traders, but they were keyed differently and pinned with wooden pegs. A few pieces of rude, axe-built furniture stood inside amid a pack-rat accumulation of several seasons.

"We'll stop here," Kordos said.

He chose a campsite well concealed by brush and allowed only a tiny cook fire of smokeless aspen twigs. Then he sent Odette to scout from the surrounding hillside.

Twilight settled. A wary anticipation settled over the camp. Kordos kept watch for Odette and cursed under his breath when he did not return. He looked around and said to Graves, "Maybe you'd better try to find him."

A gun exploded in the distance. Just one sharp crack, with echoes bounding after it.

Crossen instinctively went to one knee, his Winchester in his hands. He listened. The shot had been fired about half a mile away.

Now with the echoes gone, it seemed very quiet.

After a period of waiting, a man called from the forest. Odette. "Hello, there! Me!"

Kordos stood up and said, "All right, come on."

"Well, what was it?" he asked when Odette came in sight.

"Man. White man. He was watching us. I killed him."

"I told you not to fire your gun! I should have made you leave it in camp."

Odette wasn't cowed by Kordos like some of the others, and he growled back, "Maybe you'd rather he got loose with the big news of our coming!"

He thought it over.

"No. No, Odette, you did right. You killed him. You're sure he's dead? Where is he? I'd like to—"

"He'll wait for us." Odette leaned his rifle against a tree and looked around for something to eat. He found some bannock and commenced munching it.

"He was alone?" Kordos said it with the obvious assumption that he was, and it was like a blow in the face when Odette shook his head. "What?" he roared, "You mean—"

"Maybe he was alone and maybe not." Odette kept chewing

the bannock. He was a heavy, swarthy, taciturn man with cruel eyes. "I saw two sets of tracks."

"Then, of course there are two men!"

Kordos stood cursing in a raw whisper. "We'll have to make sure. We have to follow. We can't let anyone warn them. There aren't enough of us. If there's another man, we'll have to kill him. No. Don't kill him. Catch him alive if you can. He might tell us something. Odette, you take Marcus and get on his trail."

Odette said, "After dark I'm supposed to trail him? How, like a hound, with my nose?"

Kordos roared, "Follow him!" He watched with narrow eyes while the surly Odette put more of the bannock in his pocket and picked up his rifle to go. Then he said, "Graves, you follow the high country and try to sight him from there. Trekell, take the canoe. Go downriver. Ten or twelve miles downriver. Then cache yourself."

Trekell jerked his head at Crossen and said, "Who'll guard him?"

"We don't need him anymore."

Crossen knew they'd kill him once his usefulness was finished, but it was a shock, coming so soon. Trekell had his rifle raised. There was no chance to shoot it out.

Crossen dived, and Trekell's gun exploded at almost the identical instant.

The shot deafened him. He felt the whip and burn of powder across his cheek. He was flat, amid twigs and rough brush. He rolled over as a second bullet plowed the ground. A windfall partly blocked his way. He lunged over it, hidden momentarily from Trekell, but Kordos had his revolver out. He fired.

The bullet struck Crossen. Its impact was like a sledge against his ribs.

He was down, but instinct kept him going, crawling, clawing through brush. It seemed like minutes, but actually no more than fifteen seconds could have elapsed. Back of him he could hear the crash of pursuit.

Kordos was roaring commands. Crossen came to a crouch over the yard-high cover of fox brush, and unexpectedly, there was Trekell less than twenty feet away.

Trekell was partly turned. He tried to bring his rifle around, but there was no time.

Crossen fired with his Winchester aimed across his waist. The high-velocity slug hit Trekell and spun him on the balls of his feet. He dropped his rifle and took five or six steps before the life went out of him and he plunged face first in a tangle of cranberry brush.

Crossen barely hesitated. He rocked to his feet and ran as best he could with the bullet wound dragging at his side.

VI

CROSSEN kept running until the sound of pursuit was muffled by the forest. Blood was sponging through his mackinaw. He stopped, opened his clothing, and looked at the wound. The bullet had creased his side, nicked some of his lower ribs, and glanced away. The ribs were probably broken, but the wound wasn't serious provided he could check the bleeding.

He gathered dry moss, made balls of it the size of his fist, and pressed them to the bullet wound, afterward binding them tightly with strips torn from his shirt. He went on then, holding stiffly erect so as not to disturb the packs, and reached the river. He was now about a couple miles below camp.

The stream was too swift to ford. He followed its rocky bank for another mile, bound two logs together with wattape fibers— the tough, stringy roots of a pine that had been exposed beneath an undercut bank—and using the stock of his Winchester for a paddle, crossed.

He felt safer then. He headed into the forest, climbing, until at last, weak from fatigue, he fell on the ground and slept.

When he awakened, it was late night and the wolves were howling. He felt for his guns. The revolver was gone but he still had the Winchester. His side seemed tight, as though the skin had contracted and turned hard. It itched, too, but the bleeding had stopped.

He went on, picked a slow course across windfalls and slide rock. Through a cleft in timber he had a moonlit view of the country.

Hills rose ahead, but there were no prominent summits to justify the term "Three Sisters." A breeze came from the valley, carrying a faint tang of wood smoke.

He found a game trail, followed it until dawn, and finally stopped on a bluff overlooking the river.

He was loading his pipe with tobacco and red willow when movement attracted his eyes below.

A man had emerged from timber and was creeping forward with a rifle in one hand. He kept moving until he reached a heap of weather-whitened drift logs along a backwash, and there, resting on one knee, he peered at something upriver. It was too far to make out the man's features, but his mannerisms identified him. Paul Graves. Kordos had sent him ahead in the canoe.

Crossen's gaze went upriver a quarter mile and saw a second man, a stranger to him, kneeling at the point of a gravel bar, dipping a handkerchief, wringing it to a damp ball, bathing his face. After a minute he put the handkerchief away, picked up a rifle, and moved a swift, bounding step back to the shore.

The sun, rising, made a glare on the river so Crossen had to guess at his position, but he could see Graves crouch forward and slowly lift his rifle.

Acting quickly, Crossen levered a cartridge into the barrel of his Winchester, aimed at a spot ten feet over Graves's head, and fired.

It was extreme range, but the bullet arched close enough to send Graves diving sidewise, and thence on all fours in a mad scramble for the timber.

Crossen gave Graves no more consideration. A coward, he'd keep running. All Crossen wanted now was a sight of the other man, a chance to stop him, talk to him. He went downhill, digging the heels of his moccasins to check his descent.

A bullet stirred the pebbles five feet to one side. The sharp crack of the rifle came an instant later. The stranger was shooting at him. He found concealment in scrub pine. Below, rising in the sunshine, he glimpsed a bluish puff of powder smoke.

The man came in sight, running with a swift, animal grace through a clearing. Suddenly, with a shock, he realized it was not a man, but a girl.

She was blonde, with her hair tied in a tight knot at the back of her neck. She was dressed entirely in buckskins. They fitted her well, revealing the conformation of her young body.

He called, "Girl, wait! I won't harm you!"

She whirled and fired at the sound of his voice, aiming her rifle waist high. The bullet was wide. An instant later she was gone in the timber.

He ran until he reached the river. His wounded side burned, but he kept running. He saw her again, and he might have intercepted her, but the river intervened. He called again, but it was no use. At last, weak and sweating with a pounding pulse, he flung himself on the ground to rest. When he came to, his clothes were clammy and his teeth chattered. The side of his mackinaw was again heavy from blood. Dizziness kept passing his eyes in hot waves.

He slept again and awoke. The chill was gone, and he was thirsty. He got to his knees and steadied himself, but the click of a gun hammer jarred him to the spot.

"Stop!" It was the voice of the girl.

He rested with his hands on the ground, took a deep breath, and looked. The effort had momentarily blinded him. Then his eyes focused and he saw her face.

She was beautiful. In a city, among other white women, she'd have been beautiful. To him, a man who'd seen no white woman in better than twelve months, she was miraculous, like something out of a dream. She was a trifle under average height, very slim. Her features were delicate and perfect.

In her hands was a short-barreled rifle, a lever action gun of unusual design, some European make he'd never seen before. She kept it aimed. He could see the rear sight with the front one notched into it. She held it steady, but excitement showed in the throb of an artery in her throat.

He remained very still. He mustn't startle her. Any wrong move would bring her finger down on the trigger.

"I'm wounded," he said.

She looked at the blood-hardened side of his mackinaw and back at his face. "Who are you?"

"My name's Crossen."

"You were with them—with those men who killed Pavel."

"I was their prisoner. I got away last night about dark. They shot me in the side, but I got away. This morning I was on the hillside and saw you washing your face. They'd sent a man ahead in a canoe to ambush you, and I saw him, too. He was hiding in that backwater behind the driftwood. You'd have walked directly onto him if I hadn't shot."

He talked slowly, using as much time as he could, trying to calm her. She shifted the gun barrel, only a little, but enough so the bullet would miss if the gun discharged accidentally.

She asked, "Where are you from?"

"Spirit Lake post."

She said something in a lisping tongue he'd never heard before. It could have been Eskimo dialect, but he didn't think so. She was watching him closely.

"No savvy," he said.

"Are you a Russian?"

It seemed like a strange question. "No. American."

There was a fine excellence in her pronunciation, but English was not native to her. It added to the mystery of her being there, as though she came from another world.

She said, "Those men, why are they here?"

"A half-breed was trading some diamonds. They came north tracing them."

Her lips formed the word, "Matoos!"

"Yes, Matoos. He was from here, then? From this valley?"

"He was a thief! Is he with them?"

"Matoos is dead. Kordos killed him."

"Kordos?"

"He's their leader."

Crossen had been resting on one knee. He stood up now, and she took a quick step back. "Don't try anything, please. I don't want to kill you."

"I don't want you to, either."

She said, "What is he planning to do? That man you talk of, Kordos?"

"He thinks you have a treasure here and he's after it. He's out to get it any way he can. I suppose by killing you all, if he has to."

"Treasure?" The meaning of the word seemed to escape her.

"Jewels. Money."

"That's what he wants?" She seemed to think it ridiculous that anyone would search for such things. Unexpectedly she lowered the rifle and said, "You hate him, don't you?"

It was less a question than a plea for him to say yes. He understood how she felt. She was all alone. She needed him as a friend.

He considered for a while before answering, "Yes, I do hate him. I don't think I ever really hated a man before, but I hate him."

It had made him weak to stand. Flickers of blindness kept racing across his eyeballs. The ground seemed to tilt under his feet. He reached for a tree trunk to steady himself, but it wasn't where he expected. He had no sensation of falling, but next thing he realized, he was down, with the girl bending over him.

He said, "I took a bullet in the side. I lost some blood. I guess I—need some rest."

She quickly took off her buckskin jacket, made a roll of it, and put it under his head as a pillow. Then she opened his mackinaw and looked at his wound.

Sight of it made her take a deep breath. For a second she

seemed to be a little sick. Blood and the moss packs made it look worse than it was.

He said, "You go get me a drink. I'll take care of the bandage."

She shook her head and, tight-lipped, removed the blood-soaked moss herself. Despite pain, he was aware of the perfume of her skin and hair, the warmth of her body.

It had been a long time since he'd been that close to a white girl.

He started to speak, but she quieted him with a quick shake of her head and hurried to the river, returning with water-filled moss which she used to bathe the wound. Then she washed the bandage and put it back.

"Try to sleep," she said.

"Girl, there's no time to sleep. Kordos will be here after us."

"You can't travel."

"I'll take care of myself. You'd better get going. Warn your settlement."

She just pressed her lips tightly and shook her head. "Rest for a while!"

He lay back and closed his eyes. He had no intention of sleeping, but he did, and when he awoke the sun was noon-hot.

He sat up and looked around for the girl.

Now that the fever was gone, she seemed like part of his dream. He looked at his side and saw the neat, freshly washed bandage just getting dry. She'd been real enough to do that.

He stood up, slowly, testing his legs. He felt a little weak, but not dizzy. He'd be all right now.

The river was fifty yards away. He reached it just as a canoe came in sight around a wooded point downstream. There was one person in it—the girl.

She was good with a paddle, maneuvering the birch craft deftly though the rock-spotted current, hunting the shallows near shore. He walked to meet her. She shouted something, but her words were drowned by the rush of water. There was no chance of beaching the canoe on the jagged shore, so he waded to his knees and got hold of the gunwale.

She said, "It won't help you to get chilled."

"I'm all right now."

He put his rifle where it would keep dry and climbed over the side. The canoe slipped rapidly downstream, around the point.

"Who are you?" he asked.

Her back was turned, and she gave no sign of hearing him.

He said, "You asked me that question." Then he asked, "But of course, you had a gun on me."

"I'm—Anna."

"How did you get in this forgotten end of the North?"

"I've been here all my life."

"You were born here?"

"Yes."

He knew of no white settlement between Spirit Lake and Coronation Gulf, but his memory went back to a camp fire on the shore of Lake Grandin many years before where a renegade Indian by the name of Weasel Tail had told of a race "more white than the white men" who lived in a "castle with an onion on top, in the valley of warm waters where the muskegs meet the barrens of Windigo."

He said, "Where is this settlement?"

"I can't take you there."

"Why?"

"They might kill you."

"Who?"

"Melikov. Even my brother."

"Why would they kill me?"

"Because you're from the outside."

"Even if I saved their necks?"

She thought for a while and shook her head. "I don't know. I've warned you now. You can do as you please."

He laughed and said, "Between Melikov or Kordos, I'll choose Melikov."

VII

AFTER many miles down the swift river they cleared a point and sighted a canoe dock with a cluster of shanties and wickiups sprawled along a shoulder of bank above.

"This it?" he asked.

Anna nodded without turning, and pointed outward, beyond the Indian village, so he knew that the white settlement was still some distance away.

A tall, very lean Indian emerged from the timber carrying a rifle in one hand and ran down to the canoe float to grab the babiche line that Anna tossed to him. He made fast and said something in a spineless, lisping tongue that Crossen did not understand. The girl answered, there was a mention of Melikov's name, then she said, "This way," to Crossen and led him past the Indian village with its barking dogs and smoky smells and through half a mile of timber to the edge of a wide clearing.

The building he caught sight of there brought him to a surprised stop. It stood inside a stockade, topping a rocky knoll. It was built entirely of logs, one story pyramided on another, the whole surmounted by a bulbous cupola of a kind he'd once seen on the old church at St. Michael at the mouth of the Yukon. Lesser log structures surrounded it, some of them mere cabins, others dwellings or storehouses as much as two hundred feet in length. The stockade was made of pointed posts. It was a rough circle five or six hundred yards in diameter around the base of the knoll.

They walked up the steepening path to the closed gate. A white man with a lumpy and pockmarked face leaned from a blockhouse window to peer at Crossen until the girl said something in the same strange tongue she'd used with the Indian, and he answered, nodding violently, and hurried to open the gate.

Men and women crowded outside the log houses to stare at him. Only a couple of the men were white, the others were half-breeds or Indians. The women all seemed to be full-bloods. Anna led him up a steep pathway, past the little-used main entrance of the big house, to a door which was opened for them by an erect old man garbed in a peculiar, shirtlike capote, his loose trousers stuffed inside homemade knee boots.

A long dark passageway led to the depth of the building. She opened a second door, and they entered a room, low-ceilinged, windowless, filled with the glow and warmth of a fire.

Anna said something, and a man's deep voice answered her, calling her by name. Crossen tried to see him and couldn't. He was somewhere in shadow beyond the fire.

She said, "I have here a man who saved my life. He is wounded. His name is Crossen. He is an American."

"Melikov," the man said, introducing himself as he stepped forward. He was about sixty, not a big man, but he gave the impression of strength. He'd been blond once, but now his hair and mustache were completely white. His greeting was civil, but that was all. He made no pretense at being pleased. "Why are you here?"

"I came with Kordos." He watched Melikov as he mentioned the name, but apparently it meant nothing to him. He went on talking and told briefly the events from the time he left Spirit Lake until he'd seen Graves waiting to ambush the girl.

Anna, who'd been watching Melikov's face, cried, "It is true the man would have killed me!"

Melikov looked at her with a slight softening of his expression as he said, "Ah, Anna! How little you know about the world of men. You can travel like a deer, and shoot like the devil's own wife, but here," he smote his heart, "here, inside, you are a little white dove. What do you know about the depth of trickery to which men go to win a handful of glittering stones, to murder the ones they hate? Of course, someone was waiting to ambush you," he pointed to Crossen, "but did this man kill him? Answer, did he?"

Anna shook her head, and her lips formed the word, "No."

"Then perhaps they plotted it all together. So you would bring him here, as you have."

Crossen said, "Don't be a fool. Do you think I'd let somebody shoot me in the ribs so I could get inside as a spy?" He pulled open his mackinaw. "Look for yourself. That bullet was too close to be fooling."

Melikov lifted his shoulders and let them fall, saying "Perhaps," in a manner which he showed he had no intention of changing his mind. He reached and patted Anna on the cheek. "I am sorry, little one. Perhaps he is right and I am being the fool, but what else can I do? One mistake and it would be over for us—over for Papa-Niko—you understand? It is the old sacrifice we must make once and keep making."

She cried, "It's making no sacrifice for Papa-Niko if we turn our backs on someone who can save us."

"Eh-so," he sighed, lifting his shoulders once again. He loaded a pipe with Indian tobacco and lighted it with a branch from the fire. "Where is Pavel?" he asked.

"Dead."

His face turned savage and he cried, "Killed? Who did it?"

"Them. The strangers."

He gestured at Crossen, "Or him!"

"No!"

"You saw who killed him?"

She shook her head.

Crossen still had his Winchester, and Melikov, imagining a threat, said, "Don't try anything. You'd never get out alive."

There was someone in the shadow behind him. Crossen turned slowly and watched a man move into the firelight. The same guardsman who'd let them through the outside door. He had a rifle, cocked and aimed.

Melikov said, "Give him your gun."

"Sure." Crossen laid his Winchester on the table. Then he asked, "What are you going to do with me?"

Melikov lifted his shoulders and let them fall. The girl started to speak, but he silenced her. He said something to the guardsman, who jerked his gun in the direction of the door, a command for Crossen to go with him.

VIII

HE was taken to some rough-hewn stairs. The wound was like a weight dragging at his side. He tripped and fell and for a moment he was too weak to get up. The guard called, "Watsoo!" and an Indian boy appeared at the head of the stairs.

Crossen got to one knee and said, "Don't worry, I couldn't make it from here to the stockade."

He got up and climbed as the Indian boy backed away, watching him, and the old guardsman followed with his cocked rifle.

A door was open. It led to a barren room with a tiny cleft window and a hay-filled bunk against one wall. He lay down in the bunk, with fatigue making a hot wave through his body, and fell asleep.

He awoke with the realization that several hours had passed. He got up. It didn't make him dizzy this time, but he'd been feverish and it left him with a burning thirst. He walked to the door and asked for water. No one answered. He tried the door, knowing it would be locked. He cursed a little, spat from his dry mouth, and spent some time looking from the tiny window. The small opening through thick logs gave a narrow view of some roofs, a bit of stockade, and the steep gulch country beyond.

He sat down. Inside the house it was silent until, after the slow passage of an hour, he heard the pure, harplike sound of a stringed instrument and the singing of a girl. The beauty of it made him hold his breath to listen. He was sure the voice was Anna's.

Her song was unfamiliar, unlike any he'd ever heard. It had a sad, almost Oriental quality. She finished and he sat without moving, hoping she'd sing more, but she didn't, and there was a step out in the hall.

The door opened. An Indian woman had brought him a bowl of warm water, a towel, a comb. He cleaned up and the old guardsman took him to what was evidently the great room of the castle.

Surprise brought him to a stop just inside the door. The ceiling was two stories high, supported by pillars and beams that were simply the massive, squared trunks of trees. In a fireplace large as an average cabin a high pyramid of logs was blazing, but even such a fire scarcely illuminated the far walls, and seal-oil lamps burned in brackets around them. A table of whipsawed plank stood in the full flame of the fire, and it gleamed of silver and white cloth as no table he'd ever seen in the north.

A girl in a long, blue velvet dress came toward him. It took him a couple of seconds to realize it was Anna. Her hair had been brushed, braided, and coiled around her head. She looked taller, more womanly. She asked him how he felt, and he managed to make some sort of an answer.

There were others in the room. He noticed Melikov, five other men, a woman of about sixty. Anna took him by the sleeve and led him across the room. He thought she intended to introduce him to the elderly woman, but instead she stopped and curtsied before a very old man who was seated in a huge, carved chair.

She spoke French, not the "Coyotie-French" common in the northland, but a pure Parisian that Crossen scarcely understood, calling the old man "Papa-Niko" and introducing Crossen as their Americain visitor.

The old man kept nodding, smiling, but it was hard to tell whether he really saw or understood anything. His senses seemed to have been glazed over by the years.

"*Oui!*" he said. Then "Yes," and moved his long, transparent-looking fingers in a gesture Crossen did not understand.

"He wants you to go to him," Anna said.

Crossen stepped forward, and the old man passed a limp hand for him to shake. On his middle finger was a ring so massive it seemed to take most of his strength to lift it.

"Americain," he said. Then he gave it the English pronunciation, "American," and went on, speaking in that tongue, bringing the words with difficulty. "The American I have always admired. A brave new people, building without the slavery of custom. Of all slaveries custom is the greatest. So said Pushkin." He repeated some words in the spineless tongue which

Crossen suddenly realized must be Russian. "You have read Pushkin?"

Crossen shook his head, and the old man whispered sadly, "I have read Lincoln, you should read Pushkin."

Melikov came up and said, "Papa-Niko, would it be your pleasure to dine?"

The old man inclined his head with extreme gravity, stood gathering the rags of a once magnificent Cossack blouse about him, and walked to the chair at the head of the table.

Now for the first time Crossen had a good look at the others. Only one of the men was young. He was in his late teens, and strikingly like Anna. The others were all in their sixties or seventies.

Papa-Niko said a prayer and struck a homemade bell. At the signal, two half-breed boys came in and commenced serving dinner.

The meal consisted of roast caribou loin, tiny new potatoes and carrots, and bread made of coarse wheat flour. There were no canned foods, nothing brought in from outside. Even the salt was coarse and grayish, the product of Indian evaporation pans.

Little was said during the first part of the meal. Crossen was ravenous after a day without food, but when the edge was off his appetite he commenced to watch Papa-Niko. He wondered how old he was. Eighty, perhaps, or eighty-five. He was small, but not withered. His eyes were still intensely blue, and when he looked at things they had a childlike expression. He ate little, only a nibble here and there, pausing each time to touch his lips lightly with a very old linen napkin.

"America," he said after a long period of reverie, and went on, hunting the words, sometimes pausing for many seconds. "I heard once a prima donna from America. Your Geraldine Farrar. She is still the toast of your opera—" He snapped his fingers to remember the name. "Your Metropolitan?"

The name came faintly from the past, when he was a little boy. A star of the silent movies had been named Geraldine Farrar, but she'd been a prima donna, too. He had no idea whether she was still alive or not. "She's—retired."

"Ah, too bad. Glorious voice. We heard her, do you remember, Yakub? In the blue room where Androvitch was married?"

The old man he called Yakub nodded gravely. Papa-Niko lapsed into a reverie, his eyes almost closed, a half smile on his lips. Melikov set off on a long, determined dissertation on growing vegetables during the short season in the North, and how an extra month's ripening time could be gained by covering plants beneath cured hay just prior to August 20th when the first frost could be expected; but he failed to shift the direction of the old man's thoughts who brightened and said:

"Another—your stage star. John Drew. I must tell you of my meeting with him at Monte Carlo." He nibbled some more, touched his lips with the napkin, and apparently forgot that he'd even been talking. Dinner was finished, but no one moved, waiting for Papa-Niko. Finally he noticed, said hurriedly, "God be with you," and stood waiting to be assisted to his huge chair by the fire.

"A great actor," he said, starting in on Drew again. "I would like to have seen him in Ibsen. As the Master Builder. Or the Doctor." Then he said in French, "Did I ever tell you, Anna, of the time Ibsen was with me, shooting pigeons, at the house near Komane-Ostrog?"

The girl shook her head and sat at his feet to listen. She seemed eager, though Crossen didn't doubt she'd heard the same story innumerable times. Papa-Niko's eyes again rested on Crossen, and he said, returning to English, "He is still the idol of American womankind?"

"Who? John Drew? Not anymore."

"Eh? Such a handsome one. But he's older now. Who succeeded him?"

"As a matinee idol? Barrymore, I guess."

"Barrymore," he repeated.

Crossen thought of something and spoke deliberately, watching the old man's eyes, "You should have seen him in a Russian story called Rasputin."

The word seemed to strike Papa-Niko like an electric charge. He grabbed the arms of his chair and tensed forward, his eyes suddenly hardened, focused on Crossen's face. Melikov was there with long strides, one fist doubled, the other hand clenched on the revolver at his waist. But the fire faded from Papa-Niko's eyes and he settled back with the old, glazed look on his face.

"What's the matter?" Crossen asked of Melikov.

Melikov said, "Why did—" He forced his voice to be quiet. "I think he is tired now. Will you bid him good night."

It was a command. Crossen said "Good night," without Papa-Niko seeming to notice, and walked with Melikov to the door.

Melikov snarled, "Did you find out what you wanted?"

"I don't know what you're talking about." And when Melikov laughed bitterly, "You still think I came here to spy on you?"

"Now, I am certain of it."

"You're not very smart, Melikov. You shouldn't spend your time watching me. You should be out watching Kordos. He's probably getting ready to burn you out right now."

"Your Kordos will do nothing without hearing from you."

Melikov called out a command in Russian, and the old guardsman opened the door, his gun ready. There were two others in the hall. One was the Indian boy with a grease-dip lamp, the other a hunched, bowlegged half-breed armed with an old-time Winchester and an H.B.C. hunting knife.

"I won't cause that much trouble," Crossen said.

Melikov said something more in Russian, the guard saluted, and Crossen was walked on a winding route through rooms and hallways to a new prison room with massive log walls and a floor of solid stone.

He had a brief view of it as he was lighted through the door, then the door thudded shut behind him, and he heard two heavy bars drop in place.

IX

HE'D glimpsed a bunk against one wall. He groped and found it. His side itched a little, but food had restored his strength. He sat for a while, recalling the expression on Papa-Niko's face when the word "Rasputin" was spoken. Rasputin, a monk, an occult healer, a charlatan who'd treated the young Czarevitch Alexis, son of the Czar of Russia, for hemophilia and was assassinated in a palace plot during the last nightmare months before the Bolsheviks ended things for the royal family in 1918.

The chill of the room slowly made itself felt. There was a bear robe on the couch. He pulled it over him. He had no intention of going to sleep. He drew out his pipe and tobacco, but he had no matches. He chewed some of the tobacco. It was very quiet. He could hear only an occasional whisper of feet or the mutter of a voice outside the door.

He fell asleep. Perhaps he was asleep for an hour. Then he came suddenly awake.

He lay very still, listening, wondering what had awakened

him. He put the bear robe aside and stood up. He took a step, and suddenly he knew she was there—Anna.

"Hello!" he said.

Her voice came back, a whisper, unexpectedly close. "Yes."

He groped toward her. She was a slight figure, dressed again in buckskins. His hand closed on her shoulder. He thought for a second she was going to draw away. Then a tremble seemed to pass down her slim body and she stood still, waiting.

"Anna!" He wanted to say something, but it was a thought half formed, and nothing came to his lips. Only her name. She said "Hurry! You'll have to come with me. He'll kill you. Melikov."

"He really means it?"

"Yes. When you mentioned that man, Rasputin. He thought you knew. Perhaps you do know . . ."

"Tell me, girl. Who are you? Who really are you?"

"Isn't it enough that I'm Anna?"

He didn't care who she was, or who Papa-Niko was. He only realized that she was there, the most beautiful girl he'd ever known.

His hands closed on her arms and he drew her toward him. She came willingly. It seemed she'd have fallen without his support, as though her knees had no strength in them. Her hands were tight at the front of his mackinaw. Her head was tilted back. He kissed her again and again. He had no consciousness of time. She might have been in his arms a half minute, ten minutes. Then she pushed him away and said, "No!" like a person awakening. "You have to get out of here."

"All right."

"I have a blanket, some food, a gun. There's a trail up the steep gulch to the west. It will take you over the pass and down to a river that the Indians call the Miskootya, and after that to the fur company settlement."

"You're coming with me."

"No. No, I can't." She repeated it as though convincing herself that it was impossible. "I have to stay here."

"Why?"

"Because I have to!"

"Because Melikov says you have to? What will you do? Marry an Indian like these white men have married squaws?"

He was holding her too lightly. She gave a little sob of pain and tore away. He reached again, but she was gone in the dark.

He could hear the sliding rustle of her moccasined feet across the flagstones.

"Won't that be it?" he whispered fiercely, following her.

"No."

"Why, then?"

"Because of Papa-Niko. He loves me. I'm all he has to live for."

Papa-Niko was a god to her. He'd seen it in her eyes at the table.

He kept walking and almost ran against her in the dark. "Who is he?"

"A Russian. We are all Russians. He led us out during the revolution. We owe our lives to him."

"Russian nobleman?"

"Yes."

"He had something to do with the monk, Rasputin?"

"You guessed that! Yes. He was associated with the Grand Duke in ridding the royal family of him. Papa-Niko said if it hadn't been for Rasputin, perhaps the war would have gone better, perhaps the revolution could have been controlled. But when he died, too much harm had been done. Papa-Niko risked his life going back to see the czar. He wanted him to escape, to Switzerland. The czar would not go. He was taken prisoner and executed.

"After that it was death for any Russian nobleman that they found. I had not been born, but my father and mother and a dozen others lived through it. They lived because Papa-Niko led them eastward to Siberia, to Omsk, where General Kolak had set up a counterrevolutionary regime; and when Omsk fell to the Reds, on across the frozen tundras, month after month, until they reached Okhotsk on the Pacific.

"There they hid for months in the house of a merchant named Stein. They were carrying a fortune in jewels. Stein could have brought them passage to America, but Papa-Niko decided against it. At that time the Bolshevik secret police, the Cheka, was operating all over the world. He was afraid that even in America they'd hunt down those who were the Czar's relatives and assassinate them. Then they made the acquaintance of Captain Kablov. He was an adventurer, an aviator, who'd traveled all over the Arctic world. He told of a place in the wilderness of Canada unknown to white men where they could live in safety as long as they wanted. Under Captain Kablov an expedition was fitted out. It left Okhotsk under the Red flag.

"Three weeks later they reached Coronation Gulf. Captain Kablov had a small plane along. He flew the first trip alone and found a landing place four miles from here, along the river. He set up a temporary camp and made more than twenty flights, transporting people and supplies. Then he left, promising to return in the spring. It was the last ever heard of him.

"And they've stayed here ever since!"

"In Siberia, Papa-Niko almost lost his mind. He was very ill. The second spring Count Bakunin started for Montreal, taking some of the royal jewels with him to pay expenses, but he was never heard of again. Perhaps he was found and assassinated by the Cheka. Melikov held a meeting and announced we were leaving for the south—for the United States. I will never forget that meeting. I was a little girl. I was frightened. Papa-Niko spoke and it was the only time I ever saw him angry. He said he would give the command to leave when a command was to be given. He never has. We are still here."

"What will you do when Papa-Niko dies?"

"I don't know. I have never been anywhere but here."

"Haven't you wanted to leave?"

"Maybe," she whispered.

"I still don't know who you are."

"Papa-Niko is my grandfather. My mother died ten years ago. She was the Grand Duchess. My father was Count Bakunin. He left and never came back. The trip, I have heard, is very dangerous and long. He didn't just leave with the gems as some of them try to say!"

"Diamonds?"

"Yes. But not those that Matoos had. Matoos used to live here. He worked a year in the big house, just for the chance to steal those diamonds from Marie Androvna. Melikov knew he had them, and he always feared that some day a jeweler would identify them as royal gems so the Cheka would start tracing them."

"Girl! The Russian government is no longer concerned with the old nobility. There is no longer an army of White Russians, no sentiment to return a Romanoff to a throne. All that is forgotten history. The world—the Russians and everyone—has new problems. Bigger problems. Realize that."

"Aren't diamonds still worth money? Aren't there men in your own country of America who would sell their souls for money?"

"A great many of them."

"Then this man, this Kordos—"

She stopped suddenly. Someone was just outside the door.

X

THERE were a few seconds of utter silence. Then Anna whispered, "Old Kazin! Do you think he heard us?"

"Didn't he let you in?"

"Of course not. I came through the inner door."

He hadn't suspected the existence of a second door. She took his arm and guided him across the dark room. The door was there. She'd opened it barely enough for herself to squeeze through. It wasn't wide enough for him. The door was very heavy. It scraped and creaked as he moved it. He got through, closed it again. She stood near with something in her hands. A heavy wooden bar. She dropped it in place. The old guardsman had just entered the prison room. The glow of his lamp shone through cracks in the plank door. He shouted on finding the room empty.

She ran, leading Crossen down a hall with a dim rectangle of moonlight at the distant end. It was a relief to get outside.

They were in the shadow of a snowshed. She was breathing hard, as much from excitement as from exertion. She pointed out toward the steep hills of the back country.

"That gulch. You'll find a trail—"

"You're coming with me!"

"No."

The guardsman's shouts were arousing the house. He could hear the thud of running feet.

She said, "Here!" and lifted a pack of bedding and provisions, with one of those Russian rifles thrust through the shoulder thongs.

A man charged around the corner, almost colliding with him. Melikov.

Melikov had a pistol in his hand. He wheeled, fell toward the wall, hitting it with one shoulder. The gun was aimed, he pulled the trigger. The explosion whipped past Crossen's face so closely it blinded him momentarily, but the bullet missed. Anna had struck Melikov's arm, saving his life.

Melikov flung her away. He tried to bring the gun up, but Crossen took a long step and smashed him down with a right to the jaw.

Crossen got the pack, swung it to his shoulder, looked around for the girl. "Anna!" he called.

She was backing away. "Get out while you can."

"You're coming with me."

"No."

He started to follow her, realized she wouldn't come, turned, and ran downhill toward the smaller houses. There he found momentary concealment. A malamute sighted him, commenced barking, fighting his babiche thong. He kept running. The stockade was a couple of hundred steps farther. A gun crashed and he felt the hum of a bullet winging close. A second slug stirred pebbles that stung the backs of his legs.

He reached the stockade. It was ten feet high. He felt for finger and toe holds between the posts. He saw a ladder then. The girl had placed it there for him. A bullet tore splinters as he dropped to the far side. In another quarter minute he was in the spotty shadow of evergreens.

He found the trail. It took him along the side of a gulch, around a cliff, across loose, jagged slide rock. In the distance were three spires of stone that resembled human figures with hats on, and the final bit of Matoos's directions was explained. These were the Three Sisters.

The country became more broken, with both sides cut by gorgelike feeder gullies. The trail wound through huge boulders that had tumbled from above.

A rock came loose and fell from one level to the next with a series of hard clatters. He looked up and glimpsed bluish gun shine. A man's silhouette sharp against the moonlit cliff. He wore a hat such as Crossen had not seen in the valley. One of Kordos's men! Something in his movement even told him who it was. Jack Marsak. There'd be more of them, all of them. Kordos was waiting his chance to attack.

Crossen kept going. He stopped beneath the shadow of a rock pillar and looked around. Men were coming along the trail from the big house, following him. Kordos would lie low. He'd wait and try to trap them all. For him, it would be an unexpected piece of good fortune.

He stripped the pack from his shoulders, took out the rifle. It was a heavy gun, big bore, comparable to an old .41 Swiss. A bullet heavy enough to turn a man inside out, but with a range of only a couple hundred yards. They'd have no chance against

Kordos with his advantage of position and his high-velocity rifles.

He left the trail and doubled back, crawling over jagged slide rock. The Russians and half-breeds were closing the distance. He aimed over their heads and pulled the trigger.

The bullet, dropping, fell closer than he'd intended. A couple of the men dived for cover, the others kept on. He shifted his aim and sent three rapid shots into the rocks, high above, where Marsak was lurking.

It had the desired result. Marsak returned the fire, and an instant later Kordos's men were pouring lead down from half a dozen directions.

He stayed down, cheek pressed hard against rock and dirt while bullets screeched over him. The air smelled sulphurous from scorched rock. When the first fusillade spent itself, he inched downhill and reached the narrow bottom of the gulch.

A thin trickle of water ran among the stones. He crossed and recrossed it, moving back toward the settlement. The shooting diminished and picked up again. He cursed, realizing that they'd kept on up the gulch and now Kordos, with his superior guns, was cutting them to pieces.

Crossen cupped his hands, shouted, "Get back!" over and over.

It was futile. No one could hear him. All he could do was head for the stockade.

He struggled across rocks that choked the gulch bottom. It was too slow. He started to climb. A bullet hit and glanced like an explosion in his face.

He instinctively plunged to the protection of a rock. His right leg felt numb. He looked at it. No blood. The bullet had missed him. In falling he'd struck it over a sharp edge of stone. After a while, the numbness left and he could move it.

His rifle was gone. It lay six or seven feet away. He tried to reach it and drew another shot. He lay for half a minute, not daring to move. At the ridge crest, two men came in sight and headed down a spruce-covered shoulder of land toward the big house.

Even at that distance and by moonlight, he could tell that one of them was Kordos.

He gave up trying to retrieve the rifle. He still had the hunting knife Anna had given him. If he caught up with Kordos in the darkness of the house, perhaps the knife would be just as useful.

He inched back down the slope, feet first, flat on his stomach. He found safety again at the gulch bottom, but it had consumed time. At least five minutes now since he'd glimpsed Kordos and his companion.

There was another quarter mile of slow going, and finally he reached timber at the broadening mouth of the gulch. A trail opened, and he followed it at a swift wolf trot.

In another half hour, he caught sight of the house. It looked more massive than ever by the predawn gloom. Dark, save for a single rectangle of candlelight at one of the second-story windows.

He kept running as long as his endurance would let him, then the knoll became too steep. He bent forward and climbed hard to the stockade.

He breathed a few seconds, commenced looking for toeholds along the wall. The outer faces of the pickets had been flattened until scarcely a rough spot remained to give even a momentary purchase. He drew his knife and struck the point overhead with all his strength. Then, with one hand clutching the blade, he pulled himself up. The knife came free, and he fell. He did it over again, with the blade at a different angle, brought himself up until his chin was even with the blade, hunted a brief toehold, made a grab, and found the top of the wall. He balanced there, his waist bent over the sharp pickets, while he leaned back for the knife. It took him another quarter minute to work the point free.

Then he dropped to the ground inside.

He listened a few seconds, watched. Dogs were still barking. Somewhere the frightened babble of squaws. Dawn had grayed out the stars, but there were still great black shadows around the buildings. No movement. He climbed, found cover among the cabins, paused again to watch the big house.

He heard a woman's voice, a cry of terror, suddenly cut off. Then a gun exploded. It exploded again, and then a third time, the reports deadened by thick log walls.

He ran uphill, and once more he was beneath the roof of the snowshed. He found the door he'd escaped from. It would only lead him back to the prison room. He strode on, found a second door, entered, groped through a passageway that finally ended in the big room where he'd eaten dinner the evening before.

Coals still glowed beneath a heavy coating of ash in the fireplace. The dim light revealed no one.

He called, "Anna!" His voice, echoing in the big room, seemed very loud. No answer. He'd expected none.

Last night he'd noticed some stairs farther along the hall. He moved on, groping, and tripped over the bottom step.

He got to one knee and listened. His breathing and pulse were back to normal, and small sounds became discernible. He heard the heavy tone of a man's voice, the thud of running feet. He drew the knife, touched the needle-sharp point. It was a heavy weapon, its blade more than a foot long. He felt better with it in his hand.

He climbed, reached the second story. A door was open, with lamplight streaming from it. He looked in on a room about twenty feet square, its floor and walls covered with the skins of animals—a scene of primitive luxury.

It seemed to be deserted. Then he saw someone on the floor. It was Papa-Niko. Dead, lying on his back. He'd taken two bullets at close range, both near or through the heart.

There'd been three shots. He stood and saw a second body. The old guardsman, huddled against the wall.

He sensed someone at the door and turned. It was a woman. He ran to her. She's taken a blow alongside the head and her eyes had a staring, stunned look. "Where's Anna?" he asked. He repeated, and said, "Anna! Anna!" trying to make her understand.

Her lips formed words.

"Can't you speak English?"

He knew she could. She'd said something in English at dinner the night before.

She almost fell. He carried her to the bed. There she revived enough to whisper, "They took her. Two men. Took her away. To the canoe dock."

"How do you know where they took her?" He repeated, "How do you know?"

"I heard them say it. Twice."

Crossen left her, went outside, knowing that Kordos wanted him to follow into an ambush.

XI

HE didn't follow the trail. He cut through timber and reached the river. It was darker there, with the forest closing in. Mist still clung to the water's cold surface. He doubled back until he caught sight of the canoe dock, watched for a while. No movement. No sound except the rush of the river. The bank pitched up steeply, covered with brush and small spruce. He climbed. He was close to the trail now. He threaded his way carefully.

Suddenly the brush ended and he was in the trail.

A man was crouched on one knee, his back turned, a rifle in one hand, its butt resting on the ground. Odette, the half-breed.

Odette had been expecting him from the other direction. He sensed movement behind him, and whirled. The distance was too great for Crossen to cover. But his knife was drawn, and he flung it.

The heavy blade made a single revolution and smashed itself to the hilt in Odette's chest. Odette had his gun up. He fired as he reeled to his feet. The bullet was wild through the treetops. He fell backward, the rifle bounding a dozen feet away.

Crossen saw Kordos and the girl at the same instant.

She was at one side of the trail, her arms bound to a sapling aspen tree, her mouth gagged. Kordos was just standing, reaching for his gun.

Crossen did not pause after flinging the knife. He sprang across Odette's body, and dived headlong. Kordos tried to retreat and get the rifle up, but Crossen grabbed the barrel. Kordos took two backward steps, then, with a massive swing of his body, tore the gun free and wheeled with a returning motion, driving the steel-shod butt to Crossen's skull.

It was like an explosion in back of Crossen's eyes. Instinctively he clinched and held tight while Kordos tried to dislodge him with rib-crushing rights and lefts.

Once before, back in Matoos's cabin, he'd felt Kordos's overpowering strength. He felt it again now. It was inhuman, like the strength of a silver-tip bear.

He let go, fell back to the ground, pretending unconsciousness. Kordos reared to his full height, sucking his chest full of air. Then, with a triumphant laugh, he leaped to crush Crossen's skull under his heavy boots.

Crossen twisted over and kicked Kordos's legs from under him. Next instant he was diving for Odette's gun.

Kordos was massive, but he was quick. He hit the ground rolling, came to a crouch, and sprang. The two men collided, but Crossen stayed on his feet. He grabbed for the gun, missed. The bank fell away toward the river. He checked himself at the edge of the canoe float and lashed out with a right to Kordos's jaw.

It was unexpected enough to snap the big man's head to one side, but he didn't retreat. He had a brute's strength and a brute's resistance. He muttered thickly and rushed with both arms outstretched to grapple.

It was the thing Crossen had waited for. He seized Kordos's right arm, pivoted, and using the big man's own momentum, sent him flying over his bent back.

It was a wrestling maneuver common in a hundred villages of the Yellowknives. And there was another trick coupled with it that the Yellowknives used only in a battle to the death. He called on it now, and as Kordos was off his feet, his arm stiffly down, Crossen caught it across his knee, bent as over a falcrum.

He could hear the sharp crack of breaking bone. Kordos screamed from pain as he went down. He rose, arm dangling and useless, located Crossen and charged.

Crossen smashed him to the ground with a right and left. He reeled to his feet and Crossen put him down again. Still he wasn't out. He crawled on hands and knees. He got up, fell, got up again. He retreated. He kept weaving his battered, bloody head. His eyes were glazed, like a pole-axed beef's. He spoke, with his tongue too thick for his mouth. "I'm licked. You got the girl. Here. Take these, too." He dug in his mackinaw pocket. "These stones. They're yours. Maybe twenty thousand dollars worth. Only let me go." They were in a buckskin bag, and when he tried to hand them across, they spilled and lay gleaming on the damp, black earth. "You take 'em all. I'll get out. You'll never see me again . . . ."

Suddenly he turned and crashed through the last yards of brush and was back to the trail. He almost tripped over Odette's body. The gun wasn't where he'd expected. But his own rifle lay on the ground, twenty feet away.

He lunged. The gun was in his good hand, but he'd momentarily lost footing. He turned, saving himself by going to a crouch. The gun was angled upward across his thigh. Crossen already had the breed's Winchester. He levered and fired with one swift movement. The bullet smashed Kordos backward. Kordos tried to stand, rifle still in his hands. He fired a bullet that sliced a riffle along the wet cover of twigs and spruce needles. Then the life went out of him and he pitched face forward to the ground.

* * *

Crossen walked over and looked at him. The beating had left him dazed. He stood there almost a minute. Then he remembered the girl.

She'd fought one hand free of the babiche thongs and was tearing the gag from her mouth.

He freed her, and she was in his arms a long time before either of them spoke.

"You saw what he did to poor Papa-Niko?" she asked.

"Yes."

"What happened to the others? Our men?"

"I don't know. They were putting up a tough fight. Kordos couldn't have more than five men up there. They'll get along all right."

Indians from the wickiup village had heard the shots and were skulking through the forest to see. A squaw brought them a bowl of bark tea. Crossen drank. A quick strength flooded his body, followed by drowsy fatigue. The wound at his side was hurting again. He lay full length, eyes closed, while the squaws made moss packs and rebandaged it.

Anna said, "Leonid!"

He sat up and grabbed a Winchester. It was her brother, his head bandaged, swift-striding down the path.

Leonid ran to her, lifted her off her feet, and cried something in Russian. Then he put her down and seized Crossen's hand.

"You saved her life!"

"She saved mine."

"Where is he? That big man, that—"

"Dead."

"Ha! I knew he'd lay an ambush, but he was no match for you. When I saw you last night at the table, I said—"

"He was a good enough match for me," Crossen said. "What happened up the gulch?"

"We killed a couple of them. The rest escaped to the back country. Perhaps for reinforcements—"

"Don't worry about that. They won't be back. How many did you lose up there?"

"Kochak, Alex, and two of the half-breeds. We carried Melikov out with a bullet through him."

"He's alive then. I'd like to talk to Melikov."

"No. You can't go back there. Melikov thinks you led us into the ambush. He thinks everyone from outside the valley is an enemy. You're not safe here. You'll have to leave."

Crossen thought about it and said, "All right." He looked at Anna. "I need your canoe."

He remembered the jewels and spent ten minutes hunting them out from among twigs and spruce needles. He counted them. Twenty-four. He let them roll from one hand to the other a few times, a stream of white, red, and yellow fire. He was wondering how much they'd be worth in Montreal. A small fortune, perhaps. The stake he'd been looking for so long.

He tried to give them to Leonid, but he refused. "They're worth nothing to us here. Keep them. They'll be a little pay for what you've done."

Leonid helped him lower the birch canoe to the water. Anna held it against the current as the two men shook hands. Crossen then stepped in, knelt with a paddle ready. Anna was watching him.

He said, "My side bothers me sometimes. Maybe you could help me upstream."

"Yes," she whispered. An instant later she had the extra paddle. As they cleared the wooded point, Anna looked back and called something to her brother. A Russian word Crossen did not understand, but he knew it was farewell.

"How long will you need me?" she asked.

"To the sulphur water, to the swamps of Nipphauk, to Spirit Lake."

There was a soft smile on her lips as she said, "So far!"

"Yes, and a lot farther. A million miles farther!"

About the Editors

Bill Pronzini has written numerous western short stories and such novels of the Old West and Far North as *Starvation Camp*, *The Gallows Land* and *Firewind*. He lives in Sonoma, California. Martin H. Greenberg has compiled over 200 anthologies, including westerns, science fiction, and mysteries. He lives in Green Bay, Wisconsin.

THE BEST OF THE WEST

BY BILL PRONZINI AND MARTIN H. GREENBERG